Martin Fine Book 1

AFRICAN HUSTLE

by John Kweli

ISBN 978-1-960378-27-9 (paperback)
ISBN 978-1-960378-28-6 (ePub)

1st Edition

Book design by Anna Hall

AFRICAN HUSTLE

*To Val, who rescued this
from the trash heap.*

CHAPTER

1

THE BIG PAYOFF, Mother Africa, was so close he could taste it. Martin Fine turned to stare out the oval window at the landscape below. From twenty thousand feet, it didn't look like much: a vast brown savannah with intermittent splotches of green. The jet banked gently, and a large expanse of blue appeared under the right wingtip.

Well, it took me almost as long as Burton and Speke, he thought ruefully.

From the moment he'd first been exposed to African history, Martin had found himself infatuated. He'd read everything he could lay his hands on about the Dark Continent. He wondered if it would live up to his dreams. After all, wasn't it custom for young men of good families to be sent to the colonies to make their fortunes? Particularly if their previous careers had been as checkered as his? Somehow, those hippie, drug-dealing days in Philadelphia seemed far removed, an earlier incarnation.

"Good afternoon, ladies and gentlemen," the pilot said over the intercom. "Below us and to our right is the fabled Lake Victoria, the world's second-largest lake."

Martin tried to take another sip of his Bloody Mary, realized the hard way it was empty, and stood. After slipping past the businessman and a woman half dozing in the aisle seat, Martin drifted toward the restrooms in the back of the plane. He could sense the eyes of the passengers on him and wondered if he looked worse than he felt.

Once locked in one of the cramped bathrooms, he wiped the sheen of nervous perspiration from his forehead and checked his grubstake. It was all there: $25,000 in crisp hundred-dollar bills.

Outside, he exchanged an inviting glance with the pretty young stewardess, who slipped the intercom receiver off the wall.

A friendly warning chimed overhead as he returned to his seat.

"Ladies and gentlemen," the stewardess said, "we'll be making our final approach to Entebbe. At this time, the captain requests that you kindly fasten your seat belts and refrain from further smoking until you've entered the terminal."

Martin checked the documents in his briefcase to make sure everything was in order: passport with visa, vaccination certificates, and letter of acceptance from the university. Then he patted his money belt one last time. He would need some of it for bribes. Cash was the developing world's miracle drug, an instant cure for all bureaucratic illnesses.

The 747 shuddered as the whirring hydraulic flaps dropped, and the plane thundered directly over Lake Victoria.

Craning his neck, Martin could just make out the many fishermen in dugouts setting their nets.

Minutes later, the plane was wheels down and landing. A few battered DC-3s and a Caribou bearing the markings of the Ugandan Air Force squatted on either side of the runway. The new terminal, just completed by the Israeli government, was an appropriately futuristic-looking concrete and smoked-glass structure. Provided the air conditioning worked, it surely would be a distinct improvement over its predecessor, the corrugated iron sweatbox of unmistakably colonial origins that sat forlornly next door.

As Martin deplaned, the dry heat seared his lungs, which were more accustomed to the moldy, dank air of Philadelphia or London, though there was just enough breeze coming off the water to keep things bearable. The terminal looked sleepy. From the vigor with which the porters roused themselves and hustled the passengers for their luggage, there couldn't have been much action on tap for the rest of the day.

For all its shiny newness, the building still had that same pungent aroma of rotting vegetation mixed with vague hints of body odor so familiar to Martin from his time in the Caribbean. In fact, his hangover was contributing to a bad case of déjà-vu. The only thing missing was the free rum drink stand. Maybe he could sample some of the local brew on his way into town. But first, business: passing through customs.

Instinctively, he made for the youngest-looking officer. He would have liked to have had time to size them all up before making his choice, but there was no line. Experience had taught him that any sign of hesitation was always fatal when dealing with officialdom, so he approached the man confidently.

The young official gave him a pleasant smile as he flipped through his passport. "Good day, sah, welcome to Uganda. What is the purpose of your visit?"

"*Jambo, rafiki.* I'm going to be taking some courses at Makerere. My visa's in the passport."

"I see this is your first time in our country. I hope you enjoy your visit. I am going to give you six months. If you need more time to complete your studies, you will have no trouble getting an extension in Kampala."

"I'm sure I'll enjoy my stay. Can you tell me the best way to get into town?"

"Yes, rafiki, there are cabs outside, but do not pay more than twenty-five shilingi. The best hotel is the International."

"*Asante sana.*"

That was easier than he'd thought it would be, although between "Hello, friend," and "Thank you very much," he'd already used roughly a third of the Swahili phrases he'd memorized on the flight over. People generally liked to be addressed in their own language, even if only in greeting.

His pulse was rocketing as he pointed out his bags to the porter. Next, after scanning the line, he selected a roly-poly, jovial sort of inspector.

"Hello, sah." The moon-faced customs officer surveyed his luggage. "Two suitcases and a typewriter. You must be planning to visit us for a while. Any firearms, alcohol, or cigarettes?"

"Just a *studenti* at Makerere. No guns. You already had one coup this year. I hope there's not going to be another, or my parents will be worried. I have one carton of cigarettes and no spirits. Is there someplace I can get a beer before I catch a cab into town?"

If the customs man took offence at Martin's maladroit humor, he didn't show it.

Martin kicked himself. Stupid to be a wiseass when he didn't know the lay of the land.

"Yes, sah. On your right as you leave the customs hall. May I suggest a Nile? It is the best of our local beers." He chalked Martin's bags with a flourish and waved him toward the door.

Relief washed over Martin as he entered the grimy bar. Piece of cake. The people were loose, and the omens seemed good. A few beers for the ride, a little useful information from the cab driver, and things would be off to a good start.

A predatory-looking specimen pounced on Martin the minute he exited the terminal. "Taxi to Kampala?" The man gestured toward a dented Peugeot.

Martin sized up his opponent. "Maybe. How much to the International?"

"For you, a special price," the taxi driver said, oozing deceit. "Fifty shilingi."

Martin heard the indignant voice of a woman behind him. "You suck his blood," the woman said. "It should be no more than half of that price, even for a *mzungu*."

Martin turned toward his rescuer. She was tiny and as beautiful as she was outraged. Her skin was the blackest he'd ever seen—almost eggplant purple—and her features were finely chiseled, distinctly Egyptian, or at least the Hollywood interpretation of same.

She let him admire her for a moment before giving him an impish smile. "Is there something wrong with you, mzungu? You look at me like I am the first black person you have ever seen."

He was groping for an answer when a commotion in the parking lot opposite the terminal caught his eye. "What's going on over there?" He gestured at a shabbily clad figure racing through the rows of parked vehicles.

She made no answer as Martin craned his neck for a clearer look at the action. Two policemen were relentlessly gaining on their quarry. He was obviously a beggar, a teenager with a ratty burlap sack clutched in one of his desperately pumping arms. Martin wondered why he didn't drop the awkward burden. His gasping sobs were painfully audible as he drew nearer to where Martin and his beautiful company stood. Martin noted the boy's bugged-out, terrorized eyes.

The sharp crack of a pistol and the dull thud of the bullet hitting the boy were almost simultaneous, punctuated by an agonized grunt as he collapsed in a shapeless heap on the pavement not fifteen feet from them.

Holy shit, Martin thought. *I can't believe this is happening right in front of me.* He glanced around, everything frozen in a silent tableau. Then two policemen arrived and commenced a panting argument. Martin had never seen anybody shot before.

He couldn't tear his eyes away from the grim sight. The boy was still alive. His body twitched as he uttered slight groans. Martin found himself mesmerized by the intricate scarlet patterns the blood was etching into the pavement.

A shiny Mercedes screeched to a halt opposite the body a few seconds later, snapping Martin out of his trance. Out stepped an older white man with a bushy gray mustache, receding gray hair, and a pronounced overbite. He riffled through the boy's pockets, searching for something. When he didn't find what he was looking for, he cursed and then signaled to the limo.

The rear window rolled down, and Martin looked on in disbelief as a familiar face presented itself from the back seat of the car. It was President Amin himself, his round face and predatory gaze unmistakable. That same gaze met Martin's, and it was all the newcomer to the country could do even to breathe. Amin never looked away from Martin as he produced a pistol, held it out the window, and turned it on the boy. A shot rang out, and the boy's head exploded against the pavement.

The older white man ducked into the car, and the limousine cruised away without either man giving a backward glance.

Martin, stunned, turned to look for the beautiful woman, who was quivering with fear. She motioned for him to keep silent and then melted into the crowd forming around the dead boy. Martin started to follow her, but another mzungu, this one with a shock of white hair, grabbed him by the wrist and pulled him back.

"I wouldn't," the man said in an aristocratic British accent. "Trust me. Just go about your business."

Martin noticed something on his foot. It took him a moment to realize that the scarlet-tinged, gray-green splotch was a piece of brain matter that had clung to one of his brown leather loafers. By the time he had the breath to respond to the white-haired man, the man had already turned and was walking away.

The taxi driver smiled. "*Kondo amekwisha. Sau sau.*"

Martin had no idea what he was talking about—and didn't care. Further Swahili lessons could wait until he found a local instructor, preferably female and as attractive as the mysterious young woman who had disappeared so suddenly. In the meantime, he needed to get to a hotel, shower, and regroup. "How much for a poor studenti?"

"For a lucky mzungu, a bargain," the taxi driver said. "Thirty-five shilingi."

"Thirty with a little tour around town," Martin countered.

"You take the food from my children's mouths, but a man must work." The taxi driver grunted, and none too gently lobbed Martin's bags into the trunk.

Score one for the opposition, Martin thought. The dialogue was straight out of the movies, but so was what he'd just witnessed. He sipped on an ice-cold Nile as they pulled out of the parking lot onto a smooth tarmac road. The savannah around the lake quickly gave way to cultivated farmland, interspersed with clusters of mud and thatch huts. There were bunches of green bananas alongside the road—matoke, the staple crop, he assumed. The clay-red soil looked as though anything would grow in it.

"First time in Uganda, sah?"

"Yes, it looks like pretty country."

The light, hoppy Nile slid easily down Martin's throat as the scenery became increasingly urban. He was just beginning to come down from the airport adrenalin rush. An almost post-coital calm settled over him. The driver kept up a running commentary on points of interest as they approached Kampala. At first glance, it looked like an attractive, small-sized American city. A handful of skyscrapers intermingled with the colonial bungalows that sprawled gracefully over the gently rolling hills. The rambling shantytowns on the outskirts of town were cleaner than he had expected.

"We are coming into the center of Kampala now." The driver gestured toward a large complex of concrete sheds surrounded by a rusty corrugated iron fence. "That is Nakasero market. You can get anything you want there."

"Is that the main market?"

"For food and household goods. We are turning on to Nile Avenue now. This is where the expensive *touristi* stores are."

They drove for several blocks down the broad, tree-lined street, which was dotted with pricey-looking boutiques. Most of them appeared to be owned by Indians. The sidewalks were full, and the storefronts displayed a variety of goods that would have been of little use to the average Ugandan. They turned onto a road that meandered past luxurious bungalows with well-manicured gardens.

"This is Kololo, where most of the mzungus live. The International is just ahead." The driver pointed to a modern steel-and-glass high-rise a few blocks ahead. It looked like a nice neighborhood—but not the kind Martin wanted to pass time in during his stay. He hadn't come this far to eat hamburgers from the commissary and bitch about the servants.

A few minutes later, they drove up a steep driveway to the main entrance of the hotel.

The International didn't have a particularly African flavor. Apart from the black faces, it looked like a basic InterContinental. *Why do they always look like milk cartons?* Martin wondered. At least the beer would be cold and the towels clean. As he checked in, he was amazed to see that it was only noon. He had time for a quick nap before he started to explore town. His double room in the back of the hotel overlooked a magnificent swimming pool. He unpacked, left an alarm call, and collapsed.

CHAPTER

2

MARTIN COULDN'T TAKE *his eyes off the mysterious woman at the airport terminal. Her petite frame. Her chiseled features. She was stunning. She locked eyes with him, and everything else around them disappeared. He lost himself in her gaze as she opened her mouth to speak. But her words were drowned out by a blaring sound. Squealing brakes? Someone dragging their wheeled luggage down the tarmac?*

It was the telephone.

Martin managed to crack open his eyes and clumsily reach for the ringing phone at his bedside. "Yeah?"

"Good afternoon, sah," a man said in a polite voice on the other end of the line. "It is one-thirty."

God, it felt like he'd only been asleep for a few minutes.

Nothing a quick dip wouldn't cure. The pool was quiet, but so was everything else about the hotel. Late September wasn't the height of the tourist season. The water was as invitingly cool as it had looked from his balcony. Martin felt the travel haze clearing away as he swam a few lazy laps. Once satisfied he had exerted himself enough for the day, he retreated to an empty table to enjoy some spicy samosas and a cold beer under the shade of an oversized umbrella. Stretching out on a deck chair, he let the sun bake out the last vestiges of his hangover. It was blisteringly hot. The taxi had passed over a black line marking the equator on the drive in from Entebbe.

He let his mind drift to the mystery woman at the airport, and once more, he found himself entranced by her beauty. Her lips curled upward in a smile, but before she could speak to him in his hazy daydream, he heard a gasp nearby and willed himself awake.

The poolside banter and buzz of activity had abruptly disappeared. Martin opened his eyes to see a VIP and his entourage bustling past. The VIP was none other than Idi Amin. Martin couldn't believe they had once again crossed paths, but before he could process seeing the man for a second time since landing in Uganda, Amin stopped at his table.

"Who are you, mzungu?" The president glared down at him with a mixture of distrust and playful curiosity. "I see you this morning. What are you doing in my country?"

Martin stuttered in his response. "I'm a student, Your Excellency. I'm here to learn all about the history of your great country."

Amin reached down to take one of Martin's samosas and swallowed the savory pastry in one bite. "Mmm ... Good samosa." He returned his attention to Martin. "Be a good student, mzungu. Don't cause no trouble, and you won't have no trouble."

Speechless, Martin watched as Amin waddled off toward the pool.

Someone chuckled from behind, and Martin turned to see the same white-haired man from the airport. He was seated at a nearby table. "He'll do that sometimes," the man said in his flowery British accent.

"Are you following me?" Martin asked.

The white-haired man shrugged. "You're new here. After watching you at Entebbe, I figured you had to be."

"Been an adventure so far," Martin replied. "Like being in a movie."

"It's all of that, old cock. The problem is figuring out whether the movie's a comedy, drama, or horror. Sometimes, it's all three." He extended his hand.

Martin hesitated and then shook it.

"Major Ian Smythe-Jones," the man said. "You passed the first test. Less is more around these parts, especially when you don't know the lay of the land. Somehow, I think we might be seeing more of each other around town." He tipped his straw hat and sauntered off.

Martin shook his head. Things just kept getting more interesting. He finished his beer and samosas and then returned to his hotel room to change out of his swim trunks and into something dry.

•••

After changing some money at the *caisse*, Martin set off down the hill in the direction of Nile Avenue.

The people seemed happy as they bustled about their business. Martin, expecting a heavy military presence so soon after the coup, was surprised to see only a smattering of soldiers patrolling the streets. No shortage of deformed beggars, though. He made a mental note to select and cultivate a few. They usually turned out to be excellent sources of information. Most people considered them subhuman because of their deformities. Consequently, they often said things in front of them that they'd never dream of mentioning in front of "normal" people. Of course, he'd have to be selective. There wasn't enough money in Fort Knox to meet the Third World's needs.

A few minutes of browsing on Nile Avenue confirmed his impressions from the cab ride. Though the shops were well stocked, there was virtually nothing in them of any interest to non-tourists. He noticed that the Indian shopkeepers were starting to close up. Belatedly, he remembered that Uganda kept Muslim hours and businesses closed by three. Just as well, he thought. The heat was sauna-like, and he needed a beer to rehydrate. As he scanned the street, his eyes fastened on a shiny copper door with the magic word *bar* written on it. Looked like as good a place as any to start. He strolled up to the large colonial gingerbread structure, which turned out to be the Grand Hotel.

It felt like a refrigerator inside. Martin slipped off his shades and let his eyes become accustomed to the soothing darkness. He grabbed a vacant seat, ordered a beer, and took in the place. The vibes were good. A mixed crowd of expats and locals were shouting to make themselves heard over a thumping jukebox. Judging from the number of Ugandan ladies sprinkled through the crowd, fraternizing with the locals was tolerated. He had no doubt that it would improve his Swahili quicker than classes at the university ever would. There were also a few obvious police types sprinkled around. Why else would someone wear sunglasses inside? Since the Tonton Macoute, it was the official uniform of the security classes. At least they were easy to spot.

"Excuse me. Can you tell me if there is something caught in my right eye?"

Martin turned on his stool to see his neighbor regarding him with a good-natured grin.

He was a heavyset fellow of average height. His close-cropped blond hair and lightly accented English lent him a vaguely Germanic air. Intriguingly, his eyes were of different colors: one gold, one blue. Martin wondered which was real.

"Your English is better than your color coordination," Martin said.

"Yours is not so bad for an American, either. Have a drink?"

"Sure, a Nile. You German?"

"*Ja.* Stefan Schmidt at your service."

"Martin Fine. This looks like a pleasant spot."

"Kampala's international listening post. Just arrived?"

"Flew in this morning. Just exploring town."

"You picked the right place to start. Permit me to introduce my partner in crime, Anton Springer."

Martin nodded to Stefan's friend. "Hey, Anton. Hope he meant that literally."

"No, man. Strictly metaphorically." Anton was a familiar sort: a tall, thin black man in an elaborately embroidered dashiki. His English carried an American bite. The inflection was streetwise, but there was something strange about it, as though he'd either not been back in a while or had learned it laboriously from the movies. "Are you passing through or staying, Martin?"

"I'll be around for the next six months, taking courses at Makerere. I hope to get in some traveling while I'm over here too. I hear there are lots of things worth checking out. You all?"

"We live here," Stefan replied. "I work for a German engineering firm, and Anton does lots of different things around town."

"Let me buy you two a drink," Martin said. "You can probably give me some good tips. I thought things would be a lot more uptight after the coup. Is it as mellow around town as it seems?"

"Not really," Anton answered in a paternal tone. "This place is an equatorial iceberg. Everything important goes on beneath the surface. You'll be okay if you keep your mouth shut and your eyes open for the first few weeks."

Martin almost expected him to make the sign of the cross over him. "How's the nightlife in these parts?"

Stefan laughed. "I can see that you have your priorities in order. It is more plentiful and amusing than you would think. Anton and

I are planning on making our usual Friday rounds later tonight. Would you like to join us?"

"Best offer I've had all day. I'm staying at the International. Where and when do you want to meet?"

"In the bar there about seven." Anton signaled for his tab. "See you then."

Quite a pair, Martin thought. *They might turn out to be useful sorts to know.* He didn't believe in coincidences, only karma, and his was running well these days, so he decided to check out the market on his way back to the hotel.

It was still brilliantly hot when he emerged from the copper bar. Things took on a more distinctly African flavor as he turned down Liberation Avenue, the Third World equivalent of Elm Street. Garish signs proclaimed *World's Best Doctor of Watches* and *Clothes Surgeon*. The street teemed with hawkers selling everything from cigarettes to roasted matoke and pungent mystery meat on skewers.

The market was still in high gear, judging from the brightly dressed hordes milling about its massive iron gates. Inside, a collage of colors, scents, and sounds enveloped him. Buxom market mamas, cheerfully insulting each other as they vied for business, stood behind makeshift wooden stalls heaped with fruits and vegetables. The shouts of hawkers punctuated the constant background din of cheap transistors blaring Congolese pop music. The stench of rotting food mixed with body odor was overpowering. Little children and scabrous dogs darted everywhere, foraging for edible scraps.

As he walked down the densely packed rows of stalls, Martin quickly picked up an entourage of youngsters. They were all touching and entreating him to let them get *Bwanamkubwa* the best deal possible. He ignored them, knowing they would lose interest after a while. Judging from the amount and variety of goods displayed and the large wads of currency changing hands, the local economy was thriving. The center aisle seemed to run forever, offering everything from love potions to fake diplomas from major British universities.

After an interminable walk, Martin approached the final stretch. His nose told him that he was nearing the meat section. The feral odors of rotting flesh and fresh blood made his head swim. Whole sides of beef were being butchered none too subtly. Not the place for filet mignon. He was fascinated by the efficient disposal system. Marabou storks, large ungainly things that looked like a cross between normal storks and pelicans, devoured the bigger scraps, and African purebreds gobbled up what was left.

Enough atmosphere for today, he thought as he trudged back to the main entrance and flagged a cab.

The canned air of the hotel was a pleasant change from the fetid stench of the market. On his way upstairs, he stopped in the bar for a beer to wash the taste of it out of his mouth.

As he sat down, two Africans in shiny black safari suits slid onto the stools on either side of him. Again, the Tonton mirror shades. They were almost a self-parody, but dangerous for all that.

"Hello, you are American?" the taller of the two inquired politely. Beanpole-thin, he had sharp, angular features. His protruding forehead gave him a menacing air that was not entirely dispelled by his smooth approach.

"Yeah, the last time I looked. You must be Ugandan." Martin caught himself and eased up. Being hostile wasn't a constructive policy, especially when he was still wearing his money belt with its damning contents. He felt like a naughty little boy in the headmaster's office. He knew exactly what he was going to hear and wasn't the slightest bit interested, but he had to play the game, anyway. "I'm here to take some courses at Makerere. You have a beautiful country. I'm looking forward to my stay here."

His questioner seemed unperturbed by his petulance. "This is good. What are you studying?"

"African history. I'm very interested in the ancient history of the Baganda and Toro. Can I buy you all a beer?"

"*Asenti.* Makerere is a very good school for studying such things."

"You are not interested in modern history at all?" the shorter one interjected. His face seemed familiar, but Martin couldn't place it.

"Not really. I know what goes on generally from reading the papers in London, where I studied last year."

"What did they say about recent events?"

The old good cop, bad cop routine, Martin thought. *These guys must read the same spy books I do.* He sipped on his beer and gathered his thoughts, realizing that he had to handle this carefully. It was a real pain in the butt to have to play childish word games with these clowns. The only problem was that in spite of their buffoonish exteriors, they emanated nasty vibes.

The last thing he wanted to do at this stage of the game was arouse any official interest. "They didn't have a lot to say," Martin replied. "They seemed favorable enough, if not wildly enthusiastic. Not much is known about General Amin. I must say, from what I've seen in the short time I've been here, the people seem happy with the change."

"The general is a great man," the taller agent volunteered. "He will be good for our country."

It was a tough line to follow, so Martin figured it was as good a time as any to take a powder. His shirt was sodden. Delayed travel fatigue and the beers he'd consumed were taking their toll. He'd given enough correct answers to satisfy them for the time being. "I'm sure he will. Now if you gentlemen will excuse me, I've had a long day walking around your beautiful city. I'm going upstairs for a shower. It's been nice talking."

The tall one flipped open his wallet, flashing a card with *General Services Unit* emblazoned on it. "I am Harry Usongo. If there is anything you need during your stay, please give me a call. Our number is listed."

The short one grunted noncommittally in Martin's direction, and they departed.

While Martin was waiting for the elevator, a handsome African, nattily attired in a blue blazer with a plastic name card, winked conspiratorially at him. "Hi, I'm Joe Kaberinge, beverage and catering manager here at the hotel."

"Pleased to meet you, Joe," Martin said. "But if you don't mind, I—"

"I just wanted to tell you that you handled them well," the manager cut in. "They hassle everybody who's not a normal tourist. I'm sorry it had to happen."

Martin nodded, unsure what to say.

"If you feel like it later," Joe added in a conspiratorial tone, "join me upstairs in the Leopard's Lair for a nightcap."

This sounded fine. Martin thanked him and entered the lift.

Once in his room, he took a long shower and flicked on the TV as he toweled off. Amin was giving a chest-thumping harangue against loose sexual mores to a bemused bunch of schoolgirls in the Toro District. The general looked even more impressive on TV than he had in person. He had a way of appearing like a friendly, avuncular type, but there was something about him that disquieted Martin. Maybe it was his constantly darting, porcine eyes, a subtle, calculated menace residing somewhere just behind that jovial facade.

• • •

It was quarter to seven by the time Martin got down to the bar. He was relieved to see that the Mutt and Jeff GSU team, evidently satisfied with their conversation, had not returned. After ordering a Nile, he watched the pretty waitresses set up for the evening shift. Stefan and Anton arrived a few minutes later.

Stefan was the first to speak. "Hello, Martin. Discover anything interesting in your travels around town this afternoon?"

"Just the market. It was about what I expected. I did have a chat with two of the general's personal representatives when I got back to the hotel, though."

"GSU?" Anton whispered.

"The same. Their technique was crude. But on to cheerier subjects. What's on for my first night in Kampala?"

"How about dinner and some in-depth research into local sexual customs?" Stefan offered. "That ought to appeal to your academic bent. What kind of food do you like?"

"How about some curry? There are enough Indians around these parts. Must be some decent restaurants."

Stefan nodded. "I know just the place: Sinbad's out at Bat Valley."

"The best curry in town, combined with an incomparable natural spectacle," Anton added, adopting the spiel of a tour director.

Martin paid for the drinks, and they climbed into Stefan's battered Renault and roared off.

Stefan's driving style was not for the faint of heart, but it seemed admirably suited to local conditions. He laughed as Martin subconsciously tightened his grip on the armrest. "I see you like my driving. Actually, my style evolved after a very scientific study of local conditions. You have to drive offensively over here to survive. If I drove like I normally would in Europe, I would be terrified all of the time. I thought you might find it a little disconcerting, so I took the liberty of having Anton prepare a small religious ceremony to speed the acclimation process."

Anton reached over the seat and handed Martin a man-sized joint.

Wonderful, Martin thought. *These guys are looking more and more like my type.* He took a toke and handed it up to Stefan. "Okay, I'll bite. Why's it called Bat Valley?"

"I was hoping you would get around to that," Stefan said as he exhaled with a smile. "Oddly enough, it is because of the thousands of fruit bats that live there. During the day, they hang on the trees like pods of fruit, but at night, they fly off to feed. Quite an impressive sight. Sometimes, they seem to blacken the sun."

Martin sat back and let the reefer go to work. It was as good as he'd expected. He felt it enveloping his senses in that familiar warm blanket. This was the life, no doubt about it. They were headed out of town on a smooth tarmac road. The surrounding country was lush. Groves of banana and its sister plant, matoke, covered the rolling green hills. The villages looked prosperous. It was dinnertime, and the cooking pots were boiling everywhere.

Stefan conducted a running monologue on the charms of African women, many of whom were unabashedly taking their evening bucket baths beside the road. Every once in a while, inspired by a particularly noteworthy specimen, he would honk his horn and yell, "Look at those filet steaks! Five pounds, no bones!"

Far from being embarrassed, the ladies laughed at his attention and made no attempt to cover themselves.

"Now I know I'm going to love this place," Martin said.

"You will find the *mpenzis*—that is the Swahili for *attractive girl*—very accommodating here," Stefan said. "Things are much looser and enlightened."

Anton cleared his throat. "If you two can tear your eyes off the country's more abundant natural charms for a second, Bat Valley is coming up on the right."

It didn't look that exotic at first glance—more of a depression than a valley. A cluster of nondescript concrete buildings at one end sat against the low-slung hills. Tall trees dotted the landscape. As they got closer, Martin could see that their branches were festooned with black pods. Judging from the rapidly descending sun, they weren't going to have to wait too long to see the nightly show.

Stefan rattled to a halt in front of one of the buildings, which was decorated with a weathered wooden sign depicting a pirate. The minute they got out of the car, the aroma told Martin they had come to the right place.

Anton snapped his fingers and gestured excitedly at the nearest tree. "Look at that, man. You're right on time as usual, Stefan."

Nature quickly proved Anton right. Suddenly it was raining bats. The pods dropped slowly at first, opening magically before they hit the ground. Within minutes, they were dropping so fast, Martin could barely see the last rays of the sun through them. The whole spectacle was over in a quarter of an hour, leaving the denuded trees looking starkly forlorn against the crimson afterglow of the sunset.

Martin couldn't believe that such a natural phenomenon could unfold so close to the urban sprawl of Kampala. "That's a tough act to follow. Does it happen every night?"

"Always and forever," Anton intoned as he ushered them inside.

They were given a table directly in front of a large picture window that overlooked the valley.

Stefan waved off the menu. "How about sambosas, a vindaloo, and some chapattis?"

"Add some dal," Martin said, "and you've got a deal. I spent a lot of time in London and ate a lot of Indian food."

"Really? So did I. I went to school there for five years just after the war. That is where I learned my English."

A few minutes later, the first dish arrived, and Martin's mouth began to water.

"Ah, here are the sambosas," Stefan said. "You may have had these in England, but I doubt that you know that they originated in East Africa."

The sambosas, triangular pastries filled with curried meat and vegetables, were incendiary and delicious. Stefan explained that the English had originally imported the Indians during colonial times to build the railroad to the coast. They had stayed on to become the shop-keeping class. Over the years, they had evolved their own local variations of classic Indian dishes.

The vindaloo that followed was equally good.

Martin pushed back from the table and lit a cigarette to extinguish the fires. "That vindaloo was magical, and I'm not going to spoil it by asking what kind of meat was in it. I'm ready for anything now. What's next?"

Anton glanced at his watch. "Too early for the Big S. Shall we try the Gardenia? That's always an excellent orientation point for newcomers," he added with a smirk.

"*Ja*," Stefan said, "maybe the Fairway too. That is another good place to get one's feet wet. We will save the Appetite Afrique and the Kampala Breast House for later. We do not want him to have a traumatic experience on the first night, do we?"

"He needs at least a week of seasoning before we hit those joints."

Martin raised an eyebrow. "I take it you two are referring to establishments around town that cater to a man's every need?"

"You got it," Stefan said. "Mpenzis to make the world go round. Sussana, otherwise known as the Big S, is the best spot. The other places are usually not that interesting, unless you've been on a desert island for a long time. The Gardenia and Fairway are worth a short visit for a few laughs at the expense of the hornier members of the expat community, though. If some of their wives only knew!"

The Gardenia was a two-storied beige stucco structure with the standard corrugated iron roof. It had a pair of peeling green lattice-work swinging doors straight out of Dodge City in its heyday. A babble of voices, intermixed with snatches of James Brown's "Can't Get Enough of That Funky Stuff," assaulted them as they entered the smoky, flyblown room.

The first thing that caught Martin's eye was an ornate wrought-iron staircase that descended gracefully from the second floor. Ladies were draped along its banister like mannequins—or sides of beef. Pink and blue light from neon bulbs along the splotchy walls cast a surreal glow on the frenzied activity below.

Martin's thoughts drifted back to the airport terminal, where the mysterious woman had waited patiently, a barely perceptible grin on her lips, while he soaked in her beauty. She was exquisite. Not of this world. And he couldn't get her out of his mind.

"Is there something wrong with you, mzungu? You look at me like I am the first black person you have ever seen."

Her voice echoed in his head as he stared with a blank face at the meat market in front of him. Finally, the pulsating bass jarred him into the present.

He had to holler to his compatriots to be heard. "This place certainly doesn't lack for local color! What's drinkable? Only what they open in front of you?"

"Even then, be sure it fizzes!" Stefan shouted. "The mpenzis here are a little on the brassy side, if your tastes are so inclined."

He wasn't kidding, Martin thought. Most of them would have been at home in the sleaziest topless bar in Soho or Times Square. They were teenagers, for the most part, which wasn't surprising. Martin remembered reading somewhere that most African women were mothers by the time they turned fifteen. They certainly seemed attractive enough to the highly inebriated crowd of expats milling about in a frenzy. The whole spectacle reminded him of a tea dance at a horny boys' prep school, only the stakes were higher.

"See that guy in the blue safari suit over there?" Anton gestured to a corner by the jukebox. "He's the top surgeon at Mulago, the big hospital in town."

Martin glanced in the man's direction and watched the diminutive African drooling down the cleavage of a buxom blond-wigged mpenzi. His hands were kneading her abundant rump in a most unprofessional manner. Martin made a mental note to get up and leave the hospital if he ever had to be treated by the guy.

As he sipped his beer, he fended off the good-natured advances of several ladies. They weren't pushing the point, but the scene was getting boring. He was relieved when Stefan reappeared and suggested going to Sussana.

The ride over took about twenty minutes. Sussana was on the outskirts of town. Martin didn't know in which direction, but after Anton lit another joint, he didn't care. The large Quonset building resembled a warehouse from the outside. Only the huge parking lot and a blinking sign of pink and green bulbs gave any indication that it was a nightclub.

The first thing that caught Martin's eye as they passed through the turnstiles into the cavernous room was the huge stage at the other end. A sixteen-piece show band, complete with dancing girls, was performing "Hold On, I'm Coming." Huge potted palms stood among the tables that surrounded the vast dance floor. Though there were few dancers at this early hour, the tables were full. The bar that ran the length of the wall by the entrance stood three-deep with thirsty patrons. He could only make this out through the darkness in short bursts. Intermittent flashes from the rudimentary light show kept Martin from stumbling into the furniture.

Stefan somehow produced a table out of thin air and a waiter to take their order. "Hot enough in here for you? Do not worry.

If you don't see something that interests you soon, we will depart for the Leopard's Lair. It tends to be less crowded, especially when the hotel is quiet."

"That would suit me. I met the catering manager, Joe Kaberinge, this afternoon, and he invited me up for a nightcap. At least I'll know my way home."

"He's a nice dude," Stefan said. "One word of advice about the Lair. Lots of government types hang out there in civvies. It's not a good place for loose talk, but it's an excellent one for making useful contacts."

It didn't take long for Martin to figure out that Sussana was a place to bring dates, not find them. He signaled Stefan, and they made a hasty exit.

Martin sensed trouble outside as they neared Stefan's beat-up Renault in the parking lot.

A sketchy-looking local clad in dark, loose-fitting clothes and holding something in his right hand approached them. "You got anything for me?"

Martin spied something flash in the man's right hand and realized it was a knife. He instinctively grabbed the jacket slung over his own shoulder and wrapped it around his arm, all the while conscious of his bulging money belt hidden beneath his shirt.

"Not tonight, my friend," Stefan answered. "You best go home."

The stranger brandished the knife. "You sound like a Kraut. You mzungus are all the same: You think you run this place." He gave Anton the once-over. "What gives? What are you doing with these two?"

Stefan stepped between them. "Go home."

"You first." The stranger spit on the ground and moved closer to strike.

Just as the man reared back with his blade, Martin stepped in to disarm him. Using his jacket to block the blow, Martin soon had the man's arm wedged behind his back. A distinctive cracking sound followed—Martin could almost feel it reverberate from the man's arm—and their would-be attacker grunted in distress. Martin spun the man toward a nearby parked convertible, grabbed the knife, and drove it through the man's hand and into the roof of the car.

As the man howled in pain, Martin turned to his new friends. "Shall we go?"

Stefan looked shaken but appreciative.

Anton raised an eyebrow but said nothing.

"We shall," Stefan said.

As the three rode in silence back to the hotel, Martin glanced down and noticed a small streak of blood—his own—on his right forearm. He was still sweating but donned his jacket anyway.

• • •

From the look of the crowd in the lift riding up to the penthouse, the Lair appealed to the more upscale segment of Kampala society. It was a beautiful duplex space, with floor-to-ceiling windows that offered a magnificent view of the city at night. A balcony with a bar overlooked one end of the dance floor. The music was traditional Western disco, but the atmosphere was just as frenetic as it had been at Sussana's.

Martin sat down with Stefan and Anton, and the three men exchanged glances. Before they could unpack their encounter with the mugger, Joe approached their table.

"Good evening, Martin," he said. "I see that you have found yourself two excellent guides." He pulled up a chair and signaled the waiter before turning to Stefan. "Where have you taken this innocent visitor so far tonight?"

"The usual tour: curry at Bat Valley, drinks at the Gardenia, and dancing at the Big S. Did we leave anything out?"

"That is a pretty good start. He looks like he is doing okay for himself. What will you have?"

They ordered drinks and sat back, surrendering to the booming sound system. The dancing was a little stiffer, as befitted the mostly expat crowd. Martin was beginning to feel the effects of his long day, made longer by the violent encounter in the parking lot back at the Big S. The edges of the room were growing blurry.

Joe nudged him gently. "Would you like to come to the Bristol Bar on Sunday night for some traditional Baganda dancing? Invite anyone else you want."

"I'd love it. Consider me a definite. I'll ask the others later. Are you a Baganda?"

"Yes," Joe said with a nod. "Some of my cousins will be dancing. We should leave about six. I'll meet you in the bar downstairs. Enjoy the rest of the evening. It seems that you are in good hands." He left for another table.

Fatigue washed over Martin in waves.

Stefan tapped him on the shoulder and clucked sympathetically. "You look all-in."

"Just another night on the town."

Stefan gave him a sobering look. "You handled yourself admirably with the mugger back there. I owe you my life."

"You're lucky I had any reflexes left," Martin replied. "Tonight was a marathon."

Anton studied Martin's face. "Seems you've run a few before."

"Tonight was enough adventure for anyone," Stefan said, "myself included. We'll be going home now. If you feel like it, come out to my place for lunch."

"That sounds good." Martin thought for a moment. "I've got to arrange some wheels and do some other errands around town, so you'd better call me early."

• • •

The wait for the lift seemed interminable. When the elevator doors opened, Martin was shocked to see the mysterious woman from the airport involved in a shoving match with one of his GSU interrogators from the afternoon.

Without thinking, Martin stepped forward and pulled her free. "We meet again, and this time, it looks like you're the one who needs help."

The woman gave him a terrified look and opened her mouth to speak. She never got the chance.

"Well, if it isn't Mr. Fine, the famous American Boy Scout." Harry was his usual suave self. "I see you have met one of our delightful countrywomen." He grabbed the woman's upper arm and squeezed until her flesh turned white around his fingers. "This one is well known to me. She is a bad woman. You had better watch yourself." He threw down her arm with a cackle and strode off.

Martin turned to follow him, but the woman pulled him into the car.

"Do not go after him," she insisted. "He is a very bad man. He will make trouble for you if you interfere." She fought back tears as the doors closed.

Martin felt the adrenaline fighting against his fatigue. "I don't let anybody treat a lady like that, especially when I've had her on my mind all afternoon."

She blinked up at him with those gorgeous dark eyes.

Suddenly, he couldn't think of anything else. "You seem to be involved in all the action around here," Martin said once he'd caught up to his own head. "Who are you, and what's he got against you?"

She kissed him lightly on the lips, and there he went again, his mind gone.

"It is a long story," she said when she pulled back. "I will tell you some other time. Would you please give me ten shilingi for the taxi home?"

Of course he would. What else could he possibly have done, the way she had disarmed him so? "On one condition," he answered. "Let me have dinner with you tomorrow night."

She offered a warm smile. "I will meet you downstairs in the bar at eight."

He gave her a ten-shilingi note and ventured an inquisitive kiss before the lift doors closed, leaving only a tantalizing trace of her scent.

He still didn't know her name.

. . .

The commando stepped out of the shadows in a back alley downtown just as a sleek Mercedes rolled to a stop.

After turning off the headlights, Bertain Aka, an immaculately groomed Rwandan with dashing features, stepped out of the dark sedan. A trio of ostentatious diamond rings on Aka's right hand caught a shaft of light coming from a nearby streetlamp and sparkled in unison as the commando handed him a bulging felt pouch.

"Everything here?" Aka asked.

The commando ignored a sudden impulse to hold on to the pouch and offered a stoic nod instead. "A pleasure doing business with you."

Aka smiled, his white teeth gleaming in the darkness. "Pleasure's all mine."

CHAPTER

3

The trilling of the phone woke him the next morning.

"Good morning, sleeping beauty. It is ten-thirty. Do you know whose bed you are in?"

It took Martin a moment to register Stefan's voice. "God, is it really that late?"

"It is. I am downstairs. I figured you could use a lift around town while you do your errands."

"You're a lifesaver. I'll be down in a flash."

Stefan was waiting in the lobby with a cup of coffee for him. It was another perfect day. Martin adjusted his shades as they headed down the hill. It was a self-defense move, aimed more at protecting himself from Stefan's outrageously loud tropical shirt than the sun. As if the shirt wasn't enough to ensure high visibility, Stefan insisted on honking his horn at every mpenzi they passed and asking her if she wanted a lift. He told Martin that he knew a good place—run by an Indian, naturally—where cars could be leased by the month. The prices were the best in town, with a special rate for cash dollars.

Padwah's was located within a stone's throw of the market. The lot was loaded with new-looking Peugeots, Renaults, and zebra-striped VW buses. Stefan instructed him to haggle with

Padwah and then offer him two-thirds of the agreed-upon price in crisp hundreds. It worked like a charm. The Indian's eyes bulged when he saw the wad.

Within minutes, Martin was the proud possessor of a slightly used Renault at two hundred and fifty dollars a month. "Next, a bank, and my business will he finished."

"That is easy enough. The Bank of Uganda. They have the best facilities, including safe deposit boxes." Stefan gave him a wink. "Follow me. It is on the way out of town. You are not planning on changing a large amount of money, are you?"

"Not there. I just need some walking-around money. I figured you'd steer me toward the best black-market rate for the larger exchanges. How'd you know I was going to get a safe deposit box?"

"It seemed certain that carrying around that bulky money belt of yours was getting to be an annoyance."

"I didn't realize it was that obvious. Lucky no one's ripped me off."

"It was not that easy to see. I could tell from the way you sat down. I have worn them myself. They are not built for comfort."

While Martin completed the formalities in the bank, Stefan picked up some things for lunch.

"Next stop, Kireka," Stefan said after they reunited. "I will modify my usual pace until you are a little more used to the driving. Follow me."

They streaked out of town on an arrow-straight highway, which Martin later found out was the Jinja Road, the country's major north-south artery. It was jammed with buses and trucks. Brightly dressed Ugandans carrying bundles and baskets on their heads lined the highway. Market day. Martin had read somewhere that the main weight measurement in colonial Africa was the head-pound. The British, in their infinite wisdom, had decided that eighty-five pounds was the maximum that their laborers could carry on their heads in one load. That weight had become a standard measure. He could believe it now. Some of the precariously perched bundles defied gravity.

Just after they passed an already bustling market, Stefan turned sharply right onto a rutted murram track that zigzagged up a steep hill. They passed several villages, and everybody seemed to know Stefan, or at least his shirt. After a jarring ride that took as long as the drive out of town, Stefan braked violently to a halt in front of a white stucco bungalow. They were in a wooded clearing of about twenty-five acres at the top of the mountain.

Through the trees, Martin could make out two other similar bungalows at opposite ends of a rough triangle. The view was stunning. On one side, Kampala dozed in the noon sun. On another, Martin could just make out the tip of Lake Victoria. The third side of the clearing overlooked a well-cultivated savannah dotted by puffs of smoke from the surrounding villages.

Martin whistled as he took it in. "With all this, why leave home?"

"I try not to. Come in, and I will get my house boy, Isador, to build us a pipe."

"Now you're speaking my language."

"If we are lucky, Uganda's first white citizen, Cedric Ayres, may pay us a visit later on. He lives in the bungalow up on the left."

The house was simple but comfortable. A kitchen led to a large, airy living room with sliding glass doors overlooking the savannah. Before he knew it, Martin had a well-broken-in meerschaum pipe in his mouth and Jimmy Smith grooving in his ears. Stefan handed him a beer and beckoned him outside. The small yard ended about twenty feet from the porch and dropped precipitously through overgrown wasteland to a village about a hundred yards below.

"Are they growing matoke down there?" Martin asked.

"They are growing lots of things. Tomatoes, eggfruit, onions, as well as matoke and what you are smoking. Not a bad setup, eh?

The minute I saw it, I knew it was the place for me."

"Yeah, it's a real gem."

"Sarah, the wife of King Freddy, the kabaka of the Baganda, owns all of it. He is still in exile in London. Fortunately, Amin made his move before Obote could nationalize this place."

"Does Sarah have any more of these up her sleeve? I'm going to be looking for a place too."

"It just so happens that the third house is empty. She would probably part with it for three hundred and fifty dollars a month in those nice new bills."

Martin grinned. "I'll see what I can scare up."

"If you are interested, I can give her a call. I assume you are not that anxious to continue staying at the hotel."

"Not at their prices," Martin said with a shake of the head.

"Cedric and I would be glad to have a neighbor. You would cover our flanks from the kondos."

"Kondos? From the way you spit out the term, they sound akin to crab lice."

"Lower on the evolutionary scale, actually. They are robbers who come around after dark stealing what they can and hacking you to pieces with pangas if you resist."

"Like our friend last night?"

"Indeed. But more deadly." Stefan's face darkened, suggesting he had a story or two to tell. "Cedric is well-liked around these parts, so they tend to stay away, but I am prepared if necessary. You should have a gun. Do you know how to use one?"

"Yeah, I grew up with them in the States. My family was very into hunting. I'm also a member of a pistol club in London. Never drawn one in anger, though."

Isador, a teenager in shorts and a James Brown T-shirt, padded in on bare feet and deposited a tray of sandwiches and iced tea on the table behind them.

Over lunch, Martin inquired about the political situation.

"Pretty stable these days," Stefan answered. "It has been about six months since the coup, and Amin has consolidated pretty well. He has had help, to be sure. The coup was undertaken with Israeli support and American and British knowledge. There is still some purging of dissident tribal elements in the army, but by and large, he is in firm control. There are no problems for mzungus who mind their own business. As soon as they are sure that you are a harmless, fun-loving studenti, the GSU boys will not bother you."

Martin took another hit off the pipe. "They were apparently satisfied with their conversation with me yesterday," he said, trailing smoke. "But something strange happened when I split the Lair last night. I ran into one of the two GSU guys who hit me up in the afternoon. He was with the mystery lady I told you about, the one from the airport. They were in the elevator. I think his name is Harry Usongo. He grabbed her and got very nasty. Said she was a bad woman."

"Funny. What did she have to say about it?"

"Nothing. She said he was a bad man and that she would tell me about it some other time." Martin broke into a satisfied smile. "Dinner tonight."

"Dinner?" Stefan asked, his voice rising. "Ja, that sounds pleasant. As to your GSU friend, it is a slow time of the year, so they could be hassling her for some sex. You never know with these guys. Besides, I have yet to encounter an African intelligence service that was not overstaffed. People over here have big families, so some pretty strange types get hired."

Martin thought a moment. "Do you have any government contacts? I suppose they're rather a necessity."

"They certainly can be useful. I have Anton, who is extremely well-connected in the GSU. If you start seeing the lady and this guy is a problem, I am sure he can help you out. Contacts are not hard to get. If you hang around a bit at the right places, you will meet most of the government fellows. They are about what one would expect."

"They might be nice guys, but how well-trained are they?"

"Amin has been smart enough so far to keep as much of the civil service together as he can—tribal factors permitting, of course. They have been very well-trained. I do not know if you are aware of it, but this country has one of the highest literacy rates on the continent."

Martin furrowed his brow in surprise.

"Speaking of which," Stefan said, "when does school start?"

"Not for about two weeks. Figured I'd register Monday, find some digs, and then drive around to see some of the country. Probably I'll head up to Murchison Falls first. I'm distantly related to the old boy on my mother's side. It would be nice to be the first living relative to see them."

After lunch, Stefan ordered another pipe, and they smoked it in companiable silence. Martin felt the tension in his body dissipate. The weather was perfect, the weed was perfect, and the moment was perfect.

• • •

"My goodness! Don't you two look like the ambitious sorts."

Martin roused from his nap to see an impossibly thin mzungu, wrapped in a gaudy batik sarong that matched his badly died orange-brown hair, gently shaking Stefan awake.

"Mind if I crash for a bit, dearie?" the man asked. "I've been temporarily evicted."

Stefan opened his eyes and smiled. "Pull up a chair, Cedric, and meet Martin Fine. The newest Yank in town. Soon to be a student at Makerere."

Cedric dropped into a chair like he owned the joint. "Charmed, I'm sure. Bloody nuisance the things a man has to do around here."

"Not to be too ugly of an American," Martin said, "but exactly what do you do around here?"

"Anything a man—or what passes for one in this place—can do to make ends meet." Cedric flashed his most seductive smile and limp-wristed the glass to his lips.

"Cedric, you can spare him the show," Stefan said. "I can assure you that he is not too impressionable and that he does not swing your way."

"Well it'll be all business then," Cedric said with a performative eye roll. "Currently, I'm making ends meet by letting the frog-charge use my pad for some serious confidential business."

"The frog-charge, eh? Who is he doffing this week?"

"A cute little mpenzi from the Ministry of Internal Affairs. No pun intended, of course. They've been at it since last night. You'd think they would get tired in this heat."

Martin laughed. "All these sensitive government negotiations taking place in your home; you must be pretty well-informed about what goes on in town."

"Dearie, I know everything, down to what color underwear everybody does or mostly doesn't wear. It's what gives me my edge." Cedric glanced back at the sound of wheels spinning through the dust. "Oops! There goes the Mercedes. That's my cue, dears." He stood from the chair. "Thanks for the drink, Stefan." He turned to Martin. "Nice to meet you, Mr. Fine."

Martin waited until Cedric was out of earshot to share his thoughts with Stefan. "An interesting choice for their first white citizen."

"He is a charming fellow. Like most gays, he can be aggressive if he thinks he has something to prove. Once he realizes that you accept his sexuality, he calms down. There are a lot of advantages to having him as a friend. He is very popular around town because of all the charity work he does."

Martin glanced at his watch. It was getting on. "Listen, Stefan, you wouldn't have any spare smoke around, would you? I didn't really want to cop until I had a little better feel for what was going on."

"*Natürlich.* Three varieties to choose from. This place is a pot connoisseur's dream come true. Come inside, and I will fix you up." Stefan led Martin inside to the spare bedroom and rummaged through the closet. A few seconds later, he emerged with three tobacco tins. "Take a handful of each. I shall leave to you the pleasure of discovering which does what." He smiled. "Being of the academic bent, I am sure you will enjoy your studies."

Martin rolled a handful of each in separate strips of newspaper. "It all smells dynamite. I can think of a few folks back home who would love to have this selection. Is it easy to get weight?"

"As easy as falling off a log."

"Figured. Thought I might look into investment opportunities. This stuff fetches useful money in the States."

"That is what I like about you *Amis*: You don't beat around the bush when it comes to business. I had a feeling about you from the minute you walked into the Copper Bar the other day." Stefan waved Martin to a seat in the living room and mixed them each a stiff waragi. "Isador has the afternoon off, so it is all right to talk. First question—and if you do not want to answer, I will not be insulted: Are you really a studenti?"

"Yeah, but I'm not averse to making a little dough on the side. I've had some previous experience. In fact, I ended up over here because of my checkered university career in the States."

"I see. Are you only interested in drugs?"

"They're the only thing I know much about. But pot has a lot of disadvantages, like bulk and smell, so I'm open to alternate suggestions."

"Ja, I thought also about marijuana. I, too, am interested in making a little money on the side. Pot is not worth the risk—believe me. I have investigated things thoroughly. By the time you pay off everybody, the money is too small for the hassle. Take my advice. Leave the pot to the hippies."

"So what else do you suggest?"

"Gold, diamonds, or something similar."

"Oh, shit," Martin said in mock amazement. "I suppose you just happen to have a map to a lost mine stashed away."

"*Nein*, I am not a bullshitter. I just think they are the way to go. Actually, I have not yet stumbled upon any useful contacts."

"What about Anton?"

"He is fine to run a few ladies with, and he is also useful for fixing up a few minor hassles, but I get the impression that he is the sort of guy who enters a revolving door behind you and comes out ahead of you. I do not really trust him."

"Makes sense. Too many friends in the GSU."

"Exactly. Think about what I told you. Make your own inquiries. If you agree with me, maybe we can do some business. You need a partner to cover your ass in these matters. You also have to be patient and do some investigating. In these cases, any apple that falls directly off the tree into your lap is bound to be rotten."

Martin offered a tight-lipped smile. "Thanks for the advice." He rose and extended his hand. "For what it's worth, I had a feeling about you too. We might just make a good team."

Stefan nodded appreciatively.

"I've got that dinner date," Martin said. "Maybe you want to hook up with us afterward."

"Unfortunately, I have a business dinner tonight. In any case, I try to avoid town on Saturday nights. It's a little crowded for my tastes."

Stefan rose and walked Martin out to his car. "I would love to come to the dancing on Sunday, though."

"Great. Should be a gas. Thanks for the help this morning."

"Forget it. Anything for a future neighbor and partner. I will give Sarah a call tomorrow. Just take a left at the bottom of the hill. The road leads right into town. *Kwaheri.*"

The drive back was quick, the roads deserted, everybody taking an afternoon nap—the only way to beat the heat.

• • •

After a nap and a shower, Martin arrived at the bar at about eight o'clock that evening. There was no sign of his date, but he told himself there was no reason African women should be any more punctilious than their Western counterparts. The good news was that Harry Usongo wasn't around, either. Martin had to assume that the girl's willingness to meet him in such a visible place meant that her feud with the GSU man tended toward personal. As he thought on this, he ordered a waragi and tonic and took in the atmosphere.

"Hey, Martin, you seem to have had a busy day." Joe sat down next to him. "I saw you drive in earlier."

"Evening, Joe. Figured you'd notice the car. Can I buy you a drink?"

"A beer. I hope they gave you a Kruk lock too," Joe said with a laugh. "What are you doing tonight?"

"This lovely lady I met last night was supposed to meet me here half an hour ago. We're going to dinner at an African place."

Joe glanced at his watch and laughed. "You've probably got at least another half hour. There are only two times of day here: daytime and nighttime. Anything else is in the laps of the gods. At least you can listen to some familiar accents while you wait."

He gestured to a posse of loud, catalog-safari-clad Americans at the bar.

"Should've known you wouldn't be able to resist," Martin quipped. "Actually, I can't really cop too much of an attitude, still being a newcomer myself. It's funny how quickly your perspective changes once you're going to spend some time in a place, though."

"Too true."

"By the way, Stefan will be joining us tomorrow night. Shall we leave the arrangements the same?"

"Yes, tell him to meet us here by six-thirty at the latest. If we want a large table, we must get there early." Joe glanced at his watch again and quickly finished his beer. "I must be off. See you tomorrow."

Joe had barely left when Martin heard a familiar voice.

"*Habari*, mzungu. Were you worried I was not coming?"

Martin looked up to see the mysterious woman standing in front of his table. "No, I figured you were on Female Standard Time." He leaned back to take in the sight of her. "I must say, the wait was worth it. You look ravishing—good enough to eat."

She smiled and looked down.

"Speaking of which," Martin said, "where are we going?"

"Some place called the Arizona. I have a taxi waiting outside." With that, she was off, her alluring hips swaying.

He followed after her. "Let's pay him off. I rented a car today. The only way I'm going to learn my way around is by getting my feet wet." Martin paid the taxi driver with a flourish and then led his date to his car.

As they pulled out of the driveway, she started rummaging in her bag. A moment later, she'd lit up a joint she produced from somewhere in its depths. "Do not smoke too much of this," she warned. "It is very strong."

"I'll be careful. Actually, my biggest problem in life at the moment is not knowing your name."

She giggled—a tinkling, bell-like sound completely unsuited to her body but all the more endearing because of the incongruity. "You mzungus never like surprises. It is Mapende. Esther for short."

"Tell me something. Is mzungu an insulting term, like *honky* back home?"

"No. Translated, it actually means, 'man who walks in circles,' which is what the first white people who visited Africa did."

Makes sense, Martin thought. *An eminently African practical approach*. Fortunately, as far as he could tell, he wasn't doing a mzungu thing. They were headed in the direction of the airport.

"Take it easy," Esther said. "The military often sets up roadblocks after dark to capture kondos. They usually wave mzungus through, but sometimes they are drunk on Saturday nights, so it is better to be careful."

Martin acknowledged the warning with a nod. "I was surprised yesterday when I walked around town. There weren't too many soldiers around. In fact, I saw more policemen in their cute little uniforms."

"They move the roadblocks around, and they almost never set them up in town. Do not be alarmed, even if they are drunk. Ten shilingi will take care of any problem."

Just when Martin felt comfortable enough to speed up, a set of arc lights clicked on up ahead, shining directly in his face, bright enough to practically sear his eyeballs. Partially blinded, he braked to a halt. When his vision cleared, he could just make out a crude barricade of oil drums and planks. A handful of soldiers cradling Uzis regarded his arrival with diffidence verging on narcolepsy.

One of them, obviously an officer, approached the car as Martin rolled down his window. When the soldier saw Esther, his broad face split into a lascivious grin. "Be careful," he told Martin in broken English. "African women are very strong." With that, he waved them through.

"Mellow enough," Martin said once they had cleared the road-block. "At least he had excellent taste in women."

Esther flared her eyes in mock anger and stuck out her tongue. "You will pay for that later, mzungu. It is just ahead on the left by those colored lights. Park in the front so you can keep an eye on your car."

The Arizona looked like a real African club. No shiny Mercedes or Peugeots in the parking lot. Inside, the long, dimly lit room was furnished with rough-hewn tables covered with plastic checkered tablecloths. An art-deco Wurlitzer jukebox in the corner pumped out Congolese music. There wasn't another mzungu in sight, and the aroma emanating from the kitchen in the back made Martin's mouth water.

Esther flagged a passing waiter. "I will order."

"Okay," Martin said. "If it's something really weird, don't tell me until after I eat it." He munched on some crispy tapas in a bowl on the table. They didn't taste of much but corn oil and salt. They had an interesting texture, though. "These are great. What are they?"

"Fried locusts. You have probably noticed the children congregating around the streetlights at night. They are gathering them. Do you mind eating bugs?"

"Not if they taste good. You'll have to get a lot more outrageous than that."

She gave him that luminous smile.

"Now that I'm initiated," Martin said, "tell me a little about the local cuisine."

"A lot of the dishes are stews, and we use groundnuts in the sauces. Chicken and goat are the most common meats. There is also delicious fish from the lake called tilapia and Nile perch. The staple is matoke, which we prepare in different ways. You will like it."

They'd arrived there just in time. The place was filling up with an interesting crowd—mostly civil service types and prosperous merchants, but there were enough country people, easily distinguished by their dress, to give the restaurant a more African flavor than any place he'd been to so far.

Martin regarded Esther with a sideways grin. "So what did you really order? Sheep's eyeballs or snake stew?"

"Fried tilapia, then roast chicken with matoke in a spicy groundnut sauce. If you want more exotic things, you will have to go to the bush. Maybe I will take you to my home village one day."

"I'd be honored. Where do you come from?"

"A small village in the North. Actually, it is just over the Sudanese border. I am a Kakwa, the same tribe as Amin."

"Do you go back often?"

Darkness seemed to settle over her face then, a sorrow she hadn't practiced enough to hide. "No. I do not have much family left—only a younger brother. We were orphaned at a young age. Missionaries raised us. I write to my brother occasionally. Things are not good there. They have been fighting a civil war for nineteen years. Sometimes, I think it will never end."

"Tell me about it. There has been very little mention of it in the Western press."

"Well, it is a familiar story—for Africa at least. When the British divided up their colonial holdings, they did not pay much attention to anything but geographical boundaries. Consequently, the people in the northern half of the Sudan are predominantly of Arab and Muslim descent, and those of the South are Africans who practice animism and Christianity. The Northerners, who control the government, want everything and leave only crumbs. The South should really have been made part of Uganda. In fact, there are already a quarter of a million refugees living in camps here in Uganda. I am lucky the missionaries took me in."

She seemed to shake off the immediate sorrow, though certainly not the ghosts, just as the rest of the food arrived. The fish was light and delicious. The groundnut sauce over the chicken and matoke was hotter than anything he'd eaten in a long time.

"That was fabulous," Martin said. "But I better not eat any more or I won't be able to dance."

At once, she returned fully to herself. The way her playful smile reached her eyes said as much. "You better be able to. I need to dance at Sussana's tonight."

"I'm ready. Let's get the check."

• • •

The big S was so zooed, they couldn't find a table. It was obvious why Stefan wouldn't go near the place on Saturday nights.

"Well," Martin said, "I guess we have to dance. That's what we came here for, after all."

The dancing effort was strictly self-defense. They lasted about an hour and then struggled outside for some fresh air.

Martin wiped at the sweat dripping down the back of his neck. "Jesus, I feel like I just played in a soccer match."

"Yes, my legs are sore too." Esther's eyes glowed like pearls under the streetlight. "Let us smoke some banjii and go home. I have had enough dancing for this week."

Martin was relieved that they didn't run into any roadblocks on the way home. He figured that the soldiers were probably pretty drunk by then, wherever they were. Esther was quiet, intently smoking a huge joint. He could think of nothing to say and was relieved when they got hack to the hotel.

He turned to Esther as they approached the lobby. "Do you want a nightcap upstairs in the Lair?"

"No, get some drinks to take to the room with us. I want to make love."

His heart racing, Martin bought a few beers, and they headed upstairs. They were barely through the door when she assaulted him. She pawed frantically at his clothes. He had just enough time to put the beers down before they were on the floor.

After, they lay panting and sweating and naked beside the bed.

"I think you needed that more than I did," he said, slowly regaining his breath. "What do you do for an encore?"

She laughed self-consciously. "I was thinking of my family, which makes me have this terrible empty feeling. It is like I do not have any roots, any soul, or reason to live. Then I have to hold on to something until my head stops spinning." She looked at him then, then down at his chest. "You are very strong."

"I hope I'm around every time you feel the need," Martin quipped. "Let's take a shower."

Esther's body glistened in the soapy water, the white lather of the soap accentuating the deep purple-black of her skin. Her hands explored him. Her lips followed. When he took her again, Martin was so hard it hurt. Her nails raked his back as she locked her legs around his buttocks, arching her loins against the fulcrum of their pleasure. She shuddered and bucked in a paroxysm of lust as he jammed her body against the tiles and lost himself in her. Their orgasm was so intense that they melted on the shower floor.

Martin was the first to recover. He reached up to the faucet and flicked the cold water on and then off as Esther started pounding his chest. "I know you didn't learn to do that in missionary school."

She glanced at the bandage on his right forearm. "What happened?"

A flash of memory came to him. The mugger with the knife, Martin's reaction so sudden and decisive it shocked even him, the sound of the man's scream. "A brief encounter with the local wildlife." He rose to his feet and handed her a towel.

She gave him a skeptical gaze. "You don't strike me as the safari type."

"I'm not."

"What did you study in school?"

"Journalism." He flicked on the television and joined her on the bed.

The newscaster was doing his best Walter Cronkite impression. When he wasn't slurring his words, his English was impeccable.

Martin laughed. "Is this guy drunk or what? Look at him. He's weaving around like Ali with Frazier all over him like a cheap suit. I guess I'd be drunk too if I had to read the same bullshit press releases every night."

The commentator grew animated as he gave a rehash of an international boxing match between Uganda and Kenya. While making a particularly violent gesticulation, he accidentally knocked over a vase full of flowers that had been sitting on a pedestal behind him. He didn't miss a beat as a hand emerged from the curtains that formed an artsy backdrop to the set and righted the vase.

"Wonderful. Does he ever fall off his chair?"

Esther nodded in disgust. "He did a few weeks ago. I know him well. He is always around town drunk, but he is so well-connected that he will never lose his job."

An ad followed for batteries that would start a car enclosed in a block of ice, after which a thoroughly discordant version of the national anthem finished the broadcast.

Martin turned off the lights and slipped under the covers next to Esther. "What's up with you and that GSU guy? They may not make very good friends, but they're worse enemies."

She stiffened. "It is a long story. When I came to Kampala about three years ago, my brother came with me. We were the only two left alive in my family. My brother always wanted to join the Anyanya, but he was only fourteen then, so I brought him with me. He got into some trouble. He was caught stealing. Harry Usongo was the one who arrested him."

"So what does that have to do with you?"

"Harry arranged to get my brother out of jail and back over the border to Sudan, where he joined the Anyanya. I had to get him help. He had no papers. I needed money to get him out of jail, and I needed papers. Harry pretended to be my friend. He took me to this man who lent me money and got me the papers."

"So Harry wants you to return the favor and go to bed with him?"

"He and the man who lent me the money and got the papers are partners. I paid them back the money, but now they make me pay something every week or they will tell the ministry that my papers are false. I make very little, and they take half of it. Harry says that if I go to bed with him, he will not take any more money. I know he is lying. It is a bad thing." He could sense her gaze on him then, though he stared up into the darkness. "Sometimes, I do not want to live anymore, but what can I do?"

Martin clenched his teeth. "There must be something we can do. Don't you have any friends at the ministry who can help you out?"

"I have many friends, but they are only clerks like me with no influence." Her voice softened. "I should not be troubling you with my problems. Life is not so bad. At least I have a job and a place to live." Her warm hand slid over his chest. "I am glad I met you, Martin. You are a very nice man. Do you know you are the first mzungu I have ever slept with?" She laughed and caressed his cheek. "I was interested in you from the moment I saw you at the airport. It is funny, but I knew I was going to go to bed with you."

"Pretty sure of yourself, weren't you? What exactly were you doing at the airport, and why did you disappear so quickly? I got the feeling you knew that kid who was shot."

"I might have, but it does not concern you. Sometimes it can be just as dangerous to know too much." Her tone was final. There was no use pushing things.

CHAPTER

4

Idi Amin paced in front of a row of tall windows, his gaze fixed on the marble-tiled floor, his hands clasped behind his back. In moments like this, when he awaited information that only he had the power to produce, he felt the singularity of his position. He was alone in his purity of purpose, alone in his breadth of view and vision. He was the embodiment of the mission. Only through him could his country reach untold heights. He bore a weighty responsibility that few could fathom, much less appreciate.

He heard the double doors to the Command Post burst open and turned in time to see his right-hand man, Sergeant Major Bob Astles, stride into his palatial office with the morning sunlight beaming behind him.

Astles held a manila envelope in his right hand. The old Englishman sometimes frayed Amin's nerves: his all-too-dignified air, his stoicism and patience, the way he seemed to always agree with Amin, even while trying to talk him into another position. He was a manipulative one—that much was certain—but he used his power softly and unobtrusively, never pushing Amin beyond his breaking point. Astles was always eager to listen, and sometimes, ever so carefully, he pushed back, proving himself the only one in Amin's orbit with the courage to speak his mind.

"You have something for me?" Amin asked.

"I do indeed, My President. My sources tell me we have a snake in our midst."

Amin liked to be addressed in such formal-yet-endearing terms. And he appreciated the crude imagery. "Tell me about this snake."

"It pretends to be a loyal soldier," Astles answered, "yet it does deals behind your back, My President."

With a sigh, Amin dropped his ample frame into the chair behind his desk. "Sounds venomous. Is it deadly?"

"No, My President. From what I gather, he's more skilled at profit than politics, although he might have a friend in the CIA."

Amin felt a surge of energy as he made the connection. "So this snake has our diamonds."

"Doubtful." Astles ran a hand over his bushy gray mustache. "They're most likely in the hands of the rebels by now."

As he leaned back in his chair, Amin delivered what he knew to be a deadly smile. "Bring me this snake so I can cut off its head."

• • •

In the late morning, Stefan led Martin and Esther on a tour of the botanical gardens located on the shore of Lake Victoria not far from Entebbe. Stefan was something of an expert on the local flora and gave them an interesting tour of the extensive facilities, which he said were the best in Africa.

On the way back into town, they stopped at Esther's bungalow. While she was changing, Martin brought up the sore subject of Harry Usongo with Stefan.

"Ja, I know the type all too well," Stefan said. "There are lots of them around. I suggest you talk to Anton about the problem. It is the sort of thing he is good at fixing. I will be bringing him along this evening, so you will have a chance to talk to him."

When Martin and Esther got back to the hotel that evening, they took a leisurely shower and headed downstairs.

Joe was sitting at a corner booth. He stood and waved them over. "I hope you are ready for some real African dancing."

"I'm definitely ready," Martin said, "as long as it's the real thing, not the airport tourist variety."

Esther winked conspiratorially at Joe. "It certainly will be. I hope these mzungus know how to dance."

Stefan and Anton arrived a few minutes later. Anton had donned traditional African dress for the occasion.

Martin laughed in admiration. "At least you two look the part." He introduced them to Esther. "I think they're going to have us poor mzungus dance for our supper."

"Don't worry, Martin. If you can handle the discos in London and New York, this will be a piece of cake." Anton executed a neat pirouette. "We'd better boogie, Joe. Who's riding with whom?"

"I will ride over with Esther and Martin. No use taking three cars. It's easy to find. About a mile past Sussana's on the left." Joe signed the check, and they headed for the parking lot.

Martin turned to Esther. "I hope you're ready for a wild ride. Stefan is like a frustrated race car driver."

True to form, the German careered out of the driveway, taking the turn on two wheels.

"This mzungu drives like he is possessed." Joe tightened his grip on the seat and closed his eyes in mock horror.

Esther giggled. "You are fortunate. If it was still light out, he would go slower so he could stop and talk to every mpenzi he sees."

Joe laughed. "That doesn't surprise me. I've seen him around town quite a bit, always with different mpenzis. His attitude makes a pleasant change from the average stick-in-the-mud mzungu mentality in this town."

From the outside, the Bristol looked remarkably similar to the

Arizona, Martin thought. Blinking colored lights illuminated even the parking lot. The long, rectangular main room was much better furnished. A large brick patio opened off its rear. The room was already crowded.

Martin was relieved to see that Joe had managed to get a large table near the dance floor. "I love it! Great atmosphere! Bring on the dancing girls. I'm ready."

"Let me order some food first," Joe said. "I know what is best. We have plenty of time. The band is just setting up." He gestured over to the corner, where musicians were stacking drums of various sizes.

Martin didn't recognize the rest of the instruments, mostly stringed. "I know something about traditional African music from my studies in the States and London, but I've never seen anything like those. What are they?"

"Different kinds of zithers," Joe explained, "an instrument similar to the violin. They, too, are played with a bow. Flutes and woodwinds will also be used. The music is very complex. If you don't listen carefully, it sounds like monotonous drumming. However, once you get used to the sound, you'll be able to pick up subtle changes in the beat, which the flutes and zithers accentuate." He leaned forward in his seat, his eyes going wide. "I see that the dancers are ready to start, so you'll have to figure out the rest on your own."

The drummers came in one by one, gradually building up a hypnotic intensity. Joe was right. Careful listening revealed subtle rhythmic patterns. The flutes and zithers joined with a cacophony more reminiscent of Arab music than the traditional African music Martin had heard before. Just as he was getting used to the exotic sound, the dancers shimmied onto the floor with a rustling of straw skirts and a tinkling of ankle bells. They formed a rough circle, and the dance began.

The women were buxom, the men lithe and angular. There was no fat on either. The drumbeats coursed up their legs to their pelvises, which pulsed with a primordial sexuality. Their upper torsos seemed to be affected by rhythms different from those that electrified their lower bodies. Martin hadn't seen muscular control like that outside of the Crazy Horse in Paris. He glanced around. Everyone was entranced. The youngest of the women gyrated toward them. She *was* the music. Her eyes were glazed like those of voodoo dancers he'd seen in Haiti. She slithered toward him with all the modesty of a bitch in heat. He felt the skin on the back of his neck tingle as she straddled his legs and started humping them. He was overcome by the lusty, ammoniacal scent her body exuded. His head reeled, and he broke into a heavy sweat. Just when he thought he could take no more, the drumming built to a pounding crescendo and she collapsed, sliding down his legs in a perfect mimicry of sexual release.

The crowd leapt to its feet with a roar. Martin felt flushed like he'd just had an orgasm but embarrassed at the same time, as if he'd just been caught masturbating. He peeled off a hundred-shilingi note and gave it to the young dancer. Esther looked at him with wide eyes, and then broke into a knowing smile.

Anton snickered. "Brother, you look like you could use a drink to cool off. Stefan's jealous, but it's just as well she didn't pick him. He would've had her on the floor."

"I'll switch seats with him for the next number," Martin said. "I don't want to offend my lady."

When Esther left a few minutes later to make a short call, Anton gave Martin a nudge. "Stefan tells me that you've got a problem you need some help with."

"Word travels fast around these parts," Martin said, impressed. "Yeah, I'd be interested in seeing if you could use your good offices."

"When can we get together and discuss the situation?"

"How about tomorrow over breakfast?"

Anton nodded. "You got it. I'll see you in the buttery about eight."

• • •

Esther had left by the time Martin woke at seven o'clock the next morning. He showered, ordered some coffee, and sorted out his papers for Makerere. Boring as it was going to be, it was time to register. He didn't figure he'd be too long with Anton, so he decided to head out to the campus after their meeting.

Anton was sipping from a cup of coffee when Martin arrived at the buttery. "Greetings, Martin. The coffee here is excellent."

"Sorry I'm late. It was a little difficult getting started this morning. Did Stefan brief you on the problem?"

"Yeah." Anton paused when a waiter appeared out of nowhere to take their order. Once the waiter had finished and turned toward the kitchen, he resumed his answer. "I think we can work something out. I gather from Stefan that you have the resources necessary to fix things."

"Probably. It depends on what's entailed."

"Protection first. You must get yourself some cover if you are going to deal with a guy like Usongo. I've heard of him, and he's a nasty piece of work." Anton methodically buttered a piece of toast. "The papers will be easy to fix. They will cost about five hundred dollars."

"Damn. That's not cheap. Does that figure include your commission?"

"Certainly. They are expensive because they will be real. I assumed you wanted real ones so this problem will not occur again."

Martin nodded. "Yes, which brings us back to the sticky subject of Mr. Usongo. He's made some other rather ungentlemanly threats, which I'll leave to your imagination. I'd like to arrive at some sort of arrangement by which he loses interest."

"Yeah, man. Otherwise, he could be a problem. You definitely don't want to have him breathing down your neck the rest of the time you are here. I think I'd better set up a meeting with Ali Kilogo. He should be able to arrange the whole matter."

"Who's he?" Martin caught himself. "Or should I ask?"

"Don't. Could you see him this afternoon?"

"Sure. I'm going out to Makerere to register this morning, but I should be done by early afternoon. You could leave a message at the desk for me if I'm not here."

"You got it, brother. Thanks for the breakfast."

"Thank you, Anton. I will, of course, keep you in mind should any other problems arise."

Anton left, and Martin got directions from the hotel clerk and drove to campus, which was about five miles out of town on the Jinja Road. It looked just like a small community college somewhere in the Midwest. Almost all the buildings were modern concrete-and-glass structures. One colonial monstrosity, a castle with crenellated towers, stuck out like a sore thumb and smacked of imperial officialdom. The campus was deserted. Martin didn't see anybody to ask for directions, so he followed his hunch and walked across a tree-shaded square toward the hulking building.

Sure enough, it was the administration building. He strolled through the empty halls until he found a janitor, who directed him toward the bursar's office.

Martin nodded a greeting as he approached the clerk. "Good day. My name is Martin Fine. I'm here to register for some courses. Here are my documents."

The clerk, a middle-aged man wearing a white dress shirt, black tie, and brow line glasses, examined them briefly and handed him some papers in return. "Just fill out these basic registration forms. That is all you have to do, since you prepaid in the UK and do not require accommodation. Classes start in two weeks." He pointed toward the far wall. "The schedule is on the bulletin board over there. Enjoy your studies."

Martin explored the campus briefly, went to the bookstore, and bought his books. Given how quickly his interests in country had turned, the books felt like a prop.

• • •

A familiar Renault screeched to a halt and parked behind Martin's rental as he was locking the car outside the hotel.

Stefan stepped out of the Renault. "I can see that you've had a busy morning already."

"You could say that. What's up?"

"I was just on my way to lunch, but when I saw you, I figured I would stop and give you the good news. I tracked down Sarah this morning. She would be glad to rent you the other bungalow. Do you want to go see her tomorrow morning?"

Martin couldn't believe the news. "Stefan, you're too good to be true."

"I will pick you up at the hotel at about eight and run you over there."

"*Danke.*"

After Martin stepped inside the hotel, he stopped at the clerk's desk to pick up his key.

The clerk handed him a slip of paper. "Phone message, sah. It came in about half an hour ago."

The message said that Anton wanted to meet him at the Sultan's

Table, a restaurant on Nile Avenue, at two-thirty. Martin would have just enough time to stop at the bank on his way. *Best to be prepared*, he thought. Any dealings were going to be in cash only.

It took him a while to find the place. The Sultan's Table wasn't in any of the tourist directories, and one look at its shabby exterior explained why.

Martin entered through the dilapidated doors and scanned the moldy, peeling room for Anton. There was no sign of him, so he took a seat at the plywood bar. The room reeked of cheap disinfectant, stale beer, tobacco, and body odor—a bouquet common to dives the world over. As far as he could tell, the place had only one good point: It was deserted, aside from the bartender.

Martin cleared his throat and signaled for a Nile. The old-timer gave him a toothless smile and shuffled over to a forties vintage Whirlpool icebox in the corner.

It was hard to figure out which of the two relics wheezed more.

Martin accepted the beer and took a deep pull on the frosty brew, trying to wash the gag-inducing stench from the back of his throat.

Mercifully, Anton sidled up a few seconds later. "See you found the place."

"Yeah, what a discovery. How come it isn't written up in all the guidebooks?"

"A horrible oversight on their parts, no doubt. Come on in the back. Ali is waiting."

Martin followed Anton through some hanging beads into an even dingier back room. A corpulent, perspiring African in a stained lace suit sat at the head of a rickety card table. An overhead ceiling fan rotated lazily, barely stirring the fetid air. Ali's pinkish gimlet eyes sized Martin up as he waved them to seats.

My God, just what I need: a black Sydney Greenstreet. Martin was careful not to break eye contact with the African.

Their eyes stayed locked for thirty seconds going on five minutes before Ali gave a high-pitched chuckle and extended his hand. "Welcome, Mr. Fine. I think we can do business. Anton tells me that a friend of yours has some problems. How can I be of service?"

"First, I need citizenship papers for her. She is a refugee from the Sudan. The past three years, she has been working at the Ministry of Information, so I don't think you would be taking a chance. Second, a certain Harry Usongo, with whom you may or may not be familiar, has been blackmailing her. I would like him discouraged from this distasteful practice."

Ali clapped his plump hands, and a Ton Ton Macoute type slithered through the beads. "Waragi, *pesi pesi*." Ali wrinkled his brow in concentration while the flunky poured them all double shots of brown waragi and bowed his way back out. Like many Ugandan Muslims, Ali didn't seem to worry about drinking openly.

Martin sipped his drink. At least Ali's bona fides had been firmly established. The flunky had GSU written all over him. Martin felt surprisingly calm, considering he had his head in the lion's mouth.

Ali snapped out of his trancelike state and slapped his palm on the table. "One thousand dollars, and it is done."

Martin wondered whether he should bargain. The man was obviously of Arab descent, and it wouldn't do to be taken for an easy mark. He might need his services again. "That seems an awfully high price for such a small thing. I was under the impression that five hundred should suffice."

His reply was greeted with another thunderous silence as Ali studiously contemplated his stubby, bejeweled fingers.

Martin began to wonder if he'd misread the situation.

Suddenly, Ali looked up and gave him a charming smile. "I am so glad that you did not immediately accept my first offer,

Mr. Fine. I hate dealing with Western cretins who pay the first price they are asked. For a wise mzungu, eight hundred and fifty."

"Six should be more than adequate."

"I can take no less than seven hundred."

Martin smiled and reached into his pocket. He carefully counted out the right number of crisp bills and laid them on the table. It was more than he had wanted to pay, but not an unfair price. "What happens next?"

"Your friend will receive her Ugandan passport at the ministry tomorrow. You have my word that it will be a real one. It is a small thing to change the records at the Ministry of the Interior. After all, our esteemed leader is also a Kakwa. Now let us have another drink to seal our bargain."

Ali chatted pleasantly with Martin over drinks. It turned out that he *did* have Arab blood on one side of his family and had attended university in Cairo. He appeared intrigued by Martin's interest in African history. All in all, he seemed a pleasant, cultured type, but Martin didn't buy the facade. He knew when he was being pumped by a professional. There wasn't any doubt in his mind that Ali would kill him as quickly and thoughtlessly as he would swat a fly if it suited his purposes.

After they'd finished their drinks and small talk, Ali rose and ushered Martin and Anton out.

That was when Martin spotted a familiar face. He was so shocked to see Harry Usongo lounging at the bar that he came to a halt abrupt enough to have Anton run up on his heels. In the commotion it caused, the insolent GSU agent noticed them.

Usongo leapt from his stool and grabbed a handful of Martin's shirt. "What are you doing here, mzungu? This is not a place for a law-abiding studenti to be found."

Wincing, Martin tried to reply, but then Usongo shook him.

"I did not like you from that first day I met you," the agent spat.

"When I saw you with that Mapende woman, I knew you were up to no good. Now what are you doing here?"

Martin tried to regulate his breathing before answering. "I got lost. Stopped in for directions."

"That's not good enough."

"Okay, Harry, if you insist. I was here to see what I could do to stop you from blackmailing Esther. Face it: You're a sleazeball from way back."

Usongo tightened his grip and raised his fist. That was all Martin needed. He buried his knee in Usongo's groin and chopped down on his hand. Usongo exhaled explosively and started to slide to the ground. Martin brought his elbow up in a short arc, making perfect contact with the point of the African's jaw as it went by. Martin felt the impact in his teeth. Usongo was out before he hit the floor.

Anton's eyes widened. "Shit, Martin. They didn't teach you *that* in college."

"Sure didn't." Martin straightened his shirt and regained his breath. "Kind of unfortunate it happened, though. I have a feeling it's going to cost me some more money."

"You are right there, my friend." Ali's laugh tinkled across the room. "It was very neatly done, but it will cost you an extra five hundred. I shall have to clean up this mess by transferring him somewhere far away." He stepped over to them and kicked the limp body. "Stupid, greedy little man. I think he must have had designs on Miss Mapende. She must be as beautiful as I have been led to believe. You are obviously a lucky man, both for knowing her and for knowing me."

Martin peeled off several more bills and handed them to Ali. "It was worth it to cream that creep."

"No doubt it was satisfying, but I trust you will not make a habit of it. You seem to be an enterprising young man. I hope

that you will keep me in mind should you need any more . . .
unorthodox services."

"I certainly will. You can also rest assured that I don't wish to
make any waves." Martin gave him a half bow and exited.

Back outside on the street, Martin turned to Anton. "Can I
give you a lift anywhere?"

"No, man." Anton studied Martin for a moment. "You are a
bundle of surprises, mzungu."

"I've picked up a few interesting things here and there in my
travels." Martin reached into his pocket and handed Anton a
hundred.

"Thanks, brother."

"Think nothing of it," Martin said with a shrug. "You've
distinctly livened up what would have been an otherwise dull
afternoon."

IT WAS THREE-THIRTY when Martin got back to the International. There was no message from Esther, and it was too late to call her at the office. He took a smoke out on the balcony. *A busy three days*, he thought, but so far, his karma had been good. He'd paid too much to help Esther, of course, but his motives weren't entirely altruistic. Excellent contacts were popping up all over. All he needed was a project on which to use them. He didn't have any doubt that, in no time, plenty would present themselves. Only three days in the city had been enough to show him how Kampala was wide open for business. The only problem was going to be picking out the right investment opportunity. What the hell—he might even get in a little journalism. The ringing of the phone jarred him from his thoughts. It seemed too modern an object for Africa, and he resented its intrusion even more than he would have in the States.

Stefan's voice sounded on the other end of the line.

"Oh, it's you, Stefan. I guess I'm a bachelor tonight. Where are we eating dinner?"

"Do not sound so depressed. She is not tired of you yet. You are the best thing that has ever happened to her. Why not try that African place you told me about? Meet me for an after-work cooler at the Nile. It's just down the road from you."

"Okay. How does six sound? I need a nap."

"Ja, registering for courses really takes it out of a man."

"Believe it or not, my afternoon got interesting after lunch. I'll fill you in over dinner."

Martin stripped and showered. He was already developing a tan. His arms and legs were well-muscled, but his gut was beginning to show some flabbiness. He made a mental note to return to his daily exercise routine. The prospect of looking like some of the beached touristi whales he'd seen around the pool didn't appeal to him. The face staring back at him from the mirror as he combed his sandy-brown hair surprised him. Before fleeing Philadelphia, he'd cut off his shoulder-length hair and shaved his subversive beard, mostly to avoid recognition from anyone his dealings had offended. The effort had made him look much younger, almost straight. Even a week on, his new clean-cut image still made him look twice.

He slept deeply and dreamlessly until the alarm call woke him, then dressed and headed off for the Nile. It was the first time he'd gotten a good look at Kampala's newest hotel in the daylight. A Yugoslav construction firm had thrown up the futuristic complex in less than eighteen months—just in time for an annual Organization of African Unity conference that didn't take place, owing to Amin's coup. The building was your basic foreign-aid showcase project. Looking at it, Martin had the distinct impression that it would look as new as tomorrow for a year and as old as sin afterward.

At the Nile, he found Stefan seated at a corner table with a familiar face. "*Ach* so, Martin, glad you could make it. Permit me to introduce you to one of the few interesting expats around these parts: Major Ian Smythe-Jones."

Of course, Martin knew him at once. But here, for the first time, he got a good look at the man, with neither an impromptu execution on the tarmac nor a surprise appearance by President Amin to distract him. The major was plumper than Martin remembered. In fact, he looked like he could have stepped straight out of Wodehouse, a prototypical blimp, but his firm grip and steely blue eyes belied his rotund, almost cherubic exterior. He was about average height, and his aquiline nose stood out against the deeply etched laugh and worry lines that wrinkled his tropically tanned skin. It was the eyes that grabbed Martin, though. They'd seen everything and taken it all in stride.

"Mr. Fine and I have already met," the major said.

Stefan appeared surprised. "You have?"

"A couple of times," Martin said, but didn't feel the need to elaborate.

Major Smythe-Jones nodded. "Stefan tells me that you are from Virginia. Not Langley, by any chance?"

"Not exactly. My family comes from a small town nearby, though, and it does so happen that a lot of retired spooks make their home there. Cocktail parties are as close as I've ever gotten to that crew. My family didn't move down there full time from New York until after I went away to school. Actually, I spent most of the past four years in Philadelphia and London, attending various schools of higher and lower learning. How about you?"

"At the moment, I manage a wolfram mine up near Mbarara. I was in government service for a long spell, but the sordid details would bore you."

Stefan ordered another round, and the major launched into a string of anecdotes about his travels around East Africa during colonial times. He talked nonstop for the next half hour, telling them about the time he retraced on foot Burton and Speke's original route inland from Mombasa on the Kenyan coast to

Jinja. He was a marvelous raconteur, and it was soon apparent that the Colonel Blimp image was a carefully cultivated facade. Behind it lurked a first-class political mind and a wealth of African experience.

"Those must have been the days," Martin said. "In the forties, this place couldn't have been much different than in Victorian times. I would have liked to have seen it then."

"To be honest, old boy, it hasn't changed all that much. There's a little more of a thin, civilized veneer over things, but there's still the same cast of interesting freebooters around, though most of them these days are black." The major frowned and stirred his pink gin contemplatively before continuing. "That's really the problem with this place: Everybody's here to take something. Sometimes, as retirement looms closer, I wonder if I've missed the boat. But on to cheerier subjects. When do your courses start?"

"In about two weeks. I was thinking of doing a bit of traveling in the meantime. Murchison Falls first, I think. I'm distantly related to the old boy on my mother's side. Then all over. I met a few newspaper people in London before I left, and they convinced me to try my hand at writing some pieces. It seems that stringers are rare in these parts."

"First living relative to the falls, and all that rot. You'll enjoy the trip more with a reliable guide."

"Would you happen to know anybody?"

The major didn't hesitate. "It just so happens that I do. An old Sikh named Singh. Been on the ground a long time. He took Rommel and Goering around between the wars. Only problem is that he doesn't speak English. How's your Swahili?"

"Still of the kitchen variety, but my sign language is good."

"That should do in a pinch. I'll give him a call tomorrow. Should he expect you about the weekend?"

"Sometime Friday. Could I meet him at the lodge? Paraa, isn't it?"

"Yes, a beautiful spot too. There shouldn't be any problem. This is slack time for the touristi." The major rose. "Must be off, chaps. If there's any problem with Singh, I'll leave word with Stefan. Perhaps you can fill me in on the trip over dinner one night next week. Thanks for the grog and natter."

Stefan settled the tab, and they headed for the parking lot.

Martin felt a sense of satisfaction, almost closure, now that he had interacted with Major Smythe-Jones in a more routine situation. "That guy's some piece of work," he said to Stefan. "He's forgotten more about Africa than I'll ever learn."

"Could not have said it better, my friend."

"It sounds like a great trip," Martin hinted. "Wish you were coming."

Stefan offered a mischievous smile. "Oh, but I am. I have leave coming, and I have been meaning to do a little traveling around also. You have a partner in crime." He winked his golden eye and extended his hand.

Martin took it with a smile.

• • •

On the ride over to dinner, Martin caught Stefan up on his afternoon adventures.

"I figured Anton would be able to fix things," Stefan said.

"He was, but not without some extracurricular excitement. All in all, it was an interesting experience. In the bargain, I also met a rather dangerous guy named Ali Kidogo. Handy sort, though. He fixed up Esther's problem in no time."

"Ach so, Anton took you right to the top. There are not too many people who can say they have had pleasant encounters with that fellow."

"How about bargained him down on a price and then beat up one of his minions in front of him?"

"What!" Stefan gave him a long, calculating look. "None that I have ever heard of. Your old friend Usongo?"

Martin flashed his teeth. "None other. He wasn't very well-trained. I wouldn't give him more than two seconds in a few places I know in New York and London. Knocking him around cost me an extra five hundred, but it was worth every cent."

"Ja, it was probably very satisfying in the short term but not so great for the big picture, as you Amis like to say. You are probably no longer a harmless studenti in their eyes."

"The thought occurred. But what was I supposed to do when he grabbed a handful of my shirt and neck and got ready to unload on me?"

Stefan nodded.

"I smoothed it over as best I could afterward," Martin explained, "and Ali agreed to transfer him to their equivalent of the Eastern front, so hopefully, things will settle down. I'm pretty sure Ali saw it as just another fight over a pretty woman."

"That is possible. I hope so, because he is the wrong fellow to have taken an interest in you."

. . .

After Stefan dropped him off at the hotel at about ten, Martin headed up to the Lair for a nightcap. It was dead. Kampala evidently took Monday nights off.

Joe motioned him over to a table by the bar. "I see you survived last night's ordeal. Let me introduce you to Hal Jones, communications officer for the British High Commission, and Zack Bakazi."

Jones looked like a Celt. A luxuriant black beard obscured his ruddy, sunburnt complexion. His features were angular, his nose almost hawklike.

Bakazi was a short-but-well-built Ugandan with a viselike grip and piercing eyes. "Nice to meet you. It is always good to see some new faces. Where are you staying?"

"Here for the time being," Martin answered. "I just rented a place out at Kireka, though. I'll be moving out tomorrow."

"Then no doubt you have met the redoubtable Cedric Ayres," Hal said with a chuckle. "Not a bad sort, actually, if his act doesn't put you off."

"It didn't. I've met his type pretty often before in New York and London. As a matter of fact, I've heard some very nice things about him."

"So," Bakazi began, "you are an American studenti by way of London. How did you come to choose Uganda for your studies?"

Martin was quick with the lie. "I was studying at the School of Oriental and African Studies in London and was told that Makerere was the best university on the continent. So here I am."

Bakazi appeared drunk. His eyes bored into Martin's. "I have heard that all American studentis studying abroad work for the CIA. Is this true?"

Why me? Martin thought, sipping his beer to buy some time. "You can't believe everything you hear. For instance, the other day I heard a drunken soldier in a bar say that Amin had two journalists killed for writing about the massacres of dissident Acholi and Lango troops at Mbarara. I didn't believe it."

Hal and Joe exchanged a startled glance.

Bakazi looked momentarily perplexed. Then he broke into a loud guffaw. "Permit me to introduce myself more fully. I am Lieutenant Colonel Zack Bakazi, commandant of the paratroops. I should like to buy you a drink."

Martin felt his face burn red. "Colonel, we have an old saying in the States. Open mouth, insert leg. I just did up to my thigh."

The tension at the table evaporated, and everybody started talking at once. The ice broken, Bakazi proved to be amiable enough. He told them hilarious stories about his jump training in Israel. He also admitted having put Martin on about the CIA, but he cautioned all of them against loose talk, even in front of other mzungus. It turned out that one of Amin's closest aides was retired British Sergeant Major Bob Astles. Before departing, the colonel invited Martin out for a tour of the base.

Hal gave a relieved chuckle. "You sure lucked out there, boyyo. What you heard is absolutely true. Zack is a nice guy, but one never knows how they will react. He loved the way you called his bluff. I might add that he is a very useful sort to know, very close to his nibs. It would definitely be worth cultivating his friendship in the future."

Martin swilled his drink. "I certainly will. Never look a gift horse in the mouth, et cetera. I think I'll quit while I'm ahead." He said his goodbyes and headed for the lift.

On the ride down, he chastised himself for his impetuous behavior. *You're allowed one stupid mistake*, he thought ruefully, *but not two*. Currents and crosscurrents. Anton's iceberg analogy was making more sense every minute. Once back in his room, he smoked some banjii to unwind and then fell into a deep, dreamless sleep.

• • •

Stefan took Martin to Sarah's place early the next morning. Martin signed his lease and looked over his new digs. Fortunately, they were furnished in much the same fashion as Stefan's, so he wasn't going to have to buy a lot of things to make them comfortable.

Even better, Isador had a cousin, Reuben, who was looking for a job. Martin interviewed him and hired him on the spot.

After settling his bill at the International and packing up his things, Martin called Esther at the ministry to give her the good news about Kireka and her papers. She was overjoyed and promised him a special housewarming present, which she said she would give him in person after leaving work early. He picked her up on the way out of town, stopping at the International to buy a bottle of champagne.

Esther giggled when she saw it. "I have never drunk champagne before. I hear it does wonderful things."

"Everything you've heard is true. Besides, it's the only way to christen a new place."

Esther was enchanted with the house. "This is like a dream," she said as she took it all in for the first time. "I thought only the people in the movies lived like this."

Her naiveté charmed him. He could only imagine what she would think if she ever got to America. He opened the champagne, and they took it and a stick of banjii outside to view the lake under the hot afternoon sun. Martin wasn't sure whether it was the booze or the smoke, but it proved to be a hallucinatory experience. As they savored the view, Esther slid on top of him. Their lovemaking was passionate but relaxed, more familiar than before.

"Was that my housewarming present?"

"Yes, mzungu. It is also a thank-you for the gift that was delivered to me at the ministry this morning. Is it real?"

"Absolutely, with records to match at the Ministry of the Interior. You are now officially a Ugandan citizen. There's more. I saved the best bit of news for last. Harry Usongo has been transferred out of town."

She collapsed into him. "Is it really true?"

"All true."

"I cannot thank you enough, but you should not have gone to so much trouble. You hardly know me."

He pulled back from her embrace to get a good look at her, and to show his sincerity. "I know you enough to like you. It wasn't a lot of trouble, just a little bread in the right places."

"I cannot believe how beautiful it is here." She disentangled herself and walked to the edge of the yard. After beckoning him over, she pointed to the sun-dappled water. "It is so wonderful that you can see all the way to the lake."

He nibbled on her ear. "Tell me, Esther, can you get in touch with the Anyanya?"

She stiffened. "It depends. Why?"

"I want to do some articles on them. Think they could use the publicity."

She wheeled around to him, her gaze sharp. "You are a journalist?"

"In a way. I have some good press contacts in the UK and the States, and I figured I'd send them something. From what I hear, the Anyanya movement isn't exactly in vogue at the moment. I think that everybody could profit from the deal."

She thought a bit before replying. "I do not think that they are interested in publicity unless it is likely to be influential. They have had their hopes built up falsely many times. But if the articles were serious, they might be persuaded. I will get in touch with my contacts. When would you want to see them?"

"As soon as possible. I was thinking of going up to Paraa this weekend. Maybe it's closer to where they operate."

"I will see what they say."

He put his hands on her shoulders and looked down into her eyes. "Are you annoyed that I'm going away so soon after we met?"

She smirked. "No, Martin. I think that I can survive a few days without you. I will restrain myself from going to the Big S." Now there was a measure of hope in her expression. "Will you do me a small favor? If I get in touch with the Anyanya, will you deliver a letter up to the falls?"

"Your brother."

She nodded.

"Sure. Do I get to meet him?"

"No. You will give it to a messenger. I told you before: Even *I* cannot find him."

Martin nodded his understanding.

"There is one other thing," she said. "I cannot see you tonight. My roommate invited me to a party several weeks ago. It is at the church she goes to. I do not think you would find it very interesting. Call me at the ministry tomorrow."

Martin drove her into town and stopped at the market on the way back to pick up a few necessities for the trip. After an hour of spirited bargaining, he emerged with a stout pair of walking boots, a battered but still serviceable igloo cooler, and best of all, a hammock that would go perfectly on his front porch. He figured he was getting better at bargaining because several of the merchants had been surly as they handed over his purchases.

He spent the rest of the afternoon assembling the hammock and giving it a test run.

• • •

"Wake up, lazy mzungu dog. It is time for one of Schmidt's famous Kireka Cannonballs." Stefan shoved a frosty tumbler in Martin's hand. "Guaranteed to wake the dead. I gather from Reuben that your mpenzi has already tired of your mzungu ways now that she has gotten what she wants. That being the case, you can expose yourself to some of my not-too-bad cooking."

"I take it from your ebullient mood that you're all set for the trip." Martin took a gulp and shuddered. "What's in this?"

"Two types of waragi and other secret ingredients. Thought you might need some cheering up."

"Nothing like that. Esther had a longstanding commitment to go to some church dance." Martin thought about taking another drink, but then shook his head at the tumbler. "She seemed to get a little uptight when I asked her to get in touch with her Anyanya friends. I think she questioned my motives at first, but she seemed all right with it by the end of the discussion."

"I have no doubt it was your subtle reasoning powers that brought her to her senses." Stefan regarded him speculatively. "You are an interesting fellow, Fine: one part studenti, one part foreign correspondent, and one part smuggler. It will be interesting to see which you turn out to be."

Martin accepted the joint Stefan handed him and lit it. After enjoying a couple of hits, he stretched out lazily. He only barely registered the sound of a jeep rumbling up the hill behind them. "Yeah," he said, "they used to call me Never-a-Dull-Moment Fine. I always figured the more irons in the fire, the more chances you have. Now that that's settled, what's for dinner?"

When Stefan didn't answer, Martin looked up to see a jeep approaching. He dropped his joint into his drink. "Who the hell is this?"

"Good question." Stefan stood. "No one knows we are here."

The jeep came to a stop a few meters away from the hammock, and out stepped Major Smythe-Jones.

Martin stumbled out of the hammock and clambered to his feet. He dusted himself off.

"Ah," the major said. "I thought I might find you here."

"This is a surprise, Major," Stefan said. "What brings you all the way out here so late in the day?"

"Not to worry. Nothing to do with you." The major motioned toward Martin. "I've come for this one."

Martin couldn't hide the confusion in his voice. "Me?"

"Yes," the major said. "You've been invited to a state dinner."

Martin was lost for words. "State dinner? But I'm—"

"He is only a few days in country," Stefan said. "He is just a student."

"Maybe in his mind," the major said, waving off Stefan's concerns. "But not in the minds of some." He stepped forward and handed Martin an envelope.

Martin tore it open. To his disbelief, he was staring at an official invitation from the office of President Amin. "This is from—"

"The president, yes," the major said.

Stefan's face grew ashen. "Amin?"

The major appeared amused. "That's the one. You see, old boy, this is an invitation you can't decline."

"When?" Stefan asked.

"Tonight. Why do you think I drove all the way out here?"

Martin felt wobbly on his feet. He was stoned and a little drunk—and unsure he could believe his ears.

"You'll straighten out," the major said, as if reading his mind. "Trust me. And even if you don't, well, might be better to have a touch of the fog on for this one. Just take care with your tongue. Maybe, whenever possible, simply keep it still."

"But we're leaving for safari," Martin protested.

The major looked to Stefan for an explanation.

"We depart Thursday afternoon," Stefan said.

"For Jinja," the major said, anticipating Stefan's next words. "Then on to Paraa."

Stefan drew back in surprise. "That's right."

"Did you forget that Singh, your guide, is a friend of mine?" the major asked. "Don't worry. I'll have Martin back here in time, and

Singh will have you seeing all the game there is in a weekend." He turned to Martin. "C'mon, old boy. We'll just be there and back."

Martin looked down at his casual attire and gestured toward it. He couldn't go dressed like a tourist.

"Well, hurry along then. Have you got something suitable for dinner?"

•••

Less than an hour later, the major led Martin inside President Amin's private barracks in Kololo. Everyone was dressed to the nines, which made Martin feel self-conscious in his off-the-rack American suit. Three long, rectangular tables had been arranged in a U-shape and covered in white linen. Most seats at the head table were occupied, save for Amin's. The same men who were trying to glad-hand Major Smyth-Jones seemed confused about Martin. The major ushered them through the party and pointed to an open seat. Martin was relieved to see that the major's name was on the place setting next to his.

The feeling was short-lived. It left the moment the old gray-haired British man slid into the seat on Martin's other side. Martin remembered him as the man who'd arrived with Amin in the limousine at the airport. Whenever he thought about the moment, Martin would picture the brain matter splashed onto his shoe.

"You're—"

"Major Bob Astles," the man said.

Martin exchanged glances with a poker-faced Major Smythe-Jones and remembered the major's instructions to keep his mouth shut. It was clear Astles was there to keep a close eye on him.

All rose when Amin entered the room, and the president gestured for everyone to sit before taking his place at the head table. Servers appeared and presented a series of lavish and exotic dishes, one after the other, and Martin struggled with how to eat some of them. He slammed every drink offered him and soon found himself returning to the fuzzy-headed feeling he had been cultivating back at the hammock. He picked up a few details here and there in conversation carried mostly by the major, but he still couldn't figure out why in the world he'd been invited to something like this.

When the last plate had been cleared away, Astles stood up beside Martin. "Now if you'll all remain tucked in for a moment," Astles announced, "the president has prepared a special show."

A murmur rose up from the men gathered at the tables, with some glancing around for a sign of what awaited them. Martin looked to the major, who gave no expression one way or another.

A moment later, the front doors burst open. Two guards in formal uniform dragged forth a prisoner who had obviously been tortured and, for all Martin knew, was no longer breathing.

Casually, Amin stood up from his seat and rounded the tables.

The prisoner groaned, and the room fell silent. The only sound was of Amin's heavy boots striking the tiled floor as he strolled toward the prisoner.

Amin gestured toward the prisoner, whose commando uniform was in tatters and barely covered his broken body. "This man double-crossed me," the president said. "He thought he could make a deal behind my back. All for a handful of diamonds." With startling quickness, Amin yanked a Ka-Bar from the belt of the guard standing nearest to him, plunged it into the commando's body, and began sawing back and forth with rapid jabs from the knife.

As the commando's neck went limp, the guests looked on in silence, their mouths agape. Martin sank in his chair, wishing he could disappear.

Half a minute later, Amin was holding something. It took Martin a moment to register that it was the man's liver. Amin presented it to the captive audience. "This man betrayed me!" the president bellowed. "If you betray me, I will eat you!"

The crowd gasped silently as Amin plunged the bloody organ into his mouth and bit into it. Dark-red blood dripped down his chin. After tearing it away from his teeth, he swallowed the chunk of liver in a performative gulp.

When Amin's gaze turned toward him, Martin felt himself retch involuntarily.

The major placed a hand on his back. "I say, old boy, that's a bit rough. Shoot the cognac down, will you please?"

Martin did as he was told and collected himself, and as the cognac from his glass warmed his throat with its dry and spicy ensemble of flavors, he felt something strange wash over him. He had just seen Africa for the first time, and he knew he would never be the same.

CHAPTER

6

MARTIN DROVE TO the ministry the next day at noon and found Esther waiting for him near the entrance.

She jumped in the car and gave him a slow, lingering kiss.

It was almost enough to make him forget what he had witnessed the previous evening.

"I do not have time for lunch, but I have something for you." She wrinkled her brow in concern. "What is wrong, mzungu? You do not look yourself."

He toyed with the idea of telling her about the gruesome dinner but decided now wasn't the time. "It's nothing. What did you want to give me?"

She shoved a letter into his hand and pecked him nervously on the cheek. "My friends will also talk to you about an interview." She started to get out of the car.

"Esther—"

She brought a finger to his lips. "No words. I need some time to think. My head is whirling. The time apart will be good. I will miss you. Call me the minute you get back." She jumped out of the car and ran inside before he could say anything.

He tried to make sense of her behavior on the drive home, but the more he thought, the more confused he became. He filed it away for future reference. He finished loading the car by noon just as Isador came running up the hill a short time later to tell him that Stefan had called, reminding him to fill the car with gas and buy a map.

"My first safari," he said with a sigh as he rolled down the hill. He wished he was in a better frame of mind.

After he had gassed up and purchased a map, he drove back up the hill and charted their route.

Stefan arrived shortly after two-thirty. "The show is finally on the road. Any problems this morning?"

"Just Esther. She was a little moody when we parted."

"What was the problem?"

"It could be the Anyanya business, but then again, it could just be that time of the month."

"Ja, it is a mistake to make these things too complicated." Stefan gave Martin a look similar to the one Esther had given him just a couple of hours earlier. "And what about you? You look like someone going to a funeral, not on safari."

Martin told Stefan everything as they drove.

Stefan took a moment to absorb the grisly details. "The president is a dangerous man. We knew this already. Nothing has changed."

"I guess so," Martin said as he gripped the steering wheel. "But why did he want *me* there? Is he trying to send a message?"

"Certainly." Stefan gazed out the passenger-side window. "He wants everyone to know that he is a madman. Cross him at your peril."

Martin shuddered. "If I never see him or his goons again, it will be too soon."

The country was dull, flat, and sparsely populated. The few cars they saw were old and battered. Many showed signs of ingenious repairs with cannibalized parts. One particularly interesting specimen, a Peugeot station wagon they passed about ten miles out of Kampala, looked as though someone had flattened its roof onto the chassis with a giant hammer.

Martin tried to make the shift to tourist mode. "Are there any interesting sights on the road to Jinja?"

Stefan's eyes brightened. It was clear he appreciated the opportunity to change the subject. "Only the Madvhani tea plantation, the largest in Africa. The Madvhanis, who own it, are the leading Indian family in the country and have a finger in just about every financial pie. They give lots of money to local charities and generally do what they can to dissipate the bad feelings against the Indian community here. I am afraid it is a case of too little, too late, though."

Martin nodded. "If you ask me, they deserve most of the agro. If they hadn't been so standoffish and had made some efforts to assimilate themselves—even, heaven forbid, taken citizenship— they wouldn't be so hated. What's worse, of course, is that they're pretty damn successful. To be fair, the economy really wouldn't function without them."

"Ja, I am afraid that Amin will follow Nyerere's and Kenyatta's lead and systematically deport them anyway. It is a matter of saving face. A classic case of penny-wise, pound-foolish. They are going to end up with nothing but what they have already stolen."

Martin remembered the letter from Esther. It was just what he needed to break out of his funk. "Esther's letter included some pretty cryptic instructions: 'You will be contacted.' Straight out of the movies, but who knows? It could be exciting. I take it that our schedule isn't so onerous as to preclude a secret rendezvous or two?"

"No, we are our own bosses. Besides the de rigueur game watching, we have nothing planned. There will be plenty of time to look for trouble." Stefan slumped in his seat and dozed.

•••

They reached the Madvhani plantation an hour or so later. It was so vast that it took Martin half an hour to drive past it. No doubt they could afford a few handouts like *Sesame Street* to keep the natives from getting too restless. They rolled into the outskirts of Jinja at about five-thirty.

From the looks of it, Jinja was predominately industrial. It was smaller than Kampala, probably with a population of about fifty thousand, and much cleaner. The highway fed into the main drag, Speke Boulevard. As usual, the prosperous shops that lined it were Indian-owned. A few blocks along, they turned into a parking lot in front of a two-story stucco structure, aptly if not originally named the Jinja Guest House. The rooms weren't opulent, but they were clean and functional. More importantly, the air conditioning worked.

Martin had just finished showering when Stefan arrived with some cold Niles.

"That hits the spot," Martin said as he savored his first sip. "What's on the agenda for this evening?"

"Drinks, dinner, and a tour of the local hot spots. Not that I am necessarily inclined to sample the goods."

Dinner wasn't great, but the Honey Pot was a real African nightclub. The furnishings were rudimentary except for the jukebox, the latest Wurlitzer model, which looked ready to blast into orbit. Congolese lilted through the smoke. The crowd, entirely African, took their partying seriously.

After feeding the jukebox, Martin joined Stefan at the bar.

"Much better than Kampala," Stefan said, beaming. "More earthy, right down to the floor. The mpenzis look a lot less polished too."

They inhaled a few Uganda boilermakers, dark waragi with Nile chasers, and let the atmosphere roll over them. Nobody seemed to take any notice of them.

As he drank, Martin mused on how little he knew about Stefan. Here he was, contemplating embarking on a criminal enterprise with the guy, and all he knew about him was that he had a good sense of humor. Yet he both liked and trusted him. He guessed that he was attracted to the what-the-hell-anything-for-kicks vibes that Stefan evinced, but he also found Stefan's hints of solidity—good old-fashioned Teutonic common sense—attractive. Funny, Martin thought, how little was necessary to build a foundation of trust over here. In the States, if he'd known anyone for this short a time, he would've been barely past the name-rank-and-serial-number stage.

Stefan ordered another round and headed off for a "short call."

As Martin watched him pick his way around the crowded dance floor, he was struck by a sudden impulse and signaled to an immense mpenzi with a blond Afro wig and matching gold lamé boots. "What's your name, sweetheart?"

"Ruby."

Martin parried her neatly as she lunged for his thigh. "Did you see the mzungu who was just sitting next to me?"

She nodded.

"He told me that he likes you very much, but he's too shy to talk to you. Why don't you come over and talk to him when he comes back. His name is Stefan." He patted her capacious rump and handed her forty shilingi.

Ruby teetered back over to the jukebox and assumed a watchful attitude.

As soon as Stefan returned, she waddled toward the bar as fast as her platform heels would permit. Stefan, blissfully unaware, was chatting animatedly with Martin when she engulfed him in a full nelson. Stefan blushed from his bare ankles to the top of his ears.

Martin slid off his stool and left to make a short call before Stefan could gather his wits. By the time he returned a few minutes later, Stefan had disengaged himself, and there were only a few tinges of red showing through his tan. He was smiling, which was a relief.

"I really wanted to stick around to see how you handled the situation," Martin said, "but I didn't want to cramp your style."

"It was not that difficult." Stefan winked with his gold eye. "These can work two ways. I merely told her that you had made a mistake, and that I would give her the evil eye if she did not leave me alone. She made a hasty exit just as you returned. Reflecting on things, I wonder if I should have invited her back to the hotel with us. There was certainly enough of her for two."

"Not tonight, Josephine. Let's head outside and catch a cool breeze around the back. This doesn't look like the kind of place that stands on ceremony."

They worked their way around the side of the building and found a suitable spot.

"There's nothing like lighting up under an incredible night sky," Martin said. "At this altitude, the stars really seem to come at you, don't they?"

"Close enough to touch," Stefan replied, "like the fellow standing behind us."

Martin slowly looked over his shoulder.

A tall African was watching them impassively. He stood well over six feet and was ax-handle thin. His face was a series of interlocking bony planes—almost statue-like in their angularity. A trace of quizzical humor in the glint of his obsidian eyes softened his otherwise severe expression. Not the kind of fellow Martin wanted to see on the wrong end of a panga.

"Mr. Martin, Mr. Stefan?" he asked softly. "My name is Nathan. I hope I did not frighten you. It was easy to recognize you from Esther's description."

Martin gulped for breath. "Just give me a few seconds to shove my heart back down my throat. You do that rather well. Esther said we'd be contacted, but is all this cloak-and-dagger stuff really necessary?"

"Sadly, it is. Our presence is tolerated here, even sometimes encouraged. However, this is Africa, and a man who does not butter his bread on both sides soon goes hungry."

"I don't have the letter with me," Martin said. "It's back at the hotel."

"That is not really what I came for." Nathan filled and lit a battered pipe. "I am more interested in discussing your recent offer to Esther of some press coverage. As you know, our cause is not as glamorous as that of our brothers farther south. Some of our younger leaders, me included, are more conscious of the media's power in the West than are our elders. They are traditionally suspicious of such things. We think that it is an appropriate time for some publicity, so here I am."

Martin sat down beside him. "Why now?"

"Because that Libyan madman Khadafy has made overtures to Nimeiry concerning a union of the two countries. Certain Western powers, the US in particular, are most anxious to prevent such a union."

Martin thought for a moment. "Why would Nimeiry even consider it? He gets plenty of support from the Americans?"

"Nimeiry's main motive is to gain the military necessary support to crush us. The civil war is draining the economy, and the US does not give him enough military aid. It is the opinion of those of us who have studied in the States that the Americans might be disposed to forcing him to negotiate with us in return for a large financial-aid package. It would be a small price to pay for keeping him from getting any closer to his dream of an Islamic African Empire."

"That would make sense if Khadafy really has those intentions."

Nathan puffed vigorously on his pipe, stretched his beanpole legs, and sighed. "Do not doubt it. He does. It terrifies all of us who know much about him. Unfortunately, a lot of people think of him as a relatively harmless crackpot. I am positive that time will prove this to be a disastrous underestimation."

"Do you really have the government in such a bad state militarily?"

"It is a stalemate at the moment. We have about ten thousand men under arms and the total support of the populace. Time and a shaky economy are on our side."

"I think I can get you exposure in a lot of the big Western papers," Martin said, "but I'll have to interview some of your top people. Editors want names."

"That sounds acceptable, but I shall have to discuss it with my superiors and get back in touch. They are ignorant and suspicious of the media." Nathan rose and brushed off his pants. "By the way, Esther mentioned that you were going to be staying at Paraa for a few days. Would you be prepared to meet one of my superiors while you are up there? It is less dangerous for us to meet you in the North."

Martin nodded. "Sure. You guys move fast."

"Always. If something can be arranged, you will be contacted. Now I must leave. My watchdog will catch up any minute."

"You're being followed?"

"The GSU watches us from time to time. These days they might have more cause than usual. Khadafy has long tentacles." Nathan stiffened. "I hear him coming. Hide in the bushes over there. It would not be good for him to see you." He melted silently into the night.

Martin and Stefan slipped into the bushes as silently as they could and assumed an awkward crouch that afforded maximum cover. Within seconds, a short, squat figure ghosted around the far side of the building and came to a halt in the clearing opposite them. After sniffing the air, he crouched down and looked in the dirt. The moon was just rising, and there was enough light for Martin to make out the watchdog's coarse, pushed-in features. He stifled a gasp as a primeval frisson fluttered in his gut. It was Usongo's partner.

Evidently satisfied with his inspection, the watchdog turned and disappeared into the darkness.

"Well, well," Martin whispered to Stefan. "It's a small world. Do you know who that was? Harry Usongo's partner. At least he was when they bounced me that first day in the International."

Stefan scrambled to his feet. "Let us hope that he is now an ex-partner. I do not think that you want to run into Mr. Usongo too soon. That guy Nathan must have radar. I did not hear anybody coming."

"Like he said, in his business you have to." Martin shook his head. "Nothing like a little intrigue to liven up an otherwise dull evening."

The streets were ghostly quiet.

Stefan glanced at his watch. "They sure close this place early. It is only just past ten. Still, all in all, it has been an eventful enough evening for an innocent touristi, let alone a fledgling foreign correspondent."

"There could be some interesting pieces in it," Martin said, "provided I get to talk to the leaders. The only problem is that most people at home haven't even heard of the Sudan, let alone the Anyanya."

"I am sure that is true most places in the world, but it might take their minds off Vietnam for a while."

"True," Martin said. "Besides, guerrilla movements are in at the moment. Sometimes I wonder who's more cynical: us or them."

• • •

The next morning, Martin and Stefan headed north for Paraa. The flat, dry savannah gave way to hillier, lusher terrain. Women, babies tightly swaddled to their chests, worked the densely cultivated fields of millet and sorghum. The tableau had a certain timeless quality to it.

Martin felt like a voyeur in a time machine. "Amazing, isn't it? They look almost untouched by history. I bet you they've been farming the same way for centuries. Wouldn't the women's libbers back home just love it?"

He settled into the drive, but the very lushness of the country soon made it boring. There wasn't much traffic on the road, and they were making good time. There was just enough of the morning freshness left in the air to keep him comfortable, but he wasn't looking forward to the afternoon leg. The Renault wasn't air-conditioned.

His thoughts wandered to Uganda's future. It wasn't a new story: Virtually every modern African state was the product of the capricious whims of colonial powers. Because of the random selection of their boundaries, all of them experienced some degree of tribal and ethnic strife. Many were nonviable economically, their resources too small to support their exploding populations. They could only be kept afloat by massive injections of foreign aid.

With the breakdown of traditional society and the influx of foreign aid came the Coca-Cola culture. Martin wondered who was better off: the women toiling timelessly in the fields or their counterparts lured to the sprawling urban slums with all of the

Western ideals but no means except prostitution to attain them. One of the things that disturbed him most about modern Africa was that there were as many internal as external refugees.

If nothing else, he figured the guerrillas might be useful contacts. They were usually looking for money as well as publicity. No telling what intriguing items they might have access to. The idea of helping the guerrillas as well as himself was tempting. He'd always been a sucker for good causes.

Stefan stared at him from the passenger's seat. "You look pensive. Are you thinking about Amin's horror show?"

"No. Just Africa and what it all means." Martin fumbled with the visor to block the morning sun. "It's the world's biggest anthropological test tube at the moment." He found it hard to adopt the scientist's detached air, especially in the chaos of the real world, as opposed to the controlled calm of the research lab. "How much farther to Fort Portal?"

"We passed Tsalo a minute ago," Stefan answered, glancing down at the map in his lap. "Make it another fifty miles or so. An hour at this rate."

It seemed like less when they pulled into a ramshackle gas station and general store on the outskirts of Fort Portal. The attendant told them that it would be a good idea to gas up because supplies to the North tended to be spotty. Martin was glad Stefan had insisted on bringing along some extra jerry cans.

While the attendant was filling them, Stefan strolled inside for some sambosas and beer. He emerged a few minutes later with a half dozen sweating liter bottles and a greasy bag. "Another hundred miles to go. The last thirty are on murram roads through the game park, so they will be slower but more interesting."

Martin accepted one of the clammy bottles and took a deep swig. "Suits me. I like to get where I'm going, though I could do without the dirt roads."

After they left Fort Portal, the road moved away from the lifegiving Nile, and the cool hills surrounding town quickly gave way to dry plains. The midday sun baked the Renault mercilessly. The interior was oven-like.

Martin was sweating out the beer as quickly as he drank it. At times the shimmering heat above the tarmac was so intense he could barely make out the white lines that divided the road. "Keep the brew coming. I feel like I'm turning into a dried prune."

"*Sehr gut.* Dehydration is the main danger in this heat, but at least it keeps the dry-cleaning bills down. My sweat is evaporating so fast it is not even getting onto my clothes. I will be interested to see what our contact at Paraa is like."

"I've been thinking about that. Probably just a messenger type. You've got to feel for these people. Esther's lost her whole family, except for one brother and some cousins, and she's luckier than many. Do you put any credence in Nathan's Libya scenario?"

"Looks good on paper, but after nineteen years of civil war, I am not sure the rifts can be healed. From the American point of view, it certainly makes sense to make sure it doesn't happen. Khadafy's going to be a pain in everybody's butt before he is through. He's a card-carrying fanatic." The beers and heat got to Stefan, and he nodded off.

Martin slipped into autopilot, and after an hour or so, the country began to change again.

Stefan resurfaced with a cavernous yawn. "The country is starting to look a lot more interesting. Did I miss anything exotic?"

"Nope. Lots of scrubland. No people or cars. I figure we must be getting close to the park."

The road became more circuitous, and they made slower time over the next thirty miles. The countryside was looking more and more like Hollywood Africa.

"I almost expect Tarzan to hop out and ask for a lift," Martin said.

"Ja." Stefan pointed to a battered sign on the left welcoming them to Murchison Falls Game Park. "I like that part about not getting out of your vehicle unless accompanied by a guide. This is going to be the biggest zoo you have ever visited."

Martin shifted down as the tarmac gave way abruptly to a rutted murram track. "I read somewhere that this preserve is the size of Connecticut."

They bounced uncomfortably along for about five miles until Stefan punched Martin on the shoulder and pointed ahead to the left. "We have officially arrived. Photo op."

A pride of lions lazily sunning themselves occupied a cluster of rocks about a hundred yards off the road.

After exhausting a roll of film, they drove up to the lodge. The parking lot was empty, which surprised Martin, because the setting was gorgeous. They checked in and had Singh paged before going upstairs to shower and change. Martin's room was small, but the balcony overlooking a salt lick more than made up for the size. He had just finished toweling off when the desk rang, announcing that Singh was waiting for them in the lobby.

Singh was a small, gnarled elderly Sikh with a wizened prune for a face. Martin figured he had to be at least seventy. It didn't look like he was up to the rigors of game stalking in this heat, but his animated eyes and spry gestures as he explained their schedule to the clerk belied his age and dispelled Martin's doubts.

They would drive about ten miles upriver to a spot just beneath the falls, where they would get into a launch and float back down to the lodge. Game watching made easy. It was a good time of the year for river game, so there would be plenty about. Even better, they would be the only ones going on the afternoon trip. The clerk advised them to bring plenty of bug repellant, because the mosquitoes in the swamps next to the river were voracious.

The hot, clear day was ideal, according to Singh, for game watching. It was a tight fit in his battered Land Rover, but the abundance and variety of small game that they saw soon took Martin's mind off the discomfort of the ride.

About the only thing they didn't see was a big predator. Singh suggested that the big cats were nocturnal hunters, so they were rarely seen before noon unless they were digesting a kill from the night before.

The roar of the falls was audible for a good mile before they suddenly appeared through layers of mist. The few pictures Martin had seen had not prepared him for their awesome grandeur. The boiling mass of water roiled through jagged cataracts and plunged over polished lips of stone, falling hundreds of feet into a rocky pool. The lush green foliage on the banks perfectly framed the yellow-brown water.

The wall of noise precluded any conversation. Transfixed by the power of the falls, they stood around for twenty minutes before Singh tapped Martin on the shoulder. He gestured to a dock about five yards downstream. Martin took a few snaps, even though he knew no picture could capture the majesty and raw, elemental power of the moment. He felt like a little child again. It had been a long time since he'd been awestruck by nature.

They made their way down a precipitous track to the dock, where a large launch with a striped canopy was waiting. The river and its banks teemed with game. Large groups of hippos caroused in the shallows and lazily fed off the vegetation on the banks. Singh pointed to some ripples in a nearby pool and pantomimed a hippo running along the bottom. He ran his hands through the water, attracting the attention of a large hippo standing guard on the bank. It approached the launch with its vast jaws distended.

At a signal from Singh, the driver reached in the cooler and disinterestedly passed over a large loaf of bread. He'd obviously seen the show before. He didn't even bother to look as Singh gently laid it in the cavernous opening. The hippo closed its mouth and submerged, making noises that sounded somewhere between those of a jackass and a pig.

"Does he know that one personally?" Stefan quipped. "It looked like a set piece to me, but charming nonetheless. I'm sure that they have gotten used to the boats. Some of them probably get quite tame. It beats working for a living."

Monkeys, lizards, and hundreds of different species of birds swarmed through the dense rain forest on the banks. Tropical orchids dotted the clearings, which interspersed the vegetation.

"It's idyllic," Martin rhapsodized.

"It is pretty but dangerous," the driver replied with a laugh. "Like so many things in our country, it is not what it seems on the surface. The jungle is filled with nasty things."

"There is something that is not the least bit deceptive." Stefan pointed to a huge crocodile sunning itself on the bank. "He must be close to twenty feet long. What do they eat besides the odd delectable human they come across?"

"Small animals and fish mostly," the driver replied patiently, lapsing back into his prerecorded spiel.

Sensing his boredom, Martin asked him to get Singh to tell them about his travels with Rommel and Goering during their trip through Uganda in the thirties. Leave it to the colonel to lay on a piece of history for them, Martin thought. Singh set in with a will. Evidently, they'd insisted on conducting their hunts with military precision. Their use of Somali beaters to form pincers that drove the game to its inevitable conclusion had first amused, then annoyed Singh. There was no sport in the exercise. He hadn't taken their marksmanship as lightly. According to him, with them, it wasn't a question of shooting something between the eyes but the right or the left. The stories might have been apocryphal, but they were interesting, nonetheless.

The rest of the afternoon, with the exception of an impromptu shower from a herd of bathing elephants, was pretty much the same.

"I wonder if poaching is a problem here," Martin said as the lodge appeared up ahead.

Once again, the driver lapsed into cruise control. "It still exists locally, but the imposition of the death penalty has really cut it down. Kenya is where most of the poaching goes on these days. As long as there is a lucrative market for ivory in the Far East, it will be impossible to stamp out the trade completely."

Stefan nodded. "Natürlich. It is widely known that many in the Far East call Mama Kenyatta the ivory queen."

They returned to the lodge at about five-thirty.

Martin had showered and was sipping a waragi on the balcony when Stefan knocked.

"You got a lot of sun today," the German said after joining Martin on the balcony.

"Yeah, I'm just starting to feel it now. It has always struck me as one of life's great ironies that you never feel sunburnt until after sunset." Martin killed his drink and headed inside. "Let's go downstairs. Being on the water always gives me a fierce appetite."

The bar was packed. Evidently, a tour bus had arrived during the afternoon. Luckily, they were able to find a table in the dining room. Over dinner, Martin asked Stefan about the schedule he had worked out with Singh for the next day, and afterward, they ordered brandies and took a stroll through the gardens.

Martin scowled at the tourists. "Well, it was nice while it lasted. These camera-toting hordes are really the locusts of the twentieth century."

"Ja. Do you have the letter with you?"

"Sure do. I've been expecting a Kalashnikov-toting guerrilla to step out of the woods any second."

"We should be so lucky. It will probably be a runty school boy in shorts."

"Whatever. I just wish he'd show up. I hate having these obligations hanging over my head."

"You will not have to wait much longer, mzungus," someone said nearby. "We know that patience is difficult for you."

Stefan hadn't been too far off. The gangly youth, who'd silently materialized behind them, wasn't carrying a gun, but he *was* wearing shorts. "Do you have the letter, Mr. Fine? I still have a long way to go tonight."

"Yeah, here it is." Martin handed it to him.

"Thank you. I have a message from Nathan. He and a friend will meet you here Sunday night. He said to tell you that if you want to write a good story, you should stop at the Masirwa refugee camp. It is not far from here." The boy vanished into the bushes.

Stefan finished his brandy in one gulp. "I cannot get used to these silent entrances. Every time one happens, I can feel ten years of my life melting away. He certainly was an outgoing fellow. I may be getting too old for this."

CHAPTER

7

THEY DIDN'T SEE a single tourist bus after they left the parking lot the next morning, but they saw everything else in droves. Singh's bushcraft was extraordinary. Time and time again, he got them to within fifty feet or less of the animals.

After their breakfast break, they were crawling along the now-customary rutted murram track when Singh slammed on the brakes and gestured to a watering hole in a spindly grove of acacias about a hundred yards ahead. A warthog was slobbering up the brackish water. Martin snapped his telephoto lens on the camera and surveyed the trees. He could just make out a spotted, tawny coat outlined against the foliage.

"Leopard!" Singh hissed rather needlessly.

The warthog savored the water, blissfully unaware. The silence in the car was broken only by the clicking of the camera. Seemingly enjoying the moment, the leopard waited until the tension was exquisite. Then it sprang in a blur of yellow. The kill itself had a clean, antiseptic quality. The surgical efficiency of the operation rendered it anticlimactic. Within seconds, the leopard had dragged the carcass off into the bush. The kill seemed a fitting way to end the session: nature taking its course, as it had from time immemorial.

Martin wondered why he hadn't found it more repulsive. *Probably because it was honest.* His mind drifted to Amin's staged killing of the tortured commando, and suddenly he understood what he had witnessed: a shameless act of cruelty and petty power. Uganda's strongman president could only wield power over the powerless and the willing. A leopard in the bush, on the other hand, had to work for a living.

They made a quick turn at the lodge and headed north by ten. The country started to change drastically less than half an hour from the lodge. The semitropical foliage gave way to arid bush, dotted with clumps of acacia and gum trees. Within thirty miles, all signs of civilization had disappeared.

"Jesus, the guidebooks that describe this part of the country as inhospitable aren't kidding." Martin opened the cooler. "Just looking out the window makes me hungry and thirsty. I wonder if Singh scrounged anything for the trip."

"How about some banjii too?" Stefan asked. "It does not look like a really interesting ride."

"Banjii, sau sau, Singh?" Martin asked.

Singh took one puff of the joint and heaved it out the window. His finger-to-nose gesture needed no translating. Grunting, he opened the glove compartment and motioned to Stefan to fill his pipe from the tobacco pouch.

Stefan inhaled deeply, coughed, and passed along the pipe. "I feel like I am in a concrete mixer. Thank goodness we are in a Rover. I do not think any other vehicle could make it over this road. This country does not look like it has changed in thousands of years."

Martin nodded in agreement. "It's only eleven, and it already seems hotter than it did all day yesterday." Lulled by the banjii and the heat, his thoughts drifted lazily with the wispy cumulus clouds in the brilliant-blue sky.

They hadn't seen another vehicle or any sign of civilization for miles. It seemed they had crossed an invisible line into a time warp. Martin half expected to see the ghosts of Stanley, Burton, and Speke plodding along beside the road.

Singh nudged him out of his reverie. As the Rover careered around a sharp curve, their guide gestured to a battered metal sign by the road.

Martin could barely make out the words: *Masirwa Refugee Centre, a joint venture of the UN Refugee Committee and Uganda.*

They drove up to the camp about ten minutes later. From a distance, it resembled a Hollywood version of a Nazi prisoner-of-war camp—but not as nice. A rusted wire fence surrounded the dusty two-or-three-acre compound, and a couple of large concrete sheds, obviously administration buildings, stood in one corner. The rest of the compound was covered by every type of shanty and lean-to that human ingenuity could devise. Their arrival didn't seem to jolt the refugees out of their midday torpor. None approached them or took any apparent interest as they climbed stiffly out of the car.

As he stretched out the kinks, Martin noticed the smell and the flies. It was the usual African cocktail. Stale body odor blended with rotting food and vegetation, accented by the stench emanating from open latrines.

The flies descended on them like they were freshly butchered meat at the market. Following Singh's example, he fanned his face with his hat. It didn't get rid of the flies, but it kept them from flying into his mouth and nose.

The refugees they passed on their way to the main buildings regarded them with the same vacuous look: a combination of hunger and hopeless boredom that was so familiar to Martin from the barrios in South America. Their hopelessness was contagious. He felt inadequate, desperately wanting to do something but knowing that nothing he could do would make the slightest difference. Stefan's grim, tight-lipped frown indicated his revulsion. Martin realized that it wasn't the depressing conditions of the camp that bothered him as much as his own helplessness.

A screen door slammed, jolting Martin out of his walking nightmare, and a diminutive bearded mzungu bustled toward them with a welcoming smile. "Well, what a surprise! We don't get many unexpected visitors in these parts. The Reverend Lars Nilsen, Danish Volunteer Services. Welcome to Masirwa."

Martin performed the introductions.

The priest waved them inside. "Just passing through, huh?" He handed them some beers.

"More or less," Martin replied. "I'm a journalist researching some pieces on the Anyanya and didn't think the story would be complete without a visit to one of the refugee centers."

"In that case, you came to the right place. We can definitely use the publicity. Finish your beers, and I'll give you a tour. We have enough food and medicine at the moment, but we live on the razor's edge. Of course, as is common in all refugee settlements, we always seem to be in short supply of the most essential medicine of all: hope."

The tour was every bit as depressing as Martin had expected. Lars stopped frequently and translated for him. The stories were all distressingly similar. Driven south by the brutal reprisal raids of the Sudanese Army, the refugees had tried to eke out a living from the inhospitable land. When their few meager possessions had been stolen by bandits, they were forced to seek help at the camps.

"At first, I thought it was better than being killed by bandits or soldiers," one dignified mzee said with a sigh. "But now I am not so sure. Maybe a quick death would have been better. All I have left now are my memories, and I cannot eat those."

It was a sad litany. After several interviews, Martin felt the general hopelessness of the refugees' situation physically—an almost suffocating weight. He was genuinely moved by their dignity. Even with only rags to their name, they projected pride. He believed them when they said that charity was the last thing they wanted.

The last stop on the tour was the hospital tent.

"I've saved the worst for the last," Lars confessed. "You don't really have to come in if you don't want to. You've seen enough already to get the general picture."

"We'd like to see it, Father," Martin insisted. "We came for the whole tour, not the censored version." He shrugged. "How much worse can it get?"

Lars opened the door and ushered them in. The stench was appalling. Liberal doses of industrial-strength disinfectant were fighting a losing battle with the combined odors of excrement, putrefying flesh, and death. Martin gagged, and his eyes watered. The first patient they passed smiled helplessly at them as he voided himself in his bed.

Lars shook his head sadly. "Dysentery is a horrible disease. First, it takes away your vital fluids. Then it takes away your self-respect. Then ..."

"Can't it be cured by modern techniques?" Stefan asked, trying not to gag.

"Not if you don't get it in time." Lars looked ready to cry. "This man walked fifteen hundred miles to get here. He'll be dead before nightfall."

The first two aisles they walked down provided a textbook of tropical medicine.

Lars read the grim list in a dull monotone. "Dysentery, dengue fever, typhus, gangrene ..."

Martin closed his notebook as they approached the children's section. The diseases were the same, but the horror was accentuated by the frail little bodies. One little boy, who couldn't have been more than five, croaked, touched Martin's arm, and pointed to his lips. His limbs were like matchsticks. Every bone in his body was clearly defined through his taut parchment skin. A living mummy.

Martin poured a glass of water from the pitcher at the bedside and cradled the boy's head. The boy's neck was so hot that Martin almost snatched his arm away. Gently, he tried to dribble some water through the boy's cracked lips. The boy's frail body gave a convulsive heave that seemed to start in his toes and gather momentum as it passed through his straining ribcage until it exploded in Martin's face in one, long raking gasp. Yellow-green bile appeared at the corners of the boy's mouth, and he went limp.

Lars stepped forward and gently lifted the boy from Martin's arms. He lowered him to the pillow, tenderly closed his eyes, and made the sign of the cross. "Measles. He was running a temperature of one hundred and seven. He's in a better place now. It's a shock, isn't it? Nobody in the West dies from measles anymore. Out here, it's one of our deadliest killers."

Martin was stunned. Tears rolled down his dusty cheeks. He looked at his arms, unable to believe that the living boy cradled in them a few moments before was now a corpse.

Stefan patted him gently on the back and led him outside.

It was all a bad dream, Martin kept telling himself. *Just pinch yourself, and it will go away.* With a massive effort, he consigned the horrific image to a dark place in the back of his mind, willing it to be gone forever—or at least until a time when he could deal with it. The merciless, midday heat and the interminable dust and flies made him feel faint. He barely had the strength to make it to the temporary salvation of the air-conditioned office. The cool canned air and the ice-cold brew that Lars thrust into his hand seemed like grotesque luxuries.

Stefan looked deflated. His face seemed to have aged ten years.

Martin turned to Lars. "How do you do it every day? Doesn't it ever get to you?"

"The fact that I'm a Christian helps. Sometimes, it does get to me for about five minutes, but then something happens, and I slip back into my routine."

Martin grimaced and gestured out the window. "You have to look pretty hard to find the hand of God anywhere in this lot."

"He certainly appears to have forgotten them for the time being." Lars seemed unfazed by Martin's vehemence. "I'm not an old-school Bible thumper. I guess I took up the ministry because it was the best medium around to do good in." He paused and lit a cigarette. "To be perfectly frank, I find it pretty hard to tell a sixteen-year-old whose child has just died of any one of twenty diseases to have faith in an all-seeing, just divinity. One of the first things I was forced to learn out here was that God probably doesn't have a divine blueprint. You just have to do the best you can."

Martin mopped his brow. "After seeing this, I'm inclined to agree with you. I find your candor very refreshing. I was an altar boy when I was growing up, so I've had lots of exposure to men of the cloth. It's impossible for me to visualize any of the priests I knew holding and comforting some excrement-encrusted wretch who's dying of galloping cholera."

Stefan coughed and spit out a fly. "I do not mind swallowing them as long as they go down the right way. One thing that struck me as odd, Father, is that most of the refugees outside the hospital do not appear that ill. I did not see any signs of pellagra or the other common maladies in these situations."

"There isn't any at the moment, but don't be deceived. As I've said before, these people live on the razor's edge. Give any of them a general antibiotic, and it would work on at least six different diseases. To illustrate my point, the last time we had an outbreak of measles, six thousand died. Most were children."

Martin whistled. "Why did it happen? Is their resistance that low?"

"Both physically and mentally," Lars replied with a sigh. "If they'd had something to live for, more of them would have made it." He glanced at his watch. "Can I give you something to eat before you leave?"

Martin looked up from his pad. "I'd find it pretty hard to eat anything at the moment."

"Nothing for me." Stefan smiled weakly.

"Is there anything, no matter how small, we can do to help?" Martin asked.

"Just write your stories," Lars answered. "The world should know more of the plight of the refugees all over the continent." He smiled bitterly. "Not many of us, myself included, read United Nations reports. Before you go, I've got a gift for each of you." He rummaged through a desk drawer and handed each of them a smooth black stone. "Perhaps you will find a use for them, though I sincerely hope not. They are miraculously—and I don't use that term lightly—effective in treating venomous snake bites."

Martin noticed the stone in his hand had the greasy feel of a piece of dried tar, but it was much heavier. "How do you use them?"

"Make an X-shaped incision over the bite and attach the stone. It will stick until the venom has been sucked out. Then it will fall off of its own accord. After each use, boil the stone in milk and then soak it in water overnight. I have seen this stone cure a girl bitten on the neck by a mamba."

"Somehow it seems a little odd to accept a stone of such magic powers from a man of the cloth," Stefan remarked as he pocketed his.

"I should think my recommendation would overcome your skepticism. One thing I have had to learn out here is to use what comes to hand. It may interest you to know that I have been using a local bone healer for years."

Martin reopened his notebook. "Now that's an interesting leap of faith, Father."

"Not really. After I saw him set a nasty compound fracture by touch, no x-rays, I was convinced. It was a real eye-opener. He set the bone, applied a few herbal poultices to prevent gangrene, and sent the man home to his village. He instructed his family to hold him down at sunset each evening because he would be massaging the bone at a distance. Sure enough, the patient went into convulsions at that time every evening. The bone healed perfectly, with no shortening. The man walks without a trace of a limp today."

"That would have been good enough for me too," Martin said. "Any other good stories, or can I put this away?" He gestured to his notebook.

"Put it away, and go with God. Please send me copies of the articles if they get published."

"I will." Martin rummaged in his wallet for a scrap of paper and wrote down their addresses. "Dinner is on us, if you visit Kampala."

They went back to the Land Rover and found Singh asleep.

"Amazing," Martin said with a shake of the head. "It's got to be about a hundred and thirty in there." He rummaged through the cooler and took out all the sandwiches.

"What are you doing?" Stefan asked.

"What I can. We'll just have to prove that you can live by beer and banjii alone."

"Sehr gut. The least we can do. Offbeat man, that Lars."

"Offbeat morning too. That was one of the most depressing experiences of my life. I'm going to have nightmares about it as long as I live."

"Ja. Lars is right, though. In that situation, you just do the best you can. In some ways, it makes me bitter. If these people cannot take care of themselves, who will?"

Martin opened his mouth to reply, but Stefan wasn't done yet.

"No offence, Martin, but you haven't seen much of the hard side of life yet. When I was only slightly older than you, I was scratching out a living in postwar Berlin. Some of the more pleasant things I had to do to make ends meet were pimping and selling black-market drugs. The less pleasant I will leave to your imagination. I envy the fact that you had a childhood. I did not. One of the things you will learn—and it is a hard lesson—is that idealism doesn't leave the classroom. Maybe the great unwashed are better in their ignorance."

"Not sure about that. You've got to be better for knowing the situation exists. The rest of the touristi still think they're running around in the world's largest amusement park."

"I am not saying that compassion is bad, just that not all the world's problems are solvable or our responsibility."

Martin lit a cigarette. If someone came from Stefan's world, he thought, it all made sense. Still, on balance, bad as it was to have his inadequacies rubbed in his face, he would vote for consciousness.

Overwhelmed by the heat, the others fell asleep during the drive back. Martin concentrated on the road ahead. Singh's directions had been simple enough: Drive until he was tired.

The landscape was growing drier and emptier by the moment, a trackless void that contained nothing but itself. The heat mirages had a hypnotic effect. Martin wasn't sure when he saw the willowy silhouette of what appeared to be a vehicle a few miles ahead. He rubbed his eyes and tried to make it go away, but it wouldn't.

He slowed down as they drew closer. He could make out the driver lugging a spare tire out of the trunk.

"Poor bastard. What a place to get a flat." Martin shifted down. "We'd better see if he needs help."

Stefan had stirred and rubbed his eyes. "*Ja*, it could just as easily be us."

A few seconds later, they pulled up next to a spanking-new Toyota Land Cruiser. The driver seemed even more out of place than the car. A tall, immaculately groomed African, he wore a suit that screamed Via Veneto. The diamond rings on his fingers would have fetched millions anywhere.

"Need a hand?" Martin asked through the open window.

"*Non, merci.* The car is new, so everything should work." If the mystery man was surprised to see them, he showed no sign of it. "However, since you have been kind enough to stop, perhaps you could wait until I am sure. Then you can join me in a glass of champagne." The man extended his hand. "Permit me to introduce myself. My name is Aka Bertain."

Martin got out to shake his hand and introduced himself and the others. "It's a pleasure."

Bertain stripped off his jacket, draped it over the ground next to the flat, and began to assemble the jack. Grunting with effort, he lowered himself on to the jacket and crawled under the bumper to position it.

It all happened fast—horribly fast. Bertain screamed, his legs started shaking as though he had the ague, and then he went limp. Stunned into immobility, Stefan and Martin exchanged helpless glances. Singh, who had emerged from his comatose state, roughly shouldered them aside, grasped Bertain by the ankles, and dragged him out from under the Toyota. There was a hissing noise, and a six-foot-long snake slithered out from the same place and shot through Martin's legs before he could move.

Singh shook his head mournfully. "Mamba," he said as if pronouncing a death sentence.

Stefan sprang toward their car and started rummaging through his pack. "Find the bite," he ordered. "We only have a few minutes to see if Lars's magic stones really work."

Martin and Singh rolled Bertain over. It only took seconds to find the wound on the back of his neck, just above the shirt collar.

Stefan crouched down with his knife and swiftly made two incisions. "Lucky it was not closer to his carotid," he muttered as he attached the stone.

As soon as it stuck, they gently rolled the African back over to facilitate his labored breathing.

Singh tapped his watch and signed forty-five minutes.

"We'll know soon enough." Martin searched for a way to alleviate the tension. "I wonder what he was doing in these parts, anyway."

The time seemed to move as slowly as the sun. It was only two-thirty. Martin's brain was saturated by the day's events. He couldn't absorb any more.

Minutes—though it could have been hours—later, Bertain gave a deep groan and fluttered his eyelids. His handsome features contorted into a grimace of supreme effort, almost as if he were clawing his way back from the abyss. "*Est-ce que je suis mort?*" he rasped.

"An entirely reasonable question under the circumstances," Martin announced to no one in particular. He leaned down and whispered in Bertain's ear. "*Doucement, mon vieux. Tu as été piqué par un mamba.*"

"I hope you are not telling him that you are his maker," Stefan said.

"No, just giving him the bad news that he is going to live." Martin felt a surge of adrenalin. After being surrounded by so much death in the morning, he felt an incredible rush to snatch one back a few hours later.

Even Singh seemed elated. His leathery face split into a big grin as he rummaged through their cooler for some water. He dripped some on to Bertain's lips.

The African sat up as the color returned to his face. "I owe you my life. Look in the cooler in the back of my car. There is some champagne. A moment like this deserves only champagne. There are not many men who can say that they have survived the bite of a green mamba without the aid of an antidote. Where did you get that stone?"

"From a priest we met in the Masirwa refugee camp about two hours ago," Martin replied as he uncorked the champagne. "You're a lucky and intriguing fellow, Bertain. I, for one, didn't expect to run into somebody like you in these parts."

"My occupation quite often takes me to strange places." Bertain smiled enigmatically and struggled to his feet.

Martin assisted him over to the back seat of the Rover. "How do you feel?"

"Not too bad. Perhaps if you could help me with the tire, I will be okay to continue on."

Singh already had the Land Cruiser jacked up.

"Consider it done," Stefan said. "Are you sure you will be all right to drive?"

"Yes, but I cannot leave without properly expressing my gratitude." Bertain reached into his back pocket and pulled out an alligator billfold. After searching inside it, he extracted a cloth packet and handed it to Martin. "These are a small price for a life, but I hope you will accept them."

Martin unfolded the packet to reveal three small but seemingly perfect diamonds. He rolled the stones around in his palm, fascinated by their feel. "Are they real?" was the best he could manage.

"As real as I am."

"Do you have any more?"

Bertain smiled. "Not here and not for free, but if you were to visit me in Rwanda, we might be able to arrange something."

Martin smiled. "You're indeed an intriguing fellow. Maybe we could get together and work out a deal. Stefan and I might be interested in buying some stones."

Bertain gave them a calculating look. For a second, the suave veneer disappeared, revealing the hint of a wily leopard in his eyes. "It is possible. Of course, I will need to know a little more about you."

"Fair enough. How do we handle that?"

"It is not a problem once I have your names. As I said, my work not only takes me to interesting places; it also puts me in contact with many useful people."

"Are you serious enough to set a time and place?"

"*Pourquoi pas?* Come to Kigali next weekend. By then I will have had adequate time to understand you. Check into the Mille Collines. Do not worry. I will hear of your arrival. If you are worthy partners, I will invite you to join me for lunch at my villa in the hills." He glanced at his watch. "It is getting late, and I see that your guide has finished with the tire, so I must be off. Au revoir for now." He embraced them in turn, kissing them on each cheek in Gallic fashion, started the Land Cruiser, and drove off.

Seconds later, he disappeared into the heat mirages.

MARTIN SHOOK HIS head in wonder. "Did that really just happen?"

"These are real enough." Stefan selected one of the diamonds and presented it to Singh, who pocketed it without a word and headed for the Rover.

"He's a cool one. I'll say that for him." Martin turned to follow Singh. "You'd think it was all in a day's work."

"Who cares?" Stefan said with a laugh. "At least it means he will not tell anyone. One thing has become increasingly apparent to me: Our Sikh friend understands a lot more English than he speaks."

"I was coming to the same conclusion myself." Martin watched Singh get behind the steering wheel. "I'm glad he's taking over the driving. I'm too tired to drive a nail at this point. A shower and an air-conditioned bed are starting to look awfully good."

Stefan handed Martin a hot Nile. "That's the best idea you've had in miles."

Martin stretched luxuriously and looked around. Heat mirages shimmered in every direction. He was back in the time warp, disengaged from civilization. None of the old rules applied.

It was as if there were nothing but him and the land as it had always been. He had a feeling of completeness and serenity. No cares, no worries—they all belonged to a parallel universe. It was probably as close as he would ever get to feeling totally free. Who needed the bullshit anyway? "Mother Africa, I fucking love it."

"What is wrong with you? Has the heat gotten to you?"

"No, just digging it. Was that karma or what?"

"Ja. The only thing we have not seen are the white rhino Singh promised us."

"They don't seem that important. Feel like a trip to Kigali?"

"Natürlich. Fate seems to be pointing us in that direction." Stefan extracted the diamond from his wallet and held it up to the sun. "You know it all fits. Kigali is right where the Rwandan, Ugandan, and Zairian borders overlap. It is known as a smuggler's haven."

"Karma," Martin repeated. "That's what it is. So far, ours is good."

Stefan's face grew pensive. "I hope it does not turn the other way."

Martin slipped into the passenger's seat beside Singh and let Stefan take the back seat. "We just go with the flow. That's what I love about this place: anything can happen in the next thirty seconds." He turned to Singh. "Diamond sau sau?"

Singh grinned roguishly. "Diamond *a panna*. Mota diamond, Missouri sana," he replied with a wink.

"Was old stoneface actually making a joke?" Stefan asked.

"What passes for one in these parts, but at least it confirms his bona fides or lack thereof. He said that one diamond was okay, but more were better. Kind of restores your faith in humanity, doesn't it?"

$$\bullet\ \bullet\ \bullet$$

Back at the lodge, a half-hour shower and a nap revived Martin. He wasn't entirely sure he liked the sensation, but he felt almost civilized as he took a table on the veranda and ordered a Nile. Stefan joined him a few minutes later.

They watched the technicolor sunset in a companionable silence. A convoy of zebra-striped VW buses clattered to a halt and disgorged its cargo of touristi, shattering the moment. After Masirwa, the bustle of the lodge seemed almost surreal.

"This is probably as close as they will get to the heart of Africa," Martin mused, "but then it's as close as they want to get."

Stefan rose. "I believe that is our cue for dinner."

They just beat the crowd into the dining room, which was a good thing. Service was slow enough when it was empty. The last thing they needed was a three-hour dinner.

Afterward, they took their brandies out to the gardens.

"Let's get away from the lodge a little," Martin suggested. "I trust Nathan's abilities, but I don't have the energy to deal with any GSU representatives tonight. Especially, if it's Usongo's better half."

"Agreed. Maybe if we stay alert, we can spot Nathan or whoever first for a change."

"We appreciate your concern for our well-being, but everything has been arranged." It was the young messenger from Friday night. He was better dressed this time. The latest addition to his wardrobe was a nasty-looking machine pistol. He signaled silence and gestured for them to follow.

They didn't have much choice, so they blundered through the bush after him. They weren't exactly silent, but they managed to keep up.

Half a mile later, he led them into a clearing where a battered Land Rover waited.

The engine started as soon as they came into sight. The boy pointed them toward the back seats and gave the driver a thumbs-up before vanishing back into the bush. The driver, a squat, muscular fellow with a bushy Afro, obviously knew exactly where he was going, since he didn't bother to turn on the headlights.

Stefan's query of "Where are we going?" met only stony silence.

Martin sighed. "The strong, silent type. What else could we expect? I hope we caught the right bus. The signs are so confusing in this neck of the woods," he added, trying to dispel the tightening of his gut.

He had completely lost his bearings. For all he knew, they were headed to the Sudan. He tried to act relaxed, but it was difficult to maintain a facade of indifference when his whole body was quivering like a tuning fork. He glanced across the Land Rover. Stefan looked as nervous as he felt.

Martin had no idea how long they'd been driving when they finally stopped. Like a fool, he'd forgotten to look at his watch when they had been picked up. He had to admire their security. There was no way he could ever find the spot again. Relief flooded over him when the door opened and Nathan's taciturn face appeared.

"Nice to see you again, Mr. Fine and Mr. Schmidt. I trust you enjoyed your little moonlight drive. Once we have finished our talk, I think you will understand why we took such precautions."

"Speaking of which, I think I will wait down here by the car," Stefan said. "Too many cooks will spoil the dinner."

Nathan smiled. "Like everyone else in this business, our leader does not like to meet too many new people."

Martin turned to Stefan. "Sorry about that, but I think the man makes sense."

"Ja, in his position I would feel the same way. I will do as Nathan suggests and look at it as a nice moonlight excursion."

"How did you get rid of your guardian angel without arousing his suspicions?" Martin asked.

"He had some car trouble. A flat tire and a faulty jack—both quite common occurrences in these parts. He will curse his bad luck, but we arranged for a mpenzi to help him forget his problems. I do not think he will report the incident to his superiors." Nathan motioned for him to follow. "Our camp is just over here. Levi Sabako is waiting to give you your interview."

"How should I describe Levi?"

"A senior official will do. I believe that is the normally used expression."

"Good enough."

The camp, if they could call it that, consisted of a tattered army-surplus tent and a few plastic ground sheets spread around a sputtering fire. A small, hunched mzee was warming himself beside it. Martin wasn't sure whether the hump was caused by deformity or senility. One look at the mzee's face confirmed that it was age. Martin had never seen such a face. It was so wrinkled that it was almost shapeless. Except for the eyes, every distinguishing feature was lost in loose, hanging folds of flesh. The eyes radiated such a depth of experience, wisdom, and compassion that Martin wanted to move closer and bathe himself in the aura.

He tore himself away from the hypnotic stare and opened his notebook to an empty page. "Let's start with the basics, Mr. Sabako. How would you describe the fundamental ideology of the Anyanya?"

Nathan, who had silently slipped behind him, translated the question and the mzee's long, rambling answer. "Nationalistic. At the moment, we have not really defined any clear-cut political positions, because we are not seeking independence. What we are seeking is autonomy and a larger place in the power structure of the Sudan. For instance, at the moment, we Southerners are under the Sharia or Islamic law. This is very unfair, because we are not Muslims."

Martin continued with a series of background questions about the military situation. Even though the answers more or less confirmed what he'd already heard from Nathan and Esther, they served to get the old man into the flow of the interview. The mzee's mind was still sharp. He answered every question off the cuff, not once consulting Nathan about his facts or numbers.

Once the ice had been broken, Martin turned the discussion toward the international ramifications of the situation. "Have you been approached by the Chinese, Russians, or anybody else with offers of help?"

Levi and Nathan talked that one over for a bit. "We have been approached by the Chinese and the Russians, as well as the Libyans. Levi said to tell you that we have turned down all these offers, because their price was too high. We are too poor an area to operate as a new state. We do not have the resources. There are already too many nonviable countries in Africa. Why start another? The aid will not go on forever."

"Hasn't the Organization of African Unity helped you at all?"

Nathan didn't bother to translate the question. "Not really," he said with a sigh. "They say nice things, but they do not offer us any concrete help. There are really two reasons. First, their charter specifically precludes involvement in the affairs of member countries. Second, and most importantly, the Arab members are becoming increasingly influential due to their rising oil revenues. You can guess whose side they are on."

"What about Libya?"

Levi became extremely animated as Nathan translated the question. His answer was scathing in tone. "The mad colonel is about to propose a pan-Islamic union between his country and the Sudan. He approached us first, because he hates Nimeiry, but we turned him down. No one in his right mind will deal with that madman. He is the devil incarnate."

"If the military situation is a stalemate, what hope do you have of making a breakthrough?"

"The war is crippling the economy. We think that if a little economic and diplomatic leverage is applied by the United States, the government could be persuaded to negotiate in good faith."

"Why the US?"

Once again, Nathan paused to listen and then translated Levi's words. "To keep the Sudan in its current pro-Western alignment. They should be concerned about a possible union with Khadafy. Even though Nimeiry distrusts Khadafy, he might be getting just desperate enough to cut a deal."

"With all the suffering that your people have experienced at the hands of the government and the animosities that have built up during a nineteen-year war, do you think there can be a real reconciliation?" Martin looked directly at Levi as he asked the question.

The mzee thought a long time before answering.

"Perhaps not for my generation," Nathan said. "There has been too much pain and suffering. I think that the wounds will heal in time if a fair agreement can be reached and the Northerners stick to it. The people on both sides want peace. They do not have to love each other to live peacefully side by side."

"Do you see any kind of time frame?"

"It must be soon." Nathan made a fist and shook it. "The younger of us are getting impatient with the old ways. Many of us are willing to make any deals we have to. We do not want to waste our lives fighting and suffering."

His outburst prompted a long speech from Levi.

Nathan looked distinctly embarrassed as he translated. "He says to tell you that youth are always too impatient. They want the eggs before the chickens. When you have been lied to before, you get suspicious of easy deals. What use is it to exchange one form of bondage and oppression for another? If we are patient, the peace will come at the right time on the right terms. God willing, it will be soon."

As the interview progressed, Martin was pleasantly surprised by Levi's refreshingly simple outlook. He was apolitical, not really holding on to any specific ideology. He didn't appear naive or unaware of the political nuances of his movement's situation; he just refused to get diverted by them. He clearly realized that the long-term solution to his people's problem was not to be found in selling out to a cynical, manipulative third party for short-term gain and ultimate disillusionment.

The younger generation, as typified by Nathan, was more impetuous and inclined to go for the pragmatic, short-term solution, letting the future take care of itself. There was some merit to both positions. After all, the superpowers still hadn't realized that they couldn't buy Third World countries. They could only rent them.

Martin had heard enough. He thanked Levi and promised to get the clippings to Nathan as soon as possible.

They headed back for the Land Rover.

"Did you get what you wanted?" Nathan asked.

"Yes, he's a very impressive fellow. How old is he, anyway?"

"It is said that he was alive at the time of Gordon Pasha. He has seen many things."

Martin gave a low whistle. "I'll say he has. That would make him in his nineties. That's a lot of history."

"Will the interview get published?"

"I think so, but I can't give you my word. I'm freelancing, so the papers are under no obligation. All I can do is send it in and hope for the best."

"At least you are honest, mzungu." Nathan's expression grew pensive as he gave Martin a calculating look. "What if I could get you something really sensational?"

"Like what?"

"How about proof that the Libyans are in secret negotiations with the Ugandan government?"

"For what purpose?"

"To establish full diplomatic relations with close military and economic ties. Mutual defense treaties, military cooperation agreements, including the establishment of Libyan training bases here."

"Wow!" Martin said with a gasp. "Where does that leave the Israelis? I thought Amin loved them."

"Out of the picture. They give Amin plenty of training, but they can't give him what he wants most: cash to buy expensive new toys for his army. He has to keep the soldiers happy."

Martin nodded. "Needless to say, all of this would come as rather a surprise to the Israelis—not to mention the Americans and British who helped put him in power. They thought they had a big, cuddly lap dog. What sort of proof have you got?"

"Documents from official—though obviously ultra-secret—negotiations between the Libyan and Sudanese foreign ministers. It is all part of the package. With Ugandan cooperation in closing our bases, the Libyans can assure our defeat."

"And Khadafy has two converts for his pan-Islamic empire. Do you have the documents in your possession?"

"I can have them in your hands by early the week after next. They will have to be handled very carefully."

"Yeah, I wouldn't want the wrong people to know I'd even seen them, let alone had them in my sweaty little hands."

"If those people you mention were to find out, you would be a dead man," Nathan said matter-of-factly. "As dead as the two journalists who found out about the massacres at Mbarara."

Martin made a snap decision. It was a risky proposition, but a story could establish an instant reputation for him. "Okay, but let's keep up your usual high-security standards."

As they were approaching the Land Rover, another thought occurred to him. "Do you have any contacts in Rwanda and Kenya?"

"We have contacts in most of the neighboring countries. Why?"

"Because we might have a business proposition of mutual benefit. It could be a way of making some useful money with no ideological strings attached."

Nathan grinned. "We are always open to suggestions. I take it this proposition is illegal?"

"It all depends on your point of view. In any case, I won't have the details for another couple of weeks. When I get them, how can I get in touch with you?"

"Go to Nakasero next Wednesday at noon. Wait at the front gate. You will be approached by a deformed beggar. He will be our contact for any future dealings." Nathan glanced up at the starlit sky. "We had better go back to the lodge."

Stefan was sound asleep on the back seat by the time they had returned.

Martin didn't bother to wake him. They weren't going to get enough sleep as it was.

CHAPTER

9

TWO DAYS LATER, Martin found himself back in civilization. After visiting Makerere to explore the campus and play the role of studenti, he picked up Esther at the ministry and agreed to take her to her place so she could change out of her work clothes.

"Why don't you just pack some clothes and bring them out to Kireka," he suggested. "This drive could get tedious if we have to do it every day."

Esther stared at him from the passenger's seat. "Are you asking me to move in with you, mzungu?"

Martin hadn't really thought about it that way, but it seemed natural enough. "I guess so."

"I will on one condition."

"No, you don't have to wash my underwear."

"Oh, be serious," she said, rolling her eyes.

"That's exactly what I'm trying not to be."

"I see that, Martin. Sometimes you are very easy to know. That is why I am trying to tell you that my one condition is that you are under no obligation to me."

Martin looked into her eyes. There didn't seem to be any guile, just a touch of amusement. *That's a relief,* he thought to himself.

The implications of his casual invitation had just begun to dawn on him, and he wasn't too sure he was comfortable with them. He found it interesting that she'd sensed his nervousness before he had even become aware of it.

"Your roommate at home?" he inquired as they parked.

"No, why do you ask?"

"Because I want to try out your bed."

"It is not as comfortable as yours. Let's use the shower."

• • •

Stefan was waiting with Major Smythe-Jones when they sauntered into the Nile. "Look what I found propping up the bar."

"Well, we owe the man a good dinner for his most excellent advice on a guide. Singh made the trip." Martin introduced Esther to the major.

He bowed graciously and kissed her on the hand. "Well, well, Martin. Stefan told me your friend was attractive but not beautiful."

Esther smiled. "I bet that you say that to all the mpenzis, Major."

"Only the special ones, my dear. Bloody hell, look what the cat dragged in." The major gestured toward the entrance, where an obviously expat American was making a beeline for them. "Martin, this could be your first chance to meet someone who actually does work at Langley. Never did understand why they all wear the same uniform."

The man wore a baggy seersucker suit. At first glance, he seemed a pudgy, amiable sort. In spite of his laidback exterior, he had a certain hardness in his eyes.

"Steve Russell," he said as he gave Martin a bone-crushing handshake.

Martin introduced himself and tried to ignore the uneasiness in his gut, which he chalked up to Russell's CIA connection. As a rule, he wanted nothing to do with the agency, because anyone unfortunate enough to hook up with the CIA never got out. In some ways, he thought, they were similar to the mafia. Both organizations steeped themselves in a bizarre, ritualistic mumbo jumbo of traditions that would have been laughable if not underpinned by a strong tendency toward institutionalized violence.

Russell gave the major an appraising look and then turned to Martin. "I heard you two just returned from a trip up north to Paraa. I've been dying to get up to those parts myself. I'm sure the game was great."

"The game was outstanding," Martin said, "but I found our stop at the Masirwa refugee center to be the most interesting—if not pleasant—part of the trip."

Russell looked surprised. "Why so? It's just another depressing refugee camp. Unfortunately, they're a dime a dozen around these parts."

"I guess that's true, but I've been researching a few pieces on the Anyanya, so it was right up my alley."

"You're a journalist then?"

"No. At the moment, I'm a studenti at Makerere. I've always been interested in writing, though, and I have a few press contacts in England and the States, so this looks like as good a place as any to get my feet wet."

"Cautiously, I hope. Africa can be a dangerous place for the uninitiated to practice journalism."

"So I've heard. I plan to stick to noncontroversial topics."

The major smiled. "I've heard there's quite a bit going on up north at the moment. Did you get any interesting buzzes while you were up there?" He winked at Martin's inquiring look as Russell bent over to scoop up a handful of nuts.

"Really, Major. What have you picked up recently?" Russell's attempt at casualness didn't succeed.

"The political situation in the Sudan, of course, old boy."

"I was in Khartoum a couple of weeks ago," Russell said, "and things seemed sleepy as usual."

The major chuckled. "I've been hearing a lot of talk about secret negotiations with the Libyans. Nimeiry is getting pretty desperate about the Anyanya these days. His economy is in shambles. A deal with Khadafy might have its benefits. Surprised you haven't picked up any rumblings. The people I've talked to were pretty concerned about the situation."

"Well, I was only there forty-eight hours," Russell said with a shrug. "I'll certainly have to look into it, though it seems unlikely, in view of their traditional hatred of each other. Still, anything's possible. If those two decide to mix it up, things could get very complicated all over the region." He turned back to Martin. "Did you hear anything from your Anyanya contacts?"

Something told Martin that these two were always on duty. "What contacts?" He sighed wistfully. He wasn't about to admit to having any—not for free, anyway. "I would love to get an interview with some of them. We did get a buzz that something was going on with the Libyans from some of the refugees who'd just arrived, though. Something about Sudanese soldiers bragging that they were going to have money to buy lots of new powerful weapons soon. I just put it down to morale-boosting government propaganda."

Russell fell silent for a moment. Martin could almost see the wheels turning. Abruptly, he snapped out of his reverie and extended his hand. "Thanks for the tip."

"Just a concerned citizen," Martin replied modestly. "Please keep me in mind if an interesting story surfaces."

"I'll certainly do that. If you'll excuse me, I have a dinner engagement."

As soon as Russell was out of earshot, Martin looked questioningly at the major. "Why the free info, and where did you get it? I thought I had a hot scoop."

The major laughed in delight. "Just an ex-civil servant keeping my ear to the ground. Two reasons: One, it makes him indebted to us, which might prove useful in the long run, and two, it put him on the defensive. From my experience, the less these eager types know about you the better. He's new to Africa—the Third-World, for that matter—which makes him more dangerous."

Stefan nodded. "Agreed. The man did not even understand the equatorial iceberg syndrome."

"Nor do I," the major said, "and I've been here for years."

"Simple, Major," Stefan said with a wave of the hand. "Everything important here goes on below the surface. If you haven't figured out what's going on before it surfaces, you will get clobbered like the Titanic."

The major laughed and raised his glass in a mock toast. "Here, here. That analogy is just paradoxical enough to be apt for these parts. They would probably like it on Fleet Street." His expression turned serious as he locked eyes with Martin. "Regardless of my opinion of Russell, his warning about practicing journalism in these parts was spot on. I take it you've heard what happened to the two Yank journalists at Mbarara a few weeks ago. Take my advice, old boy. Be very careful what you do, and keep a very tight arse. This isn't a school paper lark."

It was just the kind of advice that Martin was inclined to ignore on general principle, but this was a different game, and while the major might have been old, he was as sharp as a tack and playing on his home field. "Point taken, Major. I'm a neophyte, and all advice will be gladly received." He swallowed the dregs of his drink. "I'm getting hungry. What's the game plan, guys?"

"Dinner," Stefan said, "followed by the Lair."

• • •

Over dinner, Martin finished their briefing and asked the major if he had heard of Bertain Aka.

"Yes, the name sounds familiar." The major scratched his head and frowned. "I have it now. I remember hearing somewhere that he was a useful sort of chap to know in Rwanda. There was something else about him too, but I can't drag it up at the moment. Did he by any chance mention anything about tension between the Hutus and Tutsis? I've been getting rumblings that trouble is imminent." He shook his head. "I can tell you, I don't want to be around when the balloon goes up among that lot. There's going to be a bloodbath as sure as I'm sitting here. Thousands of Tutsis will probably be killed."

"Why do they stay if they know trouble is coming?" Martin asked.

"Why did so many Jews stay in Germany? Some are leaving, but lots have no place to go. Others don't want to give up what they have and live on in the unjustified hope that the inevitable cannot happen."

"Why don't they go next door to Burundi? Surely, it's the natural place. After all, it's a mirror image. The Tutsi minority that controls things would welcome them with open arms."

"I wish things were that easy," the major said with a sigh. "You're correct in stating that a minority of Tutsis control things in Burundi, and they would no doubt like their brothers from Rwanda to come there. Unfortunately, their hold on power at the moment is quite tenuous. Large segments of the army are still Hutu, and they're in a position to make things difficult for Micombero. When he's had some time to consolidate, the situation will change. The only problem is that the Tutsis in Rwanda cannot wait."

"Ach so," Stefan said. "That short a timetable?"

"Soon. Mark my words." The major wagged his finger for emphasis. "The Parmehutu—that's the name of the ruling party in Rwanda—have recently consolidated their hold on the army. They've also moved enough of their own people into the civil service to keep things running after they make their move. That was why the Tutsi minority hung on as long as they did. The Belgians trained them. The Hutus couldn't move them out for fear of a total collapse."

Stefan laughed bitterly. "What I want to know is the name of the genius who thought of splitting the countries that way. He must have been a communist mole. What better opportunity for destabilizing the region than splitting the two countries in such a way that each tribe is a majority in one country and a minority in its neighbor."

The major offered a grim nod. "It was certainly an idiotic thing to do. Most likely, it was the usual scenario: a couple of ignorant colonial officers drawing lines on a map over brandy and cigars. It's not an uncommon situation elsewhere on the continent."

"Actually, I don't think it was an accident of history at all," Martin interjected. "It was the Brits, to be precise—no offense intended, Major—who perfected the technique of indirect rule by a disaffected minority in India. The Belgians made good use of it in their colonial possessions. Now as always happens in these matters, the hens are coming home to roost with a vengeance."

"Since we are on the subject of tribal bloodshed," Stefan said, "how are things around here?"

"Settling down, thank God. The purge is over. The general feels much more secure these days. The only sign of anything ever having occurred are the large groups of widows begging around Mbarara. Distressing, but it's not healthy to take too great an interest." The major signaled for coffee.

"When are you coming back to Kampala?" Stefan asked.

"Normally, I come up every weekend, but it just so happens I'm staying over for a party tomorrow night. Colonel Zack Bakazi, the commandant of the paratroops, is giving it. Maybe you three would like to come. I can personally introduce you to Amin. He served under me in the African Rifles."

Martin exchanged glances with Stefan. Was the major playing some kind of game? Was he hoping Martin would forget all about what he'd witnessed the last time the major had dragged him to a black-tie event? Was this some kind of test?

"Sounds intriguing," Stefan said, forcing a smile.

"Sure does," Martin lied. The last thing he wanted to do was watch Amin unleash more of his ghoulish antics. "But we haven't been officially invited. Won't that cause problems if the big guy is there?"

"Nonsense," the major waved his hand airily. "I know Bakazi quite well. It will be no problem if I bring you along. Meet me here about six, and I'll take you out there with me." He nodded to Esther. "You must come. It will raise Mr. Fine's stock with the locals."

Martin tried to ignore the sinking sensation in his gut as he extended his hand. "Thanks, Major. The party sounds great."

• • •

Martin drove to Makerere the next day to check his class schedule. Tuesday mornings and Wednesday and Thursday afternoons—he couldn't have planned it better himself. He wouldn't have any problem taking long weekends for travel.

On his way home, he stopped in Nakasero. He was intrigued by the Anyanya contact. He'd been meaning to put one of the town's beggars on his payroll. One thing was certain: Nathan's point man would have to contact him. Half the beggars in town loitered in front of the market, and he couldn't really hang a sign around his neck.

As he rounded the corner of Liberation Avenue, a sibilant hiss brought him up short. He whirled around just in time to see a crippled African scuttle into a garbage-strewn alley. Martin didn't know how the man managed to move so fast. From the looks of it, a severe childhood bout of polio had fused both his legs in a permanent kneeling position.

He was quick as hell. Martin had a hard time keeping up as the beggar scuttled through the smelly alley.

As soon as they had made a few turns and were out of sight of the road, Legs—the name was cruel but intuitive—stopped. "You are punctual, Mr. Martin." He reached into the back pocket of his grubby shorts and handed Martin a folded newspaper. "Nathan said you should take this to the terrace of the Speke. A messenger, who you will recognize, will substitute papers with you."

"When?"

"In one hour."

Martin glanced at his watch. It would be two-thirty. He decided to chat up Legs for a bit and found him surprisingly well-educated and excellently informed. He seemed an ideal candidate for Martin's fledgling private intelligence service. He was an Acholi, and some of his relatives had been killed in the recent army purges at Mbarara, so his political bona fides were impeccable. After some pro forma bargaining, he accepted Martin's proposal to keep his ears open in return for future considerations. The hundred-shilingi note disappeared magically into the folds of his tattered flour-sack shorts.

Martin arrived at the Speke as the lunch crowd was beginning to thin and was able to find an inconspicuous table in the corner. He ordered a beer and settled in, scanning the area for any signs of untoward activity. On the stroke of two-thirty, he spotted the messenger from Paraa striding quickly up Nile Avenue. He was walking faster than the rest of the crowd and glancing back frequently over his shoulder.

Martin felt a sudden frisson. There was pursuit, but it was from the front, not the back. The walk tipped him off: Usongo's partner's penguin waddle would have been comical under any other circumstances. Even if Martin could have thought of some diversion, he wouldn't have had time. The currier spotted the closing net and broke into a run. Suddenly, GSU types began coming out of the woodwork. Martin counted ten agents surrounding the helpless youth in a rugby scrum.

A Mercedes that had been sitting in the hotel driveway glided out to the melee. It was all taking place less than twenty feet from where Martin was sitting. The agents dragged their bloodied quarry to his feet as the car's tinted window rolled down.

"Excellent, you've taken him alive. Now we can find out who his accomplices are."

Martin's guts shriveled like a dried raisin. It was Sergeant Major Bob Astles. Martin was fucked if the kid lived. There was nothing Martin could do except hope no one spotted him. He might have time to get away before they made the kid talk. Everything had become very real. The major's ominous warning came to mind. Until now, Martin realized, it had been like a movie. The only problem was that he wasn't in the seats watching anymore.

At an order from Astles, the agents began to search the prisoner. With a sudden, convulsive effort, the teenager ripped free from their grip. His right hand snaked inside his shirt, and he popped something in his mouth. Within seconds, he went into convulsions, vomited on himself, and slumped motionless. Martin caught a whiff of almonds—cyanide, just like the books said.

There was a shocked silence. The agents turned toward the car, waiting for Astles's reaction. It was not long in coming. He jumped out of the car and started screaming abuse. It was the longest, most inventive burst of swearing Martin had ever heard. The GSU boys literally shrunk in place. If the specter hadn't been so terrifying, Martin would have laughed. As Astles worked himself up to a crescendo, he unholstered his pistol and fired a whole clip into the teenager's head, which disintegrated into a pinkish vapor.

Astles threw the pistol at the head of the nearest agent and climbed back in the Mercedes without a glance at the headless corpse. Everything was still. No one seemed to know what to do. Finally, Usongo's partner issued a string of orders, and the agents dragged the corpse off down Nile Avenue. The agent gave one last glance around the scene, and his eyes came to rest on Martin.

Martin felt like his bowels had been gripped by a cold fist.

Usongo's partner let his glance linger just long enough so that Martin knew he'd been recognized.

Martin's legs started shaking so much that the table began to vibrate. Luckily, the African turned and strode off before the glasses tipped over. Within minutes, conversation, albeit hushed, returned. Martin flagged a waiter and ordered a double grappa.

CHAPTER

10

MARTIN COULDN'T HIDE his hangdog expression when Stefan joined him at the hotel bar.

Stefan glanced from Martin's face to the full snifter in front of him. "What's wrong with you?"

Martin ordered him a brandy and waved him over to a quiet corner. "You'll need this when you hear what happened." He gave a full account of the afternoon's events, including his theories on what they meant.

Stefan swirled his brandy in the snifter and said nothing. Finally, he killed the drink in one gulp and gently set it down on the marble table. "The iceberg begins to surface. The screwup in security was theirs. I certainly did not mention the meeting to anyone. They might have an informer, but then again, they might not. Nathan said that the GSU had been watching them. Perhaps they got lucky."

"Yeah, we can't really do anything but watch our tails and wait. I figured I'd better tell you, though."

Stefan sighed. "We will have to keep a close eye out the next few days. If they are watching us, we can assume the worst."

"It was Astles. Everybody jumped when he said boo. He's got an awful lot of pull in these parts."

"We have been very lucky. Usongo's partner has crossed our paths without knowing it several times in the past few weeks."

Martin laughed ruefully. "Don't I know it? In the future, I'd just as soon stay out of sight and out of mind as far as he is concerned."

Stefan stared into his empty glass. "Well, *Hein*, I guess your career in journalism is going to be short-lived."

"Or at least put on the back burner for the time being. That's okay. We've got other fish to fry."

"Maybe. It all depends on how hot the fire gets."

Martin glanced at his watch and rose. "Let's head out. You can join me and Esther for dinner if you like."

"Not tonight. I am going to my boss's for dinner. I must hurry, or I will be late and his wife will be mad. She is a real stickler for detail. I think she is distantly related to Himmler."

• • •

After picking up Esther, Martin told her what had happened and then braced for her reaction as he drove.

"I am not surprised, mzungu," she said in a calm voice. "This is a dangerous game. I am sad that such a young boy was killed, but he was a soldier." She muffled a sob. "So many, so many." She seemed so small and vulnerable.

He wanted to take her in his arms, but that could come later. There were other matters to deal with first. "Stefan and I compared notes earlier. We think the GSU has an informer planted."

"More likely the Sudanese pigs," she said, spitting out the words. "I am worried about you, Martin. They have killed before when journalists knew too much."

"Even if they *do* know that I'm the one they were delivering the papers to, I don't think they'll bother me."

"Why?"

"Without the documents, I don't have a story, so I pose no threat to them," Martin answered with more confidence than he felt. "Also, the previous incident generated a lot of negative press. I don't think they want any more at the moment. They're still in the process of trying to establish full diplomatic relations with a lot of countries."

"That could be true, but I am still scared."

When they got back to the house, they stripped the moment they walked through the front door and made love on the floor. It was an instinctive act, almost savage in its intensity. They were drained afterward and wordlessly dragged themselves into bed.

· · ·

Esther's tossing and turning woke Martin from a deep sleep. It was still dark outside. He didn't want to look at his watch. If he saw what time it was, he would never get back to sleep. Esther started muttering and moaning, her movements became more agitated, and she broke out in a sweat. He took her in his arms, hoping to soothe her without waking her.

"Oh, Martin," she said and kissed him. "I was having this horrible nightmare. I just have to be sure it is not real."

"Tell me about the dream. It might help."

"It happened when I was young. My parents were simple farmers, and our life was hard but good. We had heard about the war, of course, but it had never really touched us. One day some men with guns came through the village. They took all the food they could carry and left. The next day the soldiers came." She started to cry. Her body heaved with deep, gut-wrenching sobs.

Martin held her tightly and let her take her time. He couldn't think of anything to say.

She regained her composure after a few minutes and wiped her eyes with the handkerchief he handed her. "It was horrible. They herded us into the main square. Then they raped all the women—some after they had torn babies from their breasts—and bayoneted them. When the men tried to fight back, they were shot. Then they burned the whole village. Not one hut was left standing. The soldiers were drunk and went crazy. My brother and I got away in the confusion. I don't know how we escaped. We walked for days until the missionaries found us." The dam burst, and she cried until she was cleansed.

He rocked her gently in his arms until she fell into an exhausted sleep.

• • •

Esther didn't say anything the next morning about her nightmare or their conversation, but she seemed in a pretty good mood as she dressed for work.

Maybe the purging helped, Martin thought.

"Go back to sleep. I probably kept you up half the night." She leaned over and kissed him gently. "Thank you. Now you know all my secrets."

The sound of Stefan starting his car came through the open window.

"I will get a ride with Stefan," Esther said and blew Martin another kiss as she ran out the door.

Tired as he was, Martin couldn't get back to sleep. He got up, showered, and hit the books. Keeping his student cover intact seemed doubly important. It struck him as funny that he had taken to using the spook jargon that featured so heavily in the thrillers he was addicted to. Two weeks in Kampala would do that to a man, he told himself with a sigh. The only problem was this wasn't a book, and he was being sucked in deeper.

By the time Stefan brought Esther back that afternoon, Martin had managed to make a substantial dent in his assigned reading, but he'd reached his saturation point with early Baganda history.

He invited Stefan inside for a beer while Esther showered and commenced her painstaking preparations for the party. "Notice any strange fellows with mirror shades lurking around today?"

"No, no sign of anyone. I had to run errands all over town, and I kept a sharp eye out. Maybe we are being too paranoid."

Martin shrugged. "Perhaps, but I don't know if it's possible to be too paranoid in these parts. It should be an interesting party tonight."

"Nein, it will be just another diplomatic cattle call—nothing like the savagery you witnessed at the barracks."

Martin offered a faint smile. "I hope so."

It took all of Martin's subtle powers of persuasion to get Esther ready by five-thirty. They headed to the Nile in Stefan's car. The major hadn't arrived when they got there, so they took a large table in the corner. Esther asked them to order a double waragi and tonic for her and left to make a short call.

Stefan smiled. "She is probably going off to make sure that the ride in did not spoil her hair."

"I think that she's a little nervous about meeting the general."

"Have you told her about what he—?"

"Not yet. But I will." Martin edged his chair a little closer to the table and looked around to make sure no one was listening. "How reliable do you think the major is? I'm tempted to ask him about the events of the past few days. He certainly seems to have a feel for the politics around here. But the way he invited us to this party—acting like he never dragged me to the dinner with Amin—felt like he's playing some kind of game or testing me."

"I agree. Ostensibly, he is retired, but I do not think people in his line of work ever retire completely. Do you know what he did before?"

"Outside of assuming he was a spook, nothing."

"During the Biafran War, he found himself in a rather remarkable situation. On one hand, he was seconded to the federal government as a military adviser. On the other, he also somehow managed to obtain a place for himself on the UN anti-genocide committee with free access to Biafra. As you might imagine, there was concern, if not agitation, in some quarters when his dual responsibilities were discovered. As I recall, he was forced to resign both positions in a flurry of public mea culpas. Shortly thereafter, he was retired altogether." Stefan smiled wickedly. "If you choose to believe that the Brits would retire someone with his experience, not to mention ability to speak five languages, including Russian, that is fine."

"It wouldn't seem to make much sense," Martin agreed. "You seem to know a lot about him."

"The rumor mill here is very active. What else is there to do besides drink and gossip?"

Martin wondered what people were saying about the newest American studenti to hit town. Nothing pedestrian, that was for sure. They'd invent something to relieve the tedium.

"Evening, chaps." Major Smythe-Jones took a seat. "I must say, I just saw Esther, and she was a revelation. Made me wish I was a young man again." He turned to Martin. "You said you knew Bakazi. You do seem to get around for a studenti."

Martin let the last dig pass and told the major how Joe had introduced him to Bakazi—and how icy things had gotten when Bakazi insinuated Martin worked for the CIA.

The major was still laughing when Esther returned. "I say. The mpenzis in the old days were nowhere near as ravishing as you, my dear." He rose and gallantly pulled out a chair for her. "Simply superb. I'm not going to have to introduce you. Amin will make a beeline."

Not surprisingly, the major knew the way out to the base. As they turned into the drive, two Uzi-toting soldiers snapped to attention and gestured for them to stop. The major rattled off some Swahili at them, and they waved them on. They followed the drive for about a mile until they came to a ten-foot-high chain-link fence with a proper checkpoint.

A sergeant checked their names against his list and told them Colonel Bakazi's quarters were a mile ahead on the right. The grounds were immaculate, and the troops were exceptionally well turned-out.

The major cast appraising glances at the fortifications. "The Israelis do a first-class job. I heard this base was a joke before they came in."

The colonel's quarters were in a large but simple whitewashed bungalow. A soldier waved them into a makeshift parking lot that was already overflowing with Mercedes and Peugeots, most of which bore diplomatic tags. It was obvious from the noise as they approached the bungalow's adjoining garden that the party was well under way.

Colonel Zack greeted them graciously at the entrance to the garden. "Mr. Fine, what a pleasant surprise. I am glad to see that you have met one of our country's beautiful women. Major, it is always good to see you. I hope we get the chance to talk later. Enjoy yourselves."

Martin counted seven different languages as they worked their way over to the bar. He decided on a scotch for some social lubrication. It was a bit of a shock when the orderly gave him a highball with three fingers and a lone ice cube. Esther's waragi was of similarly heroic proportions. They pushed their way over to a vacant table in the corner.

The general's motorcade arrived as they were seating themselves. Astles scrambled out of the passenger seat and deferentially opened the door on the driver's side. His rigid bearing and salt-and-pepper crew cut were impossible to miss.

Martin and the others had a clear view as Amin unfolded his massive frame from the cramped Citroen. He was immediately surrounded by a phalanx of security guards. He towered at least a head over everybody around him. Like a good politician, he stopped frequently to press flesh as he worked his way into the center of the garden.

"He has not missed many meals since the Rifles," the major noted with a chuckle. "Wait until the brouhaha dies down, and I will introduce everyone."

They didn't have to wait long. The general spotted the major, beamed, and headed for their table. Amin embraced the major and signaled for a chair.

Martin spotted a flicker of recognition on Amin's face when the major made introductions, but Amin, just like the major, maintained an amiable façade. His recent descent into barbarism was all the more frightening because no one seemed willing to acknowledge it had ever happened. It hung over everything like a menacing cloud.

The major translated as Amin made pleasant small talk. Amin told Martin that it was a good thing to study African history, because much about the present could be learned from the past.

"I can't argue with that," Martin said. "I'm enjoying my visit to Uganda and have found the country beautiful and the people hospitable."

Turning his attention to Esther, Amin flirted with her in an outrageous but courtly manner. She batted her eyes and said something in Kakwa that made him laugh uproariously. Up close, he evinced raw, almost brutal, power. Frequent broad smiles did nothing to dispel the brooding, malevolent vibes that emanated from his massive, porcine skull with its constantly shifting, beady eyes.

He continued chatting with the major for a few minutes more before rising and striding energetically over to the bar to work the large contingent of ambassadors and high commissioners gathered there. As Colonel Zack hurried over to make introductions, Astles caught his arm, nodded at Martin, and whispered something in his ear. Martin's stomach flip-flopped. What the hell did Astles want with him? As if he didn't know. Well, at least there was one comforting thought. They could hardly have him taken out and shot at a party like this. Or could they?

"For a military man, he appears to have a fair amount of political savvy," Stefan observed.

The major laughed. "He has good taste in women too. What did you say to him, Esther?"

"That is for me to know, and the rest of you to guess. I think he is a charming man as long as he gets what he wants. When he does not, I think he can be very dangerous. He reminds me of the bully in the village where I grew up."

The major nodded. "Yes, I'm afraid you're right, my dear. One must not be put off by his facile exterior. He's a master of tribal politics and very ruthless if crossed." He exchanged a knowing glance with Martin before rising from his chair. "If you'll excuse me for a moment, I must go over and pay my respects to the high commissioner."

"Mzungu, can you please get me another drink?" Esther handed Martin her glass.

Martin nodded and headed for the bar.

As he joined the mile-long line, an orderly approached. "Colonel Bakazi wishes to see you inside." He signaled for Martin to follow and headed for the bungalow.

The orderly ushered him into a spartan office, poured him a drink from the wet bar in the corner, and left him with his thoughts.

Martin hadn't gotten very far when Colonel Zack and Astles entered the office a few seconds later. It was all Martin could do not to flinch at the sight of Astles. Martin concentrated instead on lighting a cigarette and regulating his breathing. His heart palpitated wildly.

While the colonel mixed them drinks, Astles engaged Martin in some ice-breaking small talk. "I hear you've been busy since we last dined together. How was Paraa?"

Surprisingly, now that the fat was in the fire, Martin felt relaxed. He slipped easily into the company line, enthusing about what a great opportunity it was to study at Makerere. Astles seemed to know everything he'd done since getting to Kampala. That didn't disturb him much. He hadn't tried to hide anything, and none of his travels were that out of the ordinary for an adventurous tourist. The disquieting thing was that his answers didn't elicit any visible reaction. It was as if they were reciting by rote from a prearranged script. Either Martin's answers didn't make any difference, or Astles already knew what they would be. Martin steeled himself for the inevitable curveball.

"Word has reached me from various sources that you are thinking of doing some newspaper pieces," Astles said. "This upsets me. Are you aware that all foreign correspondents must register their credentials with the Ministry of the Interior?"

"I wasn't," Martin replied. "Unfortunately, I don't have any credentials—just a few contacts I picked up in London. I'm not a professional, or I would've known about the regulation. I hope I haven't done anything wrong. I just wanted to see if I could get a career going. I've always wanted to be a foreign correspondent. You know the adventure and intrigue bit." It seemed wise to come on like a bumbling Walter Mitty sort. He would pose less of a threat that way. Besides, he thought ruefully, it wasn't that far from the truth.

Outside of exchanging veiled glances, Astles and Bakazi remained silent.

"I didn't see the harm in writing a few noncontroversial pieces," Martin continued. "I have no intention of writing about anything that involves local politics."

Astles lit a foul-smelling pipe. "Just what are you going to write about?"

"Well, the refugee camp at Masirwa was pretty interesting."

"How about some articles on their guerrilla counterparts?" Bakazi asked innocently. "From what I have been told, your girl-friend Mapende has a brother in the Anyanya."

Nothing like a little Ugandan subtlety, Martin thought. "That would certainly be a good story. I was interested when she told me about him. Unfortunately, she hasn't seen him for a long time. She doesn't have any contact with him or anyone else in the movement, so no Anyanya, no story."

Apparently satisfied, Astles gestured to Bakazi for a refill. "Yes, that war has been going on a long time. Without something new, it would be difficult to sell a story." He gave Martin a sympathetic smile and changed tack. "I noticed that you were sitting at the Speke during that unfortunate incident the other afternoon."

And there it was. Out in the open.

Martin tried to play it cool. "Yes, it was a bit unsettling, but I've heard that the general's new anti-crime initiative has worked wonders. Petty criminals get shot all the time in South Philly. If you were worried about me writing about that—"

"That man was more than just a petty thief!" Bakazi barked. "He was a spy for the Anyanya!"

"A real spy that close?" Martin played dumb. "How exciting! I thought it was just another kondo."

"Yes, he had stolen some top-secret documents from the Sudanese. They alerted us, and we tracked him from the time he came across the border. If one of my overzealous colleagues had not acted so stupidly, we would have seen the person he was bringing them to." Astles sipped his drink, fixing the clear gray marbles that passed for his eyes directly on Martin's.

Martin felt like a butterfly about to be skewered. If he fielded this one properly, everything would be all right. Astles and Bakazi wouldn't have invited him on this fishing trip if they'd had anything concrete. He let his initial expression of incomprehension slip into dawning understanding and, finally, amazement. It was a masterful performance, if he did say so himself. "You mean you thought he was coming to meet *me*?" Martin laughed. "Why me? It's not like I'm an internationally known newsman or anything. I've never even had a piece published. Those guys wouldn't know me from Adam."

Astles, to Martin's amazement, looked almost sheepish.

Hook, line, and sinker, Martin thought triumphantly.

"It does seem a bit farfetched, doesn't it?" Astles admitted. "I just had a flash when I saw you at the party tonight."

"Actually, I'm flattered that you thought I was some kind of hotshot reporter. I should be so lucky. Talk to me in twenty years if we're both still around." Martin finished his drink. "It's been nice talking to you, and I'm sorry I couldn't be of more help."

Astles signaled Bakazi for refills. "Have one for the road, Mr. Fine. You've been a great help, actually, and you could be of further service." The marbles gave him an expectant look.

That was the last thing Martin wanted, but it didn't seem he had much choice. "Sure, if I can. I'd be glad to. I don't want you all to get the impression that I'm uncooperative."

"What have you read about the current regime?"

"Only a few pieces in the British and American press. I thought the majority of them were pretty fair, if a little on the cautious side."

Astles gave him a wintry smile. "I can see that you have the potential to be a good journalist. I've always maintained that the only people more evasive by nature than politicians are reporters. It goes with the territory, I guess."

Not to mention acute paranoia, Martin thought.

Astles paused briefly before continuing. "The general is concerned about his image abroad. In short, he'd like some positive press notices. I thought you might be interested in some exclusive pieces."

Martin resisted the urge to laugh. There weren't any journalists currently working in Uganda. They'd all been withdrawn in protest over the murder of the two freelancers the month before. Stefan was going to love this. "Some articles that would bolster the image of the general abroad," Martin suggested with a conspiratorial smile.

Astles turned and winked at Bakazi. "You see? I told you this was an intelligent young man." He turned back to Martin. "I wouldn't ask you to write anything that goes against the grain. We just want a few of our more positive achievements, which have so far been overlooked, to get some play."

"That sounds fair enough to me. Of course, you realize that I can't guarantee they'll get published." Martin figured it couldn't hurt to emphasize his amateur status. "How about some pieces on other countries too? I'm thinking of visiting Rwanda soon. I hear there's some trouble brewing there between the Hutu and Tutsi."

"Sure, why not?" Astles replied with a wave of the hand. "It'll serve to make our pieces look less like plants. The only sensitive area as far as we're concerned is the Sudan." He gave Martin a steely stare, and his expansiveness vanished. "We're currently involved in some very sensitive negotiations that we hope will bring an end to the stalemate. They're at a very delicate stage, and any ripple, no matter how slight, could capsize them."

"Understood."

"Good. As you may be aware, we have had some difficulties with journalists in the past. I trust those will not be repeated." Astles let the implied threat hang ominously for a few seconds before slipping back into his good-fellow persona. "Well, that concludes our business. I'm sure we can both look forward to a pleasant, mutually beneficial relationship. We'll be in touch."

Bakazi rose and escorted Martin out.

The babble of the party seemed almost surreal to Martin. He was walking on air. He'd managed to extract his head from the lion's mouth with nary a scratch. He found the combined fear and adrenalin rush exhilarating. He felt masterful, as if he was the grand puppeteer, pulling everyone else's strings. Or were they pulling his? The hell with buttering his bread on both sides, as per the proverb. He'd need a whole loaf before he was through.

"Mr. Fine," Bakazi said, "I am sure that you have begun to realize that there are many opportunities for an enterprising young man in our country. Have you encountered any interesting propositions yet?"

Martin debated how to fob off Bakazi. "So far, Colonel, we haven't encountered any sleazy individuals wearing grimy white suits with maps to lost diamond mines. It's been a major disappointment. Just kidding! I wouldn't want to get involved in anything like that. It seems dangerous enough just being a law-abiding studenti around here."

"It can be, without protection," Bakazi replied enigmatically. "Remember to keep me in mind if anything comes up."

Martin stopped at the bar on his way back. As he stood in line, he glanced at his watch. The interview had taken twenty minutes. It had seemed more like five hours.

Major Smythe-Jones joined him in line. "You look like a man who just stared into the abyss."

"I've seen much worse," Martin said. "So have you."

"About that," the major said. "I appreciate your circumspection. In Africa there are two realities: what we all know, and what we say out loud. Word will get out about what happened. In fact, it already has. That was the whole point of the general's stunt. But it's best to keep on pretending as long as possible."

"*Stunt?*" Martin couldn't get past the major's choice of words.

"That's correct, old boy. That's all it was. A bit of theater. And as you'll soon learn, it's far safer to be in the audience than on the stage."

"There you are!" Esther rushed up to them and gave Martin a quick kiss on the cheek. "We were worried about you. Where have you been?"

Stefan was right on her heels and joined them a second later.

Martin faked a smile. "Having a brief-but-informative chat with the good colonel and another government type. I'll fill you in later."

Stefan flashed him an inquisitive look. "Ach so. That is good enough for me. What do you say we head off and eat?"

"Sounds good to me. I've certainly done everything I came here to do." Martin turned to Smythe-Jones. "What about you, Major?"

"Don't worry about me, old boy. I'll find my own ride home."

$$\bullet \; \bullet \; \bullet$$

As soon as they ducked inside the car for the drive back to Kireka, Esther and Stefan jumped all over Martin.

"Easy, easy," he teased. "You're like a couple of kids the night before Christmas."

"It could affect us too, mzungu," Esther said indignantly.

"It does, and it's good news." Martin gave them a blow-by-blow account of the interview.

"So you figure that they would not have invited you on the fishing expedition if they had anything solid," Stefan said.

"Damn right. If they had an informer in the Anyanya, I'd be feeding crocs in the Nile just like those other two guys. You too, for that matter. I think we're in the clear."

Esther frowned. "It appears so, mzungu, but I am still worried about you being associated with Astles. Did you know that he is called Bullet Bob?"

"Why?"

"It is said that when Amin was having the Acholi and Lango slaughtered at Mbarara, Astles got upset about the money the ammunition cost. Instead of having them shot, he ordered the soldiers to make them stand in lines. Then he distributed a sledge hammer to the man at each end of the line. They were ordered to bash in the skulls of the ones in front of them until they were too tired to continue." Esther recited the horrible tale in a flat monotone.

Sometimes her fatalism shocked Martin. It was as if the whole scenario was inevitable, the natural order of things. From what she'd seen growing up, Martin thought, maybe it was. Life certainly seemed to be cheap in these parts.

Stefan's face was ashen as he muttered, "Charming." He looked genuinely shocked. The vision of cold-blooded, systematic slaughter probably evoked horrible memories from his childhood.

Martin didn't want to think about it, either. Having looked into Astles's eyes, he had no problem believing the story, but obsessing about it was just going to dredge up those horrible feelings of futility that the visit to Masirwa had evoked. The whirlpool was beginning to spin faster and faster. He knew he was teetering on the edge, the vortex pulling harder all the time, but he still felt in control.

Maybe the major was right: It was all theater.

Martin and Esther collapsed into bed as soon as they got home, and Martin dreamt of the encounter between the leopard and the warthog he had witnessed at Murchison Falls. The tape played on an endless loop. Sometimes he was the leopard, at other times the helpless, oblivious warthog.

CHAPTER

11

THE NEXT FEW days passed quietly and quickly. Martin played the model studenti. At first, he watched carefully to see if he was being followed, but he soon gave it up as a worthless effort. It would be easy enough for Astles and Bakazi to keep an eye on him without being that obvious. There was no such thing as a mzungu with a low profile in Kampala.

Martin and Stefan got together for their usual quiet dinner on Esther's church night. They hadn't really had a chance to talk since the night of the party.

"How are you feeling," Martin asked, "now that the dust has settled?"

"Cautious," Stefan answered. "And you?"

"My gut, for what it's worth, tells me that Astles bought my story. The one I'm worried about is Bakazi. He seemed a little suspicious."

"Funny, but when I first met him, I did not take him to be the sort that would be on the take. Maybe the major would have some good input."

"Good idea. I ran into him today in town. He invited us to lunch at the Lake Vic on Saturday. We can ask him then."

"Why not? He might have some 'buzz,' as he puts it." Stefan made them refills, and they moved out onto the porch to watch the sunset. "Since we are talking about gut instincts, Martin, mine tell me that you come from money. Why are you so interested in smuggling diamonds?"

Martin sensed a new seriousness in the German. The previous light banter had vanished as quickly as the sunlight. "Not just for the thrill of it, if that's what you're thinking, though I'd be lying if I didn't admit that I like the excitement. The truth is I do come from a wealthy family, but family money always has strings attached. I want to be free to do whatever I want, no family sanction necessary."

Stefan digested the reply for a bit. "I can understand how you feel, and I wish I had those sorts of problems." He smiled. "I just needed to have some idea of where you are coming from. This may have started out as something of a lark—good, dirty fun, if you will—but it is rapidly becoming apparent that this is very high-stakes poker, as you Amis would say."

"And you were worried that I might be a dilettante out for some cheap thrills at the expense of the locals."

"Ja, something like that. No offense intended, but you are a hard one to read, Hein. There are few people I would rather drink and whore with."

Martin felt like he was back at the playground, trying to play ball with the big boys. It was that same horrible uncertainty while they picked sides. It wasn't his physical ability that was in question. He looked Stefan right in the eye. "It was a lark the first week I was here—a hippie pipe dream—but it's all changed so fast. Amin's bloody ritual, Masirwa, Bertain Aka, the messenger, and, last but not least, my little confab with Astles. Those sorts of things all make a man sit up and take a real look at what's going on around him—and a closer look at himself. I'm in with my eyes wide open.

Not for the same reasons, but better ones. When I got here, it was for a penny. Now it's the full pound."

"Ach so, could I be seeing the slightest glimpse of the real Martin Fine? What you just said is good enough for me." Stefan raised his glass. "To crime and black mischief."

● ● ●

Martin arrived at the Lake Vic for lunch at eleven o'clock Saturday morning. To kill some time, he ordered a Nile and bought a copy of the latest edition of *DRUM*. The lady doctor's advice column was normally good for some laughs, and this issue was no exception. The first letter was from a reader who complained that his sex organ was so large that every time he sexed his girlfriend, it caused unbelievable pain for all concerned. He inquired as to whether there were any medical treatments for decreasing the size of his organ.

In a stinging reply, headed "Dear Mr. Fat Penis," the columnist told him that it was his head, not his organ, that was too fat. She advocated more tenderness in the sex act and concluded by telling him that there was no medical way to diminish nature's bounty.

"She did everything but ask the guy for his phone number," Martin muttered, chuckling to himself. He flipped to a gaudy spread on the latest fashions from Nigeria.

"Find any good advice, Mr. Fine?"

Martin closed the magazine and swiveled slowly on his stool.

A genial, heavyset African in voluminous traditional dress was regarding him quizzically. He carried a black elaborately tooled Moroccan leather briefcase in his right hand. He appeared prosperous, and the amount of gold he flashed when he smiled confirmed Martin's impression. He looked nervously around the empty bar before speaking further. "I am a friend of Aka's. Let us move to a table by the window. The barman is in our employ, but this being Africa, I am not sure what other payrolls he is on."

"So how's Bertain?" Martin asked as soon as they found a table away from prying eyes and ears.

"Very well. He sends his best wishes. He wondered if you and your friend would still be interested in visiting Kigali next weekend."

"We are, but it would be nice if we had some indication of what we would be letting ourselves in for."

"I am sure that Bertain will make that clear in good time." The man's tone was gently chiding, like that of a teacher with an impatient pupil. "Aka said to remind you to check into the Hôtel des Mille Collines and make no attempt to contact him. He will hear when you have arrived."

"That sounds like an adequate, if somewhat mysterious plan. I guess I forget how visible mzungus are around these parts."

Briefcase nodded. "For that reason Monsieur Bertain suggested that you bring your friend Esther along. It is better to look like touristi." He caught Martin's startled look and smiled. "Do not be offended that we know so much about you. Like most successful business operations, we have an extensive intelligence network. It is not difficult to keep tabs on mzungus, as you so quaintly put it. We do not like to take needless chances. While this government has proved to be extremely accommodating in most ways, they have also shown themselves to be abnormally greedy."

"I guess it can become criminally expensive keeping a retired sergeant major happy, eh?"

"I do not know anything about the personalities involved," the African replied without changing expression.

Martin decided to try another tack. "Maybe you could enlighten me on this point then. We've heard that there are some impending tribal difficulties in Rwanda. Are they going to cause any problems for your client?"

"Touché. You are better informed than we thought. After an initial period of adjustment, there should not be any problems. At the moment, things are static. Both sides are consolidating. There will probably be some movement within the next month or so. My client is prepared for any eventuality."

"Perhaps your employer can give us more concrete information on the situation. It could be a good story."

"It is possible he might, if it suits his purposes." The mask was back firmly in place. "May I tell him then that the reservations are confirmed?"

"Yes. We look forward with interest to our visit."

"Good." He snapped open his briefcase for emphasis. "It has been nice to talk to you, Mr. Fine. Do you mind if I take your copy of *DRUM*? I have a long, boring ride ahead of me." He shoved it into the otherwise empty suitcase and bowed his way out.

"Sure didn't get much out of that, did I?" Martin mumbled as he settled the drinks tab.

He changed and headed out to the pool. It was the usual Saturday crowd: half of the Italian and French embassy staffs trying to hit on stray stewardesses.

Martin ordered a beer and settled into a well-placed deck chair to watch the show.

"I think the one in the pink bikini fancies you."

Martin turned to see Stefan partially blocking the view. "Surprise, surprise. What brings you out here? I thought you were in town."

"The boss's pool. What else?" He grimaced. "It always breaks on Saturdays. Where is Esther?"

"Arriving soon from home. She had a lot of domestic chores to do. I just finished an informative chat with an associate of Bertain Aka's."

"Really? And?"

"Trip to Kigali confirmed for this coming weekend. Same plan: Check in at the Hotel Mille Collines and wait to be contacted."

"Anything else?"

"No. He was as tight as a bull's asshole in fly season, as my dearly beloved grandpappy used to say. He even beat me for a copy of *DRUM* and the drinks. I did get a slight flicker of interest when I asked him if the tribal problems were going to affect things, but that's all."

"That is a relief. If this messenger had known much, I would have been worried. In this business, it is vital to be tight-arsed. What did he say about the tribal factor?"

"No problem. They have contingency plans."

Esther appeared poolside a few minutes later. "I am glad I finished my chores early." She glanced at a shapely blond sunning herself in a string bikini. "This is a dangerous place for unaccompanied mzungus."

"Ja, Esther. A man could get himself in some delightful trouble here, but do not be too jealous. Martin has some good news for you."

Martin nodded. "Remember the trip to Kigali I mentioned? It's on for next weekend. I hear they have all of the latest fashions from Paris there."

"Are we really going?" she asked in a bubbly voice. "I cannot wait. The girls at the office are going to be jealous!"

"They will be when they see your new wardrobe."

"When are we leaving?"

Martin glanced at Stefan. "Next Thursday afternoon, if you two can get some time off."

Esther jumped in his lap. "I can't wait."

"Here, here! What's all the excitement?" Major Smythe-Jones slid into a nearby chair, making no effort to conceal his interest in Esther's shapely derriere, which her skimpy dress had slid up to reveal.

She rearranged herself in a more modest pose. "We are going to Kigali next weekend. Is it a nice town?"

"If the political situation is not too dicey, you should enjoy it very much. You will like the shopping."

"So I have heard. It is as close to Paris as I am likely to get in the near future."

"Have you been there recently, Major?" Stefan flagged a waiter. "After our discussion the other night, we are counting on you for some good info."

"Not for dogs' years. I was last there in the early fifties. Remember the trip I told you about, when I walked from Mombasa to Kampala? I passed through Kigali then. Of course, in those days, it was a colonial backwater. I have a good friend who lives there now. He has nice things to say about the place. He's always after me to visit, so I'll be able to give you all an introduction. He owns one of the big hotels there. The problem, of course, is the tribal situation, but I suppose the place won't be overrun."

"I hope things haven't changed too much from colonial days," Martin said with a smile. "A town gets dull in a hurry if there aren't a few of the old-school soldiers of fortune around."

The major laughed. "Don't worry, old boy. As I told you before, there are plenty of them left, even if they have darker complexions. There's been one other rather significant change. Most of them are working for a different type of client these days. The East and West are going to fight over Africa for the rest of the century. After all, the name of the game for the foreseeable future is resources, and a substantial chunk of the undeveloped ones are here." He flagged a passing waiter and ordered another round before continuing. "There's no doubt about it. The big boys are out in force in these parts. The funny thing is they still haven't figured out that you can't buy these countries. The waste in aid dollars on all sides makes the mind spin." He clucked. "The only ones with a clue are the Chinese. The Russians and Yanks build showcase projects that do nothing but line the pockets of the wealthy elite. The Chinese, on the other hand, build a railway that opens up large areas of Tanzania and Zambia for a cash-crop economy. Now *that's* a project with a substantial impact on a large segment of the populace."

"Do you think it could get dangerous?"

"If the balloon goes up. My man there is Hans Metzner. His hotel is called the Mille Colline. I'm sure he can point you in the right direction. Feel free to use my name with him. From what he says, things are going to get nasty very soon."

"Well, it certainly sounds like a good place for some stories." Feeling the time was ripe, Martin decided to engage in some discreet probing. "Tell me, Major." He dropped his voice to a low pitch that wouldn't carry beyond their table. "How corrupt is the current regime here?"

The major thought awhile before replying in an equally subdued tone. "No more or less so than most other military regimes in Africa. I'm not trying to be coy when I say that. They all have their price. Amin is totally corruptible. Just between you, me, and these umbrellas, he was forced to seize power earlier than he planned, because Obote was going to have him arrested for embezzling a large amount of gold."

"So even a gung-ho, ramrod-straight type like Bakazi could be had for the right price?"

"Why Bakazi in particular? I can give you chaps who are totally bent and have been for years."

"Because he seems representative of the generation of officers who might be running things in a few years," Martin replied smoothly.

"Yes. He's certainly a blue-eyed boy at the moment. But things can change in a hurry in a place like this. You can be sure he's aware of it. Don't get me wrong. I'm not down on the whole officer corps, but in the Third World, there's always a certain amount of corruption no matter how good the intentions. If it's kept within reasonable limits, things still function well."

"To be truthful, Major, corruption is a natural component of human nature," Stefan observed. "For my money, it is just as prevalent in the developed world, albeit in a more subtle, sophisticated guise."

"True enough, my boy. And some of the deals that go down in the city or on Wall Street make this lot look like right pikers."

Over the meal, the conversation switched to a fighter vein. The major told Esther about his travels in the Sudan. It turned out that he knew the area where she came from quite well. This didn't surprise Martin in the least. From what he had observed so far, the major seemed to know just about all of Africa intimately. The man's depth of knowledge sometimes intimidated him. He hated feeling like a neophyte.

After they finished their meal, the major set a date with them for lunch the weekend after next and left.

The lazy afternoon of beer drinking and sunbathing left Martin feeling relaxed—and not a little tired. He braced himself for what had become a standard Saturday evening: dinner at the Arizona followed by dancing at the Big S and the Lair. As he observed the familiar weekend cattle call at both places, he was almost envious of Stefan—until he looked at Esther's face as she danced. He realized it was her release, her fleeting-yet-much-needed escape from reality. How could he begrudge her a moment of happiness?

•••

The next five days seemed interminable. Martin was growing increasingly excited about the upcoming trip. Though Bertain Aka was paramount in his mind, he sensed it was more than that. He needed a change of scenery. He was beginning to realize what a small town Kampala really was. Even though he had avoided getting sucked into the traditional mzungu circuit, there were still a limited amount of places to go and people to meet. He was beginning to understand why people always remarked on "how nice it was to have new blood on the circuit."

He made his weekly visit to Legs on the eve of their departure. Martin had time for a leisurely chat for once, and as usual, it was time well spent. Legs didn't have any gossip that related directly to Martin, but he *did* share a few very interesting tidbits.

"The Libyans have mysteriously broken off talks with the general."

"When?" Martin asked.

"Four days ago. It's rumored their special envoy has been recalled to Tripoli. In the meantime, the American ambassador and political officer have made three visits to the government office in the past two days. I wasn't able to gather any intelligence on what was being discussed yet, but I should have details for you by the time you return from your trip."

"Thanks," Martin said and slipped Legs his weekly stipend.

On his way home, Martin mused that the news might be good for Nathan and the others.

• • •

Stefan had a Cannonball waiting. "Ready for the trip?"

"Just about. It's Esther I'm worried about. She's been so excited that she hasn't packed a thing so far. The old routine: 'I have nothing to wear.'"

"What do you expect, Hein? She is a woman first."

"Sometimes I forget. Are you getting a little excited?"

"Not until I hear the deal, if there is one. Did Legs have any-thing? I am almost beginning to think that the shooting was a bad dream."

Martin gave him Legs's latest over dinner. "It might just mean that the heat is off as far as the Anyanya are concerned."

"Perhaps. I wonder what your fellow Amis are up to."

"No doubt rushing in to fill the breach. Amin can probably be had pretty cheaply these days. He needs some shiny new toys for his tin soldiers."

"Ja, that is true. As long as they do not go toward border security."

"Speaking of which, I was thinking. Nathan and crew might have some useful information on that score."

"Maybe, but we have to get that far first."

"It would be nice to let them make a little money off the deal."

"Ach so. Do I detect a liberal in the clothing of a cynic? That is the last reason we should get them involved. In a deal like this, if you try to please too many people, you end up pleasing no one, least of all yourself."

"I guess you're right," Martin agreed reluctantly, "but it was a nice fantasy."

Stefan didn't seem to have many fantasies of his own, but growing up in postwar Germany would surely have nipped most of them in the bud. The German's pragmatism was a useful curb, Martin thought, on his own natural naiveté, which was why he made an excellent partner.

A car pulled up outside, and Esther came running in. "Are you two mzungus packed already? I do not know how I am going to get ready. I will be up all night."

"No, you won't." Martin rose and took her by the arm.

"I'm going to help you pack. You'll need all your energy for shopping."

"Before we go, you had better read this." She rummaged through her handbag and handed him a neatly folded manila envelope. "It appeared on my desk right before I left work this afternoon."

As he ripped it open, Martin noticed that it bore an official government seal. Inside, he found a series of releases about various projects that had recently been undertaken to improve the lot of the people as well as details on a large loan the government had recently negotiated with a consortium of international banks. Attached to the sheaf of papers was a brief note:

> *Dear Martin,*
>
> *I thought there might be some good pieces in this material. None of this is public knowledge, so you would have exclusives. Enjoy your trip to Rwanda.*
>
> *Best,*
> *Bob Astles*

At first, he was perturbed by the reference to the trip, but as he thought about it, he realized it didn't necessarily mean much. He'd told them about it.

"Just when I thought he might have forgotten about you," Stefan said with a sigh as he ushered them to the door.

"His type doesn't forget," Martin replied. "But at least we're playing the journalism game, so it's not necessarily a bad development."

ESTHER WAS WRINGING her hands nervously before her first flight, so Martin handed her a stiff waragi while they waited in the departure lounge.

"Thanks," she said and downed it with a grimace. "How about another?"

It was only a forty-five-minute hop from Entebbe to Kigali. Immigrations and customs were perfunctory, and they were rattling along Rwanda's only paved road, a seven-mile strip from the airport into town, within three hours of leaving Kireka.

"That was quick enough." Martin glanced at his watch. "We'll be in town by five. How did you like your first plane ride, Esther?"

"Fine, except for the takeoff and landing. There are lots of people here," she added, pointing to the tightly packed shanties that lined the road.

Stefan looked up from his guidebook. "According to this, Rwanda is the most densely populated country in Africa. It has the same population density as Hong Kong. Rwanda and Burundi were originally administered as one entity by the Germans. After World War I, they were treated to the Belgians. They were subsequently administered as part of the Belgian Congo, a little finger separating it from Uganda. For some reason, they were partitioned off at independence. Rwanda has a nonviable economy, as does Burundi, which is probably why they never joined."

Martin laughed. "They do better as foreign-aid recipients on their own. You have to give them credit, though." He pointed out the window. "This has got to be the only toll road in Africa. I never thought I'd see one here."

A few seconds later, they stopped at a garishly painted shack in the center of the road. Long striped poles protruded from windows on each side and blocked the road. A crudely painted sign on the side of the shack read, *Kigali Toll Road: STOP AND PAY OR WE SHOOT*.

"We are a poor country," the driver said in passable English. "It is the only way we can collect money to build more paved roads."

"Well, it looks peaceful enough, anyway. Are the problems over?"

"No, *Blancs*, but it is safe enough in the middle of town during the day, as long as you are not a Tutsi. After dark, no one is safe because of the curfew. It is not a good time in Rwanda." He sighed. "No touristi. We are now coming into town. If you like, I can show you around the main shopping area. It is a small city. You can walk everywhere."

The commercial area looked prosperous enough, Martin thought. The shops were well stocked, though the unpaved roads made the latest dresses from Paris seem somewhat incongruous. In contrast to the shanty settlements on the outskirts of town, there didn't appear to be that many people around.

"The people do not look very happy," Esther noted. "I do not see anyone smiling."

Martin nodded. "Not many Tutsi. Lots of military, though. Looks like it could be a pretty town. I'm surprised it's so modern. There's almost no colonial architecture."

"What there is is ersatz," Stefan said with a chuckle. "Most of Kigali was built after independence. We should get a better feel for things tomorrow when we walk around. It looks like everything is getting ready to close. Guess we are going to have a quiet evening in the hotel tonight."

Martin groaned. "That's a shame. We passed some pretty interesting-looking clubs. Maybe there's some action at the hotel."

"Plenty, Blanc," the driver said. "The hotel has the best disco in town. There is everything you need for a good time there, but you will see for yourself soon enough."

They turned onto a steep driveway a few minutes later. The Mille Colline was a low-slung white stucco structure with an intricately patterned red-tiled roof that gave it vaguely Moorish overtones. The lobby was bustling, but tourists were nowhere in evidence. They were shown to magnificent rooms overlooking the pool in the back. The hotel was situated on a rise overlooking the town. The brooding blue-gray Ruwenzori Mountains formed a spectacular backdrop.

Martin opened the doors to the balcony and drank in the view. "Sorry we didn't come at a better time, Esther. This looks like a great place when the political climate is right."

"We will just have to do everything during the day," she replied. " Can we go down to the bar? I am starving. I did not eat anything this morning. I was worried about getting sick on the plane."

They found Stefan already seated at a table on the verandah. The bar inside was packed with an eclectic crowd, and couples were dancing to the pounding disco pumped out by the best sound system Martin had heard in Africa. The atmosphere had a frenetic edge. People were partying with the grim, single-minded concentration of folks in a singles club. Martin got the impression that they weren't going to let anything interfere with their pleasure.

Stefan raised his glass. "While Rome burns. These people take their partying seriously."

"So," Martin began, "what have you picked up so far in your in-depth research with the bartender?"

"Not much," Stefan answered, "except the rather interesting statistic that thirty percent of this country's annual GNP is spent on this excellent beer we are drinking."

"As always, you're a well of fascinating, if not always useful facts, but I'll drink to that. I get good vibes from this place. They appear to have their priorities in order."

"Welcome to Kigali. You picked a hell of a time to come." A squat, balding fellow with a mischievous twinkle in his eye and a smile that lit up the room bowed and clicked his heels. "Hans Metzner at your service. I own this madhouse. It is not often that I have people recommended to me by two such disparate sources as Bertain Aka and Major Ian Smythe-Jones."

"Bertain neglected to tell us that he knew you. The major recommended you most highly as a character of the *alt schul*." Stefan smiled. "I must say that first impressions of your hotel seem to confirm that. What do all these people do at curfew time, turn into pumpkins?"

"Nein, we have a bed-and-hangover special."

Martin flagged a passing waiter and ordered another round and some cheese and crackers. "Things didn't look that bad on the drive in from the airport, though I must admit, the populace didn't appear exactly overjoyed with life."

"Wait until after dark. I hope gunfire does not keep you up. Why do you think I have the loudest sound system in all of Africa? All gallows humor aside, things are bad but not hopeless. The purges are going on mostly in government circles at the moment. The situation will get dicey if and when they spread to the general populace."

"If the Hutu have the whip hand," Martin said, "why haven't they just liquidated the opposition? That would be the logical thing to do in African terms."

"Because Kayibanda is busy papering over the cracks in his own party," Hans answered. "Traditionally, the Hutu have been divided into two groups, with the Southern faction holding most of the power. Kayibanda is a Northerner, and he has shifted a lot of his own people into key jobs since he came into power. Needless to say, this has not been popular with the Southerners who control the army. Secondly, the Tutsi ran the county's whole bureaucratic structure for the Belgians. If Kayibanda moves them out too fast, everything goes poof. Finally, the Tutsi have been promised support by Micombero of Burundi."

"The Tutsi are firmly in control there?"

"Ja, but the threat only carries weight because Mobutu virtually runs the government."

Stefan smiled. "So he is rather neatly boxed in. If he goes for an all-out purge, Micombero invades with Zairian help, or the army takes him out under the pretext of restoring stability. His only choice is to keep the pot boiling with rumors and witch hunts for Tutsi subversives."

Martin whistled. "The major said it was a classic post-colonial setup."

"Indeed it is," Hans said with a chuckle. "It is really too bad for the Tutsi, though. They are a marvelous people. Unfortunately, they are now going to have to pay a heavy price for their colonial ascendancy." He glanced at his watch. "I must be off, but I will be in the disco later. I think you will find the restaurant quite acceptable. It is not Paris, but we try."

Hans was not exaggerating. The food was the closest thing to haute cuisine Martin had tasted in Africa. *Only here,* he thought, *could I be eating foie gras while death squads roam the streets a hundred yards away.* It was an uncomfortable thought, but lacking any adequate response, he put it out of his mind.

. . .

The disco was cranked up to a feverish pitch when they walked in shortly after ten, and they were dancing within minutes. The patrons had that same deathly serious vibe of the afternoon crew. The DJ could have spun the death march, and they still would have smiled and boogied.

They collapsed after two nonstop sets.

"Even Susannah's doesn't have me in training for this," Martin said between gasps as he toweled off with a cocktail napkin. "There seems to be a manic edge to the proceedings. I think prolonged exposure could be hazardous to the health."

"Ja, but it is safer than outside. Meet Dolores." Stefan pulled out a chair for a petite mpenzi in a bright-floral mini.

She looked about sixteen, Martin thought, but in Africa it was anyone's guess. She could have just as easily been twelve or twenty. Her English was surprisingly proficient, which meant she'd probably hung around tourists a lot.

A waiter arrived with a glistening magnum of Krug champagne, compliments of Hans.

Martin drank freely, hoping the bubbly would ease him into the frenzied flow of the evening. He felt uncomfortable being a dispassionate observer of the surreal atmosphere. It didn't allow him to get so involved that he could forget what was going on outside.

Esther excused herself. "Save me a glass," she said over her shoulder as she left for the ladies' room.

A moment later, Hans appeared out of nowhere with a date who couldn't have been more than fourteen. "I thought the Krug might help to get you all into the swing of things. It soothes the exposed nerve endings." He had a drunken gleam in his eyes, and his clothing was superbly incongruous: a pink satin jumpsuit with forest-green trim matched his faux suede Beatle boots. He fit right in.

Martin suppressed the urge to laugh. "Oblivion does seem to be the answer. Any word from our mutual friend yet?"

"Ja, Bertain's wife, Celeste, is coming to pick your lady friend up for some shopping. Bertain will arrive for you two at the same time." Hans anticipated Martin's next question. "He suggested you tell your companion that you are going to an interview with a dissident."

Martin nodded. "He seems to have thought of everything. How long does this go on?"

"As long as you hold out." Hans nodded to where Stefan had been sitting with the mpenzi only a few seconds earlier. "Your friend has already left, but I think he had an ulterior motive. We do not close these days. You have to make hay while the sun shines." He winked and danced off toward the DJ booth.

Martin and Esther grabbed the lift shortly after she returned from the bathroom. She was finished. He guided her into bed, then rolled a banjii nightcap to take down to Stefan's balcony.

"Is Esther all right?" Stefan asked solicitously. His young companion was already gone.

"Yeah, just exhausted. She's probably been running on adrenalin most of the day. That can burn you out in a hurry. We'd better have some medication ready in the morning. How was your mpenzi?"

"Remarkably jaded for a fourteen-year-old. That is why I dispensed with her services early. I do not expect true love, but she was as studied as a forty-year-old war horse from the Reeperbahn. I expected her to pull out her stopwatch at any second."

They smoked in silence, watching Kigali brood in the uneasy darkness. Its repose had a fragile, tenuous quality, like the sleep of a febrile infant. Suddenly, a sharp string of gunfire crackled below them. A few deeper bangs followed at irregular intervals.

"Were those what I think they were?" Stefan asked.

Martin snorted. "They weren't caused by a truck backfiring. Just some evening fireworks to keep us excited," he added with a toughness he didn't feel.

A few minutes later, a full-scale firefight broke out. It sounded as though somebody had torched a firecracker factory. Tracer rounds lit the sky. Martin counted three separate combat zones. He didn't feel frightened, because the exchanges were taking place on the other side of town. After about five minutes, the shooting died down to scattered, sporadic pops.

"They must be reloading," Stefan whispered.

"Or running for cover." Martin grabbed his arm. "Listen, there's a chopper coming in. Sounds like it's coming from behind us."

They instinctively ducked as the chopper came in low and fast right over their heads. It screamed off in the direction of the last flashes they'd seen. Seconds later, two yellow-crimson gouts of flame blossomed below it.

"Rockets!" Stefan shouted as orange explosions lit the side of the foothills.

The chopper circled the area of the detonations, releasing napalm canisters and systematically machine-gunning the flaming corridor.

"*Gott in Himmel!* They are not playing around."

The helicopter buzzed angrily up and down until it had expended its ammunition and then flew north. Gradually, silence settled back over town.

Martin was surprised that he didn't see anyone else out on the balconies watching the show. They were used to it, he guessed.

"Every living thing in that area they hit with the napalm had to be toasted into cornflakes. Poor, suffering bastards."

Stefan's hands were trembling so badly that he had trouble holding the glass while Martin poured out stiff drinks. "Ja. If the locals consider this sort of action to be light, I would hate to see what they consider heavy."

They quietly sucked on their drinks, letting the adrenalin drain.

"Sometimes, I don't like this place at all," Martin confessed. "It can be such an emotional roller coaster. Most of the time, it's wild, wacky, and wonderful, but sometimes, it's frustrating as hell. You just feel damned helpless. What do you do—act like everybody else and take the money and run?"

"I do not know." Stefan frowned as he stared out at the dark cityscape. "I have been kicking that one around ever since our visit to the refugee camp. There really are no easy answers. Sometimes, I feel like a parent with a rebellious child. I just want to wash my hands of the whole business. I guess you just have to come to an accommodation with yourself."

"Such as?"

"Understand that you as an individual are powerless to make this—or the refugee camps—go away. You just do the best you can and hope that you have some positive effect on things. Just because your children do not do everything you tell them, you cannot ignore them. There are some lessons that have to be learned the hard way. At times, Africa forces you to confront the uncomfortable aspects of human nature. Still, I would rather have it this way than live in a thoroughly plastic culture. At least it is real. I think the West has been too protective in the Third World. We want to do all their thinking for them, and when they do not listen, we get frustrated and step back."

"Like you say, 'life's hard lessons.' Sometimes you have to put your hand in the fire. It's difficult to let people make their own mistakes. At times, it's almost as painful—not to mention frustrating—for the onlooker. I guess the important thing is not to lose patience and cop out."

Like a child briefly startled from sleep by a nightmarish dream, Kigali grudgingly dozed off again.

Martin dragged himself into bed and, remarkably, fell into a deep sleep.

MARTIN AWOKE AFTER six the next morning to a quiet but persistent knocking on the door.

"Mr. Fine, wake up."

He staggered over to the door. "Who . . . who's there?" His tongue felt like it was coated with a thick layer of chalk.

"An associate of Mr. Bertain's. We are going to see him now. I am going to wake your friend. Be ready in five minutes."

Martin performed his three-minute-shower-and-shave routine. It didn't help. If anything, he felt worse. He tried to wake Esther, but a few minutes of vigorous shaking elicited only pained groans followed by wild punches. He gave it up as a bad job and left her a note explaining that he and Stefan were going to interview some dissidents. He added that a friend of Hans's would be along to take her shopping at ten.

It was the best he could manage in his addled state. He knew he was going to be knee-deep in shit when he got home, but what was a man to do? He kissed her and waited by the door.

Thirty seconds later, they were on their way.

Stefan looked horrible. His healthy tan had given way to a pasty pallor, and his eyes were so bloodshot his irises were all but invisible. "Water—I need it bad," he croaked, adjusting his shades.

"I am definitely not as young as I used to be."

Their guide signaled for them to be silent and hustled them down the back fire escape. They didn't see a soul the whole way to the service entrance. *I'll give Bertain a ten for security*, Martin thought to himself as the diminutive African hustled them through a door marked *Maintenance*.

Hans was sitting behind a desk that bore a pitcher of Bloody Marys, a pot of coffee, and a platter of fluffy croissants. "I apologize for the rude awakening and the false information last night. Aka said you would appreciate the need for security. I must say, I thought you played the role of tourists rather well. You are going out with the laundry to a safe place. Aka's car will pick you up there. If you hurry, you just have time for a quick breakfast. I do not think you will take offense if I venture to say that you look like you could use it." The man was a marvel. He looked fresh as a daisy and showed no trace of the manic drunkenness from the night before.

"Are we being watched?" Martin asked, suddenly feeling sober.

Hans gave a barking laugh as he poured them each a tumbler of Bloody Mary. "But of course. Everyone is watched here, especially mzungus who arrive at such a crazy time for no apparent good reason. The question is by whom."

Martin inhaled half his drink in one swallow. "Point taken. I guess I'm a little slow this morning. The only thing that worries me is Esther. I couldn't wake her."

Hans waved off his concern. "Do not worry. I will take care of that. You were called out to an interview with some mysterious dissidents. I will introduce her to Celeste. There will, of course, be no mention of our mutual friend. As for public consumption, you and *Herr* Schmidt will have sustained an attack of food poisoning. The doctor will visit your empty rooms and issue instructions that you are not to be disturbed."

Stefan massaged his temples. The drink had helped his color, but his every gesture still suggested pain. "I shall remember the morning after my first night in Kigali always."

Martin smiled. "Last night was equally memorable in its own way. Somewhat similar to the Fourth of July back home. This was not the only place cooking. There was a lot of action everywhere."

"Ja," Hans said. "The Tutsis tried to liberate some prisoners. Things got pretty hot for a while. I bet your town will look absolutely normal this morning, though."

There was a knock on the door.

Hans got to his feet. "That is your ride. I am afraid the first part in the back of the van will not be too comfortable, but it will not last more than fifteen minutes."

"How much farther to Bertain's?"

"On these roads, about an hour." Hans opened the door, and two Africans trundled in laundry carts. He smiled at Martin's and Stefan's disconcerted expressions. "It is only twenty feet or so out to the van."

Stefan rose unsteadily to his feet. "You are an angel, Hans. Though I am not sure which part of the afterlife you come from. There is just one more thing I need: some more aspirin. The first handful did not do any good."

Hans reached into his pocket with a smile and tossed him a bottle of Bayer. "We think of everything. You will find additional iron rations in the car."

Martin and Stefan folded themselves awkwardly into the carts and burrowed under the dirty table linens. After a ride of less than a minute, the attendants hoisted the carts into the back of a vehicle of some type, locked the doors, and gave a knock, indicating it was all right to get out.

Martin clumsily clambered out of his cart, almost tipping it over, and took in their surroundings just as the windowless cargo van took a sharp corner. "One thing I will say for Bertain: He does have a certain style."

"Ja. Do you think all this cloak-and-dagger stuff is really necessary?"

"Before last night, I would have said no, but the situation here has obviously deteriorated. You can be sure that the local authorities are checking us out. For all they know, we might be mercenaries."

"Ach so, I must really be slow this morning. That angle never even occurred to me. Now that you mention it, they have been paranoid about that ever since the Congo troubles. Not without reason," he added with a laugh.

"Myself, I didn't really like what Hans said about it being a question of who was watching us, but I guess an atmosphere like this breeds paranoia. The better question might be who's *not* watching us."

The van broke sharply and skidded to a halt. Martin heard the sound of doors sliding shut before the van was unlocked. The driver helped them down into a dimly lit garage and brusquely gestured to a Mercedes. They ducked inside, almost stumbling over a Styrofoam cooler in the back. The African driver was just as taciturn as his counterpart in the van. He rolled up the smoked-glass windows and partition, signaling for them not to open them, and drove off.

Stefan opened the cooler. "These must be the iron rations Hans referred to. I never needed a beer more."

They greedily sucked down ice-cold Primuses like babies enjoying their first bottle in the morning. The Mercedes glided smoothly through the ghostly town. As Hans had predicted, there was little sign of any disturbance from the night before. They did pass a large burned-up section of foliage, but there were no bodies or other indications of violence. A lingering odor of kerosene and burnt rubber were the only indications of napalm. They were stopped several times at roadblocks on the edge of town, but the soldiers manning them appeared uninterested and waved them through as soon as their driver flashed a pass at them.

Once they got out of town, the car started to climb rapidly along a narrow, sandy track. Every bit of land seemed to be inhabited or under cultivation. The driver appeared more relaxed and rolled down the windows and partition. Martin figured they must be out of the roadblock zone.

They made good time until they caught up with an overloaded bus. Passing it was out of the question, so they crawled along behind, inhaling noxious black fumes as the bus corkscrewed its way up the tortuous track. The bus driver slowed down at every village and tossed a packet out the window.

"Special delivery, Rwanda style," Stefan quipped as a youngster darted out and retrieved a package of envelopes. "I cannot believe that they are farming this high up in the mountains." He pointed to some tiny figures working high above them on the terraced hillside. "It almost looks like Southeast Asia."

The bus backfired sharply and slowed further as it pulled out to pass the burnt skeleton of a car next to the road. Around it, four sausage-limbed corpses that looked startlingly like Pillsbury Doughboys sprawled in a miasma of flies. The stench forced Martin and Stefan to roll up their windows quickly as the bus stopped and a woman and three children stepped off within five feet of the wreck. The Africans crossed the road and walked off in the direction of a nearby village without giving the bloated, fly-ridden cadavers a second glance.

Martin lit a cigarette and inhaled deeply to combat the fetid stench. "And I thought the bus was slowing down to do something about it."

The driver laughed bitterly. "What can they do? Report it to the people who did it?" He spat and put the car in gear. "Just be glad you were not born a Tutsi."

A few minutes later, they turned onto a paved driveway that snaked up a steep incline toward a pink stucco bungalow.

Martin whistled. "It must've cost a pretty penny to put this in."

"I am sure it did," Stefan observed, "but without it, Bertain would not be able to get in and out during the rainy season."

The bungalow was exquisite: a pocket Shangri La, seemingly airlifted in from the south of France and deposited in the middle of the African bush. A small pool with intricate tile work shimmered invitingly in the L formed by the bungalow's two wings.

Bertain Aka greeted them at the door and pointed them toward a wrought-iron table by the pool. "Have a seat while I fix some Buck's fizzes."

"Ah, Bertain, your French heritage is showing," Martin said exuberantly as his host returned with a pitcher of iced champagne and orange juice. "This is a pleasant way to start a Sunday anywhere." He pointed off into the distance. "Is that Kigali over there?"

"Yes. It's about twenty miles away as the crow flies, thirty-five by road. Would you like to see the house?"

Bertain led them inside to a tastefully furnished living room decorated with antique African art. "The collection is my pride and joy." He showed them delicate Benin bronzes, intricate Ashanti gold weights, and priceless Dogon sculptures. "I have hundreds more in storage." He waved his hand vaguely. "These are just some of my favorites."

"I hate to think what those are worth, Bertain," Martin said. "Even to my untrained eye, they're museum quality."

"Not as much as you would think at the moment. It is only recently that people have begun to take African art on its own merits.

Up until now, most people were mainly interested in how it influenced Picasso and others. I have some more interesting things to show you in back."

"Speaking of those matters," Stefan said. "Why all the secrecy around our visit?"

"Tourists are not that common in these parts. There are at least three different agencies that will want to know why you are here."

"How did you get rid of our tail without arousing suspicion?"

"Easily. He ate his breakfast in a restaurant I own in Kigali. It is the only one open on Sunday, so that did not take much planning. It was an easy matter to arrange for his food to be laced with Ipecac, a very potent emetic. I am told that after the first few bites, he was only interested in the location of the toilet. The cook was no doubt offended, but what can one do?" Bertain rose. "I have got to go get some things, so take a swim. The suits are in the guestroom on the right. I will be back in fifteen minutes."

• • •

The water was perfect, Martin thought. Just cool enough to be refreshing, but warm enough not to require acclimatization. After swimming a few laps, he reclined on one of the comfortable deck chairs and nodded off.

A cold sensation on his navel dragged him back to reality. He rubbed his eyes groggily and looked down at his stomach. A ruby the size of a pigeon egg was nestled in his navel. The incandescent patterns the sunlight made as it was refracted through the stone painted a fascinating pattern on his abdomen. It didn't look like glass, but what the hell did he know?

Bertain was seated at the table, where he was arranging a tine of sparkling stones that looked like diamonds.

Martin rose and carefully placed the ruby on the table. "How much? Not that I can possibly afford it."

"Roughly a quarter of a million for the ruby in Europe. The diamonds are worth varying amounts, depending on the size and quality of the stone." Bertain smiled and ran his finger over the glittering line. "Of course, these are all finished. Raw stones cost less." He opened another sack and poured a pile of rocks onto the table. They didn't look much different from pebbles. "About half of these will yield gem-quality stones. The rest are commercial."

Stefan appeared entranced. "Where are they from?"

"Zaire, mostly."

Martin ran his finger over the glittering stones. "Well, it's nice to fantasize, but I think all we could afford would be some of the unfinished ones. I think we can muster about twenty thousand dollars. How many would that get us?"

Bertain looked at him quizzically for a second and then burst into laughter. "You Americans never cease to amaze me. Subtle you are not. Do you know anyone who cuts stones?"

Martin hadn't thought that far ahead. "No," he replied sheepishly. "I figured on going to Amsterdam or Rotterdam and getting the best price I could."

This bought another smile from Bertain. "Alas, mon vieux, it is not as easy as buying hashish. The diamond community is very tight-knit. They do not like outsiders. If you could get someone to cut and deal the stones for you, you would get rock-bottom prices. For the amount of stones I could give you, you might double or triple your money."

Martin glanced at Stefan, whose frown said it all. "It doesn't seem worth the risk with such a small initial stake. I guess we're not going into the diamond business, after all."

He felt like a fool. How could he have been so naive? Everything Bertain had said struck him as reasonable. He remembered reading that the diamond dealers in Amsterdam only liked to deal with the big cartels. It was very difficult for anyone but registered dealers to do business.

Bertain poured them each some champagne. "Cheer up, *mes amis*. There may be a way for you to do some business."

Martin tossed back the bubbly. He was so depressed he didn't really have any taste for it. "How? We're just a two-bit pair of pikers."

"Because there is money to be made getting these . . ." Bertain paused to pick up one of the quartz stones. ". . . to where they can be made into these." He held one of the shiny gem stones up to the sun for effect. "I am not asking you to make any decisions now, just to think about the possibilities."

"Ja," Stefan said. "Ten-to-life in the slammer."

"Or a nest egg to live off for the rest of your life," Bertain countered with a smile. "There are always risks where there are rewards. Sometimes you have to risk what you need to get what you want. It is just a question of how these two factors balance out for you individually." He scooped the piles back into their respective sacks.

"I thought you just said there wasn't much money in the unfinished stones," Martin said.

"There is if you start with enough good ones and, most importantly, know where to take them for a good price."

"Well, it's certainly food for some obsessive thought."

"That is all I am asking you to do." Bertain gave another one of his perfect Gallic shrugs. "I will put these away while you think about the proposition."

"But you do not know anything about us," Stefan said.

"I may know a little more than you think. I have good contacts in Kampala." Bertain smiled enigmatically. "Let us just say you fit my profile. Why not change while I run these back? Then we can talk more."

Martin and Stefan changed in silence.

Bertain seemed equally subdued when he returned. It was as if their relationship had changed from a casual to deadly serious one in the twinkling of a diamond. In keeping with their suddenly solemn mood, Bertain did not pour out any more champagne. Instead, he pulled up a chair opposite them and quietly enquired, "*Et alors?*"

Martin caught Stefan's half nod out of the corner of his eye. "I guess we're interested. What's the deal?"

"You will act as couriers, of course."

"Where will we be taking them?"

"Possibly Europe, but most likely Kenya."

Stefan reached for the champagne and poured them each a glass. "That seems an odd choice. What do they know about diamonds there?"

"That, mon vieux, is none of your business."

Martin caught just a glint of hardness in Bertain's eyes that he had not detected before, but his expression mellowed immediately.

"Let us get down to business."

"Okay with us." Martin smiled. "Let's start with the basics. What are we transporting, and how much are we going to get paid?"

"Three to four pounds of stones. Successful delivery will earn each of you one hundred thousand US dollars or the equivalent in the currency of your choice."

"For that kind of money," Martin said, "we aren't going to be hauling many unfinished stones."

"You are right, mon vieux. It may be necessary for me to close down my operations here until the political situation stabilizes. I may even have to take a vacation for a while. It is best to be prepared for all eventualities. Does the amount scare you?"

"No, but it leaves me with some questions. Let's hear the rest of the deal before I get to them."

"Assuming you are interested, have you given any thought to how you would want to be paid? It is a little awkward, not to mention dangerous, to carry that much money around in cash."

"You have a point there," Stefan said. "How about Swiss bank accounts? I know that they have toughened up their standards a bit recently, but I think they would be interested in that kind of money. Your man could give us bank checks in return for the stones."

"That would pose no problems for me. As long as you have the bank accounts set up."

Martin cleared his throat. "I don't mean to be pushy, but where we're slated to deliver the goods might have some impact on our decision."

"To an Asian contact on Lamu."

Stefan helped himself to a cigar from the box on the table and puffed until the tip burned brightly. "You mean the island off the coast of Mombasa? An exotic place and delightful from what I hear, but I thought it would be somewhere in Europe. That would certainly be more convenient for you."

"You are right, but circumstances beyond my control have forced me to change plans. Besides, customs there are more difficult. Lamu is not without its advantages, and it is much closer for you."

"Any suggestions as to how we get there?" Martin asked. "Definitely not by plane. That draws too much attention."

Bertain lit a cigar and thought awhile. "That leaves the train or a car. I would suggest the train. It is a pleasant thirty-six-hour ride from Kampala to Mombasa. Some of the scenery is spectacular, and the customs officers tend to be less inquisitive. By the way, I have some interesting suitcases inside. I will show them to you when we finish."

Martin frowned. "I'm not sure that I like the sound of the train. We've attracted a bit of attention in what might be unfavorable quarters in Kampala. I don't think we're being watched on a day-to-day basis, but I think our comings and goings in and out of the country are probably being monitored."

"Hmm . . ." Bertain stroked his chin. "That might explain one of the watchers who was not from the usual interested parties. Still, I have heard nothing, and my sources would probably have picked it up if it was anything serious. They are generally reliable. They *should* be. I spend enough on them. Explain."

Martin did, and Bertain thought for a few minutes before replying. "I do not think you have a serious problem. Since the incident with the American reporters, Amin has been very concerned about journalists. My sources say that you are not suspected of smuggling. The Ugandans didn't ask the Rwandan government to follow you."

Stefan poured cognacs all around. "It seems your connections are very good, Aka."

"Standard procedure. One never knows."

"Where are we going to pick up the goods? Two trips here in a month would arouse unpleasant interest."

"Yes. I have considered that. I have not yet worked out the timing or location of the delivery. The situation here is so fluid that I will probably not make those arrangements until a few days before the event. You must be prepared to move quickly."

Martin swirled his cognac in its glass. "That shouldn't be a problem for either of us. As a matter of fact, I've given some thought to potential delivery points. We want some place near the border that we can visit without attracting a great deal of attention. Kisoro comes immediately to mind. It's smack on the border, and every self-respecting tourist goes there to see the gorillas."

"*Eh bien.* Looking at the map, it is the obvious place. I think it is a good idea as long as you can arrange to tour with your own guide."

"We can," Martin replied. "I have somebody in mind who knows the whole area like the back of his hand."

"*Bon.* Let us operate on the following assumptions then. First, the pickup will be in Kisoro at a time and place to be selected later. Second, payment will be made in the way you propose, as long as there is no difficulty with the bank accounts."

"Sehr gut," Stefan said. "That leaves only the problem of how we get the stones across the border into Kenya. I do not see why we cannot use the train, Martin. If what Bertain says is correct, it will be no problem. We can always sneak across with Singh if things change. I am sure he will know where to cross unobserved."

Martin thought over the details. "Yeah, I guess you're right. It's pretty rough country through there, and we can pick up the train on the other side." He turned to Bertain. "Can you give us even a rough estimate of when the deal will go down?"

"Sometime during the next six weeks. I cannot be more specific than that at this time. I must also emphasize once again that you will only have a few days' warning. From my experience, it is best to move quickly in these matters."

Martin nodded. "There's just one question that's been rattling around my brain since you first brought up the deal. Why us?"

Bertain smiled and poured himself another cognac. "I was wondering when you would get around to that. Due to the carelessness and unseemly greed of certain members of my organization, I experienced severe difficulties with my last shipment. These have been resolved but not without some difficulties, including several surgical removals and the resignation of a high-ranking ambassador from a country which shall remain nameless."

"So you have no courier network now."

"Let us say the one I have is no longer as reliable as in the past. It did not seem like a good idea to construct another from the same sources."

"Sounds reasonable. I guess we're perfect choices. Nobody would expect you to trust mzungus."

"*Bien sur.* They do not trust them. Why should I? Actually, it was our fortuitous meeting at Masirwa that gave me the idea. My subsequent inquiries showed that you two were likely candidates."

Stefan smiled. "I guess we fit the profile, but how do you know that we will be honest?"

"Nothing is certain, mon ami, but there are several factors which lean in your favor. First, neither of you is a professional. You do not have the resources to sell the amount of stones I have in mind without my hearing about it." He gave them a shrewd, calculating look. "Second, it appears obvious to me that neither of you want to do this sort of thing for the rest of your lives. You are looking for a one-time dividend. That, in essence, is part of your appeal. Nobody will be looking for you."

"Fair enough," Martin conceded.

"Finally..." Bertain paused, his cosmopolitan mask slipping to reveal the atavistic ruthlessness of a leopard in its native habitat: confident, secure, and above all, capable of random violence.

Martin felt the frisson in his gut again. This wasn't a movie, even if it felt like one. He felt compelled by some urge to keep going, even though he knew it might be a complete mistake.

Bertain's sibilant hiss snapped him out of his reverie. "Above all, you must be absolutely sure that if you double-cross me, you will pay the full price." The calmness of the threat made it all the more menacing.

Martin glanced at Stefan, but it wasn't really necessary to say anything. He rose and extended his hand to Bertain. "*D'accord.* Let's go inside and see these suitcases."

Bertain gave them a charming smile as he rose from his chair, as if to apologize for the momentary unpleasantness, and then waved them inside.

Two American Tourister Samsonite suitcases awaited them in the living room.

Stefan laughed. "At least you got them in different colors."

Bertain ignored the remark. "Please open them. They are quite clever."

Stefan dutifully opened the nearest and ran his hand around the inside. "I have to admit they look pretty normal. Not that I am an expert."

"They are, except for one rather unique feature." Bertain flicked the combination locks to 007 and turned the release catches sideways. "Push them in."

Martin did, and the bottom of the bag opened upward in two halves. The compartment below couldn't have been more than three-quarters of an inch deep. Adequate, unless someone was going to smuggle Liz-Taylor-sized stones. "It looks pretty good, Bertain. But how did they manage to machine it so the seam doesn't show?"

"Nobody can do that," he replied, folding the two halves back into position.

Sure enough, Martin spotted a faint seam: difficult to see with the naked eye, but apparent if one ran a hand over the bottom of the bag.

"Every time you use the bag," Bertain said, "just lay a piece of this special tape on the bottom and run over it with an iron or a heated knife." He demonstrated. "Et voila, no seam."

"Love your choice of combination," Martin said. "It's somehow appropriate."

"A little whimsical, but easy enough to remember. In any event, yours will come in handy for carrying back all the clothes your lady bought this afternoon. I took the liberty of giving Celeste some money to buy her gifts. Call it a goodwill gesture. If I know my Celeste, she spent it."

"That was very generous of you, Bertain. I guess it was pretty obvious that if we came this far, we were going to go through with it. Now all I have to do is concoct a good explanation for what my business with you is." Martin sighed. "Any useful suggestions would be greatly appreciated."

"Yes. That could be a delicate situation." Bertain frowned pensively. "It is usually best in these cases to stick as close to the truth as possible. Why not show them the bag and tell them that I want you to smuggle out some documents? You could say that the papers will implicate Mobutu in mass genocide in the Shaba province. I only wish I had the documents, because it is true. It would make a great story for your papers."

"Hmm . . ." Martin thought for a moment. "That might just do the trick. You seem to have all the answers."

"I do my best. Let us have some more champagne to cement the bargain. I do not think it would be wise for us to see each other again until this business has been finished. Perhaps we can all have some champagne in Paris one day. You can always find me through the concierge at the Hotel Meurice." He glanced at his watch. "*Mon dieu*, it is almost two-thirty. Time for you all to head back. I had Hans arrange a tour of the local game park for tomorrow. It is not much compared to the ones in Uganda, but it is the tourist thing to do."

Stefan tapped his glass. "Gentlemen, to success and the good life." He tossed off his champagne and theatrically smashed his goblet against the stone wall at the edge of the pool. "My mother was half Russian," he added apologetically as the others followed suit.

"No matter," Bertain said with a shrug. "It was not Baccarat." He escorted them to the car and waved goodbye.

"*Alea iacta est*," Martin said as soon as they were out of sight.

"Translation, please?" Stefan requested. "It must be something deep if it is in Latin."

"Not deep, just appropriate, even if it's somewhat apocryphal. 'The die is cast.' One of the many quotes falsely attributed to Caesar by Plutarch and Suetonius. He's supposed to have said it upon crossing the Rubicon to usurp power in 44 BC."

Stefan lit another cigar. "It is appropriate. You know, it is funny. I thought that it would feel different now that we have taken the final step, but it is somehow anticlimactic."

"You'll feel different when the first customs officer looks at your bag. It'll be the worst five minutes of your life."

"Ja, but the rush when I walk into the Credit Suisse in Geneva should last a lot longer than five or ten minutes."

CHAPTER

14

MARTIN WOKE JUST as they reached the outskirts of town, where the pre-curfew vanishing act was in progress.

Esther was sorting through a vast mountain of packages when he got back to their hotel room. "What a haul. I'm glad I brought you this nice new suitcase to take them home in."

She threw her arms around him. "Oh, mzungu, I have never seen such shopping! Celeste was so nice. She bought all these things for me. I tried to pay her, but she would not accept any money. We went to a beauty parlor too. I had so much fun that I can almost forgive you for running off and leaving me."

"You look absolutely sensational." He playfully wrestled her toward the bed.

"Not now, Martin." She slipped from his grasp. "I have to sort through these clothes and make sure they all fit. How did your business go?"

"Fine."

Clearly excited by her new clothes, she didn't press him for details. She modeled different outfits for the next half hour. There was no doubt that she was going to be the best-dressed girl in Kampala.

A delicious scent wafted over him as she twirled and pirouetted. "Smells like she taught you about perfumes also. If my nose isn't deceiving me, that's Caleche."

Esther smiled. "I already knew about perfume. Celeste just taught me where to put it for maximum effect." She wiggled her décolletage under his nose. "Like it?"

Martin growled and pulled her onto the bed. "That's the final straw, young lady."

Lovemaking was just what he needed to unwind from the tensions of the day. Esther dozed off almost immediately, but Martin was suffering sensory overload and needed a distraction. He gently disengaged himself, slipped into his trunks and robe, and headed to the pool, where Stefan was nursing a large Bloody Mary.

"You almost look like a normal tourist, Schmidt. As long as you don't take your shades off, you'll pass."

"Ja, that is what Hans just told me. He also imparted one other interesting bit of information. You will never guess who just checked in."

"I'm all ears."

"Your dearly beloved compatriot, Russell. Bees to honey."

"Yeah, the only question is what hive." Martin spotted the CIA agent waddling toward them. "We should know soon enough. He's headed this way."

"I was surprised when Metzner told me there was another American here, but I guess I should have known." Agent Russell helped himself to a chair and flagged a passing waiter. "You guys seem to have a nose for the hot spots."

"It is a little long on local color at the moment," Martin agreed with a smile. "But the food and shopping are great. Hans Metzner really runs a first-class show."

"That he does," Agent Russell conceded. "Nice class of people too.

There are an awful lot of sharks in these waters. How long are you guys in town for?"

Stefan shrugged. "A few more days."

Agent Russell glanced at Martin. "You sure picked the right time for a story. Metzner mentioned that things have really started to heat up."

"Yeah, last night was better than the Fourth at home. What brings you here? Surely a nasty internecine spat in a godforsaken backwater like this is not of vital importance to the gray heads at Foggy Bottom."

Agent Russell shrugged. "Rwanda itself isn't all that important in the greater scheme of things. However, it does border on some of our best friends' turf."

"Burundi?"

"Try Zaire."

"I can't see how the events here could possibly worry Mobutu one way or another. The worst that could happen is that he'll get a few hundred thousand refugees. The UN will feed them for him."

Agent Russell's thoughts seemed to be elsewhere. "That's one way of looking at it," he replied distantly. After glancing at his watch, he rose. "I have to be off. Nice to see you all. Give me a buzz back in Kampala. We can swap notes over a few beers."

Stefan waited until the CIA man was out of earshot. "Just checking, huh, Hein?"

"Something like that. It seemed to me he was looking for something with that whole Zaire tangent. I'll be damned if I know what. The last thing we need is more political red herrings."

"Ja. Those fellows are paid to worry about reds under the bed. We have more important things to think about."

Martin frowned. "Like the Swiss bank accounts, for starters. I have no idea how we go about getting them."

"It would be difficult under normal circumstances, but I have a friend at the embassy who can fix it. He is the commercial attaché. Better still, his uncle is high up in the Credit Suisse."

"That's handy. Does he owe you a favor?"

"A large one, as it happens."

"Even better. Won't he be curious?"

"Natürlich, but I have already thought of a good story. I will tell him that we are doing some black-market coffee deals. It happens all the time. He will not think twice."

"How long do you think it will take?"

"I think we can do it pretty fast. He is returning to Germany on leave next week. It should not take him more than a few days to arrange things. I will have him telex them for the documents when we get back."

• • •

Martin rejoined Esther in their hotel room later that evening.

"Fear's a funny thing," he mused, suddenly feeling the weight of his and Stefan's decision. "After a while, it starts to permeate everything. You think you can ignore it or block it out, but it's always there just under the surface making you do crazy things."

An exchange of automatic weapon fire punctuated his remark.

Esther trembled. "Oh God! I hate that sound. Hold me, Martin. I know it is stupid, but I am scared."

"It's not stupid." He smoothed her hair. "I'm frightened too. All I can do is keep telling myself that they won't come into a tourist hotel."

Shooting broke out every time Martin was about to drift off, and the fighting appeared to be taking place much closer to the hotel than on the previous night. Luckily, Esther was out like a light when a huge hubbub started below their window.

Martin crept out onto the balcony and spotted a crowd of

drunken Hutu troops harassing a pregnant Tutsi woman. What the hell was she doing out? Martin wanted to creep back inside and end the nightmare, but he couldn't. Suddenly, a soldier pulled out a knife and stabbed the woman repeatedly in the stomach. He pulled out the fetus and bashed it against a light post. The rest of the soldiers urinated and spat on the corpse before lurching drunkenly down the street.

Martin dragged himself back into the bedroom. The scene kept replaying whether he opened or closed his eyes. Finally, the remnants of the Brandy bottle blotted it out.

• • •

Martin nursed another hangover the next morning in the dining room.

The conversation was desultory until Hans bustled in and ordered a hearty meal. "I am afraid things are coming to a head. The fighting last night was the worst since this whole affair started. You must leave today. I've changed your tickets. In case you're interested, your buddy Russell left early for Kinshasa. I am tempted to head out to the airport with you and take my annual vacation a month or two early."

"Ja," Stefan said, "he did seem to be in a Zaire state of mind. Could almost get a man to thinking. Are we going to have any trouble getting out if you hang around?"

"Shouldn't think so," Hans replied. "Things are quiet around town at the moment. I just got off the phone with one of my friends in the military, and he assured me that everything was normal at the airport. I do hope you will come back when things are more normal. This really is a delightful town."

Martin rose and offered a handshake. "We appreciate the hospitality, Hans. Until next time."

They returned to their rooms, packed, and left for the ride out to the airport. During the drive, Martin noticed more signs of the fighting than he had spied on the way into town. They passed more than a few smoldering shells of buildings, and there were far more soldiers than civilians on the streets. It appeared that the government had given up the pretense of business as usual. The town exuded nervous tension. Martin didn't breathe a word about the previous night. He was paranoid enough and could tell Esther and Stefan felt the same. Nothing untoward had happened to them, but they would feel a lot better when the plane took off for Entebbe.

The suitcases passed their first test with flying colors. The customs search was rather perfunctory, though they did have to part with a few shilingi "duty" on Esther's clothes. Martin was certain that none of it was destined for government coffers.

• • •

Martin spent most of the next week writing. Between composing his first series of articles and researching a paper, he didn't have time for much else. After the events of the past week, he found it therapeutic to block out all distracting thoughts and concentrate his efforts on non-paranoid pursuits. The only time he thought about the diamonds was when he was writing about the situation in Rwanda. He quickly put them out of his mind as he finished working on the stack of leads Bullet Bob had provided.

The irony of the situation struck him again as he mailed the articles off to London. He debated whether or not to mail copies to Astles and finally decided in favor of doing it. Better that he appeared immersed in harmless activities, he thought. He only hoped that he would have the last laugh.

The paper proved to be the more difficult project. He hadn't done any serious academic research or writing in more than a year, and the effort drained him. He was tired but satisfied when he handed the paper in on Friday on the way out to the ministry to collect Esther.

She looked equally tired and collapsed in the front seat. "I am glad this week is over. I thought it would never end. I do not know why I feel this way, but everything at work is old and tired. It is terrible to be bored. This is not America. I cannot just go out and find another job."

"One weekend trip, and you're jaded for life." Martin smiled as he caressed her cheek. "Seriously, sometimes it takes a while to get back in the flow of things. It'll get better or at least more bearable next week. Besides, I wasn't much help. Next week I won't be so buried in my books. We'll go out and have some fun."

"I do not mind you working, mzungu. Idle minds make for trouble." She glanced at him as though debating whether or not to ask something. Then she took the plunge. "One thing I have been meaning to ask you. What was all your business in Kigali? You do not have to answer if you do not want to."

The hell I don't, he thought to himself as he fumbled for a smoke to buy some time. He sensed that the question was a test. If she thought he was holding anything back, their relationship would never be the same. He wanted to be honest with her, but he knew the less she knew the better.

"More dissident stuff. This guy claimed to have proof that Mobutu was carrying out mass genocide in the Shaba providence. It's a good story—and probably true—but he didn't have any proof. We're waiting."

"As long as it is not going to get you in trouble with that horrid man . . ."

"Bullet Bob? No way," Martin lied.

Her nod and relieved expression indicated acceptance but didn't make him feel good. In fact, he felt like a shit. She was so trusting.

"That is good," she said. "I am only now beginning to think that everything will be all right about the Nathan thing. It is terrible to be worried all of the time. It makes me very depressed."

There was one sure cure for that, and Martin didn't hesitate. "Dr. Fine prescribes a night on the town."

• • •

The treatment worked like a charm, and Esther was back to her normal self by the time they stopped by the Lair for a nightcap after midnight.

Martin took himself off for a short call, and as he relieved himself, a tall African in a loud purple dashiki stopped at the urinal beside him.

The man's forehead was furrowed with a series of zipper-like tribal scars. He glanced over his shoulder before assuming the quasi-meditative gaze that seemed the birthright of all males at the pissoir. "I have been trying to get you alone all night, Mr. Fine. This is an unexpected opportunity, and we will not have long. Nathan would like to see you. Come to the Baganda village out at Entebbe next Wednesday at two, and he will contact you."

The African zipped up and headed toward the door before Martin could recover from his surprise—and just as a bleary-eyed, pumpkin-shaped mzungu lurched through the door and staggered over to the spot next to Martin.

The African shrugged helplessly, rolled his eyes in disgust, and ghosted out the door.

"Hell of a night for a piss-up." The mzungu punctuated his slurred words with a rumbling belch and a cavernous, tile-shaking fart. He didn't seem to expect an answer.

Martin's normally agile brain had been stunned into submission.

He hurriedly zipped up and retreated. Another assault like that and the walls might come down.

On the way back to the table, Martin passed the bandstand and noticed that purple dashiki was the bass player in the house combo. *Funny*, he thought. *I must have looked at them a hundred times and not even noticed the gun. So much for journalistic observation.* Without breaking stride, he gave the African what he hoped was an inconspicuous nod. He wondered what Nathan wanted. His initial impulse was to can the meeting. According to Legs, the Libyan scenario was looking less and less likely, so Nathan might be a little less hot. But it was still a big chance in view of the fact that Martin appeared to have Astles lulled to sleep. On the other hand, the Anyanya's network might still come in handy. Martin and Stefan needed a backup in case the train plan didn't pan out.

Esther studied Martin as he sat down. "Eh, mzungu, you look like you are asleep while walking."

"Sorry. I was miles away."

"I know it is very late for a hard-working studenti. Let us go home while you still have some energy left."

Esther was in an amorous mood, so they took a blanket out on the grass overlooking the lake. Another of the things that Martin loved about Africa was that making love outside seemed so natural, and he felt he could let himself go completely.

"Have you heard from the Anyanya recently, Esther?"

"Yes, in a way. I got a letter from my brother the other day. Why do you ask?"

"Because the bass player in the band told me that Nathan wants to see me. He caught me in the WC. I didn't have a chance to ask him anything about it."

"I do not know what he wants. You will just have to wait and see."

"That's what I figured. I'm just a little worried about the timing."

"I am sure he will be careful. I think things are better around town."

• • •

Martin dropped Esther at home the next morning for her usual weekend chores and got to the hotel about noon. Stefan and the major were sitting at a corner table on the veranda.

"I was just telling Stefan what a punctilious lot you colonials were," the major said. "Where is Esther?"

"She likes to spend a domestic Saturday at home."

"I shall miss her, but it's just as well, because I want to discuss some things with you two that are best kept between us."

"In that case, we'd better take an after-lunch constitutional by the lake," Martin suggested.

"Splendid. Even though the veranda is normally empty, it goes against the grain."

"Agreed," Stefan mumbled through a mouth of sambosa.

The major seemed preoccupied, and their conversation suffered as a result. They ate quickly, paid the bill, and headed out to the path that wandered around the lake toward the botanical garden.

As soon as they were out of sight of the hotel, the major snapped out of his mood. "I had a long talk with Hans Metzner last night."

"Quite a fellow, that Hans," Martin replied. "It turned out by an amazing coincidence he knew our friend Bertain Aka quite well."

"Yes, that's exactly what I wanted to talk to you about. What do you know about this fellow Aka?"

Martin shrugged. "Not a lot. He seems a pleasant enough sort. Very generous. I gather he's a political exile from Zaire."

"Indeed he is, old boy, and right up to his charming neck in financing a resistance movement in the Shaba province of that country."

"He really didn't seem the political idealist type, but I suppose it's possible."

"In view of the fact that his parents are rotting in one of Mobutu's jails, it's more than possible. It's highly understandable." The major took a seat on the roots of a massive banyan tree. "Do you realize the importance of the Shaba province?"

Martin glanced at Stefan, who shook his head. "We haven't a clue."

"It has the largest deposits of cobalt and uranium in the world."

"So," Martin said, musing aloud, "obviously it represents a lot to Mobutu and his cronies. It also stands to reason that Bertain isn't one of their favorite people, if they know anything about his activities. How does that affect us? We just met the guy socially a couple of times."

"Time to stop beating around the bush, chaps. I've become quite fond of you two. There are times when you remind me a lot of myself when I was younger. Aka gets his diamonds from Zaire, and Mobutu is most anxious to nip any secessionist movements in Shaba in the bud."

"Not to mention get his cut of the diamonds," Stefan added with a chuckle.

"Oh, they're a bagatelle compared to his cut from the cobalt and uranium operations. He has to have the income from the Shaba province to finance the vast patronage network that keeps him in power."

"Fair enough," Martin said, "but—"

The major motioned for silence. "There is more. Nothing's cut-and-dried, especially here. The largest buyers of the cobalt and uranium are the French and the Americans. That's why they keep propping up his corrupt regime."

Stefan offered a wry smile. "The old equatorial iceberg raises its ugly head again."

"Spare me the bad metaphors. Does this information change your minds at all?"

"If we have any plans," Stefan replied warily, "it really depends on what Mobutu knows about Aka."

"I can assure you that you have no reason to worry at the moment, but I thought that you should know all of the factors in the equation. If things get complicated, I could perhaps be of assistance to you. As you know, I have some jolly useful contacts."

Martin laughed. "Your fangs and tail are showing, Major, but I understand. Government pensions don't buy much in these days of skyrocketing inflation."

"Sad but true. I have let so many other opportunities slip by. As you grow older, you begin to realize just how tenuous your grip on things is. Besides, Mobutu will not miss it, and Aka is too much of a dilettante—albeit a charming one from what I hear—to have much of an effect on the bigger picture. Are you shocked?"

Martin shook his head. "No, Major. We value your advice a great deal. I'm sure I speak for Stefan also when I say that we wouldn't be averse to contributing to your pension fund in return for the use of your intelligence network. That is of course assuming that we do any business with Bertain."

"Good, then I will just keep an eye on things in the meantime until you reach a decision. After all, it's the dream of every man, young or old, to make his fortune in the colonies. We can discuss the vulgar details at a later date if the venture gets off the ground."

"Major, do you have good contacts with the Americans and Zairians as well as this government?" Martin asked.

"Reasonable."

"Good, because you may have to keep an eye on Russell. We just happened to run into him in Kigali. He seemed to think we were there for another story besides the Hutu-Tutsi imbroglio. I'm pretty sure he was fishing around, and there's nothing to connect us to Bertain. But he could become a nuisance if he gets interested."

The major frowned. "Sometimes these young bull-in-a-china-shop sorts can be difficult to deal with. I have an old friend in the Yank embassy in Kinshasa. He owes me a few favors from the Biafra days. I'll see what I can dig up."

They rose and headed back for the hotel.

"Two parting suggestions, chaps. I think you should do a little work on Agent Russell. Sometimes a little disinformation can go a long way. Why not go to him and say you caught a buzz on the situation in the Shaba province? You could deflect his suspicions a little by asking him if there is any truth to the rumor. Tell him that you tried without success to find some contacts in Kigali."

The idea made sense in a cockeyed way, Martin thought. If Russell already had his suspicions, they had nothing to lose and everything to gain by putting things on the table. Telling him that they hadn't been able to find a contact would remove them further from Bertain, if Russell even knew about him. It would be a piece of cake to extend his naïve journalist role to Russell as well. He might even get a career out of it. Besides, the irony of appearing too honest to be dishonest appealed to him. "I'll buy the idea, Major. He told me to give him a call. It just goes against the grain to hang out with guys like him."

"A man in your line of work can't have too many scruples. Have you ever read *The Art of War*? It's a military manual that was written roughly in the fifth century BC by Sun Tzu. It's still required reading in every military academy in the world. There's a marvelous section in the chapter on the concealment of intention where a general asks his pupils, 'Where does the cockroach hide from the tortoise?' The answer is, 'In his armpit.'"

Stefan cocked his head to one side. "I like it. What is your other thought, Major?"

"That we meet once a week. When do you think the balloon will go up?"

"We don't really know, but my guess is when putsch comes to shove across the border."

The major chuckled. "Very good. How about the International next week? Nothing like a change of scene."

They gulped cold Niles back at the hotel to seal the bargain, and the major took himself off.

Stefan shook his head at the major's back as the major withdrew. "Never a dull moment. Things could get positively byzantine any moment."

Martin couldn't help but feel the same. "I wonder how many other suspicious minds are putting two and two together at the moment."

"I hope not too many. We knew we were going to have to take care of a few people. Better the devil we know."

"That's true, but there are a few we know that I'd just as soon not deal with. Just as a matter of curiosity, what's to keep the major from going for the whole swag?"

"If he had wanted to do that, he wouldn't have had that conversation with us. He could have watched and waited and then . . ." Stefan idly stirred his drink as he watched a fly do a drunken St. Vitas's dance in the dregs. "I do not think he is that greedy. He would rather have a small piece of the pie with no risks than go for the whole bundle and blow his reputation. This way he remains an officer and a gentleman of the alt schul."

"Yeah," Martin agreed, "he's the type that couldn't stand to have his rep tarnished."

Just as they were about to leave, Agent Russell came bustling in. "Well, you all are looking pensive. Kigali get to you?"

"No," Martin said, "we just finished debriefing the major. Since I'm in that mode, do you think I could pop by your office next week?"

"Sure, the door's almost always open. What can I do you for?"

"I picked up some interesting buzz on the tail end of the trip. I thought there might be a few pieces in it. I figured it couldn't hurt to run it by you."

Agent Russell smiled. It seemed to come naturally to him, like a horse salesman always showing you more of his own teeth than the animals'. "Glad to be of help. When do you want to stop in?"

Martin tried to act nonchalant. "About three on Wednesday okay?"

"You got it."

AGENT STEVE RUSSELL'S office was a perfect reflection of its occupant: cold, efficient, and without personality. No college diploma on the walls. No picture of the wife and kids on the desk. No plant to warm up the space. It was as though everything had been moved out for a paint job and never replaced.

Martin fidgeted in the merciless chair. Like most Danish-modern pieces, it was cleverly designed so that no possible position would yield any degree of comfort to a normally shaped human body. He wished he'd brought along a magazine or newspaper. When he'd arrived punctually at three, Russell's secretary, a no-nonsense spinster type, informed him that Mr. Russell was delayed in a meeting with the ambassador and asked him to wait in the office. After offering no coffee, tea, or reading matter, she'd bustled back out to her desk in the anteroom.

Martin glanced at his watch. It had been twenty minutes and counting. So far he'd successfully passed the time trying to figure out where Russell hid the microphones, but he was losing interest in the game. He felt like he was back in prep school waiting for a vital college interview: hating the whole process but knowing he had to go through it. Realizing that his childish, antiauthoritarian streak was surfacing, he wandered out to the secretary's office to see if there was any news.

The spinster was engrossed in the latest Victoria Holt romance.

Martin tried to think of something witty to say but knew it would be wasted.

Sensing his presence, the secretary jerked her head up from her book. "So sorry, Mr. Fine. Mr. Russell just called. He's on his way down." She retreated to her book without further word.

Must be a love scene, he mused to himself as he retook his seat. At least Russell wasn't off doffing his secretary. That would have been the ultimate insult.

"Sorry about the delay, Martin." Russell looked apologetic as he entered his office. "You know how it is when you're in with the boss man."

"Yeah, I understand. Since we've already used our allotted time for small talk, I'll get right to the point. Is there really a secessionist threat in Shaba?"

Russell shot him a triumphant glance and fumbled with his pipe. "There have been some rumblings. I didn't think the Hutu-Tutsi spat was the only thing that brought you to Rwanda."

"Actually, it was, but our poolside chat got me interested, so I did a little research. The problem seems to date back to the Lumumba days."

"It's the usual thing: tribalism." Russell shook his head sadly and chewed on his pipe. For a moment, he was almost simpatico. "I don't care how condescending it is. Sometimes they really *are* like children."

"From what I understand, Shaba is strategically pretty important. Just how serious is the situation?"

"It's in the nascent stage, but it could degenerate rapidly. There are a lot of old wounds."

"Are the Russians interested yet?"

"No, they're quite occupied farther south these days. As you might recall, they're funding three liberation wars at the moment."

"Angola, Mozambique, and Zimbabwe would seem enough to keep even them busy. The only buzz I heard in Kigali was that there had been some massacres by Zairian troops, but I couldn't find anyone with hard evidence. Nobody said a thing about an organized guerilla movement." Martin paused and lit a cigarette. So far things were going well. It was time for his masterstroke. He figured if he brought up the subject of diamond smuggling, there would be no way Russell would think he was involved. "I did pick up one tidbit from a drunken Belgian in the bar at the hotel, but it was so off-the-wall that I threw it out. He said there were a lot of diamonds being smuggled out of Shaba to finance an insurrection."

Russell didn't bother to play poker. "That one would have interested me."

"I doubt it. He didn't have anything to back it up. Besides, it's a well-known fact that Zaire's borders leak diamonds. Smuggling is the national sport." Martin gave a dismissive shrug. "It's been going on for years from Shaba and everywhere else for that matter. There hasn't been a guerilla movement yet."

"He didn't give you any names?"

"Are you kidding? It was straight beer babble. If he'd given me any names, I'd probably be in Amsterdam by now."

Russell managed a tepid smile. "I'm glad we had this discussion. I have to admit I was a little worried when I saw you in Kigali. Shaba produces all of Zaire's cobalt. That makes it a rather important place to us. We wouldn't want any idle speculation in the press inflaming the situation."

"I can understand how you feel, but I don't think you have to worry too much. There isn't anything to base a story on."

"Not all journalists are that responsible."

Martin laughed inwardly. Responsibility had little to do with it. He didn't have the reputation to get a spec piece published. "You can be sure, Steve, that I will vet anything I come across with you first. I wouldn't want to compromise the national interest."

Russell rose, extending his hand. "I'm glad we worked things out. If you want some background on anything else, come on by."

•••

Agent Russell leaned back in his chair as he listened to Martin Fine help himself out. Fine offered a polite "so long" to Russell's secretary and then exited through the outer office door, which closed audibly behind him.

Fine seemed like a decent enough guy, for a petty criminal. He had to know that Russell had performed a background check on him and knew all about his drug-dealing days in South Philly, among other exploits. Or maybe not. The young man struck Russell as unusually daring, bordering on reckless. Fine came from money, which perhaps explained some of his indifference to danger. He had skated through life, although from the sounds of it, he had left America due in no small part to the growing number of enemies he'd made in South Philly, with the local mafia topping the list. He seemed destined for a similar fate in Africa, but here, far more snakes hid in the tall grass, and most of them were deadly. If Russell had learned anything about Kampala and East Africa so far, it was that everyone had an angle, and loyalty was in short supply.

Fine had been lucky to make friends with the German Stefan Schmidt, but just as unlucky to become acquainted with Schmidt's mercurial associate, Anton Springer.

As if on cue, Russell's secretary rang him.

"Yes?"

"I have a Mr. Springer here to see you, sir."

Russell smiled. "Send him in."

A moment later, Anton sauntered into Russell's office wearing a colorful dashiki that accentuated his tall, slender frame.

"Have a seat." Russell offered him a cigarette.

Anton obliged.

"I trust you made sure Fine didn't see you on your way in."

"Of course," Anton said and puffed at his cigarette as he lit it. "I am always watching, never seen."

After a short spate of small talk, the two got down to business.

"Is Fine still talking to the cripple?"

"That he is," Anton said in his street-tough accent. "And the wad of cash he usually hands him says the information must be good."

Russell sighed. He knew what he had to do, but he never liked releasing the proverbial hounds. It felt distasteful—and always like it could cascade beyond his control. "We might have to see to it that the cripple stops talking. Permanently."

Anton raised his hands in protest. "That is not my line of work."

"Understood. But I'm sure you can find someone."

"What if Fine is able to trace it back to you?"

Russell shrugged. "That might be a good thing. Maybe it'll inspire him to move on to less dangerous work—far, far away from here." He paused to reflect on the big picture. "Are we any closer to knowing who's helping Fine and Schmidt ferry Aka's diamonds?"

"Everything points to the Anyanya."

"Makes sense," Russell said with a nod.

Anton studied Russell like he was trying to put together the pieces of some puzzle. "It is none of my business, of course, but I find myself a bit confused."

"Yeah?"

"I am not sure your motives align with official American policy."

Russell laughed. "As long as we don't run afoul of Mobutu or Khadafi, I'm not worried about job security. And if I can pad my retirement along the way, it's a win-win."

. . .

Martin stopped at Nakasero on his way to the Baganda Museum at Entebbe. He gave Legs a discreet nod and stepped inside the teeming market. He was haggling over some tomatoes when he heard a hiss and caught a glimpse of the beggar scuttling off toward the meat section. Somebody was paranoid today. Having lost interest in the bargaining, Martin gave the mama what she wanted and made his way to the meat section. He remembered to breathe through his mouth as he threaded the swarming aisles, but the stench still gagged him.

Legs was waiting between two grimy chicken stalls among the piles of yellowish-purple entrails and slimy, rotten meat.

"Why all the secrecy?" Martin asked as he offered him a cigarette.

Legs struggled to answer between pants for air. "Lots of GSU in the market today, mzungu. I do not know why. Maybe a black-market sweep. It is best not to arouse their interest."

"They aren't after us, are they?" Martin was instantly paranoid.

"A panna, mzungu. I have some interesting news for you. The American Russell has been spending a lot of time with Astles."

"Any idea what's going on?"

"It is said that Astles is trying to get the Americans to make the Israelis sell some arms. Now that the Libyans have left, Amin thinks the Americans and Israelis might pay to keep them out. The army is getting restive. They are bored, and bored troops get drunk and cause trouble. It is said that Amin wants to do something with them."

"Like what?"

"Maybe he will send some to Rwanda to restore the peace. The Rwandan ambassador has been having talks also."

"How about the Zairians? I have read that Mobutu was taking an interest."

"There has been somebody in from Zaire too, but I do not recognize him. It is not the ambassador."

Martin filed that one away. "How good are your contacts in the GSU?"

Legs shifted uncomfortably, coughed convulsively, and spat. "It depends what you want. I try to stay away from them—any wise man does—but I still hear things."

"Could you find out if someone was being watched?" Martin peeled three hundred shilingi notes off his wad to emphasize the question. They vanished from his hand before he could smooth out the creases.

"Who?"

"Me and another mzungu named Stefan Schmidt."

Legs smiled. "What is your name? I call you the hundred-shilingi man."

"Martin Fine."

Legs crawled off, vanishing into the swirling crowd.

•••

Martin had to speed all the way to Entebbe, but he made it by three. A guided tour of the restored village was just starting, so he tagged along. He would have looked awfully conspicuous just standing around. Nathan would find him when the time was right.

The village had been faithfully restored to its state at the time of Mutesa, the greatest of the kabakas of the Baganda. Martin knew the history involved, but the guide spiced up the otherwise dull monologue with some informative anecdotes about the great king, including what Mutesa had done when Burton and Speke had given him a "fire stick" on their first trip through. Mutesa had demanded a demonstration of the gun's power, and Speke had obliged him by shooting a bird. The kabaka was not entirely satisfied. After ordering Speke to reload, he handed the gun to a courtier and commanded him to shoot himself, which he promptly did. Life was indeed simpler in those days, Martin thought. It must have been a great loss of face for everyone involved, with the possible exception of the kabaka.

The tour ended a few minutes later, and Martin wandered over to the souvenir stand. Although they had nothing but bad reproductions of Baganda artifacts, he browsed as if interested. He glanced at his watch. Three forty-five, and still no sign of Nathan. The tourists had left. The village closed at four. He was going to have to make a move soon.

"I do not think you will find what you are looking for here." The pretty mpenzi behind the stall stretched and winked. "About two miles back toward Kampala, you will see a murram road leading off to the right. Turn down it, and drive for about a half mile. There is a big clearing on the left with a large cotton tree. Stop there." Without waiting for a reply, she turned and started to pack up the curios.

Well, at least I know I'm not being followed, Martin thought as he walked back to his car. It had not been a complete waste of an hour. After recent events, the security couldn't be too tight.

The directions were exact, and he pulled to a stop under the canopy of the huge cotton tree about fifteen minutes later.

Nathan stepped out from behind its huge trunk before Martin

had gotten out of the car. "I hope you did not mind the ruse too much." He extended his hand. "I am glad you decided to come."

"How could I refuse? After what happened, I was glad to hear that you were still around."

"Yes, that was unfortunate. Informers are something we come across quite often these days. He was discovered and removed."

"I guess it goes with the territory. Things must be improving around these parts for you, though. I've heard that the Libyan-Ugandan connection has been temporarily severed."

"For the time being, yes, but Khadafy is not going to go away."

Martin didn't press him. He'd learned enough about African style not to rush his fences. It was a test, and he knew it. He lit a cigarette before speaking. "Are you still looking around for mutually beneficial deals?"

Nathan nodded. "Yes. As I said to you the last time, there are those of us who are looking for quicker solutions. We'd like to make some money. We need many things."

"How are your contacts in Kenya?"

"Good. What exactly do you have in mind?"

"Suppose we needed to get from somewhere in southern Uganda to the Kenyan coast and back without being detected."

"It would depend on what you were transporting. If it was not anything too bulky, the matter could probably be arranged easily enough."

"With better security than last time?"

"I think we could guarantee that. There will be very few of us involved, and I know everyone well. They are absolutely reliable."

"Could we move on short notice?"

Nathan raised an eyebrow. "How short?"

"Two or three days. There probably won't be more time."

"Sometimes things are out of your control," Nathan said with a smile. "Probably. When will you know?"

"It could be anytime. I will need a guaranteed way of getting in quick contact with you."

Nathan thought that one over carefully. "Why not Esther?"

"I may not want her involved. If anything went wrong, she would be in a terrible situation."

"I can understand that. You can pass a message through the man at the Leopard's Lair. He can always find me within a day. That is the best I can do."

Martin turned to leave. "That should be good enough. I'll be in touch as soon as anything breaks."

•••

It was six by the time Martin got back to Kireka. He showered and headed down to Stefan's for their weekly bachelor dinner.

The mad Hun was beaming like the Cheshire Cat as he put the final touches on a pitcher of drinks. Stefan handed Martin a glass and raised his own in a toast. "We are now the proud possessors of Swiss bank accounts." He reached into his back pocket and handed over a telex sheet. "The numbers are listed under machine parts."

Martin committed them to memory. "One step closer, but a long way to go until we can make our first withdrawals. I had a series of interesting meetings today. You might call it my intelligence day."

Stefan waved him out to the porch. "Tell me over dinner. How did the meeting with Russell go?"

"Pretty well, I think, though he was a little disappointed that I wasn't able to name names when I discussed the rumors of diamond smuggling out of Shaba."

"Ach so, you discussed that, did you? That was pretty bold."

"The major said that it was the best way to disarm him. I didn't think he would suspect me of involvement if I put the rumors on the table."

"Ja, that makes sense."

"Especially after I volunteered to keep him abreast of any developments in the Shaba story. I told him that I was a responsible journalist and wouldn't publish any spec pieces that ran contrary to the national interest."

Stefan looked at him with frank incredulity. "Did you really say that?"

"Sure, why not? It was gilding the lily a bit, I admit, but not that out of sync with the persona I'm cultivating."

"I guess so. What did your friend Legs have to say?"

"Nothing too earthshaking. Russell has been in to see Astles quite a few times, but usually it's been joint meetings with the Israeli ambassador."

"More toys for the army. Nice, new American ones."

"He did have one interesting item, though. He said that there's some talk going around about using some Ugandan troops to stabilize the situation in Rwanda. The Rwandan ambassador has been in also. The army is getting bored, and Amin has to come up with something to occupy them."

"Natürlich. That is always a problem with large underpaid armies in peacetime. Anyone who grew up in postwar Germany knows that. They have a habit of starting to feed on the population."

"The only other news he had was that somebody from Zaire had been in several times. All Legs knew was he wasn't regular embassy."

Stefan's face darkened momentarily. "Rwanda, Zaire, Uganda, and the Americans in the same week—all parties who would be interested in diamond smuggling from Shaba, but that is probably being outrageously paranoid."

"Unlikely as it is, I asked Legs to keep an eye on the Zairian. The danger to us will probably come from Zaire and Uganda. Personally, I think they're a little more worried about the situation in Rwanda. I also saw Nathan this afternoon."

"What did he say?"

"That the heat is off, and they're still available."

"It would be nice to have a backup in case anything goes wrong, but I am afraid their security leaves a little to be desired."

"Yeah, he mentioned that. They found the informer. He also said that if we did anything with them, it would only involve a few very trusted guys—the younger generation. I gather the elders wouldn't approve."

"Ja, I should think not. You did not tell him what we were doing, did you?"

"Do I look that stupid? I told him we'd let him know if anything comes up. The train should work out fine. If something is wrong with the deal, we probably won't even get that far, but Nathan may be our only alternative."

Stefan nodded slowly. "It is possible, Hein, but I hope not. Are we meeting the major on Saturday?"

"Yes, for lunch. Time he started earning his commission. He said he had a good contact in Kinshasa. It would be nice to know what Mobutu is thinking these days."

"Ja. What do you think our contribution to the major's pension should be?"

Martin thought for a moment. "No more than ten thousand each."

"Pounds?"

"Hell no. That would be exorbitant even by African standards."

"That seems fair. It should be enough for the old fox to make a nice down payment on a villa in Majorca. That leaves just one loose end that I can see."

"What's that?"

"She is about five feet three."

"I wish you hadn't brought that up." Martin had been avoiding the subject. *Leave it to Stefan*, he thought. Still, he was going to have to decide. There just didn't seem to be any easy way out.

"I know it is hard, Martin, but you cannot leave it dangling until the last moment. It is all right to think that Esther is an African and a fatalist, but she is still a woman. You never know how they will react. The only thing certain is that it will be in the fashion you least expect. I recently heard this great story about Haile Selassie that illustrates the point perfectly."

"I'm sure I don't want to hear it, but go on."

"It seems that there was this expat businessman who had been stationed in Ethiopia for ten years. During this period, he took a local girl as a bush wife, and their union was blessed with three children. When he was summoned back to the States, he dismissed her without as much as a thank-you."

"What a class-A shit."

Stefan shrugged. "It happens all the time. He expected to hear no more of the matter. After all, lots of his friends had done the same thing. He was greatly surprised when he was summoned to an imperial audience on the eve of his departure."

"I'll bet he was. How did the Lion of Judah come to hear of the situation? From what I've heard, he's pretty isolated from the commoners these days."

"There is an old custom in Ethiopia. Any subject can petition the emperor for redress of a grievance by hurling themselves in front of his chariot—in this case, his bulletproof Mercedes."

"Just his bad luck that he picked a liberated bush wife and her good luck that the car stopped."

"The emperor asked if the woman's charges were true. The expat made no attempt to deny them, asserting that the woman was only a market whore. The emperor asked him how much a common market whore got a night. The expat replied that the going rate was about ten dollars. To which Selassie replied, 'Then you will pay her ten times ten times three hundred and sixty-five before you leave the country.'"

"Marvelous. I can see why he calls himself a descendant of Solomon. Don't worry, Stefan. As soon as we hear something definite, I'll deal with Esther. Superficial appearances to the contrary, I'm not an ugly American."

•••

Saturday started badly. The traffic was brutal. Martin was fuming as he made his way through the lobby of the International after one o'clock.

Only a few scattered groups of touristi were present. The International was between packages.

Martin hustled over to the corner table where Stefan and the major were devouring a plate of sambosas.

"Nice of you to join us, Hein." Stefan pulled out a chair for him and signaled for a Nile. "I was just speculating to the major that Esther might have twisted your arm or some more vulnerable part of your anatomy."

"I wish. We left plenty early, but all hell was breaking loose on the road out to Entebbe. There were three roadblocks between here and her house. The troops seemed uptight too. They actually checked our identification."

"Which means it was not kondos that they were after. Any developments we should be aware of, Major?"

"Just a few rumors, old boy. Wild ones at that. A buzz started going around town last night that somebody had a go at his nibs. The roadblocks seem to confirm that something happened."

"Ja, it was certainly not unexpected. But I do not think it concerns us. Did you hear anything out of Kinshasa?"

"Not a peep. I've had my nose to the ground both here and in Kinshasa. No signs of abnormal activity. It's not unheard of for them to keep a secret, but rare. My Kinshasa source did say that they're watching the diamond market carefully, but they've been doing that for the past several months. He said that they know something is going on but don't have any specifics. That confirms what Aka told you."

"We heard that there has been activity at the State House this week. Evidently, the Rwandan ambassador has been in several times as well as a mysterious but presumably government-connected Zairian."

The major ran a hand through his brilliant-white hair. "I think I can explain that. There's been a lot of talk about sending an OAU peacekeeping force into Rwanda. Both Amin and Mobutu would like to deploy certain tribal elements over the border, so it's quite likely that something will come of the idea if the situation continues to deteriorate."

It made sense, Martin thought, particularly in view of what Legs had reported. There was little doubt that the assassination attempt, if there had been one, would have been perpetrated by the army. He turned his attention to other matters. "I know it's vulgar, Major, but what did you have in mind for your consultant's fee?"

"Fifteen thousand a man," he replied without missing a beat. "The down payment on a villa in Majorca. You'll be welcome anytime, of course."

"Twelve-five." Martin glanced at Stefan, who nodded. "Okay, Major. There's only one thing I've got to say: It sure does pay to keep your ear to the ground around these parts."

"Indeed it does. But keep in mind that it takes a long time to build up a network of contacts, and that's really what you're paying for. Now that the figure is settled, have you got any thoughts on how we might arrange payment?"

Martin gave him a sheepish look. "To be honest, Major, neither of us has given it much thought. The only thing that is obvious is that we can't pay you before the deal."

"Stands to reason. I think that with certain safeguards, I'd be willing to trust you."

"Which are?"

"Presumably you've made arrangements to be paid outside of the country. Neither of you would be stupid enough to want to have to deal with that amount of cash. I propose that you issue instructions to your bankers to transfer the necessary sums to my account upon receipt of your initial deposits. Should you change your minds, I'll then have the details of the transaction and a record of same. I'm sure that the authorities in your tax departments would be interested."

Martin mulled it over. "I think we could live with that arrangement. That could also solve the equally sticky problem of our safety net, in that we'd have an audit trail back to you."

The major hesitated and then shook hands all around. "That arrangement would be acceptable to me. I suggest a serious drink to seal the bargain."

Stefan raised his glass. "Sehr gut. I am looking forward to that first sherry in Majorca."

MARTIN ORDERED HIMSELF a plate of sambosas, and Stefan and the major stretched out for some serious sunbathing. It was one of those rare days in Kampala when there was no breeze to diffuse the heat. The shimmering water seemed to magnify the incandescent glare. Shades were a necessity, not an affectation.

"Perfect day for beer drinking," Stefan observed as he roused himself from his coma long enough to order more cold Niles. "The sun evaporates it before it gets to your gut."

His ramblings were interrupted by a sudden commotion at the pool entrance.

Martin dragged himself up on one elbow and hastily surveyed the scene.

"*Was ist das?*" Stefan asked with a frown. "I wish this was a drunken hallucination."

Martin swiveled in time to see a handful of GSU men hustle into the pool area.

Their appearance unsettled the two groups of touristi, who traded questioning glances and started whispering to each other. The spooks didn't pay much attention to any of them as they took up posts around the pool.

Martin concentrated on his sambosas. "I heard the general has taken up swimming in a big way recently. He must be coming over for a dip."

"Could be. Colonel Bakazi just walked in." Stefan discreetly monitored the pool entrance over a folded corner of his newspaper. He stifled a laugh. "Gott in Himmel, only in Africa. Turn slowly, and try not to laugh."

Amin waddled into sight, his porcine girth swathed in a pink robe with large blue letters proclaiming *Heavyweight Champion Uganda Armed Services* emblazoned on the back.

"Any bets he holds that title unopposed?" Martin whispered.

Colonel Zack smiled and waved when he saw them.

"Christ," Martin muttered with a sigh. "I hope he doesn't want to race. I'm not sure I could float at the moment."

"That is just the kind of opponent he likes." Stefan inched his chair around for a better view.

The entourage continued its slow trip around the pool. Amin stopped in front of the confused touristi and chatted for a while. Evidently, his words didn't reassure them, because they hastily scooped up their things and headed for the exit the minute he moved on.

"Our turn." Stefan rose.

Colonel Zack stopped in front of them before they could make themselves scarce.

"Hello, Colonel." Martin extended his hand. "Lovely day for a swim."

"It certainly is, Mr. Fine. I think you all have met the general before."

As he nodded, Martin tried to ignore the memory of Amin biting into the commando's freshly plucked liver.

Stefan half bowed in Amin's direction. "It is an even greater honor the second time."

Amin grunted. His beady eyes darted over them. "I trust you are enjoying your visit." He scratched his testicles and waited for an answer.

"It's hard not to with weather like this, Your Excellency. Since we last met, we've had an opportunity to do some traveling. Uganda is indeed a pearl among nations." Martin figured it was impossible to flatter the general too much.

Up close, Amin's bestial presence was overwhelming. The raw power of his huge, sweating body—not to mention his rancid body odor—couldn't be ignored.

Martin stifled the impulse to laugh. *Even his best friends won't tell him.*

Fortunately, Amin noticed the major and rattled off a spate of Swahili. Martin didn't catch a lot of it, but it was about the wolfram mine.

The major gave him a long reply, throwing in enough complicated numbers to confuse Martin.

Amin appeared satisfied. A sly look stole across his face as his eyes came to rest on the one sambosa left on the plate at their table. He reached with his massive hand and snatched it with startling speed. Then, smiling like a naughty child caught with his hand in the cookie jar, he popped it into his cavernous mouth. "Mmm..." He smacked his lips, patted his swollen gut, and belched thunderously. "Dhese good sambosas, Colonel, you order me tree dozen." He didn't give them another glance as he waddled off.

"You would not have liked that one anyway, fellows," Stefan said with a snicker. "Remind me to send him an etiquette guide next Christmas—anonymously, of course."

The water follies began with a demonstration of high diving by several of Amin's aides. Two of them climbed to the highest platform, about ten meters up. A furious altercation broke out as they took up positions. The argument grew in intensity, and Martin wished his Swahili was better. He kept glancing at Amin, who was stolidly eating his way through the huge platter of sambosas in front of him, but the general gave no sign that the disagreement was bothering his digestion.

Finally, the first officer grabbed the other by the shoulders and bellowed, "I am a major, and you are a lieutenant. I command that you jump off before me, or I will have you court-martialed."

That seemed to do the trick. The lieutenant walked gingerly out to the edge of the board and jumped. The major followed him with an almost presentable swan dive.

The major chuckled mirthlessly. "Are they supposed to strike terror into the heart of the enemy?"

"They just wanted a captive audience," Stefan countered. "Nice of you to lay on the entertainment, or is it fortuitous?"

"Damned nuisance, actually. I must say, the general still has a healthy appetite. He made a clean sweep of those sambosas." The major had to raise his voice to make himself heard over the bellowing of the aides, who were engaged in a good-natured water fight. "Oh, by the by, I had an intriguing meeting with Astles yesterday."

"We're all ears."

"He wanted me to do a feasibility study for an invasion of Tanzania."

"You are joking, or they were!" Stefan exclaimed. "The idea is madness. Did you agree to do it?"

"Had to, old boy." The major heaved a sigh. "They've got me in the palms of their sweaty little hands. You remember that spot of difficulty I got myself into in Nigeria a few years back? Anyway, his nibs has some insane notion of carving a corridor to the sea. The scary thing is they just might be able to do it. The Tanzanian Army makes this lot look like the Gurkhas."

"The Kenyans would never let him get away with it," Stefan said with a snort.

The major frowned. "If he does it quickly and presents them with a fait accompli, they might not be able to do much about it. They have their own fish to fry with Odinga and his lot."

Amin was disrobing for a swim. He ordered all the aides except one into a line at the end of the pool for a race. The odd man out unholstered his pistol and fired off a round into the air, and they all dove in. Most of the contestants were smart enough to let Amin swim past or over them, but one stubborn or stupid fellow swam strongly on, oblivious to it all. He beat Amin by a clear head and raised his arms in a victory salute.

Martin groaned. "If that guy has a brain in his head, it's lonely. I don't think I want to watch this." He started to rise.

"Don't move." The major restrained him. "They've forgotten we're here. Best not to remind them."

Amin was shaking with rage as he hauled himself out of the pool. He bellowed out some commands, and the two closest GSU men pulled the now-trembling winner out of the pool. One of the aides handed Amin a pistol, and the general smashed it into the unfortunate man's face. Martin closed his eyes and covered his ears, but he couldn't close out the repeated mushy thuds of the pistol hitting home. Finally, they stopped. Martin peered through separated fingers as Amin gave the body a contemptuous kick, spat on it, and strode off. The rest of the entourage followed, with two of the GSU men dragging the corpse by its heels.

Martin fought down the bile and glanced around the table to see Stefan with his head buried in shaking hands.

The major seemed unaffected by what they'd just seen. He rose and strode purposefully over to the bar. The attendant had long since disappeared, so he helped himself to a half-full bottle of brandy. "Steady on, lads." He poured out three stiff tots. "This will help your nerves."

It took Martin a few shots, but he finally pulled himself

together. "I'll never forget that as long as I live."

"It wasn't a pleasant sight," the major conceded. "But we've seen this show before, haven't we?"

Martin could only nod his head in disgust.

"I've heard it mentioned that the general has incurable syphilis," the major mused. "In light of recent events, I'd be inclined to agree with them."

Stefan had returned to the land of the living. "I am not going to argue with you, Major."

The major poured out the rest of the bottle in equal portions. "I think the International owes us a drink." He cleared his throat. "One more thing, lads. I hate to mention it because it's so obvious, but a word to the wise. Kampala is like a small town in many ways. If you sneeze going out the door to work in the morning, it's likely to be pneumonia by the time you get to the pub for lunch."

Martin rose. "I don't know about the rest of you, but I could use a change of scenery."

"Ja, they certainly did not seem to be worried about our presence."

"I think that they forgot that we were here, old top. I suggest that we keep it that way. We should linger until they are well clear." The major launched into a dissertation on the military problems posed by the Tanzanian operation.

Martin appreciated his efforts at distraction, but his thoughts were elsewhere. The ante was going up every minute. It was okay for him. He was involved in the deal with open eyes. He caught himself. Just how open were his eyes? If he had any sense, he thought, he'd be on the next plane out. Yet he was hooked on the adrenalin and intrigue. How often did someone get to write and star in their own movie?

"Earth to Fine." Stefan's vigorous shaking snapped Martin out of his reverie. "You have insulted one of the great military minds of the century."

"Nonsense," the major said. "Just the boring twaddle of an old soldier in his twilight years. Does today change anything for you?"

"Not for me," Martin said. "But there are other people involved."

"Hmm . . . Yes, I see. The mpenzi. She could be in a very bad position even if she doesn't know anything. You'd better give that matter some serious thought. I have to be off. They've had plenty of time to sort things out. I'll be in touch."

Stefan turned to Martin as soon as the major had left the pool deck. "What are you going to do about Esther? You cannot leave her out on the proverbial limb."

"Yeah, that's becoming increasingly apparent. I've thought of a few possibilities—the best being for Esther and me to have a public breakup. Once the deal is done, we can pick up where we left off."

"Sehr gut. That would work, but you must do it as quickly as possible. The further removed she is, the better for all concerned."

Martin nodded. "A public spat at the Big S tonight would be on all necessary desks by Monday." He gulped down the rest of his cognac. The familiar burn did little to comfort him. "Getting that far is easy. It still leaves the difficult question of how I explain it to her. I'm not enough of a shit to cut her dead."

"Ja, that would be the best way to do it. It would be most convincing, but you cannot do it if you care for her."

"I guess I'll just stick to the important documents routine. She should buy it."

"I think so. Do not be too depressed, Hein. You must do something, or you will land her in trouble."

• • •

A swim at Lake Vic and twenty minutes of meditation produced no revelations. All of Martin's previous girlfriends—if he could call them that—had broken up with him. He'd never really cared enough to do more than protest feebly for pride's sake and was usually relieved afterward.

To make matters worse, Esther was bursting with good spirits when he returned home. She was flitting around the house naked, humming cheerfully as she dusted.

His first impulse was to pick her up and carry her into the bedroom—and normally he would have—but he knew it would be a mistake. He settled for a quick kiss on the cheek and a businesslike pat on the rump.

She looked at him questioningly as he helped himself to a double waragi and plopped down on the couch. "What is wrong, mzungu? Do I not please you?"

"Esther, we need to have a serious talk." He drained his drink and tried to gather his thoughts.

"Eh, mzungu, you must be sick. You seem so different. Something is very heavy on your mind." She poured another drink and sat down beside him.

"I'm worried about you. This writing thing I'm involved in could get heavy, and I don't want you to get into trouble because of me. Things are getting crazy around here. After what I saw this afternoon, I'm beginning to think that Amin and crew are capable of anything." He gave her a brief, unedited summary of the day's events.

"Surely, they would just confiscate the papers."

He sighed. "I wouldn't be too sure of that. All the regimes around here support Mobutu. They might well decide that we're too much of a potential nuisance just to deport us. Let's face it: They've already killed two journalists. Once you've done it once . . ."

"If this is so dangerous, why are you doing it? Surely one story is not worth such a risk." She hesitated and then took his face in her hands. "I do not think you are telling me the whole truth, but I am not mad, because I think you are lying to protect me, not to deceive me."

"But, Esther . . ."

She sighed and kissed him gently. "I will do whatever you want. No strings, and no teary goodbyes. My life has taught me never to worry about the future or the past. I cannot control either."

"But what if everything goes wrong?"

"You can always find me if you really want to."

"I will. Just having this whole talk has made me realize how differently I feel about you than any other woman I've ever been with."

She gently pushed him down. "We have talked enough for now. Just love me sore, and let tomorrow take care of itself."

Martin held up a hand. "There's just one more thing. I think we should have a public spat at the Big S tonight. You know how word travels."

"So that is the way you want it." She stiffened and abruptly disengaged herself. "Making love to you will not put me in the mood for that." She gave him an intimate caress. "I hope you know what you are doing. I will dress now."

Martin felt like a prime shit. Her calm acceptance was making things much harder. His gut told him to forget the whole thing, especially when he caught sight of her arranging her hair.

She caught his glance and sent an instantaneous flash of mournful resignation before she averted her eyes back to the mirror.

They rode back to Kireka in silence. Three or four times, Martin was on the verge of saying something, but the words just wouldn't come. By the time they entered her apartment, his body was vibrating like a tuning fork.

Wordlessly, Esther undressed and made slow, tender love to him. She silenced him every time he tried to whisper an endearment.

Finally, realizing that it was a gift, he relaxed and let himself go. She worked his body methodically, bringing him to the brink time and time again, only to back off when he was within one gasping breath of attaining the release he needed so much. When the moment was exactly right, she pushed him over the edge. He shuddered, emitting a deep, primal moan as the tension spurted out violently.

She collapsed in his arms. "Do not ruin it by saying anything. You were there when I needed you. Now I am here for you."

Drained, they fell asleep in each other's arms.

. . .

It was dark when Martin awoke to the sound of screeching brakes and an overstrained engine coughing and gasping to a halt. Esther stirred beside him.

"Your ride has arrived!" Stefan called from the entryway. His face appeared in the bedroom doorway a second later. "I see you have been doing some serious training for your performance this evening. I hope you will not be nervous, but I am going to go to the Big S tonight."

"We're thrilled," Martin said. "Why don't you make us a few stiff drinks while we get decent?"

"Sehr gut. It might be easier if you are drunk."

Esther pulled on her robe and clambered out of bed. "What are we going to fight about, mzungu?"

"That's a very good question, considering I love you more every minute." Oddly enough, it was true. Martin couldn't believe how easily and naturally the words had come out.

Esther seemed to read his thoughts and wordlessly turned away from the mirror, her eyes boring into him. It was the only time in his life that he had felt relaxed—not uncomfortable and somehow unworthy—in such a naked, vulnerable state.

"It's the real thing." He reached for her. "Idiot that I am, I didn't realize it until a second ago."

He felt her heart palpitating as she molded herself to him. "Oh, Martin, I wish."

"So do I, but all the more reason to protect you."

"But why do you have to do it?"

"Because it's there. I wish I could do better than that, but I can't."

That was true enough. It wasn't logical to stay involved with Aka, particularly in view of the present circumstances. Yet Martin was on the roller coaster, and there was no way off until the ride was over.

"Maybe," he said, groping for the words, "I'll get it out of my system."

She didn't push him.

Stefan returned to the bedroom and handed them each a stiff waragi. "What is it to be? Another woman? No commitment forthcoming?"

"Much as the other woman scenario appeals to my vanity," Martin replied, "I think no commitment is better. Esther should be able to get in some crowd-pleasing licks about neocolonialist pigs, et cetera. What do you think, Esther?"

She downed her drink and tweaked his ear none too gently. "It is not far from the truth." She shooed them toward the bedroom door. "Now get out. I want to be beautiful tonight. Who knows? I might meet a normal man."

Martin grabbed a change of clothes and headed for the second bedroom. "Grab me a beer chaser for the shower, Stefan. I haven't done any serious acting since school."

"I am not so sure of that, Hein."

"Touché. For the proverbial bull in the china shop, you can sometimes be uncomfortably perceptive."

Stefan smiled and handed him a frosty Nile. "Having any second thoughts?"

"No. Esther asked the same thing. Nothing has changed as far as I'm concerned. I've got to walk on the razor's edge just to see if I can do it."

"It takes less to excite a lot of people."

"Fair point. I guess I'm just jaded."

"Ja, it can happen to anyone. All you need is a deprived childhood."

"Okay, okay, I surrender."

"Do not take it too seriously, Hein. I am just getting you prepared."

Stefan's zingers were making him do some uncomfortable soul-searching, but Martin wasn't coming up with satisfactory answers. There weren't any.

• • •

Stefan tried to diffuse the tension during dinner at the Arizona with a string of amusing anecdotes about his youthful black-market days, but he was playing to a dead audience. Martin found the food tasteless, and Esther was starting to emit nasty vibes. Evidently, the shock had worn off, and her true feelings were surfacing. *It isn't going to be difficult for her to act angry*, Martin thought.

Susannah's was bursting at the seams when they arrived.

"I'm trying to figure out when Esther started acting," Martin whispered to Stefan.

"Who says she is acting?"

When they finally got to the table, Martin threw back his double waragi and asked her to dance.

Esther appeared ready for the question. "I would not dance with you if you paid me, you bastard. You have used me like a

227

common market whore. You men are all the same."

Her anger was as real as her tears, and it struck Martin like a punch in the stomach. He felt his face flush as sweat ran down his back. "But, Esther, can't we talk? I'm sure you misunderstood—"

"What is there to understand?" The question hung like a physical barrier between them.

He didn't have an answer, but he sensed he'd better come up with one quickly. Her eyes were spitting fire.

"Bastard!" She threw her glass of waragi in his face, and before he could gather his wits, she launched herself across the table.

Blinded by the stinging spirits, he raised his arms in self-defense. Her attack stunned him. He was over on his back before he could get his breath. She was hysterical. He embraced her awkwardly, trying to pin her arms and minimize the damage from her razor nails. His eyes started to clear just as two of Susannah's "quality control technicians" arrived on the scene. It was all in a night's work for them. With well-oiled teamwork that bespoke a wealth of experience, they hoisted Esther by the arms and legs and adeptly worked their way through the agitated crowd toward the exit.

Martin staggered to his feet and followed. It was tough sledding, with half the crowd pouring outside to see the rest of the show. Spurred on by the fear that Esther might get hurt, he ruthlessly shoved his way through the melee, oblivious to the curses hurled in his direction. He burst through the door into the rapidly filling parking lot just as the bouncers were depositing Esther in an unceremonious heap.

As she clambered to her feet, Martin approached with his arms extended in conciliatory fashion. Enough method acting, he thought. She slid out of his reach, like a fighter working out of a tough position in the neutral corner, and circled him warily. Undeterred, he tried to get closer. She probably thought he was going to hit her. It hadn't crossed his mind.

Just when he thought he finally had her, she swung at him. It wasn't much of punch—more of a push, actually—but it was so unexpected that it penetrated his defenses.

Before Martin could launch a counterpunch, an elegantly attired mzee stepped between them. "Children, children, this is no way to solve your differences," he pleaded. "Let us discuss matters."

The offer appeared fair enough to Martin but evidently not to Esther, who launched another roundhouse. The mzee was prepared and ducked, but the wild blow glanced off his head, knocking off his homburg.

The crowd fell silent. It was eerie, Martin thought. Almost as if someone had flicked a switch.

The mzee stooped and picked up his hat. As he dusted it off, he turned to Martin. "Sah, I think you should take this woman home and give her the beating of her life."

The suggestion brought a roar of approval from the watching crowd. Summoning what dignity he had left, the mzee walked back toward the entrance.

The thought was tempting, and the crowd would have loved it. There was nothing Martin would have rather done than take Esther over his knee, spank her, and drag her home for some wild sex, but it wasn't in the script—assuming they were still operating from the same one. He was nonplussed, paralyzed by the intensity of his emotions.

Esther slumped to her knees and started to cry with gut-wrenching sobs that tore into Martin like a knife. He felt like digging a hole and burying himself. He felt helpless and inadequate in the face of her raw pain. He was oblivious to the crowd, who were streaming back inside and grumbling at being deprived of a finale.

"You two both deserve Oscars, Hein, but I think these will do you more good." Stefan reached in his pocket and handed Martin a pair of shades. "You are going to have a hell of a shiner tomorrow."

"That's not all I plan on having. Let's go back inside. I need a drink."

"It is time to go, Martin. You are never going to be able to drink enough tonight. You will just feel worse tomorrow."

Martin felt drained. He didn't resist as Stefan took him by the arm.

"Mr. Fine, I am so sorry to have witnessed your little contretemps."

Bleary-eyed as he was, Martin recognized the falsetto voice and bulbous frame of Ali Kilogo. It seemed an eternity since their meeting. He was surprised to see Bakazi right behind him.

"Perhaps she will feel differently in the morning," Colonel Zack suggested as he nodded his head in greeting. "While she is African, we must not lose sight of the fact that she is a woman first and foremost."

In his current state, Martin was in no condition to ponder the ramifications of Kilogo and Bakazi being together—and at the Big S, no less. He removed the shades for effect. "On the contrary, she gave every indication that the split was permanent."

Bakazi didn't change expression. "That is too bad, but there are many other fish in the sea. I am giving a small dinner party for the general and his staff Tuesday night. Bob Astles expressed interest in seeing you. He was most impressed with your articles." He turned to Stefan. "Perhaps you would come also, Herr Schmidt. There should be plenty of nice, accommodating mpenzis." He gave them a lewd wink and rubbed the generous rump of the lady draped over his arm.

She ran her pink tongue over her lips and gave them a leer.

Stefan straightened. "*Mein Gott*, Herr Colonel! You give an invitation that is difficult to turn down. We will be there."

Martin zoned out again, and a warm pink haze enveloped him as he staggered across the parking lot with Stefan guiding him.

Even Kilogo's hyena-like laughter faded in his ears. He was barely conscious of Stefan pouring him into the car and sticking a lit joint in his mouth.

"Oblivion is the only answer, my friend."

CHAPTER

17

MARTIN CRAWLED TO the shower the next morning. The events of the night before were a surreal haze. He kept looking at the bed, expecting to see one of Esther's breasts casually flopping over the sheet. Gradually, the reality sank in. Breakfast was out of the question. He settled for some strong tea, laced with waragi, and a handful of aspirin. It was one of those delicate hangovers. Every nerve ending in his body seemed to be made of gossamer glass that would shatter at the slightest noise or movement. He wondered if Esther felt as badly and comforted himself with the fact that she did. The crack of the screen door slamming jackknifed him partially out of his seat. The excruciating pain that resulted from the movement forced him back down. He hoped it was Stefan. He couldn't deal with anyone else.

"Gott in Himmel, you look awful. Have a Bloody Mary and a joint. The tea will not do you any good. I brought some medication. I knew that you would need it." Stefan offered a lopsided grin.

It was enough to snap Martin out of his depression. He belted down half the drink and took a deep toke. "Thanks, Doctor. How about the Lake Vic for lunch? I don't think I'm good for much but lying around in a deck chair at the moment. Reality can wait until tomorrow."

• • •

The Lake Vic was jumping, as usual. Martin caught more than a few members of the ex-pat community throwing covert glances in his direction. The Kampala rumor mill had been busy. He buried the momentary twinge of self-consciousness. They'd find something else to talk about soon enough. He'd burned his bridge. Now it was time to see what was on the other side.

Stefan selected a relatively secluded table and wandered off in search of a waiter.

Martin resigned himself to a wait of at least a half hour for food and drink and let himself drift off. He dreamt that he and Esther were drinking champagne in the bridal suite of the Ritz in Paris. It was a very real dream. He was looking at their naked reflections in the mirrored ceiling. Post-coital sweat beaded her ebony skin. He wanted to reach out and caress her shiny flank.

"Sah, please wake up, sah."

Blearily, Martin focused on the skinny teenager in front of him. "What do you want?"

The boy was one of the street urchins who normally hung out in front of the hotel peddling phony antiques, their sisters, and anything else that came to hand. "There is a man waiting for you, bwana. He is out in the gardens. He said you would know who he was from this." He tossed a rolled-up copy of *DRUM* into Martin's lap and fled two steps ahead of the fast-closing security guard.

Black briefcase. Martin scanned the crowd, looking for Stefan, but saw no sign of him. Knowing the mad Hun, he was probably out in the kitchen hustling lunch. It didn't matter. Martin rose and headed for the gardens. Surging adrenalin had magically cured his hangover.

The deal was about to go down. He believed in synchronicity. Things with Esther had come to a head right on schedule.

He fought the impulse to run, taking his time and watching the antics of the monkeys.

He found Briefcase about halfway down the lakeside path.

The heavyset African was wearing his usual grimy lace suit and looking more than a little incongruous as he tried to lure a monkey out of a nearby tree with a piece of bread. "Good afternoon, Mr. Fine." He inclined his head slightly toward Martin and nodded.

Seeing its opportunity, the monkey swooped down, bit Briefcase's hand, and grabbed the bread. Before either of them could move, it swung back into the tree, chattering hysterically.

"So like children—always biting the hand that feeds them." Briefcase frowned at the wound, which had started to bleed. "I hope you will be more reliable."

Martin handed him a handkerchief. "As long as the hand that feeds us doesn't bite. Does your associate have a date and place?"

"This weekend in Kisoro. Aka said to pretend to be tourists seeing the gorillas. There is a place called Lion Rock outside town. Your guide will know it."

"Any particular time?"

"Around midday."

"Where exactly are we to deliver the items?"

Briefcase smiled.

Martin realized it was a stupid question and answered it himself. "We'll find out later."

"My employer said that you would have certain information regarding financial arrangements." Briefcase handed him a piece of paper and pen.

Martin carefully wrote out his and Stefan's account numbers and folded the sheet neatly before handing it back. "I won't insult you by asking if you're going to burn it after you memorize them. Is there anything else?"

"Nothing but for me to wish you bonne chance." Briefcase extended his hand and almost smiled.

"Likewise. Tell your employer that we're looking forward to seeing him."

They parted in separate directions.

Martin was on a pink cloud as he walked back toward the pool. With any luck, he'd be back in Kampala enjoying a passionate reconciliation with Esther in less than two weeks. Champagne and roses—or the local equivalent—all the way.

He was so wrapped up in his fantasy that he collided head on with Stefan as he rounded the final bend to the pool.

"Ach so, the missing Amis. What was going on out there? I was worried about you. The waiter said you suddenly got up from the table and walked into the gardens. Almost like you were in a trance. The major is waiting back at the table."

"I just finished talking to Briefcase. Everything is set for Saturday. Noon in Kisoro. The major's timing is perfect. We have some serious business to discuss with the old dog."

The major noted their arrival over a corner of the *Times* sport section. With what looked like great effort, he tore himself away. "Glad to see that the Welsh have reverted to form in the rugby internationals." He took in Martin's bruised face and clucked gently. "Speaking of which, this morning's rumor has it that your lady would be useful in a scrum. I hear she packs quite a punch. By the time I got the gen this morning, she was credited with beating up both the bouncers as well as the mzungu."

"She certainly got into the spirit of things. I knew the rumor mill was good, but I'm a little surprised it traveled so far so fast. What do you hear from Kinshasa?"

The major eyed him speculatively. "Nothing specific, but they're on the lookout for something. I gather that the head of Mobutu's personal security, a certain Colonel Bagaza, has been coming down hard on some of the small-change boys recently."

"Maybe they're behind in their protection payments."

"Always possible." The major smiled. "In point of fact, *probable*. Still . . ."

"Do we have any problems?"

"Not at the moment, but I hope your associate's security is good. They obviously have an idea something's going on, and if they sweat the small fry long enough—"

Stefan shot Martin a glance. "Ja, ja, point taken, Major. Do we have a week?"

"As long as you're clean on this end." The major glanced around. "Has the balloon gone up?"

Martin nodded. "Yeah, I just got word. I think we're all right on this end. Nobody seems to be interested in what we're doing."

"Not until last night," Stefan interjected. "We ran into Bakazi outside the Big S. He made us an invitation we couldn't refuse. Dinner with his nibs this Tuesday night."

"Oh, I wouldn't worry about that one, lads. I'm going too."

Martin pretended to be relieved, but he feared a gruesome rerun of the first dinner party. "Well, that's nice to know. The good colonel gave the impression that it was going to be a semiprivate girlie party."

"No doubt it will be. The general has healthy appetites in that direction also. I've heard that he likes to demonstrate them in public from time to time."

"Just what we need," Martin said with a frown. "Still, after his exhibition at the International, not to mention his penchant for torturing and eating political prisoners, it would make for a pleasant change."

"Unless you are the recipient," Stefan said.

The major chuckled and waved his hand dismissively. "She won't mind. For God and the fatherland and all that rot. Besides, if she's lucky enough to get pregnant, she'll be taken care of for life." He rose, casting an appreciative eye at the shapely ass of a passing stewardess. "I wouldn't miss Tuesday for the world. At my age, chaps, a man begins to think back on lost opportunities."

Martin signaled for the check. "Just when I was looking forward to a dull week." He turned to Stefan. "I guess I'd better run down Singh. Where and when do we want to meet him?"

"I think we should leave ourselves open. Why not meet him outside the park? I'll look at the map and pick the nearest town."

"How long do you think it will take us to get there?"

"Six or eight hours, depending on the roads. We will have to leave Thursday afternoon and stop for the night somewhere along the way."

"We still going to take the train on to Kenya?"

"Natürlich. If everything is running smoothly, it is still safer than flying. I will book us tomorrow."

"Maybe it would be better not to book. It can't be that crowded this time of the year. In fact, it might not be such a bad idea to board it somewhere outside of Kampala."

"Ja, maybe at Jinja."

"I was thinking of someplace even smaller."

"We can also waste a lot of energy getting too cute."

"Point taken." Martin yawned and glanced at his watch. "Four already. I say we head back to Kireka and take care of the details later. I'm getting tired. It's not like I'm not going to have plenty of free evenings this week."

•••

Esther was only an hour or so from clocking out for the day at the Ministry of Internal Affairs when two GSU men in dark suits stopped in front of her desk. Neither man was Harry Usongo or his erstwhile partner, but her heart went straight to her throat just the same.

"Can I help you?" she asked in a faltering voice.

"Come with us, miss," the stouter of the two replied.

Her mind froze, but somehow her limbs carried her past her slack-jawed coworkers, out the front entrance, and into a black Mercedes waiting out front. A moment later, she found herself sandwiched between the two agents in the back seat and unable to escape the sticky plume of cologne wafting off the man to her right. And a moment after that, just as her brain began to catch up with the events unfolding, she was being ushered into Idi Amin's palatial office, where the leader was conferring with his right-hand man, the long-in-the-tooth Bob Astles.

Astles, leaning over the desk, looked up and spied Esther, and just like that, he bustled out of the office, leaving Esther alone with the Butcher of Uganda.

"Take a seat," Idi said. In his hands was a half-peeled orange.

Esther's eyes wandered from the orange to the stack of older, drying peels in the wire waste basket beside the president's desk.

"You are not the first to notice my predilection," Amin said. "I eat them all day—as many as I want. They give me potency."

"Potency?" Esther was surprised that she had found her voice.

"Masculinity. Virility. I suppose I could eat people, but I find human flesh to be too . . . salty."

Esther's mind whirred as she tried not to picture such a thing.

Amin waved away the thought. "So let us talk about your friend."

"My friend?"

"Yes, the American studenti. Martin Fine. I hear he is a budding journalist."

Esther tried to ignore the sheen of perspiration gathering on her forehead. "I am only his girlfriend." She stopped to correct herself. "His *ex*-girlfriend. He told me little of his pursuits. And now we are no more."

Amin seemed amused by her response. "Yes, I heard about your falling out. From what I gather, you made mincemeat of him before bidding him adieu. So your knowledge of him was limited to desires of the flesh?"

"I do not mean to give you the wrong impression," Esther said, squirming in her seat.

The president chuckled. "Relax. I do not care about your private life, Mapende. I want only to know about Mr. Fine." He paused to suck down another clump of orange wedges. "Tell me. Did he ever give you any lavish gifts? A diamond necklace or pair of earrings? Perhaps something more raw or uncut?"

Esther resisted the urge to laugh in Idi Amin's face. "No, My President. Martin is an American, but as far as I could tell, he is not wealthy. He is like other students in this country. He lives for the moment and without a care for his future."

"I see." Amin tossed the remains of his orange into the garbage bin, adding to the rind carcasses. "I will take your word for it. For now. In the meantime, do not speak of our little meeting today, not even to Mr. Fine, if you two are still in contact."

"We are most definitely not!" Esther immediately regretted her forced cadence. She felt as transparent as a ghost.

Amin's wicked smile vanished, replaced by an expression far more sinister. "I have eyes on you both. I can make you disappear if I wish. The same goes for your brother across the border. I would quite enjoy visiting him in one of my dungeons. Understand?"

Esther nodded involuntarily. "I do." She could barely speak.

"Good."

The return trip to the ministry sped by at the same dizzying rate. Buildings, landmarks, and passing cars and pedestrians amounted to no more than a blur. Esther's emotions ran the gamut from fear and protectiveness to anger and annoyance. She knew just enough to recognize how little she knew. What did Idi Amin want with Martin? And what was Martin up to? It seemed he had found trouble—or trouble was about to find him.

• • •

Martin was still muzzy when he walked back into the lifeless, empty bungalow. He showered mechanically and wondered what he was going to do with himself the rest of the evening. He decided to start with papers, but his mind wouldn't focus. His thoughts jumped alternately from fond memories of Esther to wild fantasies of the future. It occurred to him that he had spent very little time alone since his arrival in Kampala. The specter of being alone with his feelings was frightening.

Fortunately, Stefan barged in before Martin could slide into full-blown depression. He pretended to take Martin's pulse. "Ja, I thought so. A severe case of that dreaded mzungu affliction: jungle fever. The classic symptoms are too much thought followed by a paralysis of analysis." He lowered Martin's arm and shook his head gravely. "There is only one cure."

"What's that, Doc? Cut off my head?"

"Nein, action. I suggest we go to Sinbad's for a fiery vindaloo and follow it up with some serious barhopping."

"Okay with me, Doc. Anything beats sitting around in my own shit."

• • •

Stefan's prescription wasn't the perfect antidote, but it was better than nothing.

Martin felt almost okay as they headed home to Kireka. "It's going to be a busy week, but I think we have things in hand—as long as we don't get any nasty surprises Tuesday night."

"I do not think we will. The thing to remember is that we haven't done anything until Aka puts the stones in our hands."

"Yeah, I keep reminding myself of the fact. But it's of little comfort when I think about Astles and crew."

Stefan gave him a stern look. "You must be prepared in case things go wrong. This is not a little pot smuggling in the gentlemanly, ivy-covered walls of a university. Once we cross the line, it is for keeps. Your daddy is not going to be able to fix this one."

The thought was enough to sober Martin. "When we leave on Thursday, I'll be fully prepared."

"I hope so, Hein."

"Once my ass is on the line—and I'm under no misconceptions about that—I'll do whatever I have to. Is that good enough for you?"

"A man cannot ask for more."

· · ·

Martin immersed himself in preparations for the next two days. He resisted the temptation to skip his class on Tuesday. It wasn't the time to change his patterns. Singh was set to meet them Friday afternoon at Diranga, which didn't look like much on the map but was the only town within thirty square miles of Kisoro.

Martin's last stop was the bank, where he emptied his safe deposit box. He still had most of his grubstake. The unfamiliar tug of the money belt around his waist was uncomfortable yet comforting at the same time.

Stefan was impatiently waiting when Martin pulled up to the bungalow. He handed Martin a Cannonball and hustled him toward the shower. "Gott in Himmel, where have you been? We are due at the State House in thirty minutes."

"Errands. Lots of them. Just as well. It kept my mind off tonight. Are we picking up the major?"

"Nein, it is easier for him to take a cab. It is on Mutesa Drive in Kololo."

"I'm glad you checked."

They were en route twenty minutes later. The State House sat among several white stucco colonial monstrosities dotting Kampala's rolling hills. They always reminded Martin of bleached whale skeletons sprinkled helter-skelter on a beach by an absent-minded creator who'd taken himself off elsewhere. They had a forlorn quality. The outer shell was still there, but the substance had vanished.

A long line of Mercedes snaked outward from the rusted iron gates. Security was tight—not surprising in view of the recent spate of assassination rumors. Once they got to the guard post, the formalities were brief. The sergeant glanced at their passports, checked their names off a list, and waved them on.

"So much for small gatherings," Stefan muttered as he shunted the Renault into an impossibly small space in the jammed parking lot.

They lapsed into silence as they ran the gauntlet of an honor guard that lined the spacious verandah. Martin was impressed. The troops were clear-eyed and immaculately turned out in full field dress.

They stopped and ordered drinks at a small bar that had been set up to service the guests while they waited to pass through the receiving line.

The major arrived just as they were handed lethal highballs. "Evening, chaps. I must say, this is a civilized way to do things. I can recall attending some state functions where a man had to wait an hour to get a drink."

The long line moved quickly, and Martin barely had time to

finish half his drink before Amin and his entourage came into view. The general was crammed into an ornate white dress uniform that looked as though it had been rescued from the British Cultural Society's last Gilbert and Sullivan production. Martin expected Madame Butterfly to waltz into view at any moment. Amin, who was sweating profusely, looked more like a bedraggled fly in a glass of milk than a head of state.

The French ambassador was in line directly in front of them. As he reached Astles, equally resplendent in a full colonel's uniform, he said, "So nice to see you, Mon Colonel. I have not been able to find my seating arrangements on the plat. Perhaps there has been some error."

Before Astles could answer, Amin leaned across and answered for him. "Perhaps you should look at the menu, Mr. Ambassador."

Martin didn't know whether to laugh or cry. He made a mental effort to gather himself before it was his turn. His nibs was obviously in prime form. "Good evening, Your Excellency. It is an honor to be here."

Amin looked bilious. He muffled a belch, emitting a cloud of sickly sweet peppermint. With his beady little eyes, he scanned Martin's face. It was readily apparent that he had already forgotten they'd met more than once before.

Astles stepped in to the breach and wisely pretended this was their first meeting, lest he embarrass the general. "Excuse me, Your Excellency. This is Martin Fine, the enterprising young studenti I told you about. The one who has written all of those nice articles." He reached around the general's paunch and shook Martin's hand.

Amin looked suitably baffled but decided to speak anyway. He launched into a mini-tirade about irresponsible journalists, jerking Martin's arm up and down like a pump handle to emphasize his points and spraying everybody in the general vicinity with sweat and saliva as he worked himself into a frenzy. No one made any effort to intervene. Who could blame them? One look at Amin's eyes was enough. It was the first time in Martin's life he'd come face-to-face with insanity, and he had no idea how to react.

Suddenly, in mid-sentence, Amin stopped. He flung Martin's hand away like a troublesome candy wrapper stuck to his palm and switched smoothly back to his normal public persona. He acted as if nothing had happened, and so did everyone else.

That suited Martin, who raced through the rest of the line, a grab bag of civilian ministers and military bigwigs, and made a beeline for the bar.

The bartender poured him a heroic scotch and replenished it after Martin drained half in one convulsive gulp. "Some days he is like that, sah. You were just in the wrong place at the right time."

Martin hoped his words would not prove prophetic for the rest of the evening. Generous sips of scotch soon dulled the shock of the encounter. He scanned the crowd in the vast foyer for familiar faces. There weren't many. With the exception of a few ambassadors, it wasn't the diplomatic A list. There were far too many uniforms.

Martin sidled up to a table and was contemplating another drink when Astles materialized out of thin air and took a seat next to him.

No rest for the wicked, Martin thought. Just as well. He was going to have to talk to Bullet Bob sooner or later. He wasn't naive enough to think that he'd been invited to the party out of gratitude for a few minor newspaper pieces. "I see that you've picked up that useful African trait of appearing out of nowhere."

"I have picked up many useful things over here and plan to acquire quite a few more." Astles smiled and handed him a scotch. "I thought I'd save you the wait. I pride myself on the ability to know what people are thinking."

"What's the general thinking?"

"Like all of us, he can be a child at times—particularly when he doesn't get what he wants."

"I hope I never have anything he wants." Martin took a long pull on his scotch. "I just lost the only thing I ever really wanted. He's welcome to anything else."

"Yes, I heard about your misfortune the other night. There are other things more important in life."

"Like what?"

"Money. When you have it, women are no problem."

"I haven't exactly been bowled over by money-making opportunities since I arrived here."

"All you have to do is be in the right place at the right time. You seem to have a knack for getting to quite a few of the right places."

"Obviously not at the right time. I guess I can level with you, Bob. You seem to know everything, anyway. I come from a wealthy, influential family."

"You would not be the first black sheep who was shipped out to the colonies. Out of sight, out of mind."

Martin wondered how much Astles really knew. "You mean a little recreational drug smuggling or the odd map to a lost diamond mine? Not me. It's not my style."

"Well, keep me in mind. Your journalistic travels seem to take you to some intriguing spots."

"If something good comes along, I'll be sure to let you know, even if I'm not interested myself."

"I'm glad you see it that way. Kampala isn't always a healthy place to keep secrets." Astles rose. "Enjoy the rest of the evening. There will be a few interesting after-dinner activities."

Martin tried not to shudder. "I wouldn't miss it. I'm sure this will be an evening I tell my grandchildren about."

The major arrived hard on the heels of Bullet Bob. "I hope you two had an interesting chat."

Martin exhaled slowly. "Slightly more interesting than my one with the general. At least I was able to get in a word edgewise. The sergeant major wanted to be sure that I let him know about any interesting business opportunities that cropped up."

"I see. Did he know anything?"

"I still think he's fishing, but it appears that he's done some checking into my background."

"Hmm . . . I'll file that one for future reference."

"Don't research it too long. Time's a-wastin'. Where's Stefan?"

"Getting drinks. The line must be longer than I thought. I wondered where you two had got to. You were gone for so long I thought maybe you were worried about guilt by association. Tonight answered my questions. Amin is mad as a hatter. He will not remember a thing tomorrow."

"I'm sure he won't. Looking into his eyes was frightening. He just wasn't there. Talk about a thousand-mile stare."

The dinner gong sounded just as Stefan staggered up to the table with an armful of drinks.

"On the way in to dinner," Martin said, "you can tell me where you were."

"Talking to Colonel Zack. He wants to introduce us to some ladies."

"I wondered where he was. I just finished another interesting chat with Astles. He didn't specifically promise any ladies, though he did mention some exotic after-dinner entertainment."

"I thought the show on the receiving line was pretty good. Did he mention anything else?"

"Nothing specific."

They were seated at a table with a handful of junior officers and mid-level civil servants. It wasn't an A-list table by any means, which suited Martin, who was intent on blending as far into the background as possible. That was by no means an easy task.

Outside of Bullet Bob and the French ambassador, they were the only albinos in the woodpile.

Dinner was tedious. The speakers were as leaden as the food—a grayish mash of pounded cassava topped with a watery stew of indeterminate meat chunks floating in an oil slick. Martin contemplated the soggy mess and sipped his drink. *Shit on a shingle,* he thought. Army food was army food the world over.

The major toyed with his food before pushing it away uneaten. "Another liquid dinner, chaps. This is the real reason diplomats draw danger money. It looks like his nibs is getting ready to speak. He has to be more interesting than this lot."

The background babble died abruptly as Amin lurched to his feet. His white tunic showed ample evidence that he'd enjoyed his dinner. He started slowly enough, giving a long dissertation on the state of the economy. It was obvious after a few minutes that the subject bored him as much as the audience. After a particularly taxing, statistic-laden section on the trade balance, Amin lost patience entirely and threw the script aside.

"I haf enough of these things!" he bellowed. "Let us celebrate!"

Astles gave a signal, and the guards opened the doors that led onto the veranda. In marched a stream of comely mpenzis—some of them barely teenagers—clad only in skimpy G-strings. Waiters followed immediately with drinks, and the partying began in earnest. Martin didn't know whether to laugh or cry. No one was being eaten—at least not yet—but the lusty atmosphere was laced with male violence. The insanity tugged at him, luring him toward the seductive abyss, but he fought it off, squeezing his glass so hard that it exploded in his hand. The sharp pain and trickle of warm blood on his palm snapped him out of the trance. He had to get out of there. He rose.

The major gently pulled him back into his seat. "Give them a few minutes to get wrapped up with the mpenzis. No use making a scene."

The major's calm demeanor and icy self-control quelled Martin's rising panic. He stanched the flow of blood from his cut with his napkin and looked askance at the unfolding debauchery. Nearly everyone had gravitated toward the front of the room, where the girls were gyrating provocatively to disco music. Couples were pairing off.

"Not long now. Let me just do a quick recce and figure the most unobtrusive way out."

"Whatever it is, Major, it had better be quick." Martin gestured toward the corner exit, where a colonel, judging from his tunic, which was all he had left on, was servicing a mpenzi on a table. "The bolt holes are getting filled pretty fast."

The major rose abruptly. "Now is our chance." He drained his glass and threw it against the nearest wall. "We might as well get into the swing of things. Stick close to the wall. I think we can nip right out the main entrance. The guards look distracted enough."

He had that one right. A pair of buxom mpenzis had grabbed the guards by their belts and were dragging them unresisting toward the nearest dark corner.

Martin felt a surge of relief after they reached the deserted foyer in less than a minute.

Stefan was the last one out. "Mein Gott. Did that really just happen?"

"Frankly, old boy, I was a little worried that you might get into the swing of things. From what I've heard around town . . ."

The major's jibe punctured the tension, and they all broke into hysterics.

Bakazi, the last person they wanted to run into, stepped out from the shadows just behind them. "Leaving so soon, gentlemen? The evening is young, and things are just getting interesting."

Martin turned back toward Bakazi, who was hastily rearranging his trousers. From the look on his face, he'd finished his business.

That was about the only good thing about the situation. *Hell hath no fury like coitus interruptus.*

"Just a little tired is all," Martin finally said.

Bakazi offered a condescending smile. "Well, not everyone can keep up with the general. Like many of us, he enjoys a good party. Now, if you will excuse me, I have some pressing business inside." He gave them a half bow, clicked his heels, and did a smooth about-face.

No one spoke during the ride home.

The quiet, impeccably manicured streets of Kololo struck Martin as dreamlike after the chaos of the State House. It was like driving out the other side of a nightmare.

THE POOL DECK at the International bulged with pale white touristi plastered sluglike to their deck chairs. Instead of being repelled, Martin found them reassuring. They provided a false sense of normalcy. Although he resented their blissful ignorance, they'd paid the fare and were entitled.

As soon as he got the waiter's attention, he ordered lunch and took a dip. The laps refreshed and invigorated him. He could feel the adrenalin beginning to flow. As the finish line drew closer, the remaining obstacles seemed less significant. The condition was better known as tunnel vision—not always a bad thing.

Stefan was waiting for him at their table beneath an umbrella. "I have never seen so many touristi. If they only knew."

"I remember the last time we were here," Martin said as he toweled off. "It was the beginning of the nightmare that ended last night."

"I hope you are right."

"Are you still planning on coming back?"

"After last night, I am beginning to have my doubts. I was too young to really understand what was happening in Berlin those last weeks of the war, but last night, I started thinking about what you and the major witnessed at the last official dinner. Then I looked at what was happening right in front of me, and I kept getting mental images of myself as a six-year-old. I do not want to relive those times."

"Or see a lot of good people go down."

"That too. Particularly, when I cannot do anything about it."

Martin recognized the helplessness Stefan felt. He understood why the visit to the refugee center at Masirwa had depressed him so. He realized that he had never experienced the ultimate dehumanization that came from being just another statistic, a historical footnote, flotsam in the eddies of time. He'd always had at least the illusion of choice—and with it, a presumed identity.

The waiter arrived with their food. "Sorry I am so long, bwana." He looked around and shrugged.

"Asante rafiki. I understand." Martin gave him an extra generous tip. He knew with sad certainty that there weren't going to be many touristi in a few months.

The major sat down at their table a moment later. "Cheerio, chaps. I hope you have some for me. We've seen the last of the waiter for a while."

Stefan nodded to the feast before them. "Help yourself, Major. The high season must be upon us."

"The locals had better make the most of it."

"I was just thinking the same thing myself," Martin said. "Stefan and I were just discussing a one-way trip."

"Very wise too. If I didn't have a financial incentive in the mine, I would join you."

Martin grimaced, "I don't envy you, Major. But on to cheerier subjects. We're ready if you are."

"I am. Nothing has turned up, so I think you're good to go with the obvious caveats." The Major scared up a round of cognacs for a farewell toast.

They drank to the good life in Majorca and parts unknown, and the major bustled off.

•••

During his first pass through the parking lot, Martin spotted Legs and watched as the man scuttled inside the market. It didn't take long to find a spot. It was getting late. Nakasero was winding down for the day, and the suffocating press of humanity that characterized the mornings had dwindled. Martin meandered back toward the butcher's stalls. He drank in the sights and smells, which had become familiar and welcoming. He was going to miss them. Shopping back in the States was so cold and clinical. He loved the human contact of the market, the raucous, often obscene banter of the market mamas, and the good-natured cut and thrust of the bargaining.

Suddenly, he heard someone scream out in pain. The cry sounded almost animal in timbre, but it had just enough futile denial of the inevitable to stamp it as human. The placid market was shattered by a growing hubbub, and people started running toward Martin from the rear stalls. Panic soon set in, and a full stampede was in progress. It was useless to resist the flow. Just as Martin was turning to duck into a stall, he was shoved from the back and knocked to the ground.

He rose to his feet cursing and was astounded to see Anton and Usongo's partner racing down the aisle. They were brutally pushing their way through the terrified crowd. Whenever somebody turned to confront them, Usongo's partner waved a pistol in their face. Fighting panic, Martin stooped below stall counter. With any luck, they hadn't recognized him. In their hurry, they might not even have realized that he was a mzungu. He was trying to make sense of the whole thing. Seeing Usongo's partner alone would have been an unpleasant surprise, but seeing him with Anton was a shock.

Anton had dropped out of sight after their meeting with Kilogo. Martin had asked Stefan where he'd got to, and Stefan had replied that Anton periodically "disappeared," usually when he was involved in some scam that might or might not have government approval.

The exodus slowed to a trickle, and Martin forced his way to the rear of the market. He couldn't shake the feeling of impending doom that had descended upon him. The aisles were empty as he approached the meat section, and he broke into a dead run. Rounding the last corner, he gasped and came to a complete halt as though he'd run into a transparent wall. The sight that met his eyes literally knocked the wind from him.

Legs was lying loose-limbed on a wooden counter. Someone—and Martin had no trouble guessing who—had driven a machete right through his chest, skewering him to the scarred plywood. The wooden handle of the machete and the odd, contorted angle of the deformed legs made Legs's corpse look like a grasshopper that had been prepped for a collector's display case. Martin's breath came in great whooping gasps. Knowing he had to pull himself together, he tried to suck every last ounce of oxygen from the fetid air. The police would be arriving any minute. He dragged himself to his feet and braced himself to search the corpse. It was just possible Legs might have written down something.

Martin got another horrible shock when he leaned over the body. Legs's penis had been crudely hacked off and stuffed in his mouth like an obscene, cheap cigar. A quick search of the pockets of the tattered, blood-stained shorts revealed nothing.

Martin was turning to leave when he spotted a glint of white in the corpse's hand. He heard the approaching police and snatched the small piece of paper from the limp fist. Realizing he couldn't use the front entrance, he sprinted out the back gates. He found himself in a deserted back alley and ran until he couldn't hear the police whistles anymore. He leaned against a dingy wall to regain his breath and take stock. There was no one in sight, and he didn't think anybody had witnessed his dash from the market. He decided on the brass balls approach and worked his way back up Liberation Avenue toward where he had parked his car. Several policemen were dispersing the large crowd outside of the market.

Martin asked one what had happened.

"Kondo amekwisha." The fat cop yawned, spat, and motioned for him to move on.

In a town where thieves were regularly rolled up in dry elephant grass and burned to death, even the method of execution was unlikely to arouse much comment.

Martin didn't remember the piece of paper until he ducked into his car. It was still clenched in his fist. He carefully smoothed it out on his thigh. The job of deciphering Legs's spidery script wasn't made easier by the fact that it had been written in pencil on greasy paper. All Martin could make out was *Russ* followed by *Bag*, with the tail of the *g* clipped in mid-stroke.

They'd obviously gotten to him before he could finish. Legs had probably sensed he was being watched and had settled on a note as the only unobtrusive way of passing on the information. As it was, it didn't mean much. Russell was involved, but who was Bag? What, if anything, did they have to do with Martin?

• • •

Once back home, Martin poured himself a stiff waragi on the way to the living room.

Stefan let himself in. "Where have you been? You look like you have just seen a ghost."

254

"I have. The spirit of the recently departed Legs, whom I found neatly skewered to a butcher's stand with a panga. Lest I leave anything out, the kindly souls who did him in cut off his dick and shoved it in his mouth for good measure."

"*Scheissen*, In the middle of Nakasero?"

"In broad daylight, no less. It gets better. Guess who I saw hotfooting it from the scene of the crime?"

"I know I will not like it. Go ahead, tell me."

"Usongo's ex-partner and our old buddy Anton."

Stefan pondered the news while mixing himself a drink. "Life is never simple in this sleepy little town of ours."

"Here's one more piece of the puzzle for you." Martin handed him the paper. "This was in his hand."

"Hmm . . . Interesting. Our friend Russell. The termites certainly seem to be coming out of the woodwork."

"Yeah, he told me stuff about Russell before, so there's no way of being sure it pertained to us. But common sense tells me it did. There was no other reason for them to have been so obvious. It smacked of panic."

Stefan shrugged. "We already know they are suspicious, but do they really know anything concrete? This does not really change anything."

"There is also the possibility that they might think we're holding out on them even if we don't actually do anything."

"Ja, Bakazi seems to have a bug up his arse about something. With what is happening at the top, it would be a real mistake to count on them reacting logically."

"It's moment-of-truth time," Martin said and finished the rest of his drink. "I vote yes. I know it's irrational, but after what they did to Legs . . ."

"You would like to get the bastards. Not the smartest reason, but let us not dwell on that. We are probably fucked either way.

I say go also, but I believe that we have to modify our plans and operate on the proviso that they are now suspicious of us."

"Great. Where does that leave us?"

"In a more difficult position," Stefan said with a shake of the head, "but not an impossible one. All we have to do is sneak out of town. If we are not coming back, we only need two or three days' head start."

"With all the roadblocks these days, that's easier said than done."

"Not if we disguise ourselves and use a different car. As long as our two cars are here, they'll think we're around. How else can we go anywhere without being spotted?"

"What happens when they don't see us around our normal haunts?"

"My guess is that they are not watching us that closely while we are in town. We can both visit the doctor in the morning and tell him that we have the shits. It is a common enough ailment around here. It only has to hold until Sunday. Once we have the stones, we will be in big trouble if they look at us the wrong way. If Singh cannot get us across the Kenyan border undetected, then he is not the man I think he is."

"You're right. It's the only way to go. If things go well, we could be on a jet out of Mombasa before they figure anything out. What will we do for a car and disguises?"

Stefan sighed. "The car is easy. Padwah will rent us a Rover for the weekend if you give him enough of your dollars. As for disguises, we will buy some hair dye in the pharmacy while we get our prescriptions filled."

"Do you think just changing our hair color will be good enough?"

"For you, yes, as long as you change the style and length. A pair of glasses would help. As for me, I think I will shave my head and wear an eye patch. Remember: the disguises only have to get us out of Kampala."

Martin mulled over their options. "Okay, there's only one small problem left. After we've disguised ourselves, how are we going to get back into town? We can't drive, and a taxi might be dangerous."

"We will get Cedric to drive us in. I will concoct some yarn about jealous husbands. He probably will not believe it, but he owes me a few favors."

"A bit thin, but it'll have to do. What's on the agenda for our last night in town?"

"Nothing special. We must act like this is a normal night. Dinner at Sinbad's and a few drinks at the Lair."

. . .

Martin noticed the Peugeot about halfway into Kampala and alerted Stefan. It was just new enough to stick out.

Stefan went through a few halfhearted, half-speed evasive maneuvers—more for the purpose of confirming its intentions than ditching it. "This fellow is not too subtle but persistent enough."

"Maybe he's not trying to be subtle."

"They do not want to scare us off at this point. He is just an incompetent. I find that encouraging. It means that we are not suspicious enough to merit the A-team."

Stefan gave no turn signal as they approached the restaurant. His last-second turn caught their tail completely by surprise, and the driver had to brake violently to avoid running up their rear.

"Definitely, the B-team," Stefan said. "He will not cause us any problems. In fact, he may even help us."

The Peugeot tailed them the rest of the evening, but the driver made no attempt to follow them into any of the places they stopped.

There were times when Martin almost forgot they were being followed, but never completely. The driver's lurking presence was a constant reminder that the game had entered a new phase.

Neither of them had much stomach for a wild night, so Martin and Stefan stayed just long enough at the Lair to have a quick drink with Joe.

They finished their drinks and headed home. Their tail didn't follow them up Kireka Hill.

"I guess you're right," Martin said. "This guy doesn't seem like the real diligent sort. Poor bastard is going to have an uncomfortable night in that car."

"Nein, he will go to the nearest shebeen as soon as he has waited long enough to be sure we are asleep. What is doubly annoying is the fact that he will no doubt sleep better in his cramped car than I will in my comfortable bed."

"You too, huh? These butterflies feel suspiciously like elephants."

• • •

Martin hovered between drowsiness and fitful dozing until the sun rose. He was too keyed-up to feel tired. After showering and dressing, he took his morning tea out to the veranda and savored his last Kireka morning. The familiar sounds and timeless routines soothed his jangled nerves.

They left for town about seven.

The sight of their tail at the bottom of the hill jarred Martin back into reality. "Welcome to the real world. The son of a bitch looks fresh as a daisy."

"And why not? He probably drank a snoot full of waragi and slept with a mpenzi at government expense. No doubt he is presently congratulating himself on having pulled cushy duty."

"By Monday or Tuesday he will have changed his mind. Nothing like the Makynde Tap to knock a little sense into a fellow."

The mzungu doctor kept a posh office suite in Kololo. Besides being Amin's personal physician, he was rumored to have made a fortune from the discreet treatment of venereal disease. Martin had seen him a few times at parties around town and had come away with the impression that he was shifty and sharp.

There were no other patients waiting, so they were ushered right into the consulting room.

The not-so-good doctor bustled in shortly after. "You chaps are in bright and early. What can I do for you? A little penicillin for a small indiscretion around town, or is it a more serious matter?" His mouthwash was fighting a losing battle with the brandy fumes, and the veins in his chubby pink cheeks looked ready to burst.

Martin wasn't sure if he should let the doctor take his blood pressure, let alone give him a shot. "We should be so lucky, Doc. I'm afraid it's a boring case of dysentery."

The doctor looked disappointed as the possibility of a fat fee vanished. "Classic symptoms?"

"Ja, Herr *Doktor*. Loose stools and violent abdominal cramps." Stefan grimaced and puckered his stomach for effect.

"Yes, yes, I see. I take it you've had it before." It was obvious the doctor saw no reason to extend the proceedings.

"Natürlich. No visit to the tropics is complete without a case of it. It is not a difficult condition to diagnose, but when it does not go away in a few days . . ."

"Quite, old boy. I'll write you prescriptions for some Lomotil. That will stop a rhino at twenty paces. Perhaps you would like something for the pain too?"

Martin nodded. "Yeah, Doc, that would be appreciated. These cramps are something else. Now I think I know how a woman feels at the wrong time of the month." He winked at Stefan. They might as well enjoy themselves while they could.

Without further ado, the doctor wrote the prescriptions as well as a bill for the exorbitant sum—by Kampala standards—of sixty dollars. "Let me know if the condition doesn't clear up in the next few days." He ushered them out to the reception room. "You can pay the receptionist with cash or a check."

Martin shook his head as they left the clinic and stepped outside into the morning sun. "What a racket."

"Ja, I think I chose the wrong profession."

• • •

They finished their errands and were back at Kireka by nine, the sun still perched in the eastern sky.

Stefan inspected the barber's shears he'd acquired at the market.

From where Martin sat, they didn't look like the latest design but appeared serviceable.

"You will be glad to hear I had them sharpened. Who is first?"

"You are. You don't have that much hair to take off, and you've got to call Cedric and arrange a lift into town." Martin took the shears. "The last time I used these was on sheep in Mexico. I hope I haven't lost my touch."

"Just remember: I get a shot at you too."

It took Martin only a few minutes to complete the job. The change in appearance was startling. Each of Stefan's features stood out in stark relief, like pieces haphazardly stuck on a child's Mr. Potato Head toy. The effect was heightened by the whiteness of the newly shaved area.

The thought made Martin giggle. "My, my, Herr Schmidt, what big ears you have! I'll say this much for the look: It's different. You'll have to put some instant tan on the shaved part."

Stefan looked at himself in the mirror. "Ja, I look like a genie from *The Arabian Nights*. Is it not so? Maybe I should get a brass earring to complete the look."

Martin sat down, adjusted the sheet around his shoulders, and closed his eyes. He was determined not to look until the operation was over.

"You now resemble a recruiting poster for the Vietnam War," Stefan said as soon as he was finished.

The change in Martin's appearance was subtler than Stefan's. He still had enough hair left to soften his features, but he looked at least ten years younger. "I don't look that different."

"Nein, not as different as I do, but when you have dyed it, it will be enough. You do not have to fool your mother." Stefan handed him the tube of Clairol. "Get on with it. I will go visit Cedric."

"What are you going to tell him? He's going to know something's up when he sees us."

"I will think of something on the way up there. He is not that naive, so it will have to be reasonable. Probably something to the effect that we have offended the wrong people and have to leave town fast. Not far from the truth, actually."

Martin showered and dyed what was left of his hair. The inky black dye made quite a difference. His new look might not fool his mother, he thought as he stared at himself in the bathroom mirror, but just about anybody else would have difficulty spotting him.

Stefan returned a few minutes later with a bedraggled Cedric in tow.

Cedric looked aghast. "You too, dearie? This is more than I can take at this time of the morning. Get me some coffee, Stefan. I hope you realize I wouldn't do this for just anyone. You dragged me away from that divine little Italian charge. I've had my eyes on him for months."

Stefan handed him a steaming mug. "By the time you finish this, we will be ready. You will be back before he even notices you are gone. We would not ask unless it was an emergency."

"What did you do, for heaven's sake? Steal Bakazi's mistress? I always told you that your wandering penis would get you in trouble."

Stefan shook his head. "You do not want to know, Cedric. In fact, you do not know anything, and that is for your sake as much as ours."

"It all sounds frightfully Byzantine to me. What about Reuben and Isador? It's a bit rummy to leave them in the lurch."

Martin had completely forgotten about them on their day off. They'd been honest and faithful, and jobs were hard to find around Kampala. He peeled off several hundreds and handed them to Cedric. "Here's their severance pay. I'll be ready in a few minutes."

He trotted up the hill and started to pack. It took him less than five minutes to fill Bertain's Samsonite bag with the necessities. There was no point in being bogged down with a lot of stuff, but he had to have enough to look like a legitimate touristi.

On the way out, he stopped in the kitchen and threw in two bottles of waragi, the transistor radio, and the flashlight. Pausing for a moment, he took one last look around the bungalow. He wasn't sentimental by nature, but he felt a pang. There'd been some good times.

The impatient toot of a car horn tore him away.

CHAPTER

19

MARTIN THREW HIS bag into the trunk of Cedric's Austin and scrunched himself down in the back seat beside Stefan.

"Is all this cloak-and-dagger stuff necessary?" Cedric asked.

"Ja," Stefan answered with a frown. "There is a fellow in a Peugeot at the bottom of the hill who has been following us since yesterday."

"I see. Where to, dears?"

"Padwah's."

It was hot and cramped in the back of the car. The full reality of what they were doing finally hit Martin during the interminable, jolting ride down the hill. From now on, there could be no relaxing. Adrenalin surged through him, and his pulse skyrocketed as they approached the bottom of the hill. Paranoid fantasies raced through his mind. What were they going to do if the tail followed Cedric? What if Anton or Usongo's partner spotted them in town and arrested them?

"You may sit up now, dears," Cedric said in a reassuring voice. "Your friend in the government Peugeot was fast asleep. I'm using all my self-control not to ask you what's really going on."

"It is best that you don't know," Stefan said. "Take our word for it."

Martin slid up to a normal sitting position and toweled off with his handkerchief. The ride into town seemed to last forever. He chain-smoked and looked over his shoulder constantly, but he couldn't detect any other suspicious-looking cars. Every time they passed a soldier or policeman, he had to suppress the impulse to duck. He concentrated on regulating his breathing as they drove into the town center. It was time to pull himself together. He forced himself to look at every policeman they passed. None gave him a second glance. By the time they drove into Padwah's parking lot, he had regained his nerve.

"Well, it's certainly been interesting. I think I'll take myself off smartly, lest anyone see me with you naughty types. Do drop me a line sometime." Cedric blew them a kiss and departed.

"We're on our own now," Martin said as Cedric drove off. "I just hope Padwah doesn't get too suspicious."

"Of course, he will," Stefan replied. "He was born that way. Just lay the bills on his desk, and he will not ask any awkward questions. I suspect the rent will be a little higher than normal, though."

• • •

Esther felt like her head was on a swivel as she sat in the back of the taxi. To her great relief, no one followed her past the sleepy villages or up the steep, zigzagging hill to Martin's bungalow.

"I will only be a moment," she told the driver before stepping out into the blazing sun.

The clearing felt lonely. Woodland warblers called to one another from the surrounding trees, and a warm breeze rustled the tall grass at the wood's edge.

Esther skipped up to the French doors and was disappointed to see no signs of life. The place was as empty as her heart.

Where are you?

Against her better judgment, she had gone to see Martin. The risk that a government stooge might tail her seemed to pale in comparison to Martin remaining unaware that Idi Amin had taken a keen interest in him. With a hand placed above her squinting eyes, she pressed her face against a door pane and peered inside, her eyes lingering on the living room she had cleaned and tidied not so long ago to give the place a woman's touch.

"He's not home," someone behind her said in an airy British accent.

Esther whirled around to see a slight mzungu dressed in baggy shorts and a Hawaiian shirt. "You must be Cedric."

"And you must be Esther." Cedric offered a hand. "I can't believe we've never met." He glanced at the taxi waiting in the drive. "You've gone to great expense. I'm sorry Martin isn't home."

"What about Stefan?"

"He's gone too."

"Do you know where they are?"

Cedric rolled his eyes heavenward before answering. "They've left me in the dark, dearie, and I much prefer it that way."

Esther let her shoulders sag in disappointment.

Cedric studied her face. "You look positively crestfallen. Why don't you join me for a drink on my patio? I'll whip up something to refresh you."

As tempted as she was, Esther knew better than to linger. "I appreciate your hospitality, but I cannot stay. I should not have come at all."

Cedric wrapped an arm around her shoulder and walked her back to the taxi. "I understand, dearie. Give me a way to reach you, and I'll let you know the moment your man returns."

Esther felt her heart swell. It was good to know that Cedric would be watching for Martin. Even better to hear someone refer to Martin as her man.

• • •

The fee turned out to be exorbitant by any standard—yet cheap, considering the fact that Padwah didn't ask any questions. Martin felt relieved that the smarmy salesman didn't recognize either of them until they produced their passports. The only hitch in the whole operation was that the Rover was being serviced and wouldn't be ready for half an hour. It was an unforeseen delay but not a disaster.

"We might as well do something useful with the time," Stefan suggested as they exited Padwah's office. "We need some supplies for the drive. The less we have to stop, the better."

"Good idea. Why don't you get some beer and sambosas? I'm going down the road to buy some cigarettes. At the rate I'm going through them, my supply won't last the day."

"You and your Dunhills. They will be the death of you yet, Hein. Why not smoke a normal local brand? Something cheap and easy to get."

"Because they taste like sawdust soaked in cat piss."

They departed in different directions.

Martin knew of an Indian store a few blocks away on Zambia Avenue that stocked Dunhills. Imported cigarettes were sometimes difficult to find in Kampala. Not even the tourist hotels had a reliable supply. Vedha Krishna, the oily proprietor of the Taj Mahal Smoke Shop, had never let Martin down. The streets were bustling, and Martin let himself be carried along by the impersonal flow. Nobody gave him a second glance, and he began to relax into his new persona. The feeling that he was wearing a mask gradually left him.

The Taj Mahal Smoke Shop was a vomit-yellow wooden shack that clung like a crapulous pimple to a moldering adobe structure that had probably been a warehouse in its colonial heyday.

The two-story building had not aged well and had settled unevenly on its foundation. It had the warped, teetering look of a house of cards about to collapse. Some enterprising Indian had subdivided it into a warren that housed a variety of itinerant merchants.

Krishna greeted Martin effusively, even though he didn't appear to recognize him. Like most of his counterparts, he could smell the dollars in the mzungu nana's pocket. "What can I do for you, bwana? Perhaps some of the fine local cigars or some Marlboros. They are very fresh. I just got them yesterday."

"Do you have Dunhill Internationals?"

"Yes, yes. I have some."

"Good. I will take all you have."

Krishna's face darkened momentarily. "I have ten packs, bwana, but they are very expensive—twenty shilingi a pack. Perhaps I can interest you in taking half of another variety. I have a very good customer who would be offended if I did not have a supply for him."

Martin extended two twenty-dollar bills and winked. "He won't mind. He's a personal friend of mine. In fact, he sent me here."

The two bills disappeared instantly, and Martin thought he detected a flash of recognition followed by fear in Krishna's eyes as he shoveled the cigarettes into a wrinkled brown paper bag.

Just as Martin took the bag, he felt something hard and cold pressed against his back.

"Do not move, Mr. Fine. The leopard may be able to change his spots but not his voice or the brand of cigarettes he smokes."

The sibilant hiss was familiar, but Martin was too terrified to place it. If there had been any food in his stomach, he would have shit himself. "Just a minute. You have the wrong fellow. My name is—"

"Do not waste any more of your or my valuable time, Mr. Fine."

The man jammed his gun into Martin's kidney, prodding him outside and along the sidewalk.

It was the first time Martin had ever had a gun pressed into his back, and there wasn't much to be said for the experience.

"Your time is particularly valuable because you may not have much left," the man continued, "unless you answer my questions truthfully. We will take a walk to a nice, quiet place. On the way, I will tell you the story of how I was walking down the street one day when I saw a mzungu who looked familiar. His face looked different, but there was something about his walk. Then he stopped, and I heard him speak. I knew I had caught my leopard."

"That's a nice story, Mr.—"

"Kalega. You do not know me by name, but you do now. I am a friend of Harry Usongo."

"But you have the wrong man. I'll be glad to show you my passport." Martin groped for his pocket with his free hand. A handful of change at close quarters might prove quite effective.

The jab to the kidneys was so hard that it made him stumble.

"After what Harry told me, I expected better from you, Mr. Fine. I am not an amateur like that incompetent in the Peugeot. My superiors turned me down when I asked to follow you. They were suspicious, but I was sure you were up to something when I saw you in Nakasero."

Martin grimaced. "Your handiwork was effective, if not subtle. The penis in the mouth was a particularly nice touch."

"He was scum, a piece of shit floating in the gutter. It was a pleasure to silence him."

"I wouldn't have thought a man in his position would have been much of a threat."

"He was the beggar king. His network was extensive. He had much to sell and an interesting list of clients, including the Americans, Russians, Israelis, and Zairians, among others."

Martin was shocked. He hadn't known that old Legs had possessed that kind of clout.

They were approaching the end of Zambia Avenue, and the commercial traffic was thinning out. Any onlookers who noticed the gun in Martin's back gave no indication of it.

Kalega forced him several more blocks down a steep hill. The man had chosen his spot well. All of the surrounding buildings were derelict, and there wasn't a soul in sight. He turned Martin into a deserted, malodorous alley that snaked behind a large government warehouse at the end of the broad street.

They slalomed around the steaming piles of garbage that had been haphazardly slung alongside the open sewer that bisected the alley. Labrador-sized rats brazenly darted across their path.

As they approached the end of the cul-de-sac, Kalega gave Martin a violent shove, slamming him into the concrete wall of the warehouse. "Now, Mr. Fine. Please do not waste my time with lies or I will shoot you and leave you here for the rats. Even though they are well fed in these parts, I hear that they find human flesh a special delicacy. Our experiments out at Makynde have shown that they like to start with the sexual organs. Now you will tell me exactly what enterprise you have embarked on."

Martin was stunned by the violent impact with the wall. "Like I told everyone else, I'm just a journalist. I even wrote a few pieces for Astles." It was his only card, and he had to play it. Kalega and parties unknown—if there were any—were freelancing. Otherwise, he would have been taken in for questioning. There was a chance Kalega might be frightened off by the mention of Astles.

The metallic click of Kalega cocking his pistol echoed off the dank walls. "The next wrong answer will get you shot in the leg. Please believe me when I tell you that a stray shot will arouse no undue curiosity in this neighborhood. Perhaps a little information might help your memory. The Zairians have let us know that they are worried that a large shipment of contraband diamonds is about to be smuggled out of Shaba."

"It happens all the time."

The crack of the pistol and the flash of searing pain on the outside of Martin's calf were simultaneous.

"I warned you." Kalega's tone was conversational. Terrifyingly, he betrayed no trace of anger in his voice.

Martin felt like a caged mouse stuck in a Pavlovian experiment. If he nudged the wrong button, he would be zapped. No appeals to human logic were possible.

"It *does* happen all the time," Kalega said, "and they are usually brought out through Uganda. More often than not, we get word from our informers either before or after the fact. This time, we have heard nothing. That tells me that the smugglers must be using an entirely different channel. It then comes to my attention that mzungus have visited Kigali within a fortnight. No normal touristi would go to Kigali when the Hutu and Tutsi are slaughtering each other."

It wouldn't hold up in a court, Martin thought, but it was more than adequate to hang him in the present circumstances. He prayed for a distraction—anything he could capitalize on. Talking wasn't going to do him any good. He gingerly shifted his weight onto the wounded calf. It felt sound. As far as he could tell, there wasn't any bleeding. The bullet had just grazed him. He slowly turned to face the man. "Can we make a deal?"

Kalega offered the hint of a smile. "But of course, Mr. Fine. The only one possible under the circumstances. Your life for the diamonds. Where are they?"

"We haven't picked them up yet."

"Where and when?"

"How do I know you'll carry out your side of the bargain?"

Kalega trained the beady eye of his pistol on Martin's chest. "Do you really have a choice?"

"I guess not."

What a godawful place to die, Martin thought. *The veritable shithole of the universe.* He wondered what death was going to feel like. Outside the alley, a large truck shifted down, its revving engine straining to climb the steep hill.

Kalega impatiently signaled him to continue.

"We're supposed to meet at—"

The truck backfired suddenly, drowning out the rest of Martin's words, and the reverberations echoed up the alley, bouncing hollowly off the walls. Kalega was good but not perfect. He turned his head, and Martin leapt, leveling him with a crude but effective cross-body block. The impact knocked the pistol across the slimy pavement.

Martin scrambled over Kalega and dove for it. Just as his fingers grasped the butt, the African leapt on his back and enfolded the gun and Martin's hand in a vise grip. It was an unfair contest from the word go, and Martin knew it. The pistol was curving inexorably back toward his chest, and Kalega's finger was crushing his against the trigger. Desperate, Martin rose to his knees and with a convulsive effort flipped himself onto his back, hoping the impact would loosen the African's grip.

No such luck. Kalega grunted in his ear as their intertwined arms shook. Martin was able to stem the tide for a few seconds, but he was weakening. There was only one chance. He had to suddenly stop all resistance and pray that Kalega's pressure would carry him too far. It was a risky strategy. If he pulled the trigger too soon, he would do the African's work for him.

His arm weakened, and he let go. The deafening report of the pistol cut short Kalega's cry of triumph. He gurgled, shook convulsively, and fell limp.

Something warm and wet spurted against Martin's neck as he rolled off the body. A bright plume of arterial blood was geysering from Kalega's neck.

Martin staggered drunkenly to his feet. His ears were ringing as if someone had clapped giant cymbals over his head. Like an automaton, he grasped the corpse's leg, dragged it over to a pile of garbage, and kicked enough trash over it to conceal it from all but a thorough search. All but oblivious to his blood-stained shirt and the pistol in his hand, he leaned down, picked up the bag of cigarettes, and stumbled out of the alley. He trotted back up Zambia Avenue.

Martin saw no one until he reached the top of the hill, where he passed an African woman. She took one look at him, screamed, and ran for cover. He came to his senses and realized that he still had the gun in his hand. Looking around, he spotted a derelict building and plunged inside. He hastily buried the pistol and his bloody shirt in a towering pile of rubble and dashed outside.

He had to get to Stefan and the car immediately. As soon as the African woman overcame her fear, she was going to scream for the cops. He ran flat out up the street. It was no use trying to be inconspicuous. There just weren't enough shirtless mzungus in the neighborhood.

The police whistles sounded before he'd gone two blocks. They were behind him but gaining fast. It was only a matter of time before they blocked off the road in front of him. He panted for air as he veered off into an alley. So far, outside of giving him startled glances, none of the locals he had passed had made any attempt to stop him. He was in luck. The alley led to Liberation Avenue, but he had to stop for a moment to get his bearings. He wasn't sure which direction to take to return to Padwah's. It was a mistake. The whistles sounded again.

Praying he was right, he turned to the left and started running again. If he didn't spot Padwah's soon, he was fucked. He could hear the pounding of the pursuers' boots on the pavement.

Just as he rounded a sharp bend in the road, salvation appeared in the form of a huge mob gathered in front of a shopping arcade. It might not have been a full-scale riot, but it was just what the doctor ordered. Without hesitation, Martin plunged into it, blasting a path for himself with his arms and shoulders. The melee extended for at least four blocks. It was hard going but a piece of cake compared to the New York subway at rush hour.

He gasped with relief as he burst out the other side and saw Stefan waiting in the Rover. The police were nowhere in sight. He dove in the back seat and told Stefan to hit it.

Stefan gunned the motor and laid rubber. "What the fuck happened to you?"

"Are there any cops in sight?"

"Nein." Stefan made a few quick evasive turns and slowed to a normal pace. "We are clean as a whistle and headed for Entebbe Road." He rummaged through his knapsack with his spare hand and tossed a bottle of waragi over the seat. "Take some of this to calm yourself, and tell me exactly what happened."

The waragi helped. "You were right. The cigarettes almost were the death of me." Martin lit a Dunhill and told the story.

"Gott in Himmel, you killed him."

"Jesus, Stefan. It was hardly a cold-blooded execution. I didn't have a choice."

"Ja, ja, I am sorry. It was a stupid question. Scheissen, we are really in it now."

"Not necessarily. I buried the body pretty well, and nobody heard the shots. It was in a derelict neighborhood. There wasn't anyone within blocks. I wouldn't even have been spotted if I hadn't had a gun in my hand and blood on my shirt. I was in such shock that I just staggered out of the alley and started running. I'd gone several blocks before that woman spotted me."

Martin took another swig and passed the bottle back over the seat. He searched through his duffel for another shirt and put it on before climbing into the front seat. "With any luck, they'll be looking for a crazy mzungu with gun. I doubt they'll even have a good description. We look just as similar to them as they do to us."

"Especially with a gun," Stefan said. "It is difficult to notice anything else. What about the police?"

"They didn't see anything but my back, thank God. It was nip and tuck, though. If that riot hadn't suddenly sprung up . . . What the hell was going on?"

Stefan burst into laughter. "Sorry, the overall situation is not so funny, but you will no doubt see the point. You were saved by two sex-starved Africans."

"You're shitting me."

"Not at all. It seems these two Africans who worked as clerks in a shop had become highly enamored of one another. Since the Indian proprietor sleeps late and rarely appears in the morning, they had gotten in the habit of using the shop and taking an amorous coffee break behind the closed curtains. The proprietor decided to pay a surprise visit this morning. When he arrived, he was incensed to find his store locked—and even more furious when he saw the couple copulating in the window. He ripped open the curtains, exposing them to public view. They were so shocked that they became stuck. The condition occurs more frequently in dogs. I believe the medical term is *penis captivi*. The rest is history."

Martin laughed until tears ran down his cheeks. It was a cleansing laughter, releasing all his pent-up horror and shock. "The good Lord sure does work in mysterious ways sometimes. Mercy me, I guess it would really be funny if I hadn't just killed a guy." He felt the laughter in his gut dissipate. "Did you ever kill anyone?"

"Ja, once in Berlin. I was a lot younger than you, though the circumstances were quite similar. He tried to double-cross me on a black-market deal. I stabbed him with a bayonet." Stefan abruptly looked away.

"Thanks for telling me. For some reason, it makes me feel better."

"I thought it might. That is why I told you. You are the first person I have ever told."

Martin felt closer to Stefan than before. It was the first time the German had ever pulled back the shutters and allowed Martin a glimpse of his real self. *Nothing like a little bit of murder to cement a friendship*, he thought ruefully. Before he could explore the thought further, he fell into a deep sleep.

• • •

The sun hung low in the sky when Martin woke up. He felt disorientated and ravenously hungry.

They were driving along a deserted road through arid, hilly countryside.

"Jesus. I feel like I've been asleep forever. Where are we?"

"Just past Mbarara, heading southwest toward Kisoro." Stefan pulled off the road and killed the engine. "Time for a pit stop. Have something to eat, and take the wheel. I am tired."

Martin glanced at his watch as he urinated. It was four-thirty. He felt guilty for sleeping so long. "You should have woken me sooner." He opened a tepid Nile and wolfed down a sambosa. "You made good time. Any problems?"

"Nein, all is in order. There was one roadblock, but the soldiers waved the car through as soon as they saw it was mzungus. I stopped for petrol just before Mbarara, and I had the spare cans filled. The car is running fine."

"Where do you want to stop for the night?"

Stefan spread the map out on the hood. "As near as I can figure it, another two hours or so will see us up and over the Mountains of the Moon. If we camp just the other side of them, we will only have about a three-hour drive in the morning."

With that settled, the two switched positions, with Martin taking the steering wheel.

"I'm ready," Martin said before gunning the engine and pulling back onto the road.

Stefan studied him for a moment. "It is good to see that the events of the morning have not robbed you of your sense of humor."

Martin sighed. "It's not going to be easy living with what I did, but at the moment, I've got more important fish to fry. I'm sure I'm going to have nightmares for a long time."

"They will pass quicker than you think. This morning could be a blessing in a way. It burned our bridges."

Too true, Martin thought. He settled into driving and tried to picture their destination. The Mountains of the Moon were a spur that jutted westward from the main north-south axis of the Ruwenzori Range. They were unique, a geological throwback to the dawn of creation. He had read that NASA had at one time contemplated sending the astronauts to them to train for lunar missions.

The terrain grew more forbidding as they climbed higher into the foothills. The vegetation petered out into a vast lava bed pocked with mini-calderas. Here and there jagged pinnacles of granite poked defiant fingers through the uniform gray covering. A damp mist permeated the air, accentuating the unworldly, alien atmosphere. Martin felt an eerie sensation of being disconnected. It was more than just being cut off from civilization in the twen- tieth-century sense. It was almost as though he were on the edge of some spectral void, a metaphysical black hole that threatened to suck the humanity from him.

Stefan shivered and rummaged through his bag for a sweater.

"Me too," Martin said, "but it's more than the temperature. This place has some heavy vibrations."

"I am glad you said that. I thought it was just me."

This must be what space is like, Martin mused. *A sensation of total detachment.* There was a certain clarity of thought available when the psyche was unfettered by the cluttered jumble of human emotions. It was only possible in a vacuum. Very few men were ready for it, Martin thought. He surely wasn't. To experience it was to be consumed. He needed the comfort of worldly imperfections. They were something to hold on to, a part of his identity. He understood why the ancients had made such places taboo.

They crossed the snow line some thirty miles later. It was difficult to believe that they were in equatorial Africa. Martin pulled off the side of the road when they reached the peak of Mount Ruwenzori. The view was mind-boggling. To the west, the mountains sloped downward into Ituri Forest, the rainforest that blanketed the upper third of the Congo. Only the occasional silver glimmer of a lake or river interrupted the vast green carpet that extended as far as the eye could see. Pivoting slowly, Martin took in the dull-brown lowlands of Tanzania to the south and the dry plains of Kenya to the east. Their bleached pallor accentuated the incandescence of Lake Victoria.

"I make it four or five different countries." Stefan picked up a handful of snow and threw it over the precipice. "Maybe the view from Kilimanjaro is as good, but it cannot be better."

"Yeah, it's pretty overwhelming. I almost expect the devil to hop out at any minute and make me an offer I can't refuse."

"He already has."

Martin shivered. The moment gone, he strolled back to the car and took a swig of waragi, returning to the present with a vengeance. Sometimes he resented Stefan's knack for bringing him down with a thud—no doubt because he needed it.

They completed their descent at dusk, and Martin began searching for a place to stop for the night. He was drained and ready to collapse when he spotted some fields of sorghum and millet up ahead. *Nirvana!* Crops meant civilization, maybe even something to eat.

They reached the village a few minutes later. It wasn't much to look at—just a handful of tattered huts surrounded by a sagging thorn-and-raffia fence.

Martin hadn't seen any people as they approached, but at least there were a few scrawny chickens and bony goats foraging outside the compound. He pulled off the road, killed the engine, and sighed with relief. "Wake up, Stefan. We've arrived. It's not the International, but it's home for the night."

A few curious Africans peeked tentatively through holes in the fence as they unpacked.

"They do not seem overjoyed to see us," Stefan observed as he shook out his sleeping bag.

"I doubt they are. As far as they're concerned, anyone crazy enough to stop in this neck of the woods probably means trouble. Who knows? They may never have seen mzungus before. I suggest we go in and palaver with the chief."

• • •

Half an hour later, they'd successfully negotiated a hot dinner of chicken and matoke as well as a supply of water for bucket baths. As Martin had suspected, the inhabitants of the village proved accommodating enough after they had satisfied themselves that their visitors were not connected with the government.

After they'd washed and eaten, Martin and Stefan unrolled their sleeping bags near the cooking fire in the center of the village. They sat listening to the village wind down for the night. Martin found the ageless routine soothing and clung to the tenuous thread of normalcy.

CHAPTER

20

THEY WERE UP and on the road by seven o'clock the next morning.

Martin had slept dreamlessly and felt refreshed and ready to face the day. He had consigned the events of the previous day to a dark, subterranean place in his psyche. There was little traffic on the road. Only as they approached Bilarba did he see any signs of civilization. "Do you think Singh will be on time?"

Stefan glanced at his watch. "Probably. We should be there by ten. It is my guess that we will find him sleeping in the Rover somewhere not far from the main square."

"I don't think we should hang around town too long."

"Ja, no longer than it takes to find him. What are we going to tell him?"

"The best bet is the truth or a reasonable facsimile thereof. He could probably use a few diamonds to pad his retirement fund."

"Natürlich. We will not be the first people he has smuggled across the border, I am sure."

In spite of its status as the administrative center for the surrounding area, Bilarba was a sleepy place. Martin figured its population couldn't be more than a thousand. The main road ran right through the center of town.

Stefan turned down the first street after the market. "I suggest we cruise around for a bit. We will attract less attention that way."

Martin couldn't argue with that. He doubted that touristi stopped in Bilarba all that often. So far, they hadn't seen any police or soldiers, but it would be just as well to avoid them. Any they encountered would be sure to remember seeing mzungu bwanas. They might even question them out of curiosity or boredom.

They found Singh on a side street behind the local branch of the Uganda Bank. He was palavering with a street vendor. Stefan pulled to a halt opposite them and killed the engine. It was evident that the Indian didn't recognize them at first. He gave them only a quick glance before returning to his conversation. Slowly, recognition seemed to dawn on him.

Martin could see him fight the temptation to look back around. *Sly old coot*, he thought. Somehow Singh had picked up on the situation immediately. *What does he want us to do? If we sit around any longer, it will be obvious.*

As if reading his mind, Singh reached around his back as though he wanted to scratch an annoying itch and signaled them to head up the street and take their first right.

Picking up on the charade, Martin consulted the map and gestured up the street.

They spotted Singh's Rover as they turned the corner.

Stefan pulled up behind it. "There are no flies on that one. He was quick on the uptake for an old codger. I bet you he is already figuring his price."

"No bet. I think we're pushing our luck if we hang around much longer." Martin looked anxiously back up the street and spotted Singh. "Here he comes. Let's give him some money and tell him to get some supplies. We can meet him outside of town."

Martin told Singh they had decided to camp out and gave him a list of supplies and some money.

The gnarled Sikh's eyes twinkled as he told Martin to wait at an abandoned petrol station about five miles outside of town, but he didn't ask any questions.

Thirty minutes later, Singh joined them behind the station.

Over a hasty lunch of bhajias and beer, Martin gave him a discreetly edited version of the situation. Using sign language and kitchen Swahili helped the process.

Singh's eyes took on a larcenous gleam. He asked for their map and pointed to a spot on the Ugandan-Kenyan border not far from Tororo. "*Hapanna askari polizei, ni Kenya, pi Uganda.*" He gave them a thumbs-up and pointed to the Samsonites in the back of their Rover. "*Una beba nini, diamanti?*"

Martin pointed at Singh and pantomimed giving him a handful of diamonds.

"*Sau sau, bwanamkubwa.*" A vast grin split Singh's leathery face, revealing a toothless expanse of foam-rubber-yellow gum. He resembled a basketball with its bladder protruding from a ruptured seam.

"He's probably dreaming of new dentures," Martin said. "Let's make tracks."

The road began to climb steeply through foothills, and Stefan had to slow down substantially. The lush green hills were shrouded in mist. Martin could almost visualize the big apes swinging effortlessly through the trees. The road corkscrewed through the forested mountains. The temperature seemed to have dropped twenty degrees since Bilarba. Martin was glad that he had brought along warm clothes.

Stefan groaned in mock horror and pointed out his window at the tangled mass of lianas and bamboo thickets that covered the mist-shrouded hills. "So this is what we are going to have to hack our way through."

"It looks like rough enough country. I take it we're still planning to trek the gorilla."

"Why not? We still have a day and a half to kill. I am sure Singh can fix it so we do not see anyone that would get suspicious."

Martin turned to Singh. "I suppose you just happen to know a good guide too. You're good, but these mountains look like work."

Singh nodded. "*Sana sawa.* Zaccariah Missouri, sana." He mimed looking for gorillas.

"That answers that."

They entered Kisoro—what there was of it—at eight. The town consisted of about twenty stucco-and-wattle buildings. The largest appeared to house the police station and post office. There were no stores or bars. Judging from the concrete booths, the muddy square in the middle of town doubled as the market.

Stefan followed Singh's instructions and turned down an impossibly rutted track that forked right off the main road.

"Does this Zaccariah speak any English?" Martin asked.

Singh nodded. "A panna English."

"Don't worry," Stefan said. "I can translate what is necessary. I am sure Zaccariah's sign language is adequate. He makes a living taking tourists around."

Zaccariah's camp was a sprawling compound of ramshackle mud-and-wattle huts situated at the foot of a massive volcanic spur. A wizened mzee—Zaccariah, presumably—and two teenagers came to the gate at their approach. Singh greeted Zaccariah like a long-lost brother. After a long chat, he checked their equipment. He pronounced it in order, and they set off.

The first part was relatively easy. The going wasn't too steep, and they were able to pick their way around the worst of the lava beds. The morning had dawned clear, but by the time they had climbed halfway up the lava flows, the sun was completely obscured behind a dense ground mist. Martin didn't mind. He was already sweating rivers.

The going got much more difficult after they hit the rain forest. Although the two boys hacked assiduously with their pangas, dank hanging lianas slapped them constantly in the face. Martin lost track of how many times he was stung by nettles and thorns. One or the other of his legs constantly slid through gaps in the dense mat of rotting bamboo and other vegetation into deep muddy holes. By the time Zaccariah called the first rest stop, Martin was drenched in sweat and thoroughly winded.

Zaccariah calmly lit a pipe of banjii and surveyed the mountains above through a battered pair of Zeiss binoculars.

"Stefan, this isn't any Sunday stroll through the botanical gardens." Martin felt something crawling up his leg and pulled up his pants. Blood-gorged leeches were puckered up on his inner thighs. "That just makes my day." He lit a cigarette. Removing leeches by burning them off with a lit cigarette was one of the few cases where the movie tough guys actually did the sensible thing, but it required extremely steady hands. By the time he finished the ticklish surgery on both his legs, he had a pile of close to a dozen leeches at his feet.

Stefan was similarly encumbered.

Zaccariah looked down from his binoculars and smiled at the pile of leeches. He handed Martin the binoculars, directing him at a spot about two hundred yards up the mountain.

Squinting, Martin could just make out a crude bamboo nest about eight feet above the forest floor. There weren't any signs of life around it, but it was a start.

Zaccariah confirmed it by signing no further smoking.

Seeing the nest gave them a new lease on life, and they hacked their way up to it in short order. The clearing around the nest was dotted with droppings, but Zaccariah didn't appear excited. Even to Martin's untrained eye, they looked old and dry. They passed more nests in the general area, and it was obvious from the ravaged bamboo thickets that gorillas had fed there recently.

They broke for lunch about midday.

Martin rolled up his pants legs and started surgery again. "At least we know they exist." He burned a particularly plump specimen off his ankle. "Too bad they don't eat these buggers. Did you know that the average adult gorilla consumes about three hundred pounds of fodder a day?"

Stefan compared a leech from his thigh to one of Martin's. "That is fine for them, but personally, I am too tired to eat a gram."

They spotted several tantalizing signs of the gorillas during the afternoon but enjoyed no sightings.

Zaccariah called a halt at about two-thirty and signed that they would head back to the camp. Going down was quicker since they were able to take a straighter route. They staggered into camp about four, thanked Zaccariah, and agreed to meet him the same time the next morning.

"What do you think?" Martin asked as he massaged his calves. "About fifteen miles?"

"Felt like fifty." Stefan fumbled with his keys. "Now if I can only remember where I put the waragi this morning."

Martin collapsed on the front seat. "I must confess that I wasn't paying much attention. I'm going to find my sleeping bag. Maybe Singh will take care of dinner."

• • •

Martin didn't feel too bad when he woke at sunset. A delicious smell was wafting over from the campfire. "Boy, that smells good, Singh."

Singh shrugged and threw him a cold Nile before returning to his pans.

"Just in time," Stefan said with an appreciative sigh. "Keep the Nile flowing."

They dined royally on gazelle curry and chapattis and retired early. Only a few stars twinkled forlornly through the ever-expanding mist as Martin zipped himself in and dropped into a deep, dreamless sleep.

• • •

The next morning was worse than Martin had anticipated it would be. After pulling on his clothes, he walked as if on wooden legs to the fire and asked Singh for a tot of waragi for his morning tea.

Stefan wobbled over a few minutes later.

After a few sips of the stiffly laced tea, Martin felt he could talk. "Strong tea with rum was one of the major factors, along with cold baths and fagging at Eton, that enabled the Brits to hold their empire for so long."

Stefan groaned. "Ja, ja. Something like that."

"One of Singh's magic elixirs will soon fix you up," Martin said, pouring some roadies. "I'm afraid it's time to go."

Zaccariah was waiting. After a brief word with Singh, he started up the lava flows at a breakneck pace. Martin was sweating in a matter of minutes and miraculously felt better for it. They were working their way in a southerly direction, away from the nesting areas they'd seen the day before and toward the Rwandan border.

Just after the first break, Zaccariah came upon some fresh droppings. They were passing through a section of the forest where the gorillas had just been feeding. The bamboo stalks had been broken off and showed no dew.

Zaccariah examined the droppings reverently, grunted twice, which Martin took to be a sign of great excitement, and bolted. He muttered excitedly as he picked up the pace.

They sweated and hacked their way through the forest for another mile before Zaccariah stopped once again to carefully study the ground.

"We must be getting close," Martin said, surveying the ground for a place to collapse. "His blood's up."

Even Zaccariah seemed winded, but he was off again as soon as they had caught their breath. After another agonizing mile, he slowed and began to move much more stealthily. Suddenly, he came to a halt and signaled silence. He pointed farther up the ridge and signed "Gorilla" with an orgasmic intensity.

"Any closer and we'd be able to smell them," Martin said as he eased himself into a more comfortable viewing position.

A huge silverback male was standing guard over a group of a dozen females and young. The babies were frolicking in the clearing while the adults fed peacefully.

Martin was stunned. His few encounters with rather pathetic zoo specimens had not prepared him for the dignity and power of these free-ranging primates. He focused on the silverback's expressive, intelligent face. Its deeply etched lines told many stories. There was an intense spark in its eyes as it scanned the surrounding mountains for any signs of trouble.

Nobody moved for the next half hour. Martin was oblivious to the cramps in his calves. He felt an intense primordial link with the apes. As they moved gracefully through the trees, looking for choice morsels, the gorillas gradually worked their way over the ridge and disappeared from sight. The mystical link was severed.

Zaccariah left them alone with their thoughts for a while. Then he looked up at the sun and gestured that it was time to return the way they had come. Only the steady clink-clink of the boys' pangas broke the eerie, anticlimactic silence during their descent. Martin was depressed at the thought that mountain gorillas were unlikely to survive the century in their natural habitat. He made a mental commitment never to go to the monkey house at the zoo again. It would be an emotional rip-off.

When they got back to the compound, they paid Zaccariah well and took some souvenir snaps.

"I wouldn't have missed that for anything," Martin said. "Pity most people will never see it."

"Ja, there was something about it that affected me in a way I cannot really describe. I wanted it to go on forever."

Singh took one look and said, "Gorillas?"

"How'd you know?" Martin asked as he gingerly eased himself onto a stool and finished a brew in one long gulp.

• • •

Martin was still exhausted and stiff as a board when he awoke at six-thirty, but a bucket bath helped.

A few minutes later, as Stefan was opening a bottle of waragi, Martin spotted a commotion at the gate.

A tall, angular woman strode into the compound and introduced herself. "Hi, I'm Dian Fossey. I do research on the gorilla for *National Geographic*. Zaccariah told me you saw them today. What incredible luck. It took me three months to catch my first sighting."

Fossey was dressed in no-nonsense khakis and work boots. Her tough and leathery face radiated an almost mannish aura of self-contained competence. She could have been anywhere from thirty-five to fifty. For all their toughness, her features radiated a serenity that intrigued Martin. Zacariah kissed her hand with grave courtesy as Martin introduced the others and poured her a glass of waragi.

She reached into her pocket and handed Martin a note. "Bertain Aka asked me to deliver this to you."

Martin unfolded the note and read it.

Mes amis, I am glad to tell you that all appears well. I am sorry not to meet you in person, but circumstances, which I will explain to you tomorrow, do not permit it. Dian is an old friend, so I asked her to deliver the note. The meeting time must be changed. Be there early in the morning. Do accept Dian's invitation for lunch. It will leave a good smokescreen. Please be discreet with her.
A demain,
Bertain

Martin passed the note to Stefan. "Small world, isn't it, Dian?"

"Yes, I was surprised when Bertain asked me to deliver the note. He can be a very mysterious man at times, but he has helped me a lot. I still cannot get over your luck in seeing the gorillas so quickly."

"It must be something to work with them in person," Martin replied somewhat enviously.

"They are fascinating creatures," she agreed. "So similar to man in many ways, yet so different. I must admit that I sometimes have a bit of an identity crisis after I spend a few weeks in the bush with them."

"That's interesting. Schaller mentioned the same thing. How long have you been over here?"

"About three years. I get back to the States for about two months a year, but sometimes it seems pretty far away. I hope you'll come visit my camp for lunch tomorrow. My door is always open to visitors from Europe and the States. I love to hear their news. I do hope that Zaccariah is going to give us some of his delicious curry before this waragi goes to my head."

Martin found the dinner delicious as well as fascinating. Dian possessed a seemingly inexhaustible supply of interesting, sometimes humorous anecdotes about the apes. Martin detected a whiff of fanaticism, but it was going to take that and more to save the gorilla, he thought.

After dinner, she gave them instructions to her camp and left.

Martin crawled into his sleeping bag as soon as he had finished eating. He wanted to get the show on the road. Stefan seemed to feel the same way. Tension charged the atmosphere. It took quite a while for sleep to sneak up on them. Martin's thoughts were riding up and down on a manic-depressive roller coaster. One minute he was fantasizing about spending all his loot with Esther. The next he was playing back the tapes of their encounter with the leopard at Murchison Falls.

The tape always finished before he could figure out whether he was the warthog obliviously lapping up the water or the leopard calmly waiting for the perfect moment to strike. Finally, he saw Stefan and himself standing naked in a dusty courtyard. It was Makynde, and they were waiting patiently for their turn to be clubbed to death.

• • •

"Wake up. Hein, it is late." Stefan handed Martin a mug of waragi-laced tea. "You had some strange dreams last night. You kept us up most of the night."

Martin squinted groggily in the bright morning light. "What time is it?"

"About seven. Singh said we'd better hurry if we want to get to Lion Rock on time. He is going to take us on a circular path to evade the other touristi."

"Too bad there isn't any time to visit Dian's."

"It would be crazy even if we had time. She is on the Rwandan side. It would mean border guards."

Martin consigned Dian Fossey to the grandchildren file and helped pack camp.

He spotted Lion Rock two hours after they broke camp. It was easy enough to see how it had gotten its name. The volcanic outcrop resembled a lioness sunning herself after a successful hunt. There was no sign of Aka, so they set up camp. Martin took the binoculars and scanned the surrounding mountains for any signs of unwelcome watchers. It was a fruitless exercise. They could have been hiding anywhere in the boulder-strewn hills. After a few minutes, he gave it up as a bad job and returned to the makeshift tent by the car.

The sun was still struggling to break through the gunmetal-gray cloud cover but didn't seem able to make the final push.

Just as well, Martin thought. The heat was almost bearable. "Mr. Aka is ruining his perfectly punctual record."

Stefan sighed and picked up the binoculars for another scan. "Lots of things could have happened. Not all bad."

"Yes, I know. Car trouble. Border trouble. I wonder where Singh has got to."

"He walked off with his rifle about twenty minutes ago. Probably gone to look for his supper. Looks pretty barren around here to me."

"If there's anything out there, he'll find it. Let's climb up the rock for a recce. We'll be able to see more."

Stefan cocked his head to the side. "Hold on. I hear something. Over there to the right."

Martin scrambled up to the lion's head. "You're right." He spotted a vehicle leaving a dusty trail in its wake. "It's a car. Just our luck it'll be a touristi. No, it looks good. A Toyota Land Cruiser with Rwandan plates. Definitely Aka's style. About a mile off, and coming fast."

A minute or two later, Aka waved and grinned broadly as he skidded to a halt in front of their camp. "Bonjour, mes amis.

Sorry I am late, but I had a flat just over the border. Fortunately, there were no mambas around."

"We were worried about you," Stefan said.

Aka looked past them. "Where's your guide?"

"Off looking for his supper."

"Good, let's get on with the business then." Aka rummaged through the back of his car and retrieved a large burlap bag from the tire well. "Bring the suitcases." He untied the bag and poured out three smaller sacks.

"Holy shit," Martin said. "This feels like a lot more than three pounds."

"Three pounds each. I had to make an adjustment in my plans."

"How much are they worth?"

"Not as much as you would think. Some are very raw."

"What about our fees?" Stefan grumbled.

"I am willing to increase them by half. Do not be disturbed, gentlemen. The bags will hold them."

Martin laughed. "Sounds fair enough. In for a penny, in for a pound. If we're caught with this lot, the amount isn't going to make a great deal of difference. Here." He handed over his bag. "Load me up. I'll go up on the rock and keep an eye out for Singh or any unwanted visitors."

Aka flipped the suitcase open and emptied the sack's contents into the false bottom. "Beautiful sight, *n'est-ce pas*?" he mused as he spread the stones evenly around. Even in the dull-gray light, they shimmered. "These have all been selected with great care. In the right cutter's hands, they are all potential gemstones." He folded the false bottom back into place and snapped the bag shut.

Martin emerged from his momentary trance. "I hope I never see them again." He grabbed the binoculars and climbed up the rock, only to spot another vehicle fast approaching. "Shit. You expecting company, Bertain?"

"Of course not. What is it, and how close?"

"A Land Rover. No markings. One person in it."

"African or blanc?"

"African."

"Probably a guide or anti-poaching patrol, but we cannot take any chances." Aka hurriedly poured the last sack into Stefan's bag. "Get these out of sight. Hide them in the back of your Rover."

Stefan scuttled over to the car and buried the bags in the gear in the back while Aka pulled out a hamper and started spreading out lunch.

Martin felt a surge of relief when the Land Rover didn't slow. "He's not stopping!" he shouted to the others. "Motoring right on by without a care in the world. Jesus."

"Watch until he is out of sight." Aka seemed unruffled as he opened a bottle of champagne.

"While we're on the subject of arrangements, where are we dropping the stones?" Stefan looked cool enough, but he sucked down his glass of champagne like a baby taking its first bottle in the morning.

"On Lamu, an island off the Kenyan coast. You'll be handing them off to a fellow named Mukhajee Gupta."

"There'll probably only be about ten Guptas in the book," Martin quipped, gratefully accepting a glass of bubbly after finishing with his sentinel duties. "What's his address?"

"He has a large trading establishment on the wharf. Lamu is tiny. It will not be possible to miss it. He is expecting you next Saturday."

"So sad you'll have to disappoint him." The hiss was accentuated by a metallic click.

Even as he whirled around, Martin recognized the voice. It belonged to Black Briefcase.

This time he was carrying a well-oiled Kalashnikov instead of his trademark bag. "So nice of you to pack the stones for me,

Bertain, and champagne too. This really is my lucky day."

Bertain sighed and started to rise. "Luck appears to have had very little to do with it."

"Do not try anything foolish, old friend. It is nothing personal. In fact, I like you a great deal. I simply got a better offer from Colonel Bagaza." Briefcase shrugged eloquently. "Business is business."

Martin reached for a cigarette.

Briefcase responded by training his rifle on him. "Do not get any misdirected ideas. I know that you outnumber me three to one, but this more than makes up for it." He fanned the gleaming gun. "Just sit down and relax. The colonel will be with us shortly."

Martin's sphincter was galloping. Stefan looked stunned and ashen. Only Aka seemed relatively unfazed. He gestured to Briefcase and calmly refilled his glass.

Martin's mind raced through the possible scenarios, none of them good. If they were on official government business, they might just take Aka and the diamonds and split. Who was he kidding? If they were freelancing, which appeared a lot more likely, they weren't going to want any witnesses. Get 'em talking, he figured. His mind was at least working clearly, even if his hands were shaking uncontrollably. His eyes were riveted on the glistening barrel in Briefcase's hamlike hands. It was the old venomous-snake-in-the-room routine. He didn't really want to look at it, but he didn't dare take his eyes off it. "Who . . . who's Bagaza?" he asked in a quavering voice.

Briefcase laughed heartily. "He is a member of Mobutu's secret police who has had dealings with Aka and his family for years."

"*Merde!*" Aka exploded. "You can be sure he is not here in an official capacity!"

"Oh, but he is, mon vieux," Briefcase insisted. "Just think how happy Mobutu will be when he brings him your head on a platter."

"What about the diamonds?"

"For our purposes, your associates will make a successful getaway during the struggle. In reality, they and you will both just disappear. Uganda's been a pretty unlawful place since the coup—renegade army bands and all that. What are a few million more or less to Mobutu? He will be happy enough to know that you are no longer funding the rebels in Shaba." Briefcase paused to listen. "Ah, I think I hear the good colonel returning. He will be happy to see you."

Martin yawned to ease the tension. "It's either him or one of those tour buses we saw earlier."

"You mean one of those horrible VW buses with the phony zebra stripes," Stefan replied with a wink.

Briefcase almost caught himself, but his head turned fractionally. Martin lobbed his glass of champagne at his eyes and dove for his arm. The short, reflexive burst of the Kalashnikov seared Martin's eardrums as he careened into Briefcase and desperately groped for his trigger hand. They collapsed in an awkward tangle. Stunned by the noise and the body mass of the corpulent African landing flush on his solar plexus, Martin began to lose his grip on the oily barrel.

Bizarrely, the only thought in Martin's mind was how badly his adversary's breath stank. He was losing it. What the fuck was Stefan doing? Martin heard a sickening thud, and Briefcase went limp in his arms. Slime dripped on Martin's face. It felt as though an earthworm was wiggling down the bridge of his nose. He opened his eyes to see tendrils of brain matter feathering outward from a crack in the African's skull. It took Martin a few seconds to make the association. Waves of nausea washed over him, and his vision began to narrow. He struggled valiantly, but the numbing blackness was too seductive. Just before he surrendered completely, a burst of gunfire reverberated hollowly off the rock.

• • •

Esther hung up the phone at her desk and stamped the death certificate in front of her. Maintaining citizens' official birth, death, and marriage documents in the public records division at the Ministry of Internal Affairs wasn't exactly glamorous work. In fact, it could be awfully tedious at times. But it gave her something she'd never had before: security. She sometimes envied people like Martin, who seemed to take safety and comfort for granted. As generous-hearted as he was, he would never understand what it meant to live from one moment to the next with survival the only goal. Kindness or empathy for a person of means were conscious choices, not prime movers. They didn't instruct like calamity and deprivation did.

She closed the folder on her desk. Did she envy Martin? Or feel sorry for him? Maybe both. She wasn't sure. All she knew was that their fake breakup and subsequent time apart had begun to gnaw at her. In the past, she had felt connected to Martin in an almost magical way, as though she could sense what he was feeling and doing even when they were apart. Now that thread connecting them seemed to be fraying. They were still together in spirit, but the union took effort. She was beginning to forget what he smelled like, what he tasted like, what it was like to have him take her in his arms.

She stood to carry the file folder to the cabinet behind her and nearly ran into her rotund supervisor, Namazzi Akello.

"Mapende," Akello said in his usual singsong tone. "We must speak."

"Oh?" Esther leaned against her desk and waited. *What is it this time?* she wondered. An invitation to discuss her typing skills over dinner and a drink? Another useless tip on phone etiquette, delivered with a subtle-but-impossible-to-miss sexual innuendo?

Her casual indifference, which bordered on impatience, changed to concern when she saw what looked like alarm on his round face.

Akello wiped at the bead of sweat streaking down his cheek. "I am afraid I have been instructed to terminate your position."

"Terminate my position?" Esther couldn't contain the indignation in her voice. "Who gave you this order?"

Akello gazed down at his shoes and then looked to his left, seemingly determined not to make eye contact. "I am not at liberty to say. Suffice to say the decision is not mine."

Esther noticed the quiver in his left hand as he dropped it to his side. Was he trembling? She understood immediately that the order hadn't come from a manager or even a department head. It had come from the very top. It was doubtful Akello had spoken with Idi Amin himself, but no doubt one of the president's minions had delivered the order while imbuing it with his employer's unquestioned authority.

"I see," she said, unsure whether to laugh or cry.

"It has nothing to do with your performance," Akello insisted. "Your work here has been exemplary."

"Of course," she said.

Akello fidgeted before her. Then a look of judgment—almost condescension—overtook his face. "It seems your unsavory associations have finally caught up with you."

Everyone in the office knew of her relationship with Martin. In fact, she had championed the charismatic American in front of Akello precisely to ward off his clumsy advances. Now he was turning her gentle rebuffing against her.

"Fine," she said. "I will just need a moment to gather my things."

Whatever Martin was up to, whatever trouble he had found with Stefan, now touched her. She suddenly felt like an impala that had been sighted by a rogue lion. She could stay and fight, or she could turn and run. But her choice hardly seemed to matter. She could feel already the predator's jaws tightening around her neck.

• • •

"Get up, Martin!"

Someone slapped Martin's face, and a trickle of cool water brought him reluctantly to his senses.

He shook his head. At first glance, nothing had changed. The evil eye of the Kalashnikov was still staring at him, but now it was being held by a wickedly grinning Harry Usongo. Desperately, Martin tried to cast himself back into the soothing blackness, but he couldn't get there.

"So nice of you to join our little party, Mr. Fine. I was worried you were not going to be able to. That would have deprived me of a pleasurable moment that I have been looking forward to for some time."

Martin looked around. Stefan was spread-eagled face down in front of the Rover. A few feet away, Bertain lay in an ever-widening rust-colored pool of blood. His silk shirt was stitched from navel to neck with a neat line of perfectly round holes no bigger than a dime.

Another African, wearing an unfamiliar military uniform, lay in an unceremonious heap near Aka. Colonel Bagaza, Martin presumed. It looked as if Usongo and whomever he was working with were going for the whole pile. Killing Bagaza was not a risk to be undertaken lightly.

Usongo gestured with the Kalashnikov for him to stand, and Martin started to comply. Before he was halfway up, Usongo kicked him in the balls.

White stars exploded in Martin's skull as he crumpled to the ground and helplessly vomited on himself.

"That, Mr. Fine, is just a small taste of what is in store for you. I have had a few days to think about your death. You cannot imagine how happy I was when Ali Kilogo offered me the chance to redeem myself by dealing with you and your incompetent friends." He paused, carefully picked up the half-empty champagne bottle, and drank deeply. "I must say, though, that it was nice of Aka to bring so many extra stones. I will live well from now on."

Stefan interrupted Usongo's reverie. "How are you going to explain Bagaza's and Bertain's deaths?"

"By saying I got here too late, of course. But enough of this nonsense." Usongo rose and strode toward Stefan. "I have nothing against you personally, so I will give you one minute to make peace with your God."

Martin was paralyzed by pain and fear. His mind kept sending signals, but his limbs were leaden. He felt like he was in quicksand up to his neck. He wanted to close his eyes as Usongo raised the gun and aimed at the back of Stefan's head.

The crack of the rifle and Usongo's grunt were instantaneous. His chest exploded in a shower of blood and tissue.

Singh stepped from behind the Lion Rock and trotted over to them. He kicked the Kalashnikov from Usongo's lifeless hand. Not that it was necessary. There was a hole the size of a grapefruit in his chest.

CHAPTER

21

SINGH'S EXPRESSION LOOKED no different than had he just bagged two kudu for dinner.

Martin's paralysis lifted. He felt lightheaded and giddy like the first time he'd gotten high. "Out of the frying pan and into . . ." He groaned as he dragged himself to his feet. "I thought we'd really had it. I wondered where old Singh had got to."

He lurched over to the car and grabbed the waragi bottle from under the seat. Two deep swigs dulled some of the pain in his groin, but his breath was still coming in deep, whooping gasps. He lobbed the bottle over to Stefan, who was beginning to pull himself together.

Singh grabbed the binoculars and scrambled up the rock. Evidently satisfied with his survey, he climbed back down and launched into a long, excited speech. "*Pole, pole. Mimi Swahili a panna Missouri.*"

Martin turned to Stefan. "What's he on about?"

Stefan took a deep drink and passed the bottle back to Martin. "Whatever he wants, he can have it." He leaned over and gave Singh a bear hug.

Martin dug out one of the Samsonites and opened it. No further comment was necessary. He motioned for Singh to cup his hands and poured into them two generous handfuls.

Stefan reached over and added a few for good measure. "What are we going to do with them now that Aka is gone?"

"Take them to Lamu and get a good price for them." Martin replied calmly. "Gupta has to be in touch with the buyers, so we just cut our own deal."

"Sehr gut. That leaves a few small problems. The first thing we have to do is get rid of the bodies."

"Yeah. That is a good place to start. It'll give them something to think about. Bakazi and Co. might even think that Bagaza offed us and Usongo and split with the loot. We'll have to make everything, including the cars, disappear without a trace."

"Natürlich. We had better get cracking. As soon as the rest of the bandits do not hear from Bagaza, they are going to be out here quickly. No use blowing what little head start we have."

While Stefan and Martin loaded the bodies and guns into the back of Aka's car, Singh gathered some branches and cleaned up the campsite. When he finished, he looked up at the sky and said, "*Linga* Missouri."

"It's going to rain soon," Martin said, translating for him. "That should take care of the rest."

Stefan slammed the tailgate shut. "Where are we going to dump all these cars?"

"In the river. We passed a deep ford about five miles back. You can follow me in Bagaza's car. We'll leave ours as a red herring."

Martin started the motor and motioned Singh to follow. As they got under way, he checked his watch. It was only three-thirty. They could probably count on twenty-four hours before the general alarm was raised—more than enough time if they used it right. He tried to ignore the smell of fresh blood and focus on what to do next. Their original plan of hightailing it with Singh was looking less and less viable. By tomorrow, they were going to be hot as pistols. Even if they got across the border tonight, they couldn't be sure that the Ugandans wouldn't have the Kenyans hold them on some trumped-up pretext. There was only one option: the major. It was about time he started earning his money. Up to this point in time, his intelligence hadn't been worth a nickel.

They reached the river a quarter of an hour later. While Singh and Stefan went back for Usongo's car, Martin commenced the ghoulish business of searching the corpses. He had to be sure there was nothing linking them to the bodies. He was so numbed by the day's happenings that he was beyond shock. He didn't even feel a twinge of nausea.

Not too bad, he thought, when he had finished: an extra $2,000 for the war chest and lots of goodies from Aka's hamper for dinner. He wasn't particularly hungry, but they were going to have to eat, if only to maintain their strength.

Singh and Stefan were back in minutes. Usongo's Austin was a piece of cake, but getting Aka's and Bagaza's Toyotas over the ledge was a bitch. The three of them finally got them moving just enough for momentum to do the rest. Martin had chosen the spot well. The cars sank slowly in a cloud of steam and bubbles. As the muddy water rose over the bodies, Bagaza's corpse floated toward the roof, his face frozen in a death grimace. His limply flapping arms gave the macabre impression of a fond farewell.

Martin shook his head. "I don't think the bastard is wishing us good luck. What a horrible sight."

"I do not feel the slightest remorse over killing that SOB." Stefan gestured to a couple of fat crocodiles on the opposite bank. "This is perfect. By the time those fellows are through, they are going to have a hell of a time identifying the bodies."

"They'll probably get severe indigestion. Let's get going. If we're lucky, we can make it to the major's by nine."

Stefan finished the waragi and threw the bottle into the pool.

"What about Singh?"

"I worked out a plan for him. He stashes his diamonds and walks into the lodge, where he tells them a woeful tale about us being kidnapped at gunpoint. Of course, he'll suitably embellish things by moaning about his car being stolen and not getting paid. He'll be grilled for a while, but he's a tough old bastard."

"Then he waits for a few weeks and lives happily ever after. Sehr gut."

When everyone was ready, Singh hugged each of them in turn and trudged off.

"Crusty old coot," Martin said as they waved goodbye. "I even thought I detected a hint of a tear. He told me that we remind him of his own youth."

"His retirement will be more comfortable. He could not spend the contents of that sack in the rest of his life if he tried."

Martin opened the glove compartment and retrieved a map. "I'll be our navigator. Singh marked a route for us."

Stefan gunned the engine of Singh's Rover and burned rubber. Once they exited the game park, they made good time over the lightly traveled roads. They encountered no roadblocks, and no one in the towns they passed through took undue interest in them.

Martin took over at the wheel and drove steadily for the next two hours, not knowing where the energy came from. Stefan had fallen asleep beside him. There was no explaining it, but Martin felt a serenity he had never before experienced. He finally appreciated what the Japanese were talking about when they said that the high of escaping certain death was like nothing else. He'd done it twice in as many days.

His reserves drained with the sun. He caught himself nodding off twice as it set. Luckily, the road was deserted, and his violent swerves disturbed nothing. He pulled off the road and got out for a piss.

Stefan woke the minute the engine died. "You must be shattered."

"Something like that," Martin said with a grim frown. "It shouldn't be more than an hour or so to the major's."

Stefan slid behind the wheel.

Martin forced down some caviar and pate—they tasted like sawdust—and slipped into a fitful sleep.

• • •

"We are here." Stefan jarred Martin awake with a punch to the shoulder. "The major is out, but his houseboy remembers us. We may wait inside."

Martin took a moment to regain his bearings. "That's just as well. We'd better discuss a few things before he gets back. Like how much of the loot we're going to show him."

"The original amount. Before we collapse, I suggest we redivide the stones into two equal lots, leaving out a pile for expenses."

They lugged the Samsonite bags inside and redivided the stones. Stefan reloaded the cases while Martin scooped a healthy expenses pile into one of the discarded sacks and rolled it into Singh's sleeping bag.

"I think we had better stay up until the major gets back," Stefan said. "I will see if I can rustle up some coffee."

They were on their third cup when the major walked in. "Trouble, I take it?"

"How'd you guess, Major?"

"It didn't take all of my extensive deductive powers. First of all, you're sitting in my parlor when you should be speeding to parts unknown. Second, and more disturbing, you have blood on your clothes. What the hell happened up there?"

Martin told him as briefly and completely as he could. "So,

Major, it's time for you to start earning your recently enlarged fee," he concluded with a lightheartedness he didn't feel.

"Well, well. I can't say I would've done anything differently had I been in your shoes. Still, it's a hell of a mess. If we kick things around a bit, I'm sure we can come up with something."

The major's calm demeanor quieted the rising tide of panic Martin had been feeling since their arrival.

The major gave them cognacs to go with their coffees and lit a smelly pipe. "I know it stinks," he murmured apologetically, "but it helps me think." He grabbed a pen and pencil and made some notes. "As far as I see it, you have two major problems at the moment. First, getting across the Kenyan border will require new identities and papers. Astles and the others will have the Kenyans on the lookout for you on one pretext or another. Your second problem is where to hide until arrangements can be made."

"Do you have any convenient hideaways in your bag of tricks?" Martin asked.

"It just so happens I do. Either of you heard of the Ssese Islands?"

Martin nodded. "They're out in the middle of Lake Vic, aren't they?"

"Yes they are. Delightful too. I know this Indian chap, Sankara, who owns a sawmill out there. He owes me a few favors. It is very isolated. The islands' population was decimated by an outbreak of encephalitis twenty years ago. I think he could hide you fellows easily enough."

"How do we get out there?"

"By boat. I keep one on the lake. We had better get over there tonight, because it's a fair drive from here."

Martin got up and freshened everyone's coffee and cognac. "The papers really don't pose any problem, Major. Without them, we're cooked."

"I know a bloke who can fix you up, but it's going to cost a bit. You'll need something in the way of disguises also. Your appearances look superficially different. Good enough for a roadblock wave-by, but not a serious check."

"We were wondering when you'd notice, Major." Martin unrolled the sleeping bag and emptied part of the contents of the sack on the table. "This ought to cover your fee and any other expenses."

The major didn't bat an eye at the glittering pile. He spun on his chair and rummaged through the desk drawer, producing a jeweler's loupe a moment later. "Very nice too. These will certainly take care of everything. I hope you're not offended that I'm taking my payment in stones. It's not so much that I doubt that you'll get through. In fact, my opinion of your abilities has risen greatly in the past half hour. Bagaza was a nasty piece of work. I met him a few times, but, as you know, circumstances have a way of changing fast here."

"A bird in the hand," Martin replied. "We've got our passports with us if it will help."

"Sadly, no. In fact, they're a death warrant. The Ugandans are going to have the border very tightly watched. You'll need bulletproof new documents."

Martin mulled over their options. "What about the Anyanya? I have contact with them. We've already had preliminary discussions. They're most willing to help. They can use the money."

"Not a bad idea. They have a pretty decent network from what I hear."

"Good. All you have to do to contact Nathan is leave word with the bass player in the house band at the Leopard's Lair. Just say that I need his services on the deal we discussed."

"Right. I'll contact him tomorrow night." The major bounced to his feet, opened a wall safe, lobbed the stones inside, and withdrew a regulation officer-issue Webley. He spun the chamber and shoved it carefully into his waistband.

"Serious business, Major." Stefan smiled. "That pistol looks like it dates from the Boer War."

"It does. It was my father's. Still works, though—as long as you put the bullet in the right spot. Time to get cracking. I have to cover my tracks too."

Martin stood. "That shouldn't be any problem for a man of your abilities, Major. Only the houseboy knows we've been here."

"Abdul won't tell. He's been in my service for ten years, ever since Nigeria. That leaves only your car, which will be a simple matter."

"Roughly how long will all of this take, and how will we stay in touch?" Martin asked as he handed over their passports.

The major tossed them into the safe and locked it. "Difficult to say exactly. Once I've talked to a few people, I should have a better idea. I'll get word to you by midweek. If I can't make it myself, I'll send Abdul."

• • •

It was after midnight by the time they got back on the road. The major took back roads to Mbali, where the boat was waiting for them. They didn't run into any roadblocks or cars.

Martin breathed a sigh of relief when he turned down a deeply rutted track about a mile before the sleeping town. He couldn't see the lake, but he could smell the dankness of the water.

A few minutes later, they stopped in front of a ramshackle boathouse. The major unlocked the door, and they loaded their gear into an old but well-maintained power boat.

"My ace in the hole," the major said and lovingly patted the boat's wood hull. "Now if we don't run into any patrols . . ."

The water was mirror-calm, and the front had cleared over the lake, leaving the full moon shimmering. It was a beautiful night for a boat ride.

Not that Martin enjoyed it much. "Too bad we're not on a pleasure cruise, Major."

"Cheer up, lad. Things could be a lot worse. I bet you surprised yourself today."

"You're right there. Murder and mayhem isn't my bag."

"Karma. I remember the first man I killed in the war. We walked into an ambush, and he lunged at me with a bayonet. I killed him without thinking. Not much older than you. Pretty wife and kids too. I found their pictures in his wallet afterward. At least your lot killed some scum."

"True enough, I guess, but it won't make it any easier to sleep tonight."

"I can't give you any easy answers for that one. Just be glad you have nightmares. Neither Bagaza nor Usongo would have. Your capacity to feel remorse keeps you from becoming an animal like them."

The breeze cleansed Martin's mind of the day's horrors. He glanced at Stefan and saw he was sleeping like a baby.

"There's a thermos of coffee and cognac in the back." The major pointed to a leather carryall by the engine.

Martin poured two cups and passed one over. "I don't think I'll be able to sleep like that for some months."

"Yes, you will. The shock will wear off soon. Sleep's the best tonic. Take it from an old soldier. Besides, there won't be a lot to do, and you'll need to rest up on the islands. The next leg of the trip isn't going to be a joyride."

The first of the islands came into sight a few minutes later.

"How far from where we dock to Sankara's?" Martin asked.

"About two hundred yards. You will be in bed in an hour."

"What are you going to tell Sankara?"

"That you've fallen afoul of Astles, Bakazi, and crew because of political reasons. He has two brothers in jail for currency smuggling—i.e., not paying enough in bribes. Needless to say, he's not too fond of the current regime."

"That's reassuring."

As usual, the major was right. They were sitting in Sankara's sparsely furnished bungalow less than forty-five minutes later. Sankara didn't speak much English, and Martin, too exhausted to focus on the long discussion in Swahili the major had with him, waited for a translation. They concluded their business with a handshake and an embrace.

"It's all set." The major beamed. "Of course, you'll have to lie low during the day, but you should be fine after dark. The mill's about half a mile away, and the African help doesn't come around here much. The only guy you could possibly encounter is Askari, the watchman. He's no threat, Sankara assures me, because he's blind."

"A blind watchman," Stefan said with a snicker. "That's uniquely African."

"On the contrary," the major replied, "it makes perfect sense. None of his own people will steal from him. If they did, the village, which is poor enough already, would have another mouth to feed. Sankara is honored to be sheltering opponents of Amin, by the way."

"We'll dream up a good cover story in the morning," Martin said.

The major appeared satisfied. "Rest assured I'll get word to you as soon as I can. I have to leave now. The morning shift starts at eight, and I have to make your car disappear before that."

Martin hugged the older man. "What can we say?"

"I've been well paid. It's my pension, remember? Just keep a stiff upper lip." He shook hands all around and left.

Sankara showed them into a grubby back room, lit a gas lantern, and went back to bed. Martin collapsed on the dusty, mildewed mattress.

•••

They slept until Sankara woke them with dinner the next evening at sunset.

Mercifully, Martin's sleep had been deep. The alcohol, no doubt. He felt curiously refreshed. "Sure is a long way from Sinbad's," he grumbled, staring at a plate of greasy daal and chapattis that had appeared for dinner.

"Even farther to Lamu," Stefan agreed. "But at least we have a plan, which is more than we had at this time yesterday. This place gives the term fleabag new meaning. Why not head down to the water? It is almost dark."

Martin lit the lantern and used it to illuminate the rock-strewn path to the dock. A refreshing breeze cooled his skin as it rustled the dense overgrowth. "I wonder what kind of exotic fauna hangs around these parts."

Stefan paused to light a joint before replying. "Lots of monkeys, plus the odd hippo and the usual complement of birds."

"So what went wrong?" Martin asked.

"The question is not what but *how*. How did Bagaza find out that Aka was running diamonds? My money's on Black Briefcase approaching him with an offer."

Martin sucked deeply on the joint and gathered his thoughts. "I'll tell you one thing: Being stoned can't be any weirder than reality at this point. After yesterday, I'm not scared of dying anymore."

"Ja, as long as it is quick. You know it is funny, Martin, but you jumped about a millisecond before I did. What went through your mind?"

"I didn't see my life in slow motion. I was just mad. Mad at Briefcase, mad at Aka, and most of all, mad at myself, because when I looked at that Kalashnikov, I knew the diamonds weren't worth it. Isn't it funny? Two nights ago, we were joking about sliding into the heart of darkness."

"We have not even broken the ice yet," Stefan replied in a sober voice. "The next week or so, we are going to plumb the depths. I have a feeling that Astles and crew are going to make Bagaza look like he was wearing white. There is little we can do about it now but keep marching. Getting on to a more practical note, since the postmortems are not solving our problems, have you thought about a disguise yet? It has to be something they see often enough not to get excited about."

"I've got a thought, and you're going to love it. We can be men of the cloth. Missionaries on our way to a new post. Of course, we'd have to work on our appearances a bit. I take it you wouldn't have any moral scruples."

"After yesterday," Stefan said with a snort, "I do not have any left. There is a certain poetic justice to diamond smugglers masquerading as clergy. I like it. Africans as a rule do not like to mess with religious types."

"*Dominus vobiscum.*" Martin mimed a blessing, and they went off to bed high and in good humor.

• • •

The next two days were excruciating. Nothing, especially time, moved fast in the torpid fustiness of the stucco sweatbox, which Martin had dubbed the Nile Hilton. There was nothing to do but play cards for diamonds and listen to the radio Sankara had provided. Sleep provided the only relief. They were able to pass at least half the daylight hours snoozing, but Martin still had too much time to think. Every time he scratched another flea bite, he cursed his own stupidity. He felt that his mind was degenerating like the peeling, cracked walls of the mildewed bungalow. The tension and uncertainty were getting to them both. They argued about everything.

It was a relief when night came and they could get away from the damp, suffocating fog of the room. By the fourth night, they'd settled into a kind of daze. Martin guessed it was similar to the survival mode adopted by long-term prisoners. Basically, all systems that didn't pertain to immediate life were shut down. They desperately needed something to hang on to—a plan, the faintest whiff of hope, anything that would suffice to divert their minds from the interminable present.

It was a warm, clear night. They headed for the sandy beach they had discovered not far from the dock. Sankara had informed them that there wasn't any bilharzia out in the middle of the lake, so they'd taken to bathing every night. Brief exposure had already informed them that Sankara, friendly as he was, didn't count personal hygiene among his strong suits. In fact, his long-drop was positively useless if you had a nose. Even the noisome bucket in the corner of their room was preferable.

"Thank God we can swim every night." Martin scrubbed himself vigorously. "I'd hate to start smelling like our host."

"Or his outhouse." Stefan grimaced. "Even the flies do not go near it."

Martin shushed the German and then paused to listen. "Do you hear what I hear?"

"Ja, it is definitely a boat. I hope it is the good guys."

They scrambled out of the water and dressed hurriedly.

"No use rushing if it is the bad fellows." Stefan sat down to pull on his socks. "Where are we going to run to?"

He had a point. It was an island.

Martin peered intently into the darkness and caught a glimpse of the major's bright-white hair. "It's the major."

They scrambled out to the end of the dock.

The major throttled down and tossed them a line.

Stefan caught it and smiled. "Gott in Himmel, Major, you are a sight for sore eyes."

"Jolly good. I thought I might be. I have lots to report, plus all sorts of kit." He started passing up cartons.

"We're all ears," Martin said breathlessly.

With a flourish, the major opened the cooler at his feet and handed each of them a frosty Nile. "You chaps have become incredibly popular. Virtually everyone who's anyone in town is looking for you on one pretext or another. I've been thoroughly interviewed by Astles and the boys. They were perfectly pleasant about things."

"What do they know?" Stefan asked.

"At this stage, not a bloody lot, but they're covering all the angles, you can be sure. The public line is that you've been kidnapped by poachers or smugglers. Not even a whiff about diamonds."

"Are you being watched?"

"In a half-arsed sort of way. Not the A-team, though. All I had to do to get out here tonight was stash a second car by the back entrance of the mine. They had only one man, none too subtly stationed by the front entrance. They seem to have bought my story that you fellows were just drinking acquaintances."

"Maybe they think that Bagaza killed us and Usongo and scarpered with the stones," Martin offered hopefully.

"Not bloody likely. With the amount of loot involved, I don't think they'll buy anything until they see your bodies. The only sure thing is that they're entirely too slick a bunch to show their hands at this early stage of the game. Besides, there's a definite buzz that border security has been tightened. It's being billed as an operation against dissident elements."

"That's convenient. Did you hook up with the contact?"

"Yes, I passed him a note last night."

"What about Esther?"

"Joe told me she's fine. She was questioned, but it was a going-through-the-motions thing."

"Any of the embassy people been around?"

"All of them. I gave them the same casual-drinking-partners routine. It seemed to suit all of them except your chap Agent Russell. He could prove to be a nuisance before this is all over."

"Really, I thought he'd be the least of our problems."

"Well, during our conversation the other day, he offhandedly, in his best Interrogation 101 fashion, asked me if I'd heard anything about diamonds being smuggled out of Shaba. He then proceeded to give me the Zaire-is-a-good-and-needed-friend-of-the-West routine. Imagine treating me like some wet-behind-the-ears young shaver! Silly boy. I told him I hadn't heard a peep. Still, he will bear watching. Those eager-beaver Yanks can get in the way. They have so much damn money to throw about."

"Scheissen, Major, for a little bit of recreational diamond smuggling, there sure are a lot of players joining the game."

The major smiled. "Nothing is ever cut-and-dried over here. One of the charms of the place. The good news is that all these wonderful fellows aren't working together."

"Why do you say that?"

"Because they all questioned me separately. Just think: you have the GSU, the CIA, and military intelligence after you."

"We're deeply touched by their concern." Martin passed out more brews. "We've had plenty of time to think up new identities, though. How about men of the cloth?"

"Bloody marvelous once you get to Kenya, but not good enough for the border here. Even if the disguises are good, the papers will be dicey. The passports will pass a general inspection, but if they were to cable Washington or Bonn . . ."

"How long before they call off the dogs? It's not that this place isn't better than Makynde."

"I know," the major said with a sigh. "I'm sorry to say that it'll be at least another week. Possibly more."

Martin couldn't hide the disappointment on his face. "I figured as much. Being realistic, it'll probably take the Anyanya that long to arrange things."

"I'll come out with supplies, news, and some kit for your disguises this weekend. I should be able to fix the papers soon after. Hopefully, the Anyanya will have contacted you by then, so things will be more definite. I have to run. Keep your chins up. This is a very safe place to lie low."

"Thanks, Major," Martin said as he untied the bowline. "The supplies will make life a lot easier."

"Not at all, my boy. I haven't had this much fun in years. In fact, I've felt ten years younger all week."

They waved until he disappeared in the darkness.

"I love him more every minute," Martin said.

Stefan triumphantly brandished a roll of toilet paper. "This will definitely improve our morale."

CHAPTER

22

THE REST OF the week was just as boring but somehow much more bearable than the first few days. The major had included a stock of lurid spy thrillers, which offset the daytime tedium. Martin found himself thinking less of the past and more of the immediate future, but it still took constant effort to avoid stepping on Stefan's toes. The nights kept him sane. Bathing in the warm, brackish lake water soothed Martin. He could almost forget his troglodyte existence. The constantly changing night sky and the familiar backdrop of night sounds provided a reassuring reminder that he wasn't really a prisoner. Still, time dragged like they were in prison. He checked and rechecked his mental calendar. It definitely was Friday night. Had it really been a week? It seemed more like a century. He had arranged a nice surprise to celebrate their first week. Like a child hoarding the last piece of chocolate, he'd hidden it from Stefan all day. Now he was impatient to show it off.

When dusk came, Martin shook Stefan awake. "Wait until you see the surprise I have for you. I managed to scrounge a chicken from Sankara. We can barbeque it down by the dock."

"Anything but corned beef and sardines. This calls for a little celebration." Stefan grabbed their last bottle of cognac on the way out the door.

They scavenged for dry wood on the way down to the water. Stefan constructed a crude spit while Martin got the fire going. As soon as the scrawny chicken was cooking, Stefan poured out generous drinks.

Martin clinked his glass. "Wouldn't you just love to see Nathan materialize out of the jungle? I guess we ought to start thinking about a bargaining position."

"What position?" Stefan asked with a snort. "It's a seller's market. You can bet your bottom dollar that he knows who is after us and what we have."

"We still have to make him an offer. He might not know the whole setup."

"He will, Hein. Sure as I am standing here. Face the facts. We will have to give him whatever he wants. Aka is dead, and Gupta will be glad to get whatever we bring him. We are going to have to restructure the whole deal."

"You're right."

They took their nightly dip, washing and lolling about, while the chicken sizzled away.

"Best bathtub I've ever been in!" Martin exclaimed. "What a view!"

"And what a sight you two make. Shame on you, mzungus. Half the Ugandan Army is out looking for you at this moment." Nathan smiled broadly and helped himself to a beer.

Martin made for the shore. "Nathan, we were just talking about you. As usual, you caught us napping. Speaking of army sorts, there aren't any around these parts, are there? We kind of figured they'd be looking elsewhere."

"No, they are covering the borders."

"Are we really that popular?" Stefan asked as the three congregated by the fire. "We hoped that they might think we had been killed."

"In a few more weeks, they might get around to that way of thinking, but at the moment, the view in most quarters is that you are still hiding somewhere. Otherwise, they would have to accept the fact that they lost their opportunity to get what you have." Nathan took a seat and sucked down the brew as they dried and dressed. "Now, gentlemen, I think that it is time to discuss that mutually beneficial proposition that was mentioned some weeks ago."

"Okay." Martin turned the chicken. "We need to get to Lamu."

"One hundred and fifty thousand US dollars." Nathan stilled their protests with a wave. "It is not much compared to what you have. No need to play games. Our sources are good."

Martin passed out cups and poured cognac all around. "Why not just take some of the stones? That much cash could be difficult to raise on short notice."

"We can no more sell the stones than you can. I am sure that your contact can raise that much cash. He is probably an Indian or Arab. They are the only ones that operate on this level."

"We don't mind the price." Martin smiled. "After all, it's for a good cause, and you're the only game in town. We're just trying to keep things from getting any more complicated."

"That is understandable, but nonetheless, I must insist on cash. Do we have a deal?"

Martin glanced at Stefan. It was a formality. They had no choice, and they both knew it. "We do. I take it you or another representative will accompany us. Discreetly of course. What's the time frame?"

"At least another week, maybe more. It will take us that long to arrange things, and the longer we wait, the more likely they are to think that you have got away and to lower their guard."

Martin paced by the fire. "How is Esther? I'm a little worried that they might give her a hard time if they get frustrated."

"Do not worry too much about that. Remember that Astles is a neocolonialist pig. He is bound to assume that you would treat the woman just as he would: like a common market whore. What self-respecting white man would tell an African woman anything? She is being watched but not bothered. Nobody thinks you would be stupid enough to get in touch with her, but they have to cover all bets, as you Americans would say." Nathan held out his cup for a refill. "If you really care, send her a plane ticket when it is over. In the meantime, just be patient. Think of where you could be."

"How will you stay in touch?"

"Through the major. But be prepared, because you will not get much warning." He shook hands all around and melted into the darkness.

"Cheeky bugger," Stefan said with a laugh. "It looks like at least one more week in paradise."

"Not a riveting prospect. Every time I look at this place, I feel more like Kurtz."

"Ja, it does seem to grow on you. It could easily get suffocating, but we have one big advantage over Kurtz. We are not here indefinitely. Like the man said, it sure beats Makyndye Prison. The only thing that bothers me is how complicated the finances are becoming. Have you thought about Lamu?"

"Not yet." Martin winced as he pulled the sizzling chicken off the fire and set it on an old serving plate they had scrounged from their backroom lodgings.

Stefan helped himself and tore free a drumstick. "Scheissen, that is hot!"

The two were silent as they devoured the chicken.

Finally, Stefan spoke. "The real problem is time. It is going to take Gupta a while to raise that kind of cash. In the meantime, we are sitting ducks, as you Amis would say. It would have been better if Nathan took the stones."

"But not safer. The fact that he can't sell them any easier than us is our only protection against a double-cross."

"Ja, that is true, but it also works the other way. Gupta knows that the stones are useless to us. We cannot do anything with them."

"Neither can he without them." Martin lobbed what was left of the chicken carcass into the water and licked his fingers. "There's not much we can do until we meet the guy. Too much thought at this stage can be counterproductive."

"A waste for sure. You know, Martin, I would cheerfully throw all the diamonds in the lake if I could walk away free."

"Who wouldn't? This is the bottom of the fucking pit. You said it right: the true heart of darkness. Sitting in the boring boonies, surrounded by greed and corruption on all sides, and worst of all, being confronted by our own every time we look at the walls in Sankara's stinking sweatbox."

"Ach so. Beating on ourselves is not going to change the past. We must look to the present if we want to change the future."

Martin nodded. "For now, I'm too drunk to do anything but go to bed." He lurched to his feet and extended a hand to Stefan.

Drunkenly, they kicked out the embers and threw their trash in the lake. The crimson fingers of dawn peeled back the dark edges of the night canvas as they linked arms and staggered back to the bungalow.

• • •

Martin woke with a raging thirst. Groggily, he took in his surroundings. It was close to sunset, and Stefan was snoring away peacefully in the corner. He giggled to himself as he groped around for a tepid Nile. The headache was almost worth it. He felt spiritually rejuvenated. The crumbling walls didn't seem to be closing in on him anymore. He laughed uproariously.

Stefan moaned. "Not so loud. What is so funny, anyway?"

"Not much, I guess, but at least I'm laughing."

"What time is it?"

"Sundown. Time to take a dip and brush my teeth. This Nile's fighting a losing battle with the skunk in my mouth."

"You seem awfully chipper this evening."

"I feel better. I guess spewing all that shit last night helped. Now that I've seen the bottom, the only way left is up. Things just don't seem so bad for some reason."

They bathed, swam, and stretched out on the sandy beach to drip-dry.

Martin inhaled deeply. "Who needs towels with this breeze? You know, this would be a great place for a resort."

"Ja, when Amin, Astles, and crew leave, we will build it. You would look great in a white suit, and Joe could run it for us."

"Perfect."

The chugging of an outboard motor interrupted their reverie. They hurriedly pulled on their clothes and dashed to the dock.

The major had already finished tying up when they got there. "Evening, chaps. Give me a hand. I have lots of gear with me. How did the meeting go? I liked the cut of that fellow Nathan's jib. No flies on him."

"Fine. More expensive than we thought, but times are tough all over."

Stefan passed Martin a cane and a makeup kit. "Disguises too?"

"Wait until you see them," the major replied. "We must have a fashion show after dinner. Speaking of which, why don't you start a fire over on the beach?" The major pulled two black clerical habits out of a duffel bag. "These may not fit exactly, but they'll have to do in a pinch."

Martin studied the full theatrical makeup kit. "Where'd you get this?"

"A friend in the business." The major's tone precluded further discussion. "Your friend Russell has been fishing around in his normal subtle fashion. For some reason, he's taken the bizarre notion that you're involved in diamond smuggling to finance a guerilla movement."

Stefan laughed. "Now that is straight out of a thriller. That is probably the line the Zairians are putting out. They cannot afford to admit what is really going on."

After the three dined on the beach, Martin kicked out the fire. "We'd better get back up to the Ritz and get our costumes together."

Not surprisingly, the major turned out to be a dab hand with makeup. Martin wasn't sure what he had done, but when Martin gazed into a hand mirror afterward, a stranger's face stared back at him.

"How about this one?" the major said with a chuckle.

Stefan sported an unsightly mole, complete with hair, just below his nose, and a vivid birthmark on his neck, perfectly positioned so that just enough would show above his clerical collar to attract attention.

The major handed out two pairs of National Health steel rims: clear for Martin and tinted for Stefan. "Into your suits for the snaps." He fiddled with the shutter adjustment on a battered Leica.

By the time they'd found a non-peeling patch of wall for the backdrop, the major had the powerful lights he'd brought along in position. "I'd never have believed it, but you two make pretty good priests."

Martin smiled. "Can't you see my halo?"

"I hope the people checking your papers won't be aware of your more secular propensities," the major added dryly.

Stefan fingered his mole. "What about the dye and this stuff. Are they permanent?"

"The dye is waterproof, but you may have to touch it up a little as your hair grows out. The birthmark and the mole are permanent unless you have the right solvent. I'll write it down for you. Another thing: I'd advise that you start thinking of yourselves as clergy. Old habits die hard, and you cannot just walk into the first bar you pass and order a waragi—or make a pass at every attractive mpenzi you pass on the street." The major glanced at his watch. "Nine o'clock. Time for me to be off. See you toward the end of the week, chaps, or sooner if anything develops."

•••

They didn't hear a word for the next five days. They passed the time as best they could perfecting their cover stories. The major had promised them some cover letters with the official Catholic charity letterhead ordering their transfer to Lamu.

Martin perfected a convincing limp by putting pebbles in one of his shoes. Still, nervous energy consumed him.

Stefan threw down his hat. "Scheissen, I am sick of this. What night is it, anyway? I have lost track."

"If it's chicken, it must be Friday. We should hear something soon."

"If my ears do not deceive me, we will hear something in the next five or ten minutes."

The distinctive signature of the twin diesels that powered the major's boat resonated through the damp mist that often embraced the water in the early evening.

"Hallo, hallo." He was all smiles as he tied up. "Lots to report." He handed them up a couple of cartons of supplies and a suitcase.

Martin offered him a hand up. "Believe me: We're ready, Major."

"Jolly good, because it looks as though you're going sometime this week."

"Really? That's music to our ears."

"Your friend Nathan appeared at the bungalow last night. Scared the wits out of me. I thought he was a kondo. Came bloody close to shooting him."

Stefan snickered. "Sehr gut. It is somehow reassuring that an old hand like yourself can be caught napping. What did he say?"

"One day this week, and not much else."

"Well, it's better than a kick in the teeth," Martin said with a sigh, "but I wish we had some idea of how we're going. What's new in town?"

"Not much. The dogs are still out, but they seem to be losing heart for the chase. They're still going through the motions, of course, but I get the feeling that they're beginning to think that you two have got away."

"That'd be a break, for a change. Any word on Esther?"

"She's as well as can be expected, though rather worried about you. Your lot will be disappointed to hear that you're no longer the hot gossip item in town."

"I'm devastated. Who pushed us out of the headlines?"

"Another assassination attempt last week. Some silly bugger threw a grenade at the general. Hit him right on the chest. There was only one problem: The bloody berk forgot to pull the pin."

Stefan shook his head in disgust. "Scheissen! Like most bastards, this one has nine lives."

"Too bloody right. There are increasing signs that his nibs is really starting to lose control. It's rumored that he has resurrected the Tripoli scenario and is about to open up diplomatic relations with the Libyans. There's more: Prominent former politicians have disappeared recently. It's said that they've been taken to detention camps."

Martin frowned with disappointment. "Sounds as though the country is over the hump and starting down the slippery slope. It's a damn shame, not to mention waste."

"On to more cheerful topics, lads. I have your papers with me, and I must say, my man did a first-class job." He opened the suitcase and handed each of them a buff-colored envelope. "Take a look at your new personae."

The major hadn't exaggerated.

As Martin studied his papers, he couldn't help feeling like he was staring at official documents. "They look good to me. I take it you composed the covering letters. The names are priceless: Stefan Buber and Martin Luther. It's wonderful that you're so ecumenical."

"Bit of an inside joke. I must be off. I have business in Kampala tonight. It's slow-going these days because of all the roadblocks."

Martin cast off the painter. "Will we see you again?"

"Over a bottle of bubbly somewhere."

"Thanks for everything, Major. You've been like the naughty uncle everyone should have."

"Not exactly racy magazines I've been passing you, though. I must say, I've grown fond of you chaps. I wouldn't have done this just for the money."

"Nice of you to say that, even if you don't mean it. You really couldn't have made this up."

"No, laddies. As they say, this is Africa."

Martin allowed himself a chuckle at the wry quip. "I just hope Nathan and crew show up."

"They will, old bean. They can't afford not to."

Stefan snapped off his best salute. "To better times in better places."

"Aw, come on," Martin said. "I'm going to miss the Sankara Hilton."

The major gently motored away. "Godspeed. If you make it, you'll be the better for this. A man always is after a journey into the belly of the beast."

Then he was gone.

...

The days crawled by with no word from Nathan to relieve their growing tension. They stewed during the sweltering days and drank heavily at night. There were times when Martin wanted to scream—and did. Not that it sped anything along.

At last, Friday arrived. They spent all day packing.

The fortnight in the mildewing Sankara Hilton had done wonders for the Samsonites. They'd lost the conspicuous sheen of newness and assumed a well-used look.

Two weeks in the Sikh sweatbox would do that to anything, Martin figured. He suddenly realized that he didn't know what their quarters looked like from the outside. They'd never seen it in daylight. Just as quickly, he realized he didn't care.

They put almost all of their clothes in a pile for their host.

Martin regarded the heap with regret. "Our host is going to be the best-dressed Sikh in the Sseses, that's for sure, but clergy are supposed to be beyond sartorial elegance." He remembered their expense stash of stones in the sleeping bag and removed them before consigning the thoroughly molding sack to the gift pile. After finishing up, he made the sign of the cross. "I just pray they get here tonight."

"Ja," Stefan mused, "I shall drink one with him even though I cannot stand the stuff. On to business. We have wallowed in nostalgia enough. What sort of contribution should we make to Sankara?"

"Something righteous. How about a thou?"

"Fair enough. That leaves us a good reserve."

"We shouldn't need that much. We're priests, remember? We're not exactly going to run around living high on the hog."

"Unfortunately, you are correct, but we may also have some serious nonclerical expenses. This living the holy life could be taxing. The eye of the needle, and all that."

"It's not so hard if you try. You're beginning to sound like a man of the cloth already."

•••

Sleep was elusive. They were still awake at dawn. Time seemed to inch by.

Martin caught himself looking at the sun every few minutes in a vain effort to hasten its path across the morning sky. If anything, it moved even less perceptibly than the hands on his watch.

They gave Sankara his gift when he visited during the lunch break. He was overwhelmed and burst into a stuttering spate of incomprehensible Hindustani.

Afterward, they resumed their sweaty vigil, and after systematically drinking their last case of Nile, they catnapped until sunset.

Stefan stared blankly out the window. Silently, he offered Martin a joint.

"No thanks. I'm too tense. How about a dip?"

Stefan tensed. "Nein. I think I hear a boat."

They bolted out to the top of the hill.

"You're right," Martin said, panting, "and it's headed this way. Just pray it's Nathan."

The boat's phosphorescent wake snaked across the turgid water. It was a good fifteen minutes before it got close enough for them to make out the shape.

"It doesn't look like a patrol boat." Martin peered into the darkness. "It's not!" he shouted in relief. "It's a dugout. It's got to be Nathan."

By the time they got to the dock, Nathan had finished securing the boat.

Martin was the first to greet him. "Are we glad to see you!"

"I have no doubt that you are, mzungus. Are you ready? We have a long ride ahead of us."

"Where?"

"I will tell you once we have started. Get your things. I want to be off in ten minutes."

They rushed up to the bungalow, gathered their Samsonites, and were back on the dock in five.

Nathan flipped on a small flashlight to help them stow the bags. When he got a good look at their appearances, he laughed. "I have to hand it to you, mzungus. You change every time I see you. I only recognized you because I was expecting you."

"Wait till you see the rest of our disguises," Stefan said with a chortle. "But we are saving that surprise until we get where we are going."

"That is a good idea. I am afraid the ride will be wet."

Martin didn't look back as they left the dock. The Ssese sojourn wasn't a part of the trip he particularly wanted to remember. He kicked a full jerry can at his feet. "What gives, Nathan? Are we going across the lake to the Kenyan side?"

"Yes. That is, of course, assuming we do not run into the odd patrol boat. Not to worry." He smiled cheerfully. "They are usually drunk on Saturday nights."

"It is reassuring to hear that some things do not change." Stefan started their last bottle of cognac on its rounds. "How long will this little ride take?"

"We should be in by dawn." Nathan glanced at a pocket compass and adjusted course slightly. "I will try some of that."

"Where do we go from there?" Stefan asked.

"We land a few miles from Kericho. The train to the coast stops there."

"How are things around town? Are they still after us?"

"They are still watching the land borders and the airport very carefully, but who really knows what they are thinking? There has been some trouble around town. Their minds are probably on other things."

"Ja, we heard. Too bad they did not get him. Probably would save a lot of trouble later on."

"It is true," Nathan said, anger sounding in his voice. "He is going to open relations with the Libyans soon."

Martin wiped his mouth after another drink. "An ominous thought. Will it affect you all?"

"It very well could. There is no doubt in my mind that the man is crazy. I am sure that he is going to throw out all the Indians too."

"All at once? Jesus, that'll be a hell of a mess." Martin shuddered as another sheet of spray plastered him.

Nathan shrugged. "Well, the price of copper is going through the floor. That means big economic trouble, and he has got to blame somebody."

Martin couldn't help but acknowledge Amin's political savvy. "Very neat. He blames the Indians and gets a loan from Khadafy to balance the books. He may not be an intellectual heavyweight, but he doesn't lack for animal cunning. We're getting out just in time."

The three men lapsed into a gloomy silence.

Gradually, Martin's mind was jarred into submission, and everything melted into a soggy blur.

Nathan's throttling down returned him to his senses. "Pass me those jerry cans. It is time to refuel."

Martin took the opportunity to light a smoke and have a swig of cognac.

Stefan was slumped over, dozing fitfully.

"How are we doing?" Martin asked. "I've completely lost track of the time."

"About four more hours. Not a very pleasant ride, I am afraid."

"Yeah, I've got to admit it might have been a lot more interesting in daylight."

Nathan silenced him with an abrupt chopping motion. The African's body stiffened into the posture of a bird dog on point. "If that noise is what I think it is," he whispered, "our trip might get very interesting shortly."

The muffled chugging of a heavy diesel engine grew increasingly clear. The mist and darkness would give them a little extra time but not much.

"Shit, you can bet it's not a fishing boat at this time of night."

"A patrol boat, mzungu. They are the only things on the water at this time of night with a diesel engine."

"So why don't we bolt? He won't hear our engine over his own noise."

"Because in the highly likely event it is a patrol boat, they already have us on their radar. The boats are Israeli-supplied with special anti-infiltration sets. The Israelis have had some problems with terrorists, so their boats are well-equipped to pick up small craft."

Nathan motioned for silence once more and began rummaging through the rucksacks under his seat. In no time at all, he had assembled an Uzi. The steady thrum of the diesel was getting closer all the time. It was a funeral dirge.

Martin couldn't believe it. For some idiotic reason, he'd assumed that they would be safe until they hit the Kenyan shore. His bowels rumbled.

Nathan handed him a round softball-sized object. "You are about to get a crash course in grenade-throwing. Pull the pin and stick your finger in the trigger mechanism."

Martin stared blankly at him. The monotonous chugging pounded a terrifying chant into his psyche. He was doomed.

Suddenly, a white-hot pain exploded in his jaw, forcing tears.

"Snap out of it, mzungu. We have but a slim chance if you do your job—and none if you do not." Nathan snatched the grenade from his hand, tore out the pin, and jammed his index finger under the handle. "Like this. Do not worry. You have three seconds after you take your finger out before it will go off."

Martin's brain switched back on. "Okay, Nathan. I'm back in the land of the living."

"If by some chance it's a Kenyan boat, keep the grenade covered in your lap. If it's Ugandan, I will maneuver us into a good position, and we will open up. I don't have to tell you that we don't want to be taken alive." He moved himself into a better firing position and flicked off his safety. "Hold on with your non-throwing hand, and do not move before I do. They have deck-mounted fifty-calibers. We will be dead in an instant if we do not move at exactly the right time."

Up ahead to their right, a brilliant white finger probed the inky darkness.

Stefan stirred but didn't wake. How could he sleep through the noise?

Martin, feeling helpless while the boat edged closer and closer, fought off the insane desire to stand up and shout anything to relieve the tension.

They were pinpointed and blinded by the harsh glare of the searchlight before the thought died. It took the sleek patrol craft five more agonizing minutes to come within hailing distance. Now Martin knew how the fly felt after it had stopped struggling in the web.

"Heave to and prepare to be boarded, or we will blow you out of the water!" The tinny, metallic rasp of the bullhorn gave the man's voice an unworldly timbre, but the reality of the command was chillingly clear.

As the patrol boat throttled down and banked smoothly to a halt about ten feet away from them, the choppy wash rocked the dugout.

Stefan finally stirred.

"Now what would two mzungus and a presumably innocent fishermen be doing out on the lake at this time of night?"

Even though the light was focused somewhere over their heads, it was still too bright for Martin to see any of the occupants of the patrol boat. But he didn't need to see to recognize the high-pitched eunuch's voice. It was Ali Kilogo. The last rat out of the woodpile. Martin could visualize his beanbag body shaking with mirth.

"Our boat broke down," Martin lied, "and this nice gentleman saved us."

Kilogo cackled, unable to restrain himself any longer. "Very good, Mr. Fine. I do not know if I could have done any better myself on such short notice. Your disguises are not bad for amateurs. I am so glad we ran into you. I have had some rather choice accommodations prepared for you for the past two weeks. It would have been most disappointing if you could not have joined me."

Martin ignored the chill running down his spine and keyed in on Nathan's throttle hand. Vague movements told him that the crew was preparing to lower a boat. Kilogo would tire of the game soon. He wasn't the type to waste time on useless chatter when he would soon have their undivided attention.

"How'd you know we would be here?"

"A little birdie told us, but you will soon know everything. My men are just lowering the raft over the side. We shall have plenty of time to discuss these matters."

Martin was groping for a follow-up when Nathan's knuckles went white on the throttle. In one smooth motion, Martin flipped the poncho off his lap and lobbed the grenade at the searchlight. The banshee snarl of their revving engine and the chatter of Nathan's Uzi were almost simultaneous, and Martin was thrown back over his seat by the concussion of the grenade's blast.

The patrol boat vaporized in a sheet of purplish-yellow flame, and suddenly, unbelievably, nothing was left but a churning, boiling mass of water. White-hot debris rained down all around them. One hulking piece landed about thirty feet in front of them and continued to blaze. It was the rubber raft. Incredibly, it had come through the blast intact. The same couldn't be said of its occupants, who were shriveling into little balls like pieces of paper burning in an ashtray.

Gagging, Martin grabbed the gunwale and puked over the side until there was nothing left and then continued the exercise for several minutes.

"Better they than us," Nathan said solemnly. "The thermite is most unpleasant, but it is effective. That was the first time I have ever used it." He passed over the cognac.

Martin took a deep swig and mouthed a silent prayer of thanks. He glanced at Stefan, who seemed to be stunned into catatonic shock. "Think they had any friends around, Nathan?"

"I doubt it. Given the nature of our cargo, the fewer people who knew, the better. Too bad I could not wait to hear who broke security, but I had to move before the raft hit the water. That was when the majority of the crew was occupied."

"God, I hope they didn't get Esther. Did she know the details?"

"No. I saw her this morning. I doubt it was her."

CHAPTER

23

THE SOUND OF the boat's engine throttling down woke Martin, who needed only a moment to orient himself.

Nathan grunted and pointed ahead to a low-slung, brooding mass silhouetted against the rapidly brightening horizon. "Kenya."

It was the magic incantation.

Stefan roused himself and glanced at his watch. "Four-thirty. In by five, Nathan?"

"Yes. Nice of you to join us." Nathan reached into his breast pocket. "Here is a schedule for the train. We should have time to tidy up some before we have to head to the station."

"How far from town are we going to hit shore?" Stefan asked.

"About five miles. It is market day on this side, so we should be able to catch a cab or a ride with no difficulty."

"You seem to have thought of everything." Martin raised the depleted cognac bottle in a mock toast. "You're coming with us on the train?"

"Of course, but in a third-class compartment more suited to my humble status as a farmer."

Martin turned to Stefan. "It sure is nice to see you back in the land of the living."

334

"Ja, that was some show. I thought we were finished, so I kept my eyes shut."

Nathan gazed toward the shore. "We were lucky, very lucky. I hope that you have not used up all your luck, because you are going to need some for the rest of the trip."

It was almost light when they landed on a deserted strip of beach in a rocky cove. They clambered out and unloaded their gear.

When they had finished, Nathan gestured up to the point about fifty meters away. "Pull the boat up there." He handed them the bowline and jogged off.

By the time they had eased the boat up to the point, Nathan parted some branches, revealing a cave big enough to hide the boat.

"Looks like you have done this before," Stefan said as they tied down the boat.

Nathan carefully adjusted the bushes. "My return ticket. Let's build a fire and make some tea. I have the necessary ingredients in my bag."

The fire felt good, Martin thought. So did the cognac-laced tea.

Nathan chuckled as they spread their habits out to dry. "I see what you mean about your disguises. An excellent choice."

"Sure looks desolate enough around these parts," Martin said.

"It should be," Nathan said. "It is Kenyan government property. They set it aside about ten years ago for a commercial fishing development. If they ever received the money, it was diverted into Mama Kenyatta's purse."

"Probably." Stefan checked their clothes. "Getting nice and dry. What do you say to heading into town? Maybe we can get some breakfast before the train leaves."

They changed. Martin felt physically revived with semidry clothes on and some warm tea in his gut, but his battered psyche was still operating mechanically, as though he was disconnected from reality. He carefully selected a few pebbles from the beach to aid his limp. It was a long, tedious slog up to the road. Luckily, the first vehicle that passed—a pickup truck—stopped.

From the sounds of it, the driver was a government agricultural official, but Martin couldn't be sure as he listened to Nathan converse with the man in rapid Swahili.

Martin's first exposure to Kenya was somewhat disappointing. The pictures he'd seen had whetted his appetite for the spectacular highlands of the escarpment or the arid game country of the Great Rift Valley. Only the brightly colored dress of the locals en route to the market interrupted the dull brown of the surrounding countryside.

Kericho was a good-sized town—the local administrative center, Martin guessed. They were dropped off at a large square opposite a bustling market. Nathan led them into a humble restaurant just outside the market's massive iron gates. Several constables leaving the restaurant didn't give them a second glance as they passed each other in the doorway. The fried eggs and toast were greasy but satisfying.

"How long to the train?" Stefan asked.

"An hour or so," Nathan said, sipping his coffee. "We shall walk to the station when we finish. You will have to change some money to buy the tickets."

"At least we don't seem to be attracting any attention."

"There is no reason that you should. An inspired choice of disguise. There is a large mission not five miles from where we sit."

• • •

The station was deserted. They were the only people waiting on the platform for the train. Martin felt like the walls of the waiting room had eyes. *Just paranoia*, he thought. *Your best friend for the next few weeks.* As expected, the clerk was only too happy to accept dollars in payment for their tickets and return Kenyan shillings in change. The rate was probably horrible, but they needed some pocket money.

The train pulled in about half an hour later.

"Unbelievable. It is on time to the minute," Stefan announced. "What a specimen too."

The staccato pants of the locomotive had an almost human quality not unlike those of an out-of-shape runner trying to regain his breath.

"A real iron horse."

Nathan cleared his throat. "This is where we part, gentlemen. I will be back in the third-class carriage with a compatriot. If you need anything, let us know."

Martin and Stefan found their compartment in the front of the old but very comfortable first-class coach.

"This is definitely the life!" Stefan said as he collapsed on the plush seat.

Exhaustion from the night's journey was setting in. Martin didn't fight the hypnotic sound and motion of the train. Time would pass more quickly if he slept.

He dreamt in excruciating technicolor. Esther was slowly sinking in a quicksand-like pool of diamonds. The more she struggled, the deeper she sank. He was running to help, but he was too far away. Her piteous moaning for help tore at his gut. He was too late. Just as he came within an arm's reach, a stream of glittering diamonds poured into her mouth as she disappeared.

Suddenly, she was there, in the light of day, sobbing quietly in front of him. The side of her face was swollen like a blowfish's. He rubbed his eyes, trying to erase the image from his mind. Something cold and oily was pressed against his cheek.

It was a gun, and Zack Bakazi was holding it. There was something sexual about the way he was caressing Martin's cheek with it. "Nice of you to join us, Mr. Fine." He smiled without the slightest hint of humor. "Your clothes will probably be of great assistance to you where you are going."

"Esther, what are you doing here?" Martin asked in a croaking voice.

"She just had to see you one more time. Is it not touching?" Bakazi handcuffed Martin, Stefan, and Esther to their respective armrests. "Do not be sad. You are going to be together forever."

"Oh, Martin," she said, sobbing. "I did not want to tell them anything, but they drugged me. They kidnapped me on my way home from work yesterday."

"Thank God they didn't torture you."

"There was no time to," Bakazi said. "Kilogo is not the only one with informers. Astles and I have our sources in the Anyanya also. One let us know on Thursday that something was going on, but he was not able to get any details, except that you were crossing the lake by boat. That is why I had to bring the lovely Mapende along. She was my trump card."

When Bakazi stretched his leg to counter what appeared to be a cramp, Martin's hand rose instinctively, but the handcuff brought him up short. It saved his life.

The gun never left Martin's temple as Bakazi continued. "Our contact reported that Nathan had not made any arrangements for a car, so I guessed you would be taking the train, and Kericho is the only stop near the lake. Verifying that in Kampala would have been too time-consuming, so I brought Mapende along. Besides, I am not an insensitive man. I thought that the two lovers would like to see each other one last time."

"To have done otherwise would have meant involving the Kenyans," Martin said.

"Yes, that was a factor in my decision. Nobody in his right mind wants to involve the Kenyans in anything where there is even the slightest hint of money these days. Mama Kenyatta. Need I say more? There was also the thought of using Mapende for leverage in the event you had sent the stones ahead. I must admit that I am most curious to hear how you avoided Kilogo."

"We didn't. He's probably giving the fish at the bottom of the lake indigestion at the moment."

The news had no visible effect on Bakazi. "A pity, really, but taking the long view, it just means more for Astles and myself. I am not altogether sure that the always-resourceful Kilogo was going to share the stones with us. Kilogo obviously underestimated Kaberinge as well as you. Now . . . where are the diamonds?"

"False bottoms in the suitcases." Martin kicked one of the bags in disgust. "Just set the combo to double-O-seven, set the catches in the center position, and push. I hope they bring you as much bad luck as they've brought everybody else."

Bakazi didn't acknowledge the remark. He carefully edged one of the bags over with his foot. His eyes and gun never left his captives for a second, which didn't seem necessary. He fumbled with the catches with his free hand. "Wonderful." He beamed as he felt around in the compartment. "I will examine and savor them later."

Stefan shifted position. "What is next? Not that we really want to know."

Bakazi consulted his watch. "We reach the Maleri tunnel in about twenty minutes. If you have ever been through a tunnel in a train, you know how much noise there is. Nobody will notice a few pistol shots. I will fingerprint the guns—I brought along a spare, of course—and scatter a few diamonds around. It will seem obvious that you thieves had a falling out. As for myself, I shall get off the train at Nairobi as scheduled. Naturally, I am traveling on a false passport. Good planning is the key to the success of any operation."

"Looks like you have everything covered." Martin inched his hand slowly toward his pocket. "How about a last drink and smoke for the condemned?"

"Come, come, Mr. Fine. I expected better from you."

Martin shrugged. "It was worth a try." He turned to Esther. "I'm sorry it came to this. I love you, and I hope we meet on the other side."

"I love you too, mzungu." Her eyes misted over as she grasped his hand fiercely, incapable of saying more.

Stefan looked ready to wet himself.

Martin wondered what he looked like to the others as the train chugged relentlessly onward. *So this is it*, he thought. His calmness in the face of the overwhelming unfairness of his situation surprised him.

Bakazi drew another .45 from his pocket. "Say your prayers, if you know any. You have about five minutes."

Martin was the first to notice it. "What's that smell? Is something burning?"

Acrid smoke billowed into the compartment, and Martin heard a muffled shout of "fire!" followed by pounding on the door.

Bakazi cursed and leapt catlike to his feet. He shoved one of the pistols back in his waistband, opened the door, and peered around the edge, carefully shielding the other gun with his body. Then he grunted sharply and staggered backward as Nathan burst through, shoving a burning wad of newspaper into his startled face.

They collapsed on the floor in a grotesque parody of lovemaking as the train thundered into the tunnel. The muffled report of a pistol and the red-hot burn on Martin's cheek were simultaneous, and soon the compartment reverberated with the guttural sounds of a desperate struggle. Martin wanted to kick the writhing mass at his feet, but it was so dark that he couldn't see who was who. Esther's hysterical screams punctuated the two combatants' animal grunts. The dull report of the gun reverberated off the walls again, and Martin felt Esther go limp in the seat next to him.

"Oh God, no!" Martin fumbled desperately for his Zippo. Finally, he managed to extract the lighter from his pocket and thumb its flint wheel.

The flickering flame showed Bakazi lying on top of Nathan with his whitening knuckles in a vise grip around Nathan's throat. A splash of crimson was slowly widening on the back of his khaki safari suit. The smell of hot, fresh blood mingled with the cordite fumes.

Esther's eyelids flickered, and she moaned.

"She is all right," Stefan said. "I am not so sure about Nathan."

"I am okay." Nathan grunted as he shoved Bakazi's body off his chest with a convulsive heave. He gingerly massaged his neck. "We must get rid of the body while we are still in the tunnel. Where did he put the keys to the cuffs?"

"Top pocket." Stefan was already fumbling for them with his free hand.

Nathan found the key and released them. "Quick! Give me a hand. We have only a few more minutes."

Together they wrestled the ungainly corpse off the floor and onto their shoulders. It was a struggle, but they managed to force it out the window.

"Good thing he was a military man and did not like sambosas as much as the general," Stefan panted.

Martin dribbled some waragi into Esther's mouth while the others tidied up.

"Is it over?" she asked in a choked voice.

Martin hugged her and rocked her in his arms. "It's over, and we'll never see that SOB again."

There was an authoritative knock on the door. "Is everyone all right in there? We smelled smoke."

"Everyone is okay." Stefan looked around carefully before partially opening the door. "One of my friends got careless with a cigarette and set a newspaper on fire." He cracked the door a little further and handed the conductor a burnt copy of the *Daily Nation*.

"You should really be more careful. You could have caused yourselves serious harm. The attendant will leave your tea outside the door." The conductor clucked reprovingly and bustled off.

Stefan shut the door and collapsed with the others. "That was the icing on the cake. Pass me the waragi. I do not care whether I am a man of the cloth or not. I need a stiff drink."

"After you. I could use some disinfectant." Martin fingered the shallow furrow the bullet had left on his cheek.

Stefan grabbed the waragi and examined the wound. "Not good enough for a purple heart. In fact, it looks like Esther scratched you." He turned and offered the bottle to Nathan. "Not that I am complaining, but just what brought you up here?"

"Sixth sense. I cannot explain it, but I had a feeling that something was wrong. I hope you do not think me too greedy, but I am asking for a bonus," he added with a chuckle.

The train finally clattered out of the tunnel into the bright daylight.

"I had better get back," Nathan said, blinking. "I hope he did not have anyone with him."

"A panna," Esther replied. "He was too greedy. Why did you mzungus not tell me that you were smuggling diamonds?"

"We could have," Martin said, "but we didn't want you to get involved. Would it have changed anything?"

"No." Esther frowned. "I would have loved you just as much, though I hate myself for my weakness."

Martin caressed her cheek. "We all have to live with our weaknesses, Esther. Believe me: Stefan and I have had plenty of time to reflect on ours the last two weeks, and it hasn't been easy."

Stefan yawned. "It may only be ten-twenty in the morning, but I am ready to collapse. It has been a tough twelve hours. What are we going to do about sleeping arrangements? I would think that you two would like some privacy."

"What about Bakazi's compartment?" Martin asked.

Esther rolled her eyes. "We were riding in second class. He was a cheap bastard to the end."

"Why not ask the conductor if there's a spare first-class compartment?" Martin suggested. "The train seemed pretty empty when we got on."

"What will you tell him about me? Remember: you are priests."

Stefan laughed. "Ja, the lady has a point. She is too pretty to be a nun. We had better say that she is our secretary. He won't believe us for a minute, but it doesn't matter. It is not unheard of for ministers to have bush wives."

Martin found the conductor down the corridor. As expected, a first-class car was available. Martin quickly arranged to take the adjoining compartment. The conductor didn't bat an eyelash when Martin handed over some shilingi and told him that Esther was their traveling secretary. He accepted the money with a world-weary look.

After the conductor had finished preparing their compartment and had returned to his cubbyhole at the end of the car, Martin and Esther took up residency.

She ran into his arms as soon as they got through the door. "Did you know that I have always had a secret desire to make love to a priest?"

• • •

They were awakened at four o'clock by a discreet knock on the door.

"*Raus, raus.* Nathan is here for a council of war." Stefan handed Martin and Esther each a steaming mug of waragi-laced tea. "Sleep well?"

"Like a dead man," Martin said, unable to resist. "You guys don't look any worse for the wear, either." He nodded to Nathan. "How's the neck?"

"Better. A little waragi helps. I have made a careful survey of the train, and it seems Bakazi was alone."

Martin wasn't surprised. "As Esther said, he was a greedy bastard like the rest. You know, if I didn't have so much personal inconvenience and time invested, I'd just throw the damn stones out the window."

"What?" Stefan spluttered indignantly. "I have paid my dues, and I, for one, plan to collect. Besides, we will need the money to start over again. If any of this gets out, our names will be dirt."

"No way will it be mentioned outside of Uganda, Zaire, and maybe Rwanda. When we get back, we just announce that we escaped from the poachers, bandits, or whatever and resume our normal lives. Of course, I don't think we'd be well-advised to take any business trips to those countries in the near future."

Stefan replenished their teas. "You are sure there is no chance of Zaire applying for extradition? The diamonds did originate from there."

"What would they have but their word against ours? Sure, we knew Aka, but we never met him that day. Singh's not going to spill the beans."

"What about the bodies, including Bakazi's?"

"I'm positive the good colonel made damn sure nobody saw him enter this compartment, so there's no way we're connected. As for the others, they won't find them until the next dry season.

By then, there won't be much left—certainly nothing to link them to us. I made sure of that when I cleaned out the Rover."

"Ja, I guess you are correct. Mobutu does not give a shit about the diamonds. To him they are a piss in the pot. He has what he wanted out of the deal: no more financing for the separatist movement in Shaba."

"And we'll get a school named after us in the southern Sudan. Right, Nathan?"

"Something like that," Nathan replied as he rose to leave. "I will return before Nairobi."

"He left quickly." Stefan rubbed his eyes. "There was something queer in his tone, but I am too tired for such subtleties. I wonder what got into him."

"I sensed something too." Martin exchanged glances with Esther, whose furrowed brow suggested she shared their concern. He took a deep breath, determined for the moment to rest and recover. "Let's just relax and enjoy the rest of the ride." He glanced out the window at the changing landscape, which was growing more verdant by the second. "It looks like we're beginning to pass through the highlands now."

The countryside was incongruous for equatorial Africa. Plump dairy cattle grazed contentedly on lush pastures.

"I expect to see a fox hunt come charging over the hill any second," Martin said.

"It is possible," Stefan said. "I have heard that they still ride to hounds in these parts, but do not worry. By tomorrow morning, we will be back in equatorial Africa with a vengeance. Down into the Rift Valley and up the escarpment at dawn. I am told the view is memorable. We should reach Nairobi about eight. Then on to Mombasa through great-game country."

"When do we get in?"

"About six."

Esther poured herself the last mug of tea, and the train pulled into Eldoret, the administrative center of the "white highlands" a few minutes later. The quaint little station house would have looked completely at home in the Cotswolds, Martin thought. He was disappointed that darkness was upon them, because he'd read that the highlands were an interesting area, a climatic and geological aberration. Dubbed the African Alps by the white planters who'd flocked there in the 1920s, the large plateau in central Kenya was blessed with some of the most fertile land on the whole continent and the mild climate to exploit it.

The attendant knocked on the door and announced that dinner was being served in the dining car.

Stefan rose to his feet with a contented sigh. "That is our cue."

"No," Martin said. "*Yours*. Someone has to stay and guard the stones. Bring some back for us."

Martin was famished. He realized he hadn't eaten anything since breakfast.

Fortunately, Stefan was quick. The food was surprisingly good, and Martin felt much better after he'd finished. *How things change*, he mused to himself. A month earlier, he would never have been able to enjoy a large dinner hours after somebody had been shot to death at his feet. The thought was disquieting, and he wasn't so sure it was a positive step in his spiritual growth. He shook it off. As Stefan had said, "Life's hard lessons."

Martin and Esther retired after eating. Exhausted, they undressed and lay in each other's arms.

Esther's gentle strength bathed him. "This all must have been terrible for you, mzungu."

"No worse for me than you. Do you understand why I didn't tell you everything?"

"Yes, Martin, I know that you did it for my own good. I did not believe you were a bad person. Do the killings weigh on your mind?"

"Yeah, they bother me, but as the major told me, I should be glad that I've still got a conscience, which is more than can be said for most of the other bastards playing this game. What really bothers me about the whole affair is my own weakness, which got me involved in the first place. I'll never look at life the same way again. My innocence is gone."

"That is not necessarily a bad thing. When you have no illusions left, you cannot be disappointed anymore."

"And nothing left to hide behind, either. I did a lot of thinking about you while I sat around that stinking hut in the Sseses. I realized that all the excuses I'd made—'She won't leave Africa,' 'We're too different,' and the like—were just a shield. I was scared of making a commitment. That's what I feel worst about at the moment: not having been honest with either you or myself. I've been cheating both of us."

"I love you even more for saying that. I knew that you were fighting with yourself, but if I had said anything to make you realize the truth, you would have run. You would have buried yourself even deeper behind those walls that mzungus are so good at building. Do you remember what I said the first night we met?"

"You mean about Africans being able to sense what mzungus are feeling better than we can sometimes? Yes. I was thinking of it the other day. I can't hide anymore. It doesn't work."

She gently rolled on top of him. "I feel like this is the first time we are really making love."

CHAPTER

24

MARTIN AND ESTHER woke to a none-too gentle pounding on the door. "*Achtung!* This is your tour conductor. Tea is up, and dawn is on the way. The escarpment will be in sight any minute."

By the time they roused themselves and dressed, the first crimson fingers of dawn were tickling the edges of the black sky.

Esther admired the view and kissed him lightly on the cheek. "Just for us."

The crimson and orange worked their way in from the outer edges of the celestial canvas, framing the mist-shrouded mass of the escarpment. The antediluvian monolith grew larger as they approached, until it blocked the whole horizon. And the first tentative rays of the sun illuminated its craggy, inscrutable face.

Rock of Ages, Martin thought.

"Worth getting up for?" Stefan asked.

"Mother Africa," Martin said with a reverent sigh. "It's seen them all come and go."

"Ja, it has been here for a long time. I hope the mist clears by the time we get to the top. I would hate to miss the view back down the valley."

The train had slowed perceptibly. The locomotive's panting

resumed its almost human timbre as they began climbing a tortuous series of switchbacks.

"What a change from last night," Martin remarked as they observed the dull-brown checkerboard emerging from the evaporating mist.

"Ja, this is more typical of most of the country. Kenya is pretty dry compared to Uganda. They do not have the Nile. The view is incredible. I feel as though I can see to the end of the continent."

Martin couldn't see the Atlantic, but when they reached the summit, the view wasn't a disappointment. The terrain changed completely up on the escarpment. It was greener than the lowlands and obviously more fertile. Large villages were sprinkled on either side of the tracks, and there was abundant traffic on the numerous roads that crisscrossed the vast plateau.

The skyline of Nairobi came into sight about an hour later.

"Looks like most European cities from here," Martin said.

"It is a lot bigger than Kampala." Esther appeared entranced. "How many people live there?"

"About one and a half million," Martin answered. "Roughly five times the population of Kampala."

The skyline might have been distinctly Western, but the slums they passed through on the outskirts were eminently African and much more squalid than the shantytowns around Kampala. Open sewers meandered through the festering piles of garbage that lay among the cardboard and tarpaper shacks. The stench was appalling even from the moving train.

Stefan wrinkled his nose. "Mein Gott. These settlements look like something the dog threw up on the carpet. It is a shame that any human has to live like this. Every time there is a drought in the north, which is pretty often, the population swells by about fifty thousand. The children look malnourished."

Martin sighed. "Lots of pellagra. I've always found it one of nature's greatest ironies that the main symptom of chronic starvation is a swollen gut."

Nathan knocked and entered. "Good morning to all. I trust you were awake in time to take in the view from the top of the escarpment?"

"It was memorable," Martin replied. "How long do we stop in Nairobi?"

"About forty-five minutes. Why?"

"I was going to get off and change some money. We're running low on Kenyan, and we get into Mombasa late."

"There should be a bank in the station. I will come with you, but I think that everyone else should stay on board. There is no purpose in arousing any undue attention. I am meeting someone here, so I will get the latest news from Kampala."

"Let's hope nobody was waiting for Bakazi."

"There will not be anyone," Esther said. "I was with him the whole time, and he did not tell anybody where he was going."

Martin shook his head in disgust. "That figures. He was probably planning to siphon off a few of the stones before he turned them over to Astles."

The station was a madhouse. Market day, judging from the bundles and baskets that everyone in sight was carrying. Nathan asked the nearest policeman where the bank was, and they pushed their way through to it. Martin didn't feel as naked as he had at Kericho. He got a nasty surprise when the clerk asked him for his passport, but it passed muster. He even remembered to sign his alias on the foreign exchange chit.

Nathan headed off to find his contact, and on the way back to the train, Martin stopped at a vendor's and bought some cold beers, newspapers, and cigarettes. The train chugged out right on schedule. They spent the rest of the morning reading.

• • •

Martin had to admit that the ride was getting boring. They had descended slowly to an arid plateau during the morning, but the promised game proved to be sparse and unexotic. They saw only one herd of elephants and no lions. "If this is the best Kenya's got to offer," he said, "I'm glad I spent my time in Uganda."

"Ja, fortunately, it is only a few more hours until we get to Mombasa, thank God. What is the drill once we get there?"

"Check into a hotel and figure out how we get to Lamu the next morning." Martin reopened the window. It had been getting progressively hotter as they neared the coast. The compartment's fan needed all the help it could get. "I was figuring on renting a car. The disguises and papers seem to be holding up, and we wouldn't attract any more attention than we would riding in native buses."

Stefan nodded. "It would be safer to have the mobility. Scheissen, it is getting hot in here! We must add a swim to the agenda tonight. Have you given any thought to a plan of action once we hit Lamu?"

"I have. It's difficult to make any firm plans before we scout the lay of the land, but there's one thing I think we have to do right away: Stash the stones. They're our only bargaining chip."

"Natürlich. I hope that we can find somewhere safe that is reasonably accessible. We will have to be careful, though. Lamu is such a small place that Gupta will probably know of our arrival within minutes."

"You're right The disguises won't do any good. The minute they see the Samsonites, they'll know. I think we had better buy new bags in Mombasa. Now that we've crossed the border, we don't need the Samsonites. I just wish we could can this priest routine. It's definitely cramping my style."

Stefan shrugged. "It is worse for me. I do not have an amorous secretary along. We cannot afford to take the chance that they are still looking for our old selves. For now, the advantages far outweigh the discomforts."

Esther frowned. "There is one problem I have been thinking about. What do I do for a passport?"

"Ach so. That is a problem."

"Not really," Martin replied. "I figure Mr. Gupta should have the resources to get us one. He's just going to have to do a little work for his money."

Nathan entered a few minutes later, listened patiently to their plans, smiled, and said, "The ferry from the mainland does not take cars. There are virtually none on Lamu. Everybody goes around on foot. I checked. There are regular tourist buses that run every morning between Mombasa and the ferry."

Stefan chuckled. "See what a little local knowledge will do for you? So, Nathan, where are we staying in Mombasa?"

"I know a hotel on the beach that should serve our purposes perfectly. It is not quite as luxurious as the newer ones but very comfortable. It is just the sort of place clergy would stay."

"Do you get a commission too?"

"No, but I am working on it. We are due shortly. I will meet you on the platform. Let us try to get out of the station as quickly as possible. There are always police around."

Relaxed yet excited, Martin packed his things. "Boy, I can feel that ocean now!" he said as they stepped off the train.

Nathan and his companion, a dour beanpole with vivid tribal scars etched into his hatchet face, argued at length with the cab driver before agreeing on a fare to the hotel. Martin was tempted to tell them not to worry about it but decided it was better not to let them know that the "priests" had plenty of cash.

Most of the action in Mombasa sprang from the strip of glossy milk-carton hotels lining the beach. There was the usual resort potpourri of rip-off duty-free shops, restaurants, and nightclubs advertising native floor shows.

The Mombasa Inn proved to be a colonial throwback. A rambling buff-colored building, it seemed to be suffering from an identity crisis and didn't know whether it wanted to be an overgrown bungalow or a Victorian gingerbread mansion. The flamingo-pink shutters tilted the scale in favor of the latter. Architecture aside, it was on the beach and boasted air conditioning, which, judging from the lobby, more or less worked.

"I'm not sure I'm going to be able to sleep in a bed with real sheets," Martin said with a laugh, "but a shower will pose no problems." He sniffed himself and frowned.

It was still the slow season, so they were able to rent adjoining rooms on the beach side. Nathan and his partner went upstairs, but the rest of them went to the hotel store and brought some ugly, overpriced swimsuits.

They were down on the beach in fifteen minutes. The sun had already begun to set, but the sand was still baking. The gently swelling ocean was bath-tepid.

"God, that felt good," Martin said as he toweled off. "I wonder if we can get a decent meal around these parts."

"I will ask on the way up," Stefan replied. "This living like a normal human being could grow on me."

The restaurant wasn't anything special, but the fish had been caught that day.

"Normalcy returns." Stefan said with a belch. "Some of those clubs we passed on the way over looked awfully tempting. It has been a long time for a young, healthy sort like me."

Martin gave him a look of disapproval. "Remember what you said on the train?"

"Easy enough for you to say. You have a bird in hand. Seeing all those mpenzis in the flesh gets a man to thinking."

Martin picked up the pace as they reached the tawdry section of the strip.

Even though the bodies being displayed were brazenly brassy, Stefan was having a hard time keeping his eyes off the wares. With what looked like a conscious effort, he tore his eyes away from the leering invitation of a rumbustious mpenzi clad in purple spandex hot pants and green leather boots with gravity-defying platform heels.

They settled for a bottle of cognac on the beach. The warm cotton-candy breeze off the moon-dappled waters gently bathed them, soothing their accumulated tensions. The rumbling ocean provided a low, rhythmic underpinning to the deep treble of the bullfrogs and the soprano trilling of the cicadas. Martin felt that he was finally in the eye of the storm. The bottle circulated methodically. No one spoke. The mood was too fragile. It was just the mental recharge they needed before the final lap.

Back in the womb at last, Martin lost track of time until lights started going off up and down the beach. Esther took his hand and nodded toward the hotel. Reluctantly, he followed. Upstairs, they lay in each other's arms. Making love didn't occur to Martin. It would have been redundant.

• • •

The next morning, Martin and Esther took an early-morning dip and strolled into the deserted dining room.

Stefan arrived a few minutes later. He looked viciously hungover but seemed cheerful enough. "*Guten Tag.* I ran into Nathan on the way down. The bus leaves at ten." His bloodshot eyes roved the room for a waiter. "More coffee, please. I need it bad."

"Good," Martin said. "That should give us time to shop for a few things we need, like suitcases. Esther needs some clothes."

"Natürlich. I could use some too. I doubt that we will find anything appropriate in these parts, but at this point, I would settle for some clean shirts, socks, and underwear. Nathan can meet us at the bus. He knows where we are going."

Nathan was amenable enough. They paid their bills and caught a taxi to the shopping area. The selection was better than at the hotel, even if the prices were the same.

Martin raised an eyebrow toward their escort. "Nathan's not taking any chances, I see."

"Ja, I noticed. Scarface has been right behind us ever since we left the hotel. Such a lack of trust. It must be our clothes."

They reached the bus depot at about nine and took turns going to the bathroom to switch suitcases.

The bus had seen better days, and the countryside was brown and boring, so Martin and Esther napped for most of the three-hour drive. The ferry terminal was a rusting pile of corrugated iron. Its lack of air conditioning and the warmth of the refreshment kiosk's beverages confirmed the impression that the tourist boom hadn't extended to Lamu. Still, the shortcomings were easy enough to overlook, Martin thought. The end was in sight.

"Remind me to write to the Ministry of Tourism." Stefan fought down the warm brew. "Amazing how quickly one becomes used to the benefits of civilization again."

"These days, only the hippies visit Lamu. They go there to smoke pot." Nathan pointed to a stoned pair of longhairs who appeared to be the only other passengers. "The ferry leaves in half an hour and is about an hour's ride," he added over his shoulder as he strolled to the end of the pier to wait with Scarface.

Martin glanced at the androgynous blue-jeaned couple, but they avoided his gaze and scuttled outside like a pair of suddenly exposed land crabs. His thoughts fleetingly turned to his good old carefree days. Maybe it was his priestly garb.

Stefan offered an encouraging smile. "Cheer up, Hein. It is not all bad to be in the real world. Do you think we are near the finish?"

"No. The fun's just beginning. Sometimes, I wonder if it will ever be over."

They strolled over to where Esther was waiting.

"I wonder what the ferry will be like," Martin said.

"We shall know soon enough. I see it coming." Stefan grimaced.

"My God," Martin said as he studied the relic steaming toward them. "It's the Show Boat's sister. They don't build them like that anymore. Haven't for fifty years."

The boat had certainly seen better days. It looked exactly like a Mississippi riverboat minus the paddle wheel. The gingerbread lattice work that surrounded the passenger accommodation on the upper deck gave it an impossibly top-heavy look. The engine wheezed and whistled like an old man with emphysema.

"Christ," he muttered. "If we blow on that thing the wrong way, it'll turn turtle. We may just have to walk on water."

"It was designed for fresh water and a very shallow draft," Stefan said as he observed it with a practiced eye. "As long as it stays calm, we will not have any problems. But do not expect a very comfortable ride." He turned to Esther. "Do you get seasick?"

"I do not know. I have never been on a boat before." She regarded the wallowing craft dubiously.

The ride was as miserable as Stefan had predicted. Martin was glad they hadn't eaten since breakfast. No one got sick except the hippies. He was tempted to offer them some waragi, but one look at their ashen faces told him that it wouldn't do any good.

Martin was distinctly relieved when Lamu's squat outline appeared on the horizon. From a distance, the town could have been confused with a fishing village in the Aegean. Whitewashed houses mounted the rolling hills. The terrain appeared arid and rocky. As they got closer, the port took on an Arab flavor. Dhows dotted the muddy green waters, and the slivered minarets of several mosques punctured the skyline.

"I read that this used to be a major shipbuilding center for the slave trade," Martin said as they docked at a ramshackle pier.

Deciding on a hotel was no problem. There was only one. As usual, Nathan just happened to know where it was. Fighting off a few lackadaisical hustlers, they followed him up the winding, narrow streets. There was a distinct Moorish feel to the ornate tile work on whitewashed buildings that pinched the one-or-two-person-wide streets. Things were quiet.

"The town still looks pretty Muslim to me," Martin said as they approached the modest guesthouse. "Mind you, that's not necessarily a disadvantage. There won't be much nightlife to tempt Stefan."

"There is no electricity except for the places with generators," Nathan announced. "There are not many missions around here either."

"Among the infidels, eh?" Martin chuckled as they walked into the cool, dark lobby.

They had the guesthouse all to themselves. The clerk, obviously glad to have visitors, true believers or not, during slack time explained in fractured but comprehensible English that most of the hippies preferred to stay in the cheaper guesthouses on the beach.

"Is it far to the beach?" Martin asked. "We're dying to take a dip."

"Not at all. You will be able to see it from your balconies. Just walk down past the pier. At the other side, you will find the market square. Once you cross it, the beach will be about two hundred meters ahead." He completed the paperwork and showed them to their rooms. "We have a generator," he announced proudly. "The electricity comes on at sunset. Will you dine with us?"

Martin handed him some shilingi. "We don't know yet. We'd like to explore town."

The best that could be said about the rooms was that they were clean. A delightful, balmy onshore breeze wafted through an intricately arched doorway that opened onto a balcony with a postcard view of the harbor.

Shortly after unpacking, Martin and Esther met in Stefan's room for a council of war.

"Not much on furniture, but the view is great, and believe it or not, the beer is cold." Stefan handed them each a Tusker, the local brand.

Martin savored his first sip. "That covers a multitude of sins in my book. Let's adjourn to the balcony. I don't think this town has changed a hell of a lot from Burton and Speke's day."

"Except that they do not sell human merchandise in the market now," Esther quipped.

Stefan chuckled. "Touché. Right, ladies and gentlemen, to business. What is on the agenda after a swim?"

"Reconnoiter town, locate a stash, and Gupta's," Martin said. "In that order."

"How are we going to ditch Nathan and Scarface? Once they have Gupta, they have all the pieces of the puzzle. I am not saying that they are bent, but after the past three weeks, I cannot trust anyone."

"Agreed," Martin said with a nod. "We'll certainly have to ditch them when we transfer the stones, but first we have to find a stash. While we're doing that, we might as well act normal."

"I also do not feel too good about leaving the suitcases around unattended."

"We can't, but at the moment, I don't have any idea how we're going to carry four pounds of stones each."

They remained stumped as they enjoyed the next round of beer.

Then Esther's face brightened. "I bought some nylon stockings today. You could use them as belts. They would fit under your shirts if you are careful packing them. I will go get them."

"Smart girl," Stefan said admiringly as she bustled out.

It took a while, but they managed to divide up the stones and make two serviceable, if not comfortable, belts.

Martin tied on the last of the belts as Stefan headed for the door. "We'd better tell Nathan and Scarface that we're headed out for an exploratory walk and a dip. No use getting them excited. I'll stop by their room on the way downstairs."

• • •

"That was easy enough," Martin said as he joined Stefan outside. "They'll be keeping an eye on us—that's for sure. We're going to have to keep our eyes peeled."

Stefan hunkered against a wall to let a laden donkey pass. "My feeling is that as long as they can keep at least two of us in sight, they will not worry. There is no way we can get off the island without them knowing about it."

Martin smelled the market well before they reached it. It was the now-familiar African mélange of excrement, body odor, and rotting vegetables and fruit mixed with the pungent stench of smoked fish. Something else gave it an Eastern tinge. Martin decided it was the racks of drying herbs, especially the cloves. As he had expected, the crafts section boasted many fine examples of wood and ivory carving. Some of the inlay work was fabulous.

Stefan glanced over his shoulder for the twentieth time since they'd left the hotel. "Do you see what I see over on the left of the square?"

Martin did a slow pan before arriving at the area in question. His effort to detect a tail drew a blank, but he hadn't expected anything else. "I see what you mean. It's right where it's supposed to be."

One glance was enough to confirm the obvious. Gupta's was the commercial hub of Lamu. The cluttered windows were crammed with everything from lawn mowers to jewelry.

"Definitely our kind of place," he Martin said, laughing. "If you've got the money, he's got it or will in the next twenty-four hours. By God, there's even a restaurant next door."

"Sehr gut. That settles dinner for tonight then. A good vindaloo will be just the ticket."

The town petered out after the market, and they found themselves on a rutted track that paralleled the white sandy beach. They stopped to remove their shoes. Stefan gestured to a group of hippies smoking a huge joint on the teetering porch of a dilapidated bungalow fifty feet ahead.

One of the hippies waved them over. "New in town?"

"Yeah." Martin accepted the proffered joint. "Just got in this morning. Looks like a pretty mellow place."

"The best, man. The weed's dynamite, and the living's cheap. You all sure don't look like you've been over here long." His glance took in Martin's and Stefan's fish-belly white complexions.

"We have not had a lot of time to sunbathe so far on the trip," Stefan replied glibly as he took a deep hit. "We are missionaries."

"No shit." A look of incredulity overtook his face. "You're having me on. With her?" He eyed Esther suspiciously.

"The Lord's flock is large," Stefan intoned. "Seriously, we really are priests. This fine young woman is our secretary. Not all men of the cloth are as out of touch with reality as you might think."

"Guess not. Far out. No offense intended, ma'am." The hippie inclined his head in Esther's direction. "Hey, people, these guys are priests."

The rest of the group appeared to be too high to be impressed.

"My name's John Stallings." He extended his hand.

"Martin Luther." Martin introduced the others. "John, where does everybody hang out here?"

"Mostly on the beach, man. Follow me for the tour."

They followed him up the kiln-hot beach. Spindly citrus trees of every description clung precariously to the jagged lava flows that bordered the sand, their delicious scent wafting over them. A few date palms were scattered here and there, but the island was certainly no Garden of Eden. After about a mile, the guesthouses gave way to a ragtag assortment of tents and lean-tos.

John came to a halt outside a fairly large encampment. "This is where I get off."

"What is farther up?" Stefan asked.

"Beach for another mile or so. Then rocks beyond the point. Nobody really goes up there, especially the natives."

"Why is that?"

"Some heavy local taboo, man. Something to do with the slave trade in the old days. The people that have been up there say it's just rocks."

Martin extended his hand. "Thanks for the tour, John. I'm sure that we'll be seeing you around the next few days."

"For sure, man. Probably at Tetley's, the restaurant next to Gupta's. That's the only place to eat if you're not cooking for yourselves."

Esther waited until they were out of earshot to comment on their new friend. "That is the first hippie I have ever seen, except for pictures in *DRUM*. He was very nice, and he did not appear to have crab lice like the articles said he would."

Farther up the beach, the sand gave way to lava. Even though the water's constant lapping had worn away most of the jagged edges, it was hard going.

Stefan signaled a halt when they got to the point. "Phew! I have not walked this much in ages," he said between pants. He capped his hands over his eyes and gazed back down the beach. "Nothing in sight but heat mirages. This looks like promising territory."

"Sure does," Martin said. "We'd better start looking. It's getting late. The light won't last forever."

They fanned out and reconnoitered the general area around the point.

A few minutes later, Martin found the perfect location and gave a shout. He triumphantly pointed to an indentation two feet deep at the base of a large lava outcrop that somewhat resembled a hand giving the thumbs-up. "Can't miss this, and it's well above the high-water mark. Plenty of loose rocks around to cover them with too."

Stefan cleaned out some seaweed and rotting vegetation. "It will do. Now all we have to do is to be sure we are not being watched."

Esther ran back around the point and then returned with good news. "There is no one in sight."

"No place for them to hide, either. There's no cover in these parts." Martin slipped off his belt and buried his stones.

Stefan followed suit. "It is not a masterpiece of subtlety, but it should work."

CHAPTER

25

FOR THE FIRST time in weeks, Martin started to think that they might actually pull it off, but he tried to suppress his optimism. There were still plenty of problems—the cash, a passport for Esther, etc.—but he made the return trip in silence, determined to make time.

It was six by the time he, Esther, and Stefan returned to the guesthouse. Exhausted but satisfied with the day's work, Martin showered and ordered up some beers.

Nathan knocked and entered just as Martin had finished dressing. "You have taken a lot of sun."

"Sure did." Martin handed him a Tusker. "Here's another hundred dollars. You might as well enjoy yourself—not that there's much to spend it on here."

"Thank you. You seem to have plenty of cash."

"We brought some extra with us in case of emergencies. It turned out to be a good idea."

Nathan shuffled and looked embarrassed. He resembled a little child trying to screw up the nerve to ask for a toy he knew he didn't deserve.

"Go ahead," Martin said. "What's on your mind?"

"Well, I was just wondering if you are as honest as you seem."

"Is that all? We're just not that greedy. Besides, we wouldn't have gotten this far without you." Martin felt insulted by the question. "If you really want to know, we're looking forward to having a school named after us."

"I am sorry. I should not have questioned your motives, but then again, diamonds seem to do strange things to some men." Nathan nodded goodbye and left.

Stefan arrived on his heels. "What did he want?"

"A little spending money for starters. He was also a little curious as to why we hadn't tried to do a bunk."

"Suspicious bastard. Almost makes you wonder about his motives."

"Not really. You'd probably think the same way if you were in his shoes. Besides, he's the only person connected with this whole deal that doesn't have pure greed as a motive."

"Ja, that is true, but sometimes fanaticism can be more dangerous than pure greed."

Martin ordered up more beer, and they watched another technicolor sunset while they waited for Esther to get ready. The view from the balcony was eerily timeless. The jumbled hodgepodge of mud-and-stucco dwellings flowed down the gentle incline to the very edge of the limpid grayish-green water. Nothing visible to the naked eye indicated they were in the twentieth century. The brightly colored lateen sails of the dhows floating in the harbor heightened the Arabic atmosphere.

It was difficult to imagine that black Africa lay less than fifteen miles across the water. Once again, Martin was struck by that wonderful sensation of being a voyeur with his own personal window into the past. Esther's arrival snapped him back to the present, and they headed off to eat.

The clerk stopped them on the way out and loaned them flashlights, explaining that there were no streetlights. The flashlights came in handy before they were halfway down the hill. The moon clouded over, and inky blackness settled over the town.

Martin felt as though thousands of eyes were boring into his back as they walked the labyrinthine alleys. He was jumpy until they reached the square.

Petley's was another Hollywood set plunked down in Africa. The overhead fans struggled valiantly against a pall of stale tobacco and alcohol. Somehow the potted plants that dotted the place managed to survive, even thrive. Only the lanterns and brass spittoons were missing, but they'd probably been removed only recently.

"This is a perfect place for a dubious deal," Stefan said. "I am waiting for a flunky to step out and say, 'Lights, camera, action!'"

It took a few minutes, but they finally made it to the bar. A table was obviously a long-term proposition, so they ordered some Tuskers. At first, their habits aroused some interest, especially among their neighbors, who deferentially moved and provided seats, but the curiosity soon wore off.

A few minutes later, a gentlemen of obvious Hindu origin bustled up to them. The cloying odor of his pomade wafted over them as he nervously patted a pair of magnificent mutton chops into place. He had that fig shape common to all truly corpulent people, but he evinced shrewdly calculating vibes as he surveyed their habits. He was good, though. He didn't blink when he saw Esther. By the time he was finished, Martin knew that his credit rating had already been assessed to the nearest penny.

"So sorry you have had to wait, Fathers. If I had known in advance, I would have held a table for you."

"That's all right, Mr.—"

"Gupta." He perched himself precariously on a stool that appeared out of thin air.

Martin introduced the others. "Looks like you've got a very prosperous establishment here."

"There is not much competition, but people have been kind enough to say that my food is good. I must say, we do not get many visitors who aren't hippies these days. It is a welcome change."

"We are actually over in Africa on church business," Stefan replied. "But we had a few free days and were told that this was a very good place to relax. It really is beautiful here. The beach is so unspoiled."

"Please call me Mukhajee." Gupta snapped his fingers for another round. "Where have your travels taken you so far?"

"Only to Kenya, but we are scheduled to visit Tanzania next week. Our church has several large missions there."

"Oh, I thought you might have been coming in from Uganda. Your church also has several large establishments there, if I am not mistaken. They tell me it is a very beautiful country—certainly exciting enough these days. I have been meaning to visit myself, but . . ." He glanced around the room and shrugged.

"With the store next door, you must be terribly busy." Martin nodded sympathetically. "We were hoping to get to Uganda this trip, but it wasn't possible to fit it into our schedule."

"I see your table is ready." Gupta rose and escorted them over to a prime table overlooking the market square. "If you need anything to make your stay more comfortable, please contact me at the store. I have an office in the back." He bowed obsequiously and waddled off.

"Sehr gut. It appears as if he is still expecting visitors from the West bearing gifts."

"Well, you've got to admit," Martin said, "we do look a little out of place here."

"Ja, that is why I tried to put him off a little with our itinerary."

Esther giggled. "You two make very convincing priests. I think twice every time I kiss Martin."

Martin found the food delicious and interesting. Most of the dishes were intriguing combinations of Arab and Indian cuisine.

"I do not think that there will be much nightlife around to tempt you, Stefan," Esther said in a teasing voice. "Unless, of course, some of these hippie mpenzis catch your eye."

"No, not tonight. I am tired. That walking today almost killed me. We have not had that much exercise the past few weeks. I am ready to head home for bed."

Martin continued to press him. "Just think, Stefan. The sexual revolution is in full swing less than one hundred yards from where we're standing."

"Please, I do not want to think about it."

• • •

They lolled on the beach the next morning and headed back to Petley's for lunch.

Martin figured it would be quiet at noon. "Have you thought about our new position with Gupta?" he asked Stefan as they approached the square.

"Nein, you?"

"Nope, but the first thing I'm going to do is arrange Esther's passport. Then I figured we'd come up with some samples and talk turkey."

"That is reasonable enough. I think that we should ask for double on general principle. I do not know about you, but I feel like I have aged ten years in the past three weeks. My retirement is looming larger every day."

"We have to keep one thing in mind, though. Gupta's an Indian, so he'll be as slick as his pomade."

Petley's was as quiet as Martin had hoped. Hippies didn't as a rule make for an early lunch crowd. The waiter took their orders and agreed to notify Gupta of their arrival.

Not long afterward, Gupta appeared. "Good morning. You must have enjoyed your dinner, if you're back so soon. How can I help you?"

Martin smiled. "Perhaps we can help each other, Mukhajee. I believe you've been expecting us."

Gupta's affable manner changed immediately. "I thought it might have been you last night. Come back into my office. You can eat while we talk."

He bustled them back through a warren of narrow passages and overstuffed storage rooms to a spacious modern office.

"It certainly looks like you're well prepared for any emergency, Mukhajee." Martin plopped down on one of the modern Danish swivel chairs that dotted the large room. "I take it you heard about Aka."

"Indeed, I did. A sad business. He was a very close friend. We had done business for years."

"Are you still prepared to carry out your end of the deal?" Stefan sniffed the contents of a Baccarat decanter on the sideboard and helped them all to large scotches.

"But of course, assuming you have the stones."

Martin sipped his scotch. By God, it was good to taste Glenlivet again. "We do, but some things have changed. The first thing we need is a passport for our assistant here."

"That's easy." Gupta rose and slid aside a garish print on the wall behind him, revealing a massive wall safe. He opened it, took out a large manila envelope, and threw it on the desk. "What nationality? I should think Ugandan or perhaps Tanzanian."

Martin raised his glass. "I thought you looked like a man of some resource. Tanzanian is probably safer. Of course, we'll need a Kenyan entry stamp for last week."

Gupta smiled. "By coincidence, I just happen to have one of those also. Perhaps your assistant would like to go back and have her picture taken while we discuss the pressing business at hand." He rang a bell on the desk, and a clerk led Esther off.

Martin reached into his pocket and tossed a toilet-paper-wrapped package onto the desk. "We also try to be as efficient as changing circumstances permit."

Gupta pulled a large contraption out of a cabinet next to the desk.

"I've never seen a scale like that before," Stefan said, moving his chair closer.

"It's a gravitational weight measurer. All elements have their own distinctive gravitational weight." Gupta fiddled with the knobs for a few minutes. "Yes, they are definitely what I was expecting. Where are the rest?"

"Somewhere on the island," Martin replied offhandedly. "As I said, there have been some changes since we negotiated our original deal with Aka. Our expenses have escalated rapidly, as needless to say, have the dangers we've had to face."

Gupta gave a studied sigh of resignation. He examined another of the sample stones through the jeweler's loupe. "I am aware of that. What is your price?"

"Before replying," Martin said, "I'd like to fill you in on a few facts you might not be aware of. The consignment that we have in our possession is well over twice the size of the one we were expecting to deliver."

That got Gupta's attention. He dropped the loupe and rolled his eyes heavenward. "Yes, I can see how that would change things. Aka must have suspected that somebody was onto him."

"Looking back on things, I'd say that's a logical assumption. He dropped a few hints to that effect, but we were so caught up in our greedy little fantasy that we ignored them. No matter now. We're here, and that's all that counts." Martin gathered his thoughts. "Our first problem is that we've had to make certain commitments to get out of Uganda."

"They were onto you too?"

"From the beginning, evidently. Either Aka's assistant told them at the same time he told Bagaza, or the late colonel formally asked them for help. It doesn't really matter at this point. What is important is the fact that we had to enlist the services of the Anyanya—a group you may or may not be familiar with—to help us out of the country. Two of their representatives are with us, anxiously awaiting their fee of one hundred and fifty thousand big ones."

Gupta whistled tonelessly and took a big gulp of his drink. "That certainly is a lot of money."

"Good help is hard to find in these parts, but nevertheless, a small price, you'll agree, from our point of view. I might add that I don't think it would be a good idea from anybody's point of view to think about not paying. After all, they've already killed several people getting us here."

That earned Gupta another large gulp. "I have heard of them. I think I can have their money together within a few days." He mopped the sheen on his forehead and extended his glass again. "Now. As to you all—"

"We're not that greedy," Martin said and smiled. "But we have to take into account the increased size of the consignment and the fact that you no longer have to pay Aka's cut. Half a million a man would be satisfactory."

Gupta spit scotch all over his expensive silk shirt.

"What a waste of good scotch," Stefan said. "Let us look at the numbers. We are dealing with six or seven million dollars' worth of stones, not two or three. I do not know what your arrangements were with Bertain, but you must have been giving him at least fifty percent. Even paying us a million, you still stand to make a lot more than you planned on. With that much loot, you can go back and buy your home village in India."

Gupta recovered fast. "Yes, yes, you are right, of course. I was just a little shocked by the numbers at first." He mopped his brow again.

"That's the spirit." Martin offered an encouraging smile. "Let's discuss the boring details."

"That should be very simple. You bring in the stones, and I will transfer the money into your accounts. You have the numbers with you?" Gupta was all business again now that his Oscar performance had come to naught.

"Mukhajee, Mukhajee," Martin said, chiding him. "Surely you don't think us that ignorant. After all, we had the brains to get this far. When you bring us bank checks on the Credit Suisse for the correct amounts, we will bring you in the stones, and good riddance. It's a small island, and we're not going anywhere. You know where to find us if we try to welch on the deal."

Martin could almost see Gupta's calculator at work.

"I think we can work something out," he finally said with a sigh. "You mzungus drive a hard bargain."

"Save your sob stories. They're wasted on us." Martin frowned. "We've seen a lot of people killed over these stones, and we don't have any illusions left. Where's Esther, by the way?"

"Outside. I'll have her sent in." Gupta left the room mumbling to himself.

"Poor guy," Stefan said deadpan. "We should all have his problems."

Martin raised his glass. "To the finish line."

Esther walked in a few minutes later holding her new passport. "This Gupta is efficient. Is everything all right?"

Stefan pulled over a chair and handed her a glass. "Evidently. Mukhajee was a little hesitant at first, but he soon saw reason—or, should I say, dollar signs."

Esther turned to Martin with a worried expression. "Is it really almost over? I almost do not dare hope."

"Five days at the most. Wouldn't you agree, Stefan?"

"A week from now you could be drinking champagne at the Ritz." Stefan lurched unsteadily to his feet. "Time for a long nap."

Martin pushed himself away from the table and stood. "Yeah, a nap sounds like just the ticket, especially since there isn't any scotch left. I think we'd better brief Nathan too."

The afternoon sun went right to Martin's head. He felt giddy and lightheaded—a combination of the booze and the relief. The market was winding down for the afternoon siesta, and most of the vendors were shuttering their stalls. Martin thought he caught sight of Scarface lurking behind a fruit stand, but he was staring straight into the sun, so he couldn't be sure. It didn't matter much now. The deed was done. He had to struggle to maintain his priestly bearing as they walked across the square.

• • •

Esther woke Martin with a cold beer at about six that evening.

He made it disappear in one greedy, gasping swallow. "Christ, what a headache. No more than I deserve for drinking scotch at noon in the tropics." He stumbled off to the shower.

Stefan was chatting on the balcony with Esther when Martin was finished.

"Have you talked to Nathan?" Martin asked.

"Ja, I ran into him after we got back. He was happy. We are having a celebratory dinner at Petley's tonight."

"You mean we're actually going to get to hear Scarface talk?"

"Fortunately not. Nathan said he sent him back to the mainland to make arrangements for their return trip."

"Funny, I could've sworn I saw him lurking around the market as we left Gupta's. If it *was* him, it's no big deal. He was probably on his way to the ferry. Still, something about him gives me the willies."

"It is his eyes," Esther said. "There is nothing behind them. No matter how deep you look, you see emptiness. They are the eyes of a killing machine. I have seen many like him in the Sudan. They have seen so much killing that they become mindless. All they have left is the violence."

. . .

Gupta had regained his oily affability by the time he seated them at the best table in the house. He smiled when they ordered champagne and beamed like the Cheshire cat when Martin insisted on paying for it. Once again, Martin felt he had a hollow leg. Nathan seemed to catch the mood. He let down his guard enough to tell some comical stories of his student days in London. It was nice to see his human side for a change, Martin thought.

They were all singing by the time they staggered home, but it didn't matter. The town was asleep. Esther's lovemaking was perfectly suited to Martin's mood: frenetic.

CHAPTER

26

THEY PLAYED TOURIST for the next couple of days. Martin considered it a perfectly pleasant but tedious existence. He didn't understand how the hippies could do it for so long, even doped out. Gupta was away, probably on the mainland sorting out things. Nathan wasn't around, either, which was vaguely disquieting.

Gupta resurfaced on the third day and sent word to the guesthouse that he'd like to have lunch with them.

"Thank God!" Martin exclaimed, crumpling the note. "I'm bloody sick of the sand and sun." He scratched his peeling forehead.

"That makes two of us," Stefan said. "I do not know what these hippies are smoking, but it does not do the same thing for me. I feel I have spent a month here the past few days."

Gupta was in an expansive mood as he ushered them into the office a few minutes later. He poured champagne all around. "To the successful completion of our business, gentlemen."

"I hope that means that everything we discussed has been arranged." Martin savored the perfectly chilled wine. Everyone in this business seemed to have expensive tastes.

"Yes, yes. I will have your checks by late tomorrow afternoon."

Martin fought to restrain his jubilance and remain businesslike. "You'll have the stones an hour later. We'll be glad to be rid of the damned things and be on our way. Speaking of which, are there any direct flights from Mombasa to Europe these days?"

"Yes, one a day. I thought you might be interested in them, and I will be glad to book seats as well as arrange transport to the mainland in time for you to make it."

Martin exchanged glances with Stefan. "Sounds good. What will be the exact timing on things?"

"You will come here at about four o'clock tomorrow," Gupta answered. "I will have your checks and tickets."

"Good," Martin mumbled through a full mouth. "As soon as we're satisfied, we'll bring you back the stones as promised."

They finished their lunch and took a bottle of champagne to the beach.

"This isn't going to do much for our image," Martin said. "But who gives a shit? We're only a day away from the end of the rainbow. I can't believe that it's almost over."

"Do not get too excited until tomorrow evening," Stefan cautioned.

"I really think we got it this time." Martin gulped down a glass of champagne and jumped into the ocean.

He was just emerging from the surf when Nathan arrived.

"Looks like everything is almost done," Nathan said with a smile as he threw Martin a towel.

"We've missed you the past couple of days," Martin said.

"I was over on the mainland taking care of some business." Nathan helped himself to the bubbly. "When do we get our money?"

"Tomorrow around five," Stefan replied.

Martin noted Nathan's cool detachment. "You don't seem to be particularly excited."

"I will be excited when I am back in the Sudan with the money." Nathan heaved a heavy sigh. "It has been a long trip. I hope it has been worth it for everyone."

They celebrated through the night. Martin lost track of the champagne they'd bought from Gupta on the way home.

Esther was the first to drop out at about ten. "Somebody is going to have to take care of you mzungus in the morning." She kissed each of them solemnly and staggered off.

Martin felt the ball in his stomach beginning to shrink. "You know, Stefan, I wouldn't trade the past few months for anything."

"Speaking for myself, I would not, either, as long as I get that check in my sweaty palm. The only thing I ever expected to get out of this deal was richer. I do not even want to consider the possibility of not getting the loot."

He had a point, but mercifully, Martin was too far gone to think about the finer implications. "I'm finished. See you in the morning."

Martin stumbled back to his room and staggered over to the bureau to empty his pockets. A wadded-up handkerchief caught his eye. With sudden recognition, he unfolded it. It was their miscellaneous expense stash of diamonds. He had forgotten them when he had loaded his belt. Esther must have found them. *I don't deserve her*, he thought to himself. He refolded the package and hid it in her suitcase. Better that she have an emergency reserve in case anything went wrong. He knew Stefan wouldn't mind. After tugging off his clothes, he collapsed on the bed.

• • •

Martin had no idea what time it was when he woke up. Miraculously, he wasn't hungover, but the medicine ball was back in his gut.

Esther handed him a towel as he climbed out of the shower. "It is good that you are finally awake. You were dragging some cows' hides last night."

He kissed her. "Translation, please."

"Snoring. I have finished packing."

"Sorry, it's this knot I have in my stomach. I guess it's not going to go away until everything is finished. What I really need is something to eat. What time is it, anyway?"

"Almost eleven."

"You're kidding. Is Stefan up yet?"

She smiled. "I heard groans when I passed his room. I think that he is up but not too happy about it."

Martin threw on some clothes. "We'd better get going."

Stefan knocked and entered a second later. Wordlessly, he clinked his Tusker against Martin's.

Martin recoiled in horror from the ghoulish specter. He turned to Esther. "Do I look that bad?"

"A little better, but not much. You both need some food." She clucked maternally, shooing them toward the door.

"And the beach to try to bake out some of last night's excesses," Martin replied, massaging his temple. "Let's just get some sandwiches downstairs. I don't think I could handle anything heavier at this point."

They packed some sandwiches and as much cold beer as they could carry and walked to the beach. Nervous energy was gnawing at Martin's vitals. He felt like he was wired on Methedrine. If time had dragged in Sankara's sweatbox, it positively crawled on the beach.

Esther seemed to sense Martin's mood and tried engaging him and Stefan in light conversation but dropped it after a few minutes.

Stefan broke down first. "Scheiss, enough is enough. It is

three-thirty. If we walk slowly, we will not get to Gupta's until after four."

They ran into Nathan and Scarface at the end of the beach.

Nathan took one look at them and fell into line.

"Why don't you have a drink with Esther while we conduct our business?" Martin suggested to Nathan as they approached Gupta's.

Gupta was terse and tight-lipped as he led them back to the office. He pulled out a large, battered leather briefcase and set it on the desk. He flicked open the catches. "It is all in here."

Stefan handed Martin an envelope with the Credit Suisse logo and counted cash. The bank checks were inside just as big as life. They were dated two days prior and obviously had been flown in by a special courier. Whoever Gupta's partners were, they ran quite an operation. Martin tried to visualize what a million would look like but couldn't.

Gupta mopped his brow. "I guarantee that the cash is all there. I counted it myself."

Stefan gave Martin a thumbs-up. "*Richtig*, it appears to be." He finished his scotch and closed the briefcase. "Do you mind if we take this along? I think our associates might have need of it."

Gupta shrugged in assent. "I will be counting the minutes until you return."

"You mean you're not coming with us?" Martin asked.

"Like you said, it is a small island."

"Very well. We'll see you in about an hour."

There weren't any paying customers in the restaurant at that hour, but there were a few service types setting up for the evening shift, so Martin nodded for Nathan and Esther to follow. Nathan didn't need any telling. His eyes never left the battered suitcase in Stefan's hand. Martin carefully surveyed the area but didn't spot any signs of untoward activity. They turned into the first empty alley behind the square.

"Okay, Nathan," Stefan said. "It is burning a hole in my hand. You take it."

Nathan rested the case on his knee and flicked the catches. Once he caught sight of the bills inside, he hurriedly closed it.

"It is all there." Stefan extended his hand. "It has been nice knowing you, Nathan. Maybe we will look you up in the Sudan one day."

Nathan shook hands all around. "Come see your school."

Martin watched him leave and then sighed in relief as soon as he was alone with Stefan and Esther. "Let's go finish the deal. My stomach is already starting to feel better."

Stefan glanced at the sinking sun. "You two start out. I will go back to the guesthouse and get the flashlights. It looks like we are going to need them."

"Good thinking. We'll take our time."

Esther grabbed Martin's hand as they began their walk. "Is it really over?"

"All but the shouting. You can start thinking about your wedding gown." He suppressed the urge to skip and sing as they made their way up the beach.

Stefan caught up with them about halfway to the point.

"Everything Jake back at the guesthouse?" Martin asked.

"Seemed to be, except for one thing. Nathan and Scarface had already checked out."

"That's odd. I wonder why they're making the crossing at night."

Esther agreed. "It seems a little strange."

"Perhaps not," Stefan said. "They are probably scared sitting on all that money. In calm waters, the crossing to the mainland is nothing compared to the one across the lake."

"True enough," Martin replied and picked up the pace.

They reached the point just as the sun was making its final plunge.

"Appropriate timing." Stefan gestured upward. "The end of the road. A mighty long and winding one, I might add."

"Well, what the hell are we waiting for?" Martin started digging feverishly.

Stefan joined in, but Esther disappeared behind the thumb-shaped boulder to make a short call.

"Raise your hands and step back very slowly." The English was heavily accented, but the meaning was all too clear.

Martin swore and rose to his feet with exaggerated slowness. His gut was dropping rapidly. Who the fuck could it be? His mind skipped through the possibilities: Astles, the police, a henchman of Gupta's . . .

"You may turn around now, but do so very slowly."

It was Scarface. Martin did not know which was uglier, the well-oiled Kalashnikov in his hands or the grimace that was obviously as close as he could get to a smile. The final termite out of the woodpile. The most obvious yet least expected. An insane thought flitted through Martin's consciousness: A man could almost get used to staring down the barrel of a gun.

"Lie down and spread your arms and legs as far apart as they will go." Scarface was obviously operating from a script.

"Just take the fucking stones, scumbag!" Martin screamed, hoping Esther would hear. She was their only chance. He assessed the odds as he lowered himself slowly onto the cold lava. Scarface was a pro and a good twenty feet from them. They wouldn't get halfway before a burst cut them in half.

Suddenly, Scarface grunted in pain, and a large rock bounced off his head. Martin leapt to his feet and charged as the Kalashnikov barked staccato in his ears. Just as Martin grasped the slimy barrel, he heard the flat crack of a pistol, followed by a dull thud that sounded like someone beating the dust from a carpet with a broom.

Esther lay rag-doll still in front of Scarface.

Martin tugged at the Kalashnikov, but before he could dislodge it, Nathan stepped from behind the boulder and leveled a .45 at him.

"Do not even think about it."

Martin let the barrel slip from his grasp and sank to his knees. A second later, he was vomiting uncontrollably.

Scarface staggered to his feet. "Hog-tie them. Now."

Nathan wrinkled his nose as he searched Martin's pockets.

Martin barely noticed the sour smell of bile. He was too busy looking at Esther's lifeless corpse, which was sprawled over the hole like a mother protecting her child.

Nathan finished his search, pocketing the checks and checking their bonds. Satisfied, he rolled Esther's body away from the hole.

"Such a waste," he said, "but at least she died for a good cause."

"What?" Martin asked. "Lining your pockets?"

"How could you think that?" The injured pride in Nathan's voice was palpable. "It is all going to the movement. Your greed opened the window for me to negotiate a better deal with Gupta."

"*Schiesse!*" Stefan cried. "What did you sell us out for?"

"An additional half a million. You should not complain. You are going to get away with your lives, which is more than Mapende can say."

Martin blinked in confusion. "You're not going to kill us?"

"Why? You are hardly going to the authorities, are you? No, we shall leave you bound and gagged. Someone will find you tomorrow with nothing worse than a sunburn."

"That's big of you. What about Esther?"

"We will dump her body in the ocean, where nature will take its course. There are many sharks out there."

The vision of bloody-snouted sharks savaging Esther's corpse was too much to bear, but Martin had nothing left in his stomach to expel.

"Get a grip, Mr. Fine. I am going to gag you again. If you choke..." Nathan rummaged in his knapsack and gave them each a slug of waragi. "I am not an unkind man. In other circumstances, I would like to think that we could have been friends."

"How stupid are we?" Martin said. "We thought you were the one person we could trust. You were the only one with a pure motive."

"That was and is still true. The movement has to be bigger than any one individual. In the end, your greed got you where you are. Gift-wrapping it in misguided Western liberalism at the last second was pathetic. In a funny way, Astles, Bagaza, and the rest were more honest."

Fuck me, Martin thought. The truth really hurt.

Scarface finished stuffing the knapsack with the diamonds, and at a signal from Nathan, tossed Esther's body into the sea.

Nathan hurled the Kalashnikov into the rising tide as well. "One last bit of advice. You will find everything, including your tickets, in your rooms. Gupta has left the island for the next two weeks. You need to cut your losses and leave. There is nothing left for you here."

Then they were gone.

CHAPTER

27

THEY WERE LEFT in the dark with their thoughts. Martin realized it was time to start thinking for a change. He'd been reacting blindly since getting off the plane those long weeks ago.

Stefan started slithering around.

"What are you doing?" Martin asked.

"Looking for that waragi bottle. He left it here. If we can find it and break it, we can cut the ropes."

It beat thinking. They crawled around like confounded crabs for several minutes before Stefan gave a triumphant shout, which was followed by the sound of shattering glass. Awkwardly, they maneuvered themselves into a back-to-back position and started sawing away. Like most things, it was much harder than it appeared in the movies. Martin felt blood running down his arms well before the soggy ropes parted.

He staggered down to the water and, after carefully removing his cigarettes and tossing them onto the dry beach behind him, flung himself in face-first to scrub himself and his clothes.

After stumbling out, he lit a cigarette and spread out his clothes to dry. "Like the man said, we're alive. What next?"

"There does not seem to be much to discuss," Stefan replied. "We do what the man said: Slip quietly out of town and cut our losses. We should have enough left in the room. We'd better get a move on if we want to make that plane."

They made good time back to the guesthouse, where the clerk agreed to arrange a ride to the mainland for them while they packed.

Martin shaved, showered, and changed into his priest's habit. His gut should have roiled when he saw Esther's clothes hanging in the closet, but all he felt was numbness. *That's a problem*, he thought, as he mechanically shoved her clothes into the bag. The answer to her disappearance was simple. He'd just tell the truth: She had left with the others yesterday.

As Martin and Stefan paid their bills, the clerk told them that he'd arranged for a fisherman that he knew to run them over to the mainland. They would probably arrive a little after the ferry, so some cabs would be around still. He handed them a flat manila envelope. "Mr. Gupta left this for you last night. I hope you had a pleasant stay on Lamu."

"Memorable," Martin said, "if not enjoyable."

He was in a daze during the walk to the docks, oblivious to the rising heat and the smells that he'd found so exotic the day before. They found the boat without any problem. Stefan went off to make a short call while Martin haggled over the price and loaded up.

Stefan returned a few minutes later and lobbed a bottle of waragi to Martin. "Medication. Dr. Schmidt insists. It will not change anything, but at least it will dull the pain."

The boatman cast off and cruised out of the harbor at a good clip. Martin didn't look back. He slugged the waragi and thought about Esther and how much she would have liked London—what could have been. She'd given him the ultimate gift—the keys to unlock his own emotional vault—but he'd been too stupid, scared, or whatever to take them until it was too late. Tears welled in his eyes, and he was teetering over the abyss again.

Stefan handed him a joint. "Do not do it to yourself. It will not change anything."

"You're right," Martin said with a sigh. "It's hard not to. She gave me so much, and look what I gave her in return."

"You gave her more than you realize. You were the only person who ever really loved her. At least she knew love before she died. That is more than a lot of people in her situation can say."

Martin mulled over the thought while the boat ate up the miles. Their luck was in for a change. They arrived just after the ferry, so they had no problem catching a ride to the airport on one of the tourist buses.

Stefan consulted his watch. "The flight does not leave until six. That ought to leave us adequate time to buy some junky airport art to show we've really been here. We will have a hell of a story to tell."

"I don't plan on telling it to anybody," Martin said. "I don't consider it one of my shining hours."

"You will tell," Stefan said with a snort. "Just wait until you are a doddering old fool, sitting on a rocker on the porch with a bunch of shiny-eyed kids at your feet. You will tell."

"I might just tell it to the major if I see him again," Martin agreed. "I guess my attitude will change with time."

"Think we will have any trouble at the airport?"

"Don't see why, after all this time," Martin replied with a smile. "We're just a couple of innocent priests going about our business. Then we visit our respective consuls in London and report our passports missing. We'll be back to our normal identities in a matter of days."

"At least superficially," Stefan said as he gazed out at the brown countryside. "In spite of everything, I shall miss this place."

"I'll be back," Martin replied with certainty. "I've left too much of myself here not to."

They were dropped at the airport at about four-thirty.

Martin picked up his bag and left for the restroom. "You go on ahead and save me a place. I just realized that I have my money belt and some clothes of Esther's in the bag. I was in such a funk that I just shoved them in with everything else."

He selected an empty stall in the bright, tourist-clean restroom, rummaged through the suitcase, and retrieved the belt. As he buckled it, he noticed Esther's purse. He opened it, and the first thing he came across was a letter addressed to him. It could wait until the plane. After pocketing it, he sifted out a few other possessions of hers and wadded them into a ball, which he shoved in the corner. No use opening himself up for any awkward questions at customs.

Stefan was just checking in when Martin found him. The clerk made only a perfunctory examination of their passports and clipped their tickets. Next, immigrations—the first time their passports would be thoroughly scrutinized.

Martin wasn't even nervous. He figured nothing worse could happen.

It was a breeze. The officer glanced at their habits and stamped the page without looking.

Martin made a beeline for the bar. "I don't care whether I'm in mufti or not."

"Permit me to buy you two a drink. It's the least I can do."

Martin should have been shocked to see Agent Russell, but somehow it made sense. He looked eminently spookish in a seersucker suit. Martin didn't know whether to laugh or cry, so he settled on silence.

"The disguises are good," Russell said. "I would never have known."

Stefan bristled. "Except?"

Russell smiled. "Let me buy you each a double before we begin. You're going to need it."

• • •

Martin took a solid belt off his Remy Martin. He didn't have any idea what Russell was about to tell him, but he was sure he wasn't going to like it. *Funny*, he thought. *The last tar baby out of the briar patch was an albino.*

"First, I want to say that I'm terribly upset that your friend Esther got involved. It was one of those unforeseen quirks." Russell, obviously in no hurry, paused to sip his drink.

Martin wondered if the CIA agent knew how close he was to being a dead man.

Stefan, perhaps sensing Martin's mood, prodded Russell to continue. "Go ahead. Spit it out."

"Oddly enough, it all started with a conversation I had with you guys. I saw the wisdom in what you were saying about forcing the Sudanese government to negotiate a settlement with the Anyanya. The best way to do that was to make the Anyanya strong enough so that Nimeiry knew it was a no-win situation, but I couldn't force the dunderheads at Foggy Bottom to fund them. It all looked like a dead end until Nathan contacted me a few weeks ago."

"With an offer neither of you could refuse." Martin could see it all, but he let Russell fill in the blanks.

"Needless to say, I was a little surprised to hear that you were involved in a diamond scam—and more than a little perturbed when Langley ordered me to terminate the operation at all costs. They count Mobutu too good a friend to let the Shaba insurrection go on."

"So we were expendable?" Martin should have felt mad, but all he could muster was resignation.

"If there was any chance of the deal going through. I was a little panicked when you dropped out of sight."

"Why didn't you stop things right away?"

"Because Bagaza only informed me the day before the deal went down. He obviously wanted to do things his own way. I knew that he planned to pocket all the loot, but I didn't give a shit as long as it didn't get to Shaba. When Nathan came to me a week later, it seemed like the perfect way to ease you guys out alive."

"And fund the Anyanya," Stefan said with a sigh. "Very neat. But what happens with Gupta's share?"

"Are you kidding? None of the rest of the bandits involved in this deal could give a shit about Shaba. Once Aka was removed, that factor was a nonstarter."

Martin signaled for another round. "One last question. Why did Nathan come to you at all, and why didn't he operate solo?"

"Couple of reasons. One, he needed me to keep the Kenyans off his back. They'd evidently caught wind of what was going on. That was no problem. We own Kenyatta. Second, and most important, he needed our network to buy the arms and smuggle them into the Sudan."

"Wheels within wheels," Martin muttered. "You know that less than two minutes ago I was thinking very seriously of killing you? Why tell us all this?"

"Because you'd done me a few favors, and Langley was interested in seeing if you two felt like doing some further work. There are worse ways to make a living."

Martin rose and cocked his right.

"Don't," Russell said, his voice cracking. "There are two rather hefty fellows not twenty feet from here who'd love to see you try. Look, I'm sorry about that. I didn't want to make the offer. It was orders. I'm sorry about everything, as a matter of fact. I know how you feel, but you've got to realize that you're far better off than if I hadn't been around." He rose and dropped some shilingi on the counter. "One last thing. You're clean stateside as far as any legal concerns go. Though, needless to say, I wouldn't visit Zaire or Uganda in the near future." He turned and walked off without looking back.

Martin's eyes followed him. He was shocked to see Anton and an obvious goon lounging at the magazine counter. As Russell came abreast of them, Anton shrugged eloquently, flashed Martin the peace sign, and turned to follow his boss out.

Stefan rolled his eyes and rose. "Would you like some cigarettes and waragi from the duty-free?"

"Yeah, the usual," Martin replied numbly as he glanced around the spanking-new terminal, trying to gather his thoughts.

The place was so new that it hadn't had any time to acquire an African flavor. Martin surveyed the hordes of babbling touristi descending on the duty-free counters like locusts.

"Mein Gott," Stefan said, "it is mortal combat out there. I have never seen anything like it."

Martin raised his glass. "To the real Africa—the other two-thirds of the iceberg. May the rest of the locusts never discover it."

Stefan clinked his glass and slapped him on the back. "Upon my word, I think you are beginning to show some signs of life."

"Pan Am flight number 745 is now boarding," a woman said in a pleasant voice over the intercom. "Will passengers holding tickets please proceed immediately to gate six for embarkation?" Even her voice was white and ersatz—no doubt reassuring for the touristi.

Martin spun in a slow three-sixty wheel as they crossed the tarmac to the plane. Even in the midst of the noxious, jet-fuel-laden fumes and the shriek of the engines, he felt the magnetic pull through his feet. Something was always boiling below the surface in Mother Africa. Suddenly, he realized why he felt so comfortable. The chaos and anarchy were the closest thing he could call home. He knew he'd be back somehow, someway. It wasn't rational, especially after what he'd been through, but that was why the feeling was so compelling. He boarded in a daze and collapsed in his seat.

• • •

Idi Amin stood on the terrace and leaned against the stone wall overlooking the palace grounds. Something about the way the sun hit the canopy of mahogany trees below returned him to a more innocent time. He longed for the freedom of youth, when a boy could wander the woods, dig in the dirt, or simply listen to the wind whip through the tall grass.

He felt his jaw tighten. The majestic beauty of his homeland fought a never-ending war against abject poverty and petty corruption. All of Africa's contradictions seemed to converge on Uganda, which would always be at the center of the bloody conflict.

The sound of leather soles on the stone expanse behind him alerted him to the presence of his most trusted adviser.

"And what have you learned?" he asked without turning around.

Bob Astles joined him at the wall and hunched ever so slightly to take in the view. "We lost the diamonds."

"How?"

"It seems several men, including those in your employ, were at cross-purposes. Each man had his own agenda, and the only thing those agendas had in common was perfidy."

Amin shook his head in disgust. "Each man will pay dearly."

"They already have," Astles said as he turned to face Amin. "To the last man."

Amin felt fury well up inside him. He didn't know whether to laugh or cry. "And what of Aka? Has he gone to meet his maker too?"

"You'll be pleased to know that the answer is to that question is a resounding yes."

"What about the American?"

"Ah, Mr. Fine," Astles said in a wistful tone. "It seems someone in the CIA was looking out for him and his German sidekick." A hint of admiration sounded in his voice.

"I suppose Mr. Fine reunited with his lover as well. Did the two fly off into the sunset together?"

"Ironically, she died the same way the others did: in a hail of bullets."

"That is not irony, Mr. Astles." Something akin to joy darkened Amin's heart. "That is tragicomedy."

"Indeed, My President. She was the only one who didn't care about the diamonds. And yet she paid the same price as the others."

"Yet Fine and the German live on." Amin tried to shed the news like an old skin. "It matters not. The land we see before us will outlive us all." He broke into a bitter frown. "Even me."

• • •

"Sir, would you like a drink before takeoff?" The stewardess was plastic-pretty. Somehow, they always looked like the mask would crack if you touched their face. "I wasn't sure whether I should wake you."

"I wasn't sleeping," Martin said, "just remembering my trip."

"Was it good?"

"Good? I don't know. It was intense. As real as life gets."

"Yes, I've often wanted to get into the bush and see the real stuff, but somehow we never seem to get away from the beach." She wandered off, the professional patter finished.

As Martin maneuvered his pillow into position, he felt the envelope in his pocket. Esther's letter. He'd forgotten it completely. As soon as he opened it, a wadded handkerchief fell out—their emergency stash that he'd left in her room.

Dearest Martin,

If you are reading this, then I am dead. I have always had what you mzungus call the second sight. Someone in my family always has, and I was the one cursed this generation. It is not a gift, but a burden. I knew from when we met that things would not end well. I am not sad, and don't you be. You made me very happy. So take these and make a dream come true for both of us. I love you.

Esther

How like her, he thought. No maudlin self-pity, just calm acceptance. He stuffed the letter back into his pocket and fingered the stones. They would buy a good-sized dream. How practical, and how African! A Western woman would have told him to keep them always as a remembrance. A fulfilled dream would be infinitely more satisfying.

Suddenly, the dam burst. Before he knew it, he was laughing and crying at the same time. Sobs wracked his body. He fought to keep from plunging over the edge into complete hysteria.

"Are you all right, sir?" The stewardess's concern pulled him back from the edge.

"It is all right," Stefan reassured her. "I will take care of him."

Gradually, the sobs gave way to giggles until he was laughing so hard he thought he would piss himself.

"Gott in Himmel, man! Get a hold of yourself!" Stefan slid into the aisle like he was preparing to slap him.

"I'm okay." Martin raised his arm in defense.

"So what is this all about?" Stefan asked. "Delayed reaction?"

"No, Stefan." Martin put the stones in his hand. "Just life's hard lessons."

JOHN KWELI is an old hand in Africa, having endured sixteen coups, six civil wars, two genocides, and many other things best forgotten. His is a false name, but everything in this book happened, as the guilty know.